Chaotic Haunts

Chaotic Haunts

Sarah Eriksen

Chaotic Haunts

Book 3 of the Chaos Guardian Series

Sarah Eriksen

Copyright © 2022 by Sarah Eriksen

Cover art by Misty Choate

All rights reserved.

All character in this work are fictitious. Any resemblance to persons living or dead is purely coincidental.

ISBN-13: 9798848873672

Sarah Eriksen

To all the people who feel a little lost and lonely at times, and the friends that get us through it.

Chaotic Haunts

Sarah Eriksen

Other books by the author
The Chaos Guardian Series
Chaotic Devices
Undead Chaos
Chaotic Haunts

Sarah Eriksen

Acknowledgements

Thank you to my friends that helped me with this book. It wouldn't have happened without Kari, Sarah W, April, Rachel.

Thank you to my friends that helped me create the weird worlds in this book. While a lot of this is straight from my own mind, there are a lot of touches thanks to Sarah W, Joseph C, Robin and her tabletop gaming friends, and my writer group friends who are always supportive.

Special thanks to Dan Q. Without him, we would never enjoy the mystery of Declan's disappearing pants.

Chaotic Haunts

Sarah Eriksen

Chapter One

An earsplitting roar echoed through the corridor of the derelict space station. Skye squeezed herself into a tight space between two computer banks, trying to get out of the line of sight from the blood-smeared window. The faint hum of the life support and artificial gravity machines was noticeable between a blaring alarm and the roars of the giant aliens on a free-for-all rampage.

There were only three of them that she knew of, but one was more than enough of a problem. They were roughly eight feet tall with claws, fangs, deadly venom that killed on contact, a sense of smell that put a bloodhound to shame, and a really bad attitude.

They were certainly up there with any number of creatures she had ever fought. They were problematic and very hard to kill. Only they belonged in this part of the universe. Although maybe not the whole running loose on a space station part.

She was starting to question why she was in her current predicament. Never mind that she had been told to help her cousin Kyadara by her boss, the god Amonir. A rescue mission on a research space station had sounded exciting, but soon as she arrived, it was clear that a few details about the entire situation had been entirely wrong.

She had teleported to the location her cousin gave her where the distress signal originated from. Except, it wasn't the advanced and high-tech facility it should have been. The space station was quite old, derelict, and full of the bloody remnants of dead space pirates. Not that she could identify much of anything from the gore that was left. Other than the rampaging aliens on the loose, nothing added up.

An enormous shadow darkened the room as something crossed in front of the window. She was masking noises and her scent with her powers. But that didn't stop her from pressing back further into her small hiding spot.

She didn't like the restrictions that came with operating in an advanced galaxy with space travel and vast technology. No flashy magic or invisibility was feasible, for the moment at least. The thought made her feel both relieved and uncertain.

The instructions Amonir had given her to control the telltale glow and sparks of her new powers had worked…at first. It was getting harder to rein in the flows of energy. She seemed to be able to operate comfortably with the tiniest things or when unleashing a massive amount of power. Anything in between was a struggle. And most of the time, she needed to operate in the vast area in between.

The shadow shifted as the alien sniffed at the gore-smeared window, its breath fogging up the bloody surface. Skye's skin crawled as the alien's claws screeched across the metal of the door like nails on a chalkboard. The shadow shifted again and disappeared as the alien skulked down the hall.

Skye reached out with her mind to make sure it kept heading away from her and let out the breath she had been holding. She knew she had blocked the sound of her breathing from being heard, but there were some things you couldn't control in intense situations like that.

She peeked out of her hiding space and glanced at the window, half expecting the alien to pop back into sight like a bad monster movie. Her lips twitched with a silent laugh at her imagination. She snuck to the controls, her mind finding the information she needed. A few taps on the console and the window panel darkened so she could move around without worrying about being seen.

"Honestly, Kya, I've fought some horrifying things before. But this…is actually kind of terrifying. How can you stand doing this stuff with your powers so limited?" She had done a lot of undercover and stealthy jobs before, so she was used to hiding in suspenseful and sometimes nerve-wracking situations. But this was a whole new level of tension.

Sarah Eriksen

"Welcome to my world, cousin. And they aren't too limited. You just have to be creative with technology so it's more easily explainable." Kya teased.

"Call me old-fashioned, or lazy, but I kind of like the combination of plausible explanation and gods sort of blurring over the obvious stuff." She was kidding, of course. It was normal for guardians to have to come up with believable explanations while trying not to use flashy magic that required a divine intervention. She squashed down the troubled feelings trying to bubble to the surface again in response to the thought of flashy powers.

"That happens all the time too," Kya replied.

"Well. All this hiding from scary aliens and not being able to be invisible is fun and everything, but you asked me to come to this small room to do something fancy and high-tech for you. So, what do you need me to do?" She was having fun, despite the dangerous aspects of the situation.

"Let me in for a bit?"

She opened her mind up to her cousin, allowing Kya to see through her eyes.

"It's to your left." She followed her cousin's direction. *"There. That's the console you want."*

Skye moved to where Kya indicated and sat gingerly on the edge of the blood-stained chair. She stared blankly while reaching out for the knowledge she required to use the highly advanced technology.

A fraction of a second later, the information poured into her mind, and she snorted softly. Super high-tech devices, and it was one glowing green button to click to open up the communication channel so Kya's people could start accessing the system.

Skye said, *"So, a couple of hours ago, you told me we needed to save some famous research scientist from what sounded like a much nicer place than this."* She didn't finish explaining the discrepancies.

"Whoever sent the distress signal did a great job rerouting and masking the data. It took Rachel and Tate a good amount of time to figure it out. Sorry, no scientist in need of rescuing." She sounded impressed by the person's skills.

Chaotic Haunts

"Any idea who could have sent the signal?" Skye was curious. Considering the bloody alien massacre, a distress signal made sense, even if it was made to look like it came from someone else.

"Hopefully, we'll figure that out as soon as we get into the systems. It could be a trap set by the pirates who were here."

Skye's instincts flared up. She wasn't so sure that was it. "I might not be familiar with how things work here. But I don't think a trap involving massive rampaging murder aliens roaming free seems like a solid plan. I mean, I would think there are a lot of other ways to trap people that don't involve potentially being maimed and eaten."

"You do have a point there."

Skye frowned absently, sending her mind out as she asked, "Did you scan for signs of life?"

"We did a basic scan, but nothing came up. Not even the aliens. The security is impressive considering it's so run down."

Skye fought off a laugh and teased, "I meant with your magic powers, cousin." She could feel Kya's consternation at missing the obvious.

"There is someone else alive on the station." Kya found the mental presence at the same time Skye did. Contrary to popular belief, minds didn't broadcast thoughts like a radio, but they were recognizable if you knew what to look for. "Not surprising, it's still not the researcher, but it would be worth finding them if you can."

"It'll be a walk in the park." She glanced at the bloodied key card lying on the equally gore-covered console. It was all that was left of whoever had been in this room. "And by the park, I mean a terrifying space horror movie set. I'm ready to go when you are."

"It'll be just a few more moments for all of us to get into position so we can give you a better idea of what's going on." She hadn't explained the details, but it was clear from the security, both the original and the pirates' additions, that their presence would be noticed if they weren't careful.

"Any clue what this place is or what happened?" She wanted to know who she might be dealing with who could send a distress signal with that skill level to hide its true source. She didn't have to know a lot about the technology of this world to know it was impressive.

"As far as who built it, not a clue. More recently, I'd say the pirates must have stumbled across it and decided to make it theirs. A fully *functional space station of this size would make a decent base in this sector for pirates wanting to branch out into bigger things."*

"Like smuggling giant alien monsters?" Skye asked wryly.

"Exactly. Things like that fetch hefty sums on the illegal market."

"Didn't seem to work out too well for them."

"No, it didn't. But that might be why someone sent an encrypted signal to call for help."

Skye mentally nodded. It did make sense. *"Fun. Space pirates. Well, dead space pirates. And a mystery person who sent a super high-tech distress signal. And for some reason, you need my help to run around as a distraction."* As jobs went, it wasn't the strangest she'd ever had.

"From the initial scans we are getting, this place will take some time to hack into. My job is to make sure it's locked down and secure. That way no one else thinks it's a perfect location for their home base. There's just something odd about it."

"You mean other than the bits of dead bodies everywhere and the rampaging aliens?"

"That's sadly not too unusual in this part of the universe. But something tells me there's more to it." Kya's shrug was apparent in her mind voice. *"I'm guessing that's also why you're here, not just as a distraction. Although I wasn't given anything specific, so your guess is as good as mine for most of this."*

Skye laughed and asked, *"So how exactly does a crew of four people take over a massive derelict space station?"* The curiosity was back. She was getting small glimmers of information on how to stay alive in this place, but she didn't need to be an expert in technology for that.

"Fancy high-tech stuff." A small device appeared in front of Skye, and she grabbed it out of the air. *"That's an earpiece so my crew can talk to you. Tate is headed to the command deck so they can hack into the systems and get control of everything. They have remotely accessed the security files and have the layout of the maintenance shafts along with the regular maps. They'll be in touch if there's anything they need you to do while they make their way."*

Skye had already mentally mapped out the entire station for herself. *"Is your crew used to the things we can do without fancy technology?"*

"They know what I'm capable of for the most part, and they know you have some of the same abilities. They won't question every little thing

Chaotic Haunts

you do that is unusual for a normal person since they are used to weird guardian tricks. I warned them you are far more reckless and wilder than I am, though." She teased again.

"I'm sure they don't believe you, but you tried." She laughed. Her cousin was a trained elven battle mage as well as a guardian. She was one of the least reckless people Skye had ever met. *"I know I have to keep things on the down low while I'm here. But for how long?"* Kya's crew might know about guardian powers, but there were other things to consider. Like massive murder aliens running amok.

"As soon as Tate can gain control of the security system, they can make sure the pirates and any previous occupants don't have remote access to the station. The last thing we need is you lobbing creation energy around on a camera that someone else has access to."

"That makes a lot more sense. I should probably get headed to our mystery presence before a rampaging alien finds them. If that's not going to be a problem." She didn't want to move until they were ready but didn't want to wait too long. Powers or not, sneaking around was one of her skills.

"You should be fine now. Tate will let you know once the cameras are secure."

Skye slipped the device into her ear, pleasantly surprised by the comfortable and secure fit. She flipped the tiny switch and heard a faint hum of static as it connected.

She was grateful for the ability to download knowledge to her brain when she needed it. She didn't have a problem not knowing things, but it was much more convenient not to have to constantly ask how everything worked when dealing with advanced technology.

She picked up two stun batons Kya had sent her way, getting a feel for their weight. They felt lighter than they should, but she knew they were reinforced with some sort of metal or alloy that didn't exist on Earth.

They weren't her swords, but she could work with them. She slipped them into sheaths on her thighs for fast access if she needed them. She had copied Kya's space mercenary gear to not look out of place in case she was caught on a camera.

She was armed but hoped she didn't have to get into close contact with the aliens until Tate had control of the cameras. She wasn't confident she could block the sparks and fire if she had to use her powers, and she was sure she'd need them if the aliens got too close.

"Skye, can you hear me?" Kya's voice sounded in her ear.

"Loud and clear, cousin." She reinforced her bubble of masking energy, blocking her voice from traveling a few inches away from her head. Thankfully, small touches of creation energy didn't set off the flashy sparks and glow of coldfire if she focused.

A soft voice said, "Hello Skye, I'm Tate. I'll be keeping an eye on what you're doing and let you know if we need anything specific. Kya sort of gave us a rundown of what you can do."

She heard the hesitation in their voice and reassured them. "Don't worry. I'm the total destructive force of nature with a complete disregard for my own personal safety. I can track your location and the big angry aliens at the same time." Mystery person aside, she was also going to be keeping the aliens busy and away from wherever Tate was.

They laughed. "Good to know. I'm guessing you won't require any help with directions either?"

"Probably not too much, but if you see something, call it out. It doesn't hurt." She'd rather have all the help and warnings she could get.

A deeper voice spoke with a dry tone, "Out of curiosity, are you as prone to blowing things up when you're irritated like Kya is? Because it can be dangerous on a space station."

Kya's reply was lightning fast. "She makes me look calm in comparison, Wes."

Skye laughed at their teasing. "Hey now, everyone always says you're more terrifying than I am."

"Trey and Declan hardly count as everyone. And we both know Kyleeria is the scary one." Kyleeria was Kya's twin sister and a high priestess of the moon in the elven kingdom of Solunaria on the planet Arborea. Skye's aunt had married the elven king, and their children all had impressive powers.

"I won't argue there." Skye joked.

"Wes and I are in place now. Rachel, is the hangar still secure?"

"Yes, boss. The hangar is fine. No aliens down here. Just keeping the engines running in case we need to make a spectacular exit. Or if some other pirates decide to come home at the wrong time." Her voice was a balance of cheerful humor and dry sarcasm.

"Good. It's go time. Good luck, Skye. Don't have too much fun."

"Sneaking around deadly alien monsters on a rampage to rescue a random unknown person on a derelict space station is the absolute definition of fun."

Sarah Eriksen

Chapter Two

Skye took a deep breath and headed to the door, double-checking that her scent and sound were masked. Invisibility and teleportation were out of the question now that she was on the ship. At least until the crew had control of things. She was more than capable of moving without being heard, but she needed an edge if she wanted to remain unnoticed by the aliens.

She had used the access tunnels to sneak into the small communication room when she first arrived. It was easier to explain how she had gotten there if anyone happened to have access to the cameras. Now she was seeing, and smelling, what the aliens had done to the pirates they had found.

The destruction was impressive, as were the bloody remains and horror movie-type trails of gore. She searched further with her mind and found the alien that had passed her hiding spot was in the commons area. The other two were on the middle level at the moment, and so was the person who had sent the signal.

The space station was a circular structure made up of three large rings around a large central complex. The command deck was located at the top of the station. There was a wide thoroughfare around the center with halls connecting to the outer rings. Ramps branched off and down to the lower levels with elevators spaced evenly around, giving multiple access points to each ring.

The lowest was comprised of a handful of docking bays and hangars with vast cargo storage areas filling the remaining space. The middle level was full of small rooms, with doors lining the entire outer ring on both sides. There was a medical facility in the middle of the commons area.

The top level had more rooms and access to the control deck. There appeared to be a commerce and trade area with a lounge and restaurants around the main shaft. Or at least what was left of them. It had been abandoned for a long time.

Skye pressed the door control, masking the sound as it opened. Smears of blood and gory remains covered the hall that headed to the commons area and the central lift shaft. She had to get to the middle ring to find the source of the signal and be in a position to distract the aliens while the others made their way up.

She snuck down the hall, delicately stepping over and around the carnage while keeping mental tabs on the alien on her level. It was on the far side of the outer ring. They certainly moved fast when they wanted to. She reached the end of the hall and leaned against the wall, searching with her mind before turning the corner into the corridor that would take her to the inner ring.

More trails of blood and mostly unidentifiable remains showed the path the alien had taken through the outer ring. She picked her way silently down the grisly hallway and scanned the open area near the commons. She knew where the aliens were, but it was always better to be cautious when operating in unfamiliar territory.

The ramp to the middle level was wide and ended on a flat walled platform with two more ramps on either side heading to the lower level. The visibility wasn't the best, but it gave her options and wouldn't be as noisy as the lifts.

She searched for the two aliens on the middle ring. One was on the far side of the outer ring, close to where Tate was heading. The other was at the bottom of one of the ramps below her.

She took a quick peek over the railing and recoiled in revulsion at the sight below. She had seen plenty of horrifying things as a guardian, but that did not make the violently dismembered bodies being eaten any more pleasant.

"Careful, Tate. One of the aliens on the middle level is near where you're heading right now." They weren't in any immediate danger but needed to be careful.

"Thanks for the heads up."

She focused on the mind of the mystery person and took a second to take a closer mental peek at their location and get a better sense of who it was. He was locked down in a small area below the medical facility. His mind didn't give off any bad vibes or warning signals. Other than a large dose of apprehension, he seemed pretty normal.

The only ways into his hiding spot were a tiny maintenance shaft and a narrow personal elevator. He was safe enough for the time being, not that she wanted to leave him alone much longer.

Skye crept down the ramp furthest from the alien. It was busy eating the unlucky pirates who had met their end at the bottom. She needed to get it away from there so she could move.

There was an open door to a small office off the side of the ramp. She slipped inside, searching for something to use as a distraction. She picked up some kind of high-tech tablet, weighing it in her hand. It was heavy enough that it should make a fabulously loud noise if she threw it.

She crept back up the ramp to the middle point. She took a quick mental look to make sure she had a clear shot and threw the tablet in a powerful controlled arc to the upper level, where it crashed into the wall.

The alien screamed and barreled toward the noise, its claws digging into the metal of the floor. Skye ducked out of sight below the railing of the upper ramp.

She wasn't easily frightened, as a rule. It was the upshot of being a guardian. This was an entirely new kind of situation for her. And while she wasn't afraid, the suspenseful nature of her movements added a different type of thrill to everything.

Kya said, "Hold on, I should be able to get that one further away from you. I'm going to send one of the lifts to the upper level." A loud whooshing noise sounded from above, and the alien snarled and ran away. The noise drew the other one away from Tate too.

"Maybe they should invest in quiet elevators on space stations in the event of a horrific alien being set loose," Skye said dryly.

"You're not wrong. Things like this happen more than you would think, so it's surprising someone hasn't come up with it." Kya replied while the others laughed at their commentary.

"*Alien monsters let loose on space stations is seriously common?*" She wasn't as surprised as she sounded.

"Says the girl who recently battled necromancers and a horde of zombies?"

"Fair point." Skye had saved an entire world from an army of undead and their necromancer masters not too long ago.

Tate asked with a laugh, "How many zombies are in a horde?"

Wes said, "You're going to ignore the necromancer part of her statement?"

"Well over a million zombies," Skye answered honestly. The fact that they were comfortable talking out loud while they were all currently sneaking through a space station told her Kya used her powers to help mask her crew's noises.

"I might not get to use my powers openly, but can you blame me for keeping them safe? It gives us an edge for sure."

"Not judging at all."

Her reply had barely left her mind when a large explosion from below shook the entire station, swiftly followed by a series of smaller explosions.

"Rachel, what's going on down there?" Kya asked.

"A few more pirates decided to come play, so I'm giving them a friendly welcome. It's fine."

Kya asked blandly, "Are you blowing up the entire hangar?"

"Not the entire hangar, just the entrance. I'm making it hard for them to land. I locked down the other bays too. They won't be getting inside any other way."

Wes said, "There are a few more ships incoming. Scans show they're smaller craft, but they must have detected us here. Rachel, you might want to take the fight outside the hangar. Tate, you better move faster."

Skye checked on the aliens. "Looks like our rampaging alien friends are very interested in the shootout down there. Anything you can do to keep the two up top? I need to check in on our mystery person and make sure he isn't causing us problems."

Rachel said, "I got it. A flashy and ineffective burst of plasma against the shields on the windows up there should distract them for a bit."

Skye heard a few muffled impacts above her, along with an echoing set of roars fading away. "Nice job."

"What can I say? I'm a giver. I'll see if I can distract the other one as I make passes." The third alien had moved toward the lower level, but a blast of purple energy lit up a window in the distance, and it screamed, running to the outer ring.

"That was very colorful, and it worked. Thank you." Skye said, running toward the medical center. Rachel's strategic blasts bought everyone more time. Now all she had to do was figure out who had sent the signal and if he was a threat.

Skye slapped the key card against the panel by the door, masking the whooshing noise with a touch of energy as it slid open. She had a much clearer feel for the emotions of the mystery man now. He was nervous and a little afraid, which made sense considering the situation.

The elevator was at the bottom. He must have taken it to get to his hiding spot. She didn't want to give him a warning, so the maintenance shaft was her best option for a sneak attack.

She removed the panel without letting a hint of sound escape and dropped silently down the shaft, landing in a crouch in the narrow space. She could feel that he was tense and alert for danger. There was no way she was going to sneak up on him, and no way she wasn't going to scare him.

The time for stealth was over. She kicked the panel open and popped into the room, rising to her feet and disarming him before he finished raising his weapon.

He stared at her in shock, fear rolling off him in waves. She stepped back, letting go of his arm, and took a good look at him. He was tall with a lanky, muscular build, sandy blond hair, and dark brown eyes. His clothing wouldn't have been out of place in a Sci-Fi movie or video game.

His emotions calmed down as he watched her, surprised that she wasn't attacking him. She could sense a variety of feelings, primarily fear and worry, with a good dose of confusion. He didn't give her any bad vibes. If anything, she rather liked what she felt. He was a genuinely decent person. It was time to find out what he was doing.

She tilted her head to the side and pointed a finger at him. "You are not an eighty-year-old galactic award-winning female research scientist." His lips twitched with a hint of a smile, and she continued, "But you did send a signal disguised like it came from one. I'm going to need you to explain a few things." A roar echoed from above, and she glanced up. "And quickly, if you don't mind."

He followed her gaze and asked in surprise, "Your crew didn't take care of them yet?"

She shrugged. "It's a work in progress. Who are you, and why did you send that very sneaky signal? Please be honest. I don't have time to call out a bunch of lies. And believe me, I'll know if you're lying."

He looked surprised but answered her quickly. "My name is Korbin Das'an, and you could say I procure goods for people. Usually, things that are hard to come by for various reasons." His expression had a hint of pride in his skills.

Skye pressed her lips together to fight a smile. His name was almost dead on perfect for a character in one of her favorite movies. "So, you're a space pirate who smuggles illegal contraband?"

His expression was mildly offended as he said, "I'm not a space pirate. A smuggler maybe, but not a pirate."

"If you say so. This station was full of space pirates." She gave him a pointed look. "And three super angry aliens took care of them. Yet here you are, in a small room, totally safe, sending out distress signals with someone else's identity."

He answered with a rueful smile. "When you put it like that, it doesn't sound great. I delivered some cargo and was headed back to my ship on the docking level when the aliens got loose. So, I ran. I stole a key card off one of the pirates before the aliens got too far, and I was able to lock myself down here."

He rubbed his hand over the scruffy stubble on his chin and continued. "I took a job that led me out here. My contact didn't tell me they got the contract from a pirate crew. I might be a smuggler, but I don't deal with pirates if I can avoid it. Especially when they start trying to branch out into bigger ventures."

"Like giant carnivorous aliens?" Another screaming roar punctuated her sarcastic comment.

"Exactly. I figured I'd be able to wait until they got things under control. Then I heard the screams, and it didn't take long to figure out I wasn't going to get out of here without help. So, I sent out a signal. And yes, I did fake who it was from, but only to get a faster and more serious response."

Skye knew he was telling the truth, and her senses told her he was sincere. "Pretty risky still, depending on who showed up."

"I'd rather get arrested for smuggling than get eaten by an alien." He shrugged, a hint of a grin on his face.

Kya spoke in her mind, *"There's an extra earpiece in your pocket now. He might be an asset where he is, and I trust your reading of his emotions. At the very least, we can stay in contact with him while you round up some aliens."*

Skye sent a silent acknowledgment to her cousin and said aloud, "That does seem like a sound choice. Here's the deal. You're safe enough here for now." She handed him the earpiece. "That'll put you in touch with my cousin Kya's crew, who are taking over the station."

"Kya? You mean the enforcer Kyadara?" He sounded impressed.

"Yeah, you know her?"

"Her reputation, yes." He looked at the earpiece in his hands and then at Skye, at a loss for words.

She grinned mischievously and asked, "Wondering why I'm not locking you up like a criminal to be dealt with later?" He nodded. His eyes full of worry.

Skye took pity on him. "It's hard to explain, but I know you told me the truth just now. And I know you're a good person. Just go with it." She winked at him, feeling his confusion grow.

"If you say so." He flipped on the earpiece.

"Kya, Tate, Rachel, Wes, this is Korbin Das'an, space pirate." Her grin was full of mischief.

"Smuggler," Korbin said firmly, shaking his head at her with a grin.

Kya said, "Nice to meet you, Korbin. Unfortunately, we don't have time for too much chit-chat, but any insight you can offer will be helpful. Do you know how many pirates there are in this crew?"

Korbin said, "I don't know too much about the station, but I heard enough conversations to know there were at least six other ships they were waiting to return."

Rachel chimed in. "I've only seen four so far. Strike that. My long-range sensors are picking up two more ships. Are you sure about the numbers?"

"I can't be completely positive, but it's what I heard."

Kya thanked him and said, "Skye, we could use you out there. They're getting wise to Rachel's blasts, and Tate has to be able to move."

She knew what that meant. "You got it. I'll go make a ruckus so you guys can get moving faster." She checked with her mind and sighed. The aliens on the top floor were going to be an issue now. "How long will it take you to work your magic so no one else can see things?"

Tate said, "Not too long, a few minutes."

"Oh good. Because I'm about to do something completely insane, and I might need that sooner rather than later."

"What are you going to do?" Kya asked with a slight tone of worry.

"Well, it sounds like more pirates will be arriving shortly. Rachel, any issue with stopping them from landing?"

"At the moment, no. I've been giving them a good show and keeping them occupied, but eventually, they'll get to the hangar no matter how hard I try."

"Well, three horrific rampaging aliens might get the pirates out of our hair for a minute. Tate needs a clear path. So, I'm going to round up all three and bring them down to meet our space pirate friends in the hangar." She shrugged at Korbin, who was shocked, terrified, and more than a little speechless.

Wes chuckled and said, "Kya wasn't joking about how reckless you are. But that should work. Tate, do you think you can get Rachel into one of the other docking bays once things settle?"

They replied, "Shouldn't be a problem."

Skye stepped into the elevator and gave Korbin a reassuring smile. "You'll be safe here."

"Are you really going to go and—" His voice trailed off.

"Run around like a maniac and get murderous rampaging aliens to chase me to the hangar to take care of some space pirates?" She nodded her head with a comical expression. "Yeah. I'll be fine. I do this kind of thing all the time." She managed to not laugh at his look of consternation as the door closed.

She crept to the closest ramp to go to the upper level. "Ready when you are."

Kya said, "Be careful, cousin. I do *not* want to explain to mother how you met your end on a space station."

Sarah Eriksen

"You know me."

"Exactly."

Skye ran up the ramp dropping her bubble of silence and yelling, "Leeroy Jenkins!" at the top of her lungs, her voice echoing across the space station.

"What does that mean?" Tate asked with a laugh.

Kya sighed. "Just go with it."

Skye laughed and waited for the massive alien to catch sight of her before launching herself over the railing of the ramp. She landed at the bottom, solidly on the middle level. She needed to hold their attention, and the empty space had quite the echo. She started loudly singing one of her favorite songs as she ran around the main hall on the inner part of the middle ring.

A loud crash heralded an alien's arrival on her level. The other one on the top ring was running toward the sound of her voice as it echoed up the ramps she ran past.

Wes quipped, "We get free entertainment as well as a great distraction. The volume is impressive."

Rachel said, "I'm more impressed at how fast she's moving and that she can sing that well at the same time without running out of breath."

Wes said, "Think how the pirates must be reacting to this."

Kya said, "Good thing our reputation can handle it."

Rachel asked, "You assume anyone will be left alive to notice?"

Skye laughed while singing, which added some interesting new notes to a rather serious song. The third alien roared and ran toward her from the outer ring.

She said, "I've almost got them all." A crashing sound from above confirmed it as she passed a ramp. "Any reason for me to not head to the hangar yet?"

Rachel said, "I'm clear of the station. Two ships of pirates have landed. I let them scan me and put on a show of fleeing in terror."

Tate said, "It looks like they are leaving their ships. I've jammed their ability to scan your location and the aliens, but I'm sure they've noticed something by now."

"Can you shut off the lights on the lower level by any chance?"

"Absolutely, but will you be okay in the dark?"

"Not a problem."

"Consider it done."

Skye dashed around the inner ring, the three aliens behind her. She didn't want to risk another lap to get to the ramp closest to the hangar the pirates were in. The open space around the central shaft would be too tempting for the massive and agile aliens to not leap across and corner her. She threw herself over the railing of another ramp, taking the fast route down to the now dark lower level.

Sarah Eriksen

Chapter Three

Skye did a broad scan with her mind as she ran through stacked cargo containers. She was on the opposite side of the station from the hangar she needed to get to. She wrapped herself in silence and climbed up the large, stacked containers, using the barest hint of energy that thankfully didn't glow. She could get away with some guardian tricks in the dark, but not if she was sparking and glowing with coldfire.

The aliens snuffled around in the darkness at the entrance to the cargo hold. They had lost sight of her but had not given up the hunt yet. She sprinted silently across the tops of the containers, hurtling over empty spaces in between.

She reached the last one and dropped to the floor, landing in front of the door and pressing the button to open it. The whooshing sound caught the attention of the aliens. Screams of rage competed with the sound of claws scraping metal as they fought to move through the narrow spaces between the containers.

Now that she had their attention again, she ran across the floor of the empty and sealed hangar, picking up speed in the open space.

Tate said, "I have control of the systems. I should be able to track your location with the earpiece Kya gave you. I don't have control over the cameras yet."

"Awesome. Can you close the doors behind them as they follow me? That should give you another safe hangar." She hurried into another cargo bay full of massive metal crates and nimbly climbed to the top.

Chaotic Haunts

"Absolutely. You're almost to the pirates. You'll probably run into some of them in the dark."

"Not unless they're on top of cargo containers."

Tate spoke slowly as they concentrated on what they were watching. "The aliens are almost out of the hangar…and there. They're in the cargo bay. Skye, can you block the sound from the door closing so the pirates don't hear it?"

"Done and done." They wanted the pirates to stay unaware of anything suspicious going on. Thankfully, silence seemed to be one of the few things she could pull off without the magical fanfare.

"Thank you. The hangar is secure now. Rachel, I can open hangar five for you."

"I'm good out here, for now, just keeping an eye out for any stragglers. I'm cloaked, but leave it sealed to be safe. I'll let you know if I need a fast landing spot."

Skye crouched down at the edge of the last container, studying the pirates below her. The aliens had been distracted by the door closing on the far side of the cargo bay, and the pirates were none the wiser.

She took a moment to find the other pirates in the hangar ahead. A few were heading toward the inner ring and the ramps. Her cousin and Wes were moving through some maintenance shafts near the outer ring of the middle level. They were setting devices that would allow them to do something fairly spectacular, she was sure.

"Kya, how much more time do you need?" She slipped into mind-to-mind communication without thinking about it.

"We're almost done. We split the difference and met in the middle. Once the devices are set, the station will be shielded from any outside hacking, and we'll have total control."

"Alright, I'll work on the other problem here." She bit her lip while she thought. She could wrap herself in invisibility, but that would make it harder to play bait. As tempting as it would have been to let the aliens handle the pirates, she didn't love killing people, even when they were absolute monsters themselves.

She felt confident that with the aliens providing a distraction, she'd be able to round up the pirates and trap them. With the lights out on the station, they resorted to night vision tech or flashlights to help them see.

Sarah Eriksen

It was pure luck that the aliens hadn't seen the lights yet. She needed to get the pirates isolated and safely out of the way.

She carefully opened up the barest trickle of energy, keeping a tight grip on it to prevent herself from sparking. It flowed over her body in an invisible shield that would protect her from stray globs of venom and any weaponry the pirates had.

Invisibility wasn't a good option, but there were other ways of going unnoticed in the dark. She kept her mental stranglehold on the trickle of energy and pulled darkness around her body like armor. She jumped off the edge of the container and dropped to the floor in front of the pirates.

They didn't see her in her shadowy disguise. There was a small storage closet with a door nearby that would make a great makeshift jail cell. She wasn't above messing around with them a little bit to get them inside it.

She tapped one in the middle of his chest with a firm jab of her finger. He jumped back in confusion. Her voice sounded unnaturally loud in the darkness as she whispered, "I'm going to give you five seconds to run to the small closet to your left before I get the attention of the big scary aliens that are locked in here with us."

She summoned a small flash of energy at the far end of the cargo hold, and the aliens screamed, pouncing toward the light hidden behind large shipping containers. The pirates glanced around in confusion, their weapons raised.

She said, "Five." Another flash of light elicited more roars, closer this time. "Four." The pirates bolted. She followed at a slow jog raising her hands and risking another touch of energy.

Their weapons flew out of their hands as they ran into the room. She closed the door behind them and punched the control panel on the outside, destroying it and locking them in. She flicked away the faint sparks that flurried around her fingers, hoping they were too pale to be noticed.

The aliens screamed and roared, crashing into the cargo containers as they charged toward the slight noise the door had made. She sprinted across the remaining space of the cargo hold to the next hangar. They wouldn't be too far behind, but there were enough containers in the way that would slow them down.

Snippets of information on how to disable the ships flowed into her mind as she snuck toward the handful of pirates standing guard. The ships' lights made a bright spot in the darkness inside the hangar. She'd have to move fast to go unnoticed.

She dragged the edge of the darkness with her as she attacked. She disarmed and knocked out the pirates with a few well-placed punches and kicks. Their weapons slid off into the shadows as she hauled the bodies into the ship and sealed them in.

She ducked under the hull and placed her palm against a metal panel. She sent a contained fizzle of electricity into it, shorting out the wiring in the engine in a chain reaction.

The aliens were close enough to be heard by the pirates at the other ship. They had a great sense of self-preservation and bolted inside, closing the door before any of their friends could hope to run to them from the far side of the hangar.

They had just made her job a lot easier. She shorted out their engine with another small electrical burst. They would be safe enough where they were for the moment. Especially since there was live bait outside the ship. She placed her hand on the door, heating the metal and melting it shut so they wouldn't be able to escape.

She frowned as a faint hint of sparks flickered over her fingers again, and she forcefully reduced the amount of energy she was drawing, letting out a frustrated sigh. She knew she shouldn't be too hard on herself. It was going to take time to get used to limiting the energy she used. The fact that it was the total opposite of what she was used to was starting to make her feel unbalanced, and she didn't like it.

Two aliens crashed into the hangar, a bent and twisted piece of a cargo container tumbling across the floor in front of them. They paused to sniff the air and listen for their prey.

She asked, "Hey Tate, do you have control over the doors in the whole station?"

"I do. What do you have in mind?"

"I'm currently herding pirates out of the hangar with aliens. Maybe you could strategically give them places to hide and lock them in? Oh, and shut off the lights on the other levels too, please."

Tate said, "That sounds like a blast. Kya was right about you."

Skye laughed. "Can you close off the cargo hold? There's one alien in there still, and it'll help encourage the three pirates I locked in from thinking about escaping."

"Done." The doors whooshed shut, and she dropped the shadows around her, making her body visible to the aliens' heightened senses as she bolted straight toward them.

One alien noticed her immediately and charged forward while the other raged at the closed door. She swerved to miss a glob of venom and then launched herself into the air. She took advantage of gravity to drop into the alien's neck, shoving it to the ground. Her body met resistance, and she used it to flip away.

"I've got a few pirates locked up on the middle ring, but there's a handful moving to the upper level," Tate said.

"You're safe, right?" She snapped her fingers, a tiny invisible explosion popping in the air behind her and getting the attention of both aliens.

"Yep, they won't be able to get to me."

Skye ran up the ramp and turned down the wide corridor around the middle of the station, the aliens snarling and screaming as they gave chase. She sensed another, calmer presence behind her. It was following her path and matching her pace.

A quick mental peek came up with nothing, so she touched the presence lightly and felt the person's startled reaction. To her surprise, careful but clear words formed in his head so she could pick it up.

"It's Wes. Kya asked me to follow you while she finishes up."

Skye shook her head and replied in his mind, *"In case I need help?"* It didn't bother her in the slightest. She was a little out of her depth. *"You two could have said something."*

His mind voice was strong and clear. He must have been used to talking like this with Kya. *"My apologies for not warning you. We do have to get the aliens locked down eventually too. I'm here to assist."*

"Any idea where to trap them?"

"There is a good-sized hall on the upper level that should hold them. If you can lead them in there after the pirates are locked up, I'll close the door behind them and put some questionably legal tech on it that will prevent them from escaping."

"Questionably legal, I like it."

"Can you see where I'm talking about?" His question included a mental projection of the location.

"Got it. You're pretty good at this mind-to-mind stuff."

"Something about my heritage makes it easy. Kya has been helping me learn. It still feels different from normal talking, but it's certainly convenient."

"It gets easier over time."

Tate said, "Skye, the pirates on the top level are trying to barricade themselves into a defensive position in the center."

"Of course, they are." She slid around a corner and ran to the upper level.

"Watch out, Wes. I'm going to slow them down to give myself a few more seconds" She felt his acknowledgment.

She slammed her hand onto the ground, and a shimmering trail of ice spread across the metal. She sent a jolt of force down the ramp as the alien's feet met with the slippery surface. The icy metal shifted, and they slid into a tumbled heap at the bottom.

The ice disappeared as she ran the rest of the way up, wrapping herself in shadows again. She had at least managed to control the sparks this time around.

She put on a burst of energy-enhanced speed and leaped over the railing into the common area where the four pirates were barricading themselves. She didn't have time to come up with a delicate solution, so she lunged straight at them.

She punched the first one in the face, wrapping him in shadows as he slumped down. His body slid across the floor into the darkness as she moved to the next one. Skye dropped down and swept out her leg, making him fall to the floor. She lightly touched his head, knocking him unconscious and sending him into the shadows.

The last two pirates searched the darkness frantically as they tried to figure out what was attacking them. They stood back to back, and Skye moved lightning fast, slamming their heads together and knocking them out. She wrapped energy around them and hauled them back where they'd be out of the way.

Her timing was impeccable. The aliens had finally untangled themselves and reached the top of the ramp.

Sarah Eriksen

Kya said, "We have full control of the ship, so don't hold back anymore, Skye."

"Oh good." She dropped the shadows and the tight control she had on her powers. White and dark blue sparks flickered erratically around her before her body erupted into a blinding blaze of coldfire. The aliens screamed in rage and ran toward her.

She headed to the hall Wes had shown her. They followed in a frenzy, bottlenecking for a moment at the entrance. The door closed behind them after they entered, and a pale blue flicker of electricity shimmered across seconds later.

Wes said, *"Can you distract them while I head to the other door? I'll let you know when I'm ready for you to exit."* He wasn't worried about her ability to handle herself.

"Got it."

She launched herself at the alien in front of her, turning her body and slamming her right leg into its torso. It flew across the room and crashed into the wall. She continued her momentum and spun so she was facing the other one.

Her right arm flew forward, punching the alien hard enough that she felt a crack as her fist sunk into its chest. The alien's body finally caught on to the fact that it had met an object with far more force, and it flew backward, screaming.

She ran forward, twisting her body to dodge a glob of venom and leaping over an angrily slashing arm. The alien sunk its claws into the floor as it pushed itself up. She turned to face it, a small, concentrated ball of incandescent fire forming between her palms.

The fireball slammed into the alien, knocking it over as the coldfire burnt through its tough skin. She casually raised her hand and redirected the venom back into the other alien's face. It screamed horribly as its own venom burned its eyes.

"Okay, I'm ready whenever you can get through the door," Wes said.

She bolted out of the room, sliding to a stop against the wall and releasing the creation energy swirling in her. The coldfire died down with a few fitful flickers.

A strange metal device appeared on the door, and electricity shimmered out of it in a contained field. The air in front of her wavered as Kya's crewmate dropped his stealth field. He was a tall man, with

Chaotic Haunts

deeply tanned skin and dark hair. His eyes were a startling gray, and a scar ran down the right side of his face.

"I thought Kya's powers were impressive, but yours are certainly…flashy."

Skye laughed wryly and glanced down at the fading sparks. "It's a bit of a recent development. And an annoying one. Being on fire is a little inconvenient at times."

Wes chuckled. "It certainly makes you stand out."

Tate said, "It was hard to see what was going on with how brightly you were glowing. Next time we should just start with that. No one would know what is going on with that much glare."

Kya said, "We still had to get control of the space station, so it wouldn't have changed the outcome."

Wes replied, "And the pirates did have a line to the ship, so maybe we don't want people to know about bright shiny magical powers."

Tate asked sarcastically, "Whose side are you on, Wes?"

"Kya's, obviously. She's the boss. And she's a lot scarier than you."

Skye laughed. Their banter reminded her of her friends. "We should probably secure those last pirates I knocked out. Korbin? You've been rather quiet. How are you holding up?"

"Oh, I'm fine in my little closet down here listening to the bizarre and confusing conversations you've been having. It's definitely educational, and I kind of wish I had seen the flashy powers." His sense of humor fit in with the rest of them.

Tate said, "Skye, I'll open the door to a room you can lock them in that's not too far."

Kya said, "Turn the lights on while you're at it. Korbin, you can head up to the top level if you want. The station is secure, and we have some things to discuss."

"Of course." Korbin seemed to be taking everything in stride.

Rachel spoke, "Can you open up one of the hangars for me to land in? It's all clear out here."

Tate replied, "Go to the same one you landed in before. Skye took out the pirates, and you can disable the ships while you're there."

Skye said, "The ships are already disabled, I shorted them out with some lightning, and there are pirates locked in them. I did melt the door shut on one ship to trap them inside, so that'll be fun to open up."

Rachel laughed. "Kya, you never said your cousin was this much fun."

"I thought it was implied in the reckless behavior statement." Kya teased.

Wes raised his eyebrows at the pile of pirates Skye had left and laughed. "I wish I could have seen how you did that."

Tate said, "It was like shadows were beating them up and swallowing them. It was kind of terrifying."

Skye shrugged nonchalantly. "It worked."

Wes frowned. "Are they going to stay unconscious while we drag them to—" his voice trailed off as the four pirates floated up off the floor and started moving toward the open door. Weapons drifted off of them and dropped to the ground.

He smiled at Skye in amazement as he took in her raised hand with small sparks flickering around it. She flashed a half grin, revealing a hint of a dimple on her cheek. "No need for us to work hard. I did just run a few miles on this ship." The pirates slumped to the ground gently, one of them raising her head and blinking in confusion at Skye before the door closed.

Kya and Korbin walked up one of the ramps nearby, studying the mess that was the main hall. Kya said, "Those things certainly did a number on everyone who was here before."

Skye asked Korbin, "Is there a lot of money smuggling those things? It seems like it's not worth the risk if they…you know…kill everything in sight, including the people smuggling them."

Korbin seemed surprised that she asked, and more surprised when the others waited expectantly for him to answer. He said, "It's a lot of money. But I personally never believed it was worth the risk. That and I don't like trafficking living things."

"Space pirate with standards. I can respect that." Skye winked at him, laughing as he muttered 'smuggler' back at her.

A door whooshed open in the center column, and Tate walked out. They had dark skin, braided black hair with a greenish cast, and an intricate cybernetic implant attached to their temple over startling blue eyes.

Tate said, "This place is weird."

Wes asked, "Do you mean the aliens and pirates? Or the station in general?"

"The station. There are multiple doors on the middle level that are obviously doors, but there's no way to open them. It took forever to find actual functional doors to lock up those pirates." They exaggerated since it only had taken them a few minutes at the most.

Kya's brow furrowed, and she asked, "Is there another control section?"

Tate shook their head. "That's the only place on board. I scanned for everything I could. There seems to be space on the other side of them, but it's empty."

Skye said, "That's probably the real reason why you're here." They looked at her in surprise. "I don't know much about being a guardian in a fancy high-tech galaxy, but why would you get sent here to handle a couple of rampaging aliens that ate everyone else? Seems like this place was handled."

She glanced apologetically at Korbin and continued, "And you probably weren't sent here to rescue a smuggler who was in the wrong place at the wrong time."

Kya said, "Maybe you should have a job like mine."

"No thanks. I have enough fun blowing up monsters and saving random worlds from rampaging hordes of undead. I like not having to behave with my powers all the time."

Tate laughed. "If I could do what you did, I'd feel the same."

Korbin finally said, "I might feel the same too, if I had a damn clue what any of you were talking about. Jobs? Guardians? Hordes of undead?" His tone shifted and became contrite. "I don't mean to sound ungrateful, but I'm still wondering why you haven't locked me up like you did with the pirates."

Wes shrugged and said, "The boss trusts you, so you're good." He jerked his chin toward Kya, which only prompted Korbin to look more confused.

Kya gazed at him sympathetically. "We'll have to fill you in on some serious details, but you are welcome to join my crew if you want." Amonir must have told her to share the knowledge of guardians with him.

Korbin nodded his head, curiosity and excitement evident in his grin.

Kya continued, "We have our work cut out for us with the aliens, pirates, and doors that aren't connected to the control center."

Skye said, "Well, cousin, it's been…fun. Even if I had to play chase with horrifying aliens. Declan is going to be so jealous."

Kya burst out laughing. "I'll ask him for help next time. I must say, it was enjoyable working with you. It certainly made my job a lot easier. We'll have to do it again sometime."

"Absolutely, without the murderous rampaging aliens, though. You should stop by for a visit one of these days anyway. Bring your friends if you want to frighten them with us crazy Earthlings you're related to." She winked at Kya's crew, getting grins from them and more confusion from Korbin.

Kya laughed. "I'm not sure they're prepared for that level of insanity."

"It was nice meeting all of you. See you around." Skye smiled and teleported back home.

Chapter Four

It had been a few weeks since the spectacular ending to a zombie invasion on the world of Meriten and Skye's subsequent space adventure shortly after. The end of summer had been uneventful guardian-wise, with only minor border infractions and no end-of-the-world situations.

Rhaeadr, the guardians' friend from Meriten, had finished training with his cousin Eric and returned home. He stayed in touch with Skye, although their romantic relationship had died down to a close friendship.

Skye spent her days dodging her unhygienic and rather pathetic stalker, Vincent Shadoweaver while running her shop and surviving the summer influx of tourists. She spent her free time trying to gain some semblance of control and balance with her new levels of power.

She hadn't had much success. If anything, it seemed to be getting worse. Small and quick uses of energy were easy. Anything bigger was an internal struggle to maintain control of the power surging through her. Amonir had been conspicuously avoiding conversations, leaving Skye on her own to figure it out.

All her life, she had had impeccable control over her powers. She had always been confident in her abilities, knowing exactly what she was capable of and how far she could push without hurting herself. For the first time in her life, she wasn't sure how to handle her powers, and she didn't know how to fix it.

She held her fears and doubts close inside, keeping her usual quick-witted, confident self in front of her friends. It was easier to act like things were alright. Her twin could pick up on hints, but she had figured out how to hide the real depth of her internal struggles from him when they were teenagers.

Trey relied on her strength and self-assurance to bolster his own emotions and confidence, so she did her best to hide her worries away. He had already been struggling with the shift in her powers and felt guilty about how he had treated her.

She felt lost and more than a little lonely, despite being surrounded by people who cared about her. The job on Meriten had been a small hint at what her life as a guardian was becoming. Her powers set her apart, and her inability to control them terrified her.

There was a bite in the air as Skye headed to town. It was mid-September, and this high in the mountains, fall was announcing its arrival. It was her favorite time of year. Cooler weather, pretty leaves, and an excuse to wear her geeky hoodies, comfy jeans, and sneakers. Not to mention Halloween was just around the corner.

Most guardians loved Halloween and Skye was one of them. It was one of the few holidays where they could let loose with their powers. They couldn't go overboard, but it was fun to make a kid's eyes widen by adding a touch of real magic to the day.

She pulled into the parking stall, waving at Ian, who had beat her by a few seconds. "Hey, Mr. Punctual, what's up?"

Ian made a face at her. "I have to be punctual. Otherwise, you might fire me. Then you'd have to put up with Trey and Declan's help all the time, which would only make you beg me to come back. And I'd rather save you from that awkwardness."

Skye gave him a considering look. "You make a valid point."

"Anything fun and exciting on the crazy magical guardian front?" Ian started making himself a latte.

"Not really. Same old, same old. I won't say it's been quiet, but it's been pretty typical. Life-sucking shadow monster one day, helping a lost fairy return home, rescuing Trey from a vicious pixie ambush. Typical."

"Your concept of typical is getting less crazy but is still crazy. Want a caramel macchiato?"

"Do I seriously need to answer that?"

"No. That was a dumb question on my part." Ian laughed and started making her favorite drink.

Chaotic Haunts

The day passed slowly, kids were back in school, and the tourists were mostly outdoors hiking in the pleasant autumnal scenery. It was Thursday, so their weekly gaming night was already scheduled.

Skye took advantage of the slow afternoon to work on her other job, writing articles for a local paper. She was curled up in her favorite chair, typing away on her laptop. It was a good distraction from her worries.

She was staring blankly out the window, thinking about article ideas, when a conversation between two teenagers caught her attention. They were talking excitedly about a real haunted house a few miles away. It was the right time of year for the thrill of ghosts and hauntings, but it was probably something completely unrelated that was causing the phenomenon.

Ghosts were real, but guardians didn't normally interact with them. Barring certain situations based on gods arguing it out and telling a guardian to step in, they didn't mess with the afterlife. Gods had any number of ideas on hereafters, and some liked the option for spirits to linger on.

It was rare for a ghost to cause problems on Earth that called for an intervention from a guardian. All-in-all hauntings were pretty trivial compared to the other monster situations out there.

Skye's brain wandered back to the job at hand. Haunted house aside, she should write up some Halloween-themed articles. She made a mental note to ask the editor to get her a list of anything noteworthy to feature in the upcoming months. She was lost in her thoughts when the door chimed, and a feeling of dread swept over her.

"My beloved Skye!" Vincent must have been fighting a cold because his typically high-pitched voice had a decidedly nasal tone that was painful to hear.

Skye growled to herself and looked up, choking back a laugh. His outfit was even more bizarre than usual. It appeared to be a white tuxedo ensemble from a decades-old wedding. Surprisingly, it was too large for his oversized frame. Rather than looking more tasteful than his usual undersized clothes, it hung off him like a stretched-out tent. To add to it, he appeared to have stuffed a crocheted doily into the neck of the suit in an attempt to replicate a cravat.

Sarah Eriksen

Skye sighed and said, "Go away, Vincent." She leaped out of her chair and retreated to the counter, ducking safely behind it. Safe being relative against the force that was Vincent's obsession with her.

"I have an invita—" his voice cut off with a hacking cough.

Ian interjected in a rare moment of confrontation. "Vincent, you really shouldn't come in here coughing all over the place. Do you want Skye to get sick? I mean, that'd be terrible, wouldn't it?"

Skye piped in, "I'd be out for days, maybe even a week or two." She never got sick. Being a guardian guaranteed good health and the ability to avoid common illnesses.

Vincent halted his slow forward momentum, confusion written all over his face. It was clear that he wanted to hand her the crumpled and rather disgusting invitation but was torn about making his beloved sick.

Ian was enjoying himself far too much. There was a wicked glint in his eyes as he said, "Rhaeadr would probably be extremely upset she got sick. He would probably have to come back to take care of her."

That sealed the deal, and Vincent backed up, wheezing in terror. Rhaeadr had scared him to death by gazing threateningly at him a few weeks before. Vincent opened the door and turned, drawing in a deep breath to deliver a dramatic line and breaking into another coughing fit. He shook his fist with the crumpled invitation at them and tripped his way out of the door, red-faced and gasping.

"I wonder how long the threat of Rhaeadr being here will work." Skye contemplated.

Ian shrugged and said, "If it ever stops working, you could probably ask him to pay a visit and renew the dread?"

"I'm sure he'd do it in a heartbeat." She said with a giggle.

Skye was closing the blinds as the boys arrived for their Thursday night gaming. Declan set the boxes of pizza on the table in the middle of their usual arrangement of comfy seating. Ian poured coffee into a carafe for fast refills. Napkins, plates, and bottles of water were already in place. All they needed was to set up their laptops and log on.

Ryan dropped energetically into his usual spot. He had been absent most of the summer while helping out his family. This was the first time in months they had all been able to get together to game for one reason or another.

Chaotic Haunts

Before they could get logged into their game, Ryan asked excitedly, "Have you heard about that haunted bed and breakfast that's been on the news? It's completely insane sounding! Things moving on their own, doors opening and closing by themselves, strange noises and voices, crying. And it's only thirty minutes down the road!"

Declan scoffed, "Probably just some mischievous brownie, or fairy, or gremlin…I could go on, but I'll save myself the breath."

Declan's sarcastic tone didn't faze Ryan. "You can be all guardian-y on me if you want, Declan, but it sounds legit to me. They invited some ghost hunters in, and they caught some apparitions on camera."

All the guardians smiled, not wanting to ruin his fun, except for Declan, who couldn't resist. "Orbs? You mean balls of dust? Or a full-blown apparition? Because I have another list of things that could appear to be an apparition."

Ryan grumbled, "I'm sure you do. But I still want to check it out. I guess the owners opened it up for people to explore and see for themselves."

"Making money off their haunted house? Smart." Declan nodded approvingly, and Trey smacked him lightly across the back of his head.

"You can't blame them. None of us have been called in to handle it, and it's still supposedly going on, so it might be legit." Trey said.

Skye agreed with her twin. "Poltergeist activity isn't unusual, and actual hauntings can and do happen."

Ryan turned to Ian and asked, "Want to go with me? These guys are no fun in haunted houses. Real or Halloween jump scare types."

Ian was confused. "You go to real haunted houses? And why are you no fun? I mean, I'd get why you're no fun in the whole Halloween gimmick ones. With your job, they would be kind of lame in comparison."

Eric answered, "Declan isn't wrong. A lot of times, hauntings aren't hauntings. They're other creatures that make people think things are haunted. Sometimes they're real, though. I can't speak for anyone else, but I've been to a real haunted house. My family's castle in Ireland has actual ghosts roaming about. They like to knock things off tables when they're being exceptionally annoying."

"Skye and I have been to a few ourselves, and like Eric said, it's usually something else. And the real haunted houses are kind of boring when we go." Trey shrugged apologetically.

Skye said, "What they aren't saying about why we are no fun in a real haunted house is that we can't see any of the ghosts. So, unless they're throwing axes across a room or knocking things down and moving chairs and doors, we get nothing. Can't even sense them. Not a creepy feeling. Nothing. Totally ghost and haunting deficient."

Ian opened his mouth, a perplexed expression on his face, and Skye interrupted him, "We can see them if we channel some creation energy, but then they know we're guardians, and they hide. Why are we no fun in a haunted house? We can't see anything, or we make them hide."

Declan snickered. "We're total buzzkills for avid ghost hunters." He blocked Trey's hand before it hit his head and wagged a finger in his face. "Not this time, pixie-bait!"

Ian sighed in acceptance. "Okay, so you guys really would be no fun at a haunted house."

Ryan sighed and said, "That's what I'm saying. Nothing scares these guys."

Declan smirked and shot a sideways glance at Skye. "That's not true—"

Skye glared at him. "If you say anything about paranprids, I will shove that entire piece of pizza you're holding into your mouth. All of it."

Declan glared eloquently back at her and let out a delicate cough. "I was going to say, have you ever seen Trey ambushed by pixies? Thank you very much."

Skye gave him a suspicious look and sipped her coffee. Trey raised his hands in a confused and defeated gesture and muttered, "What is with the teasing about pixies tonight?"

Eric said, "There are some things out there that would scare any of us for different reasons, but ghosts and jump scares don't quite make the cut."

Trey said brightly, "But hey, if you take us to a haunted house and something scares us, you should probably be terrified."

Skye gave him a 'what the hell' gesture.

Ian shook his head. "That doesn't make it any better, you know?"

Ryan was undeterred. "I seriously am going to go check it out. Do any of you want to go with me? Even you boring old guardians."

The guardians' faces went slightly blank for a second. Declan laughed. "Well, I guess we're going to go with you, Ryan. We just got told." He tapped his temples with his index fingers.

Ryan's face fell. "You mean it's probably not a real haunted house?"

Skye's expression was comically confused. "I'm actually not sure that it's not. Amonir wants us to see what's going on. Something is off about it." She gave him an encouraging grin and offered, "Maybe there are some real ghosts still."

Trey said, "Better get all six of us booked for the bed and breakfast for tomorrow night."

"I'll try, but it'll probably be too short notice to do it." Ryan grabbed his phone to pull it up and not interrupt his gaming.

Declan smirked and said, "I think you'll be amazed at the sudden availability."

Ian looked around at the guardians and asked, "Wait, six of us? I get to go on an investigation with you?"

Trey nodded. "We'll need your help if there are any real ghosts. You two get to be our warning system."

Ryan exclaimed, "Holy shit, they had a bunch of cancelations, and I got all of us in."

"Just like magic…or obvious divine intervention." Declan laughed.

Ian asked in disbelief, "A god interfered so you guys could get rooms at a haunted bed and breakfast?"

"Pretty much." Skye shrugged.

"Does he ever take requests for premium vacation spots?"

The next day flew by at the shop, despite Ian's millions of questions about ghosts and hauntings. Skye answered him with her usual attention to detail in between making coffee and helping customers. She welcomed the distraction since it took her mind off her own issues.

The sun was starting to set, and the winding road through the mountains gave a beautiful view of the changing leaves on the higher slopes. The haunted bed and breakfast was the next town down the scenic route.

Sarah Eriksen

It wasn't long before the highway turned into another ski resort town. The sky was aglow with twilight, and the first impression of the old bed and breakfast was that it could very well be haunted. It was built in a Victorian style and certainly gave the impression that it would have at least one ghost lurking in its dark hallways.

Declan voiced the same impression. "I think a house that looks like this is supposed to be haunted, by default. All we need now is a dead tree and some lightning to make it complete. Maybe a wolf howling in the distance."

Ian asked, his voice baffled, "Why do we need a dead tree and lightning?"

"To set the mood, of course."

Skye rolled her eyes. "Don't encourage him. Besides, it's obvious that the owners take great care of their yard. A dead tree wouldn't last more than the time it'd take to remove it." Her observation was accurate. The yard, or what they could see in the bright light from the porch, was well maintained.

They grabbed their bags and headed to the door. It was opened by the young couple who owned the bed and breakfast. They wanted to greet their guests personally.

"Welcome! If you are seeking the excitement of a true haunting, you've come to the right place!" The young man said with enthusiasm.

On the surface, they seemed excited. Only there was a hint of strain around their eyes, a tension that spoke of trouble. They hid it well, but they would have to for the guests.

The house was huge, with more rooms than their group would be taking up. There were three floors total and a closed-off attic above. The second and third floors were identical. They had a sitting room for the guests if they were inclined to socialize, and four bedrooms lining a hallway with a spacious bathroom at the far end.

The owners gave them a tour, explaining where the various disturbances happened. The third floor had a shadowy apparition that materialized at the end of the hall. The second floor had a phantom door that appeared during the night.

The closet doors in most of the rooms opened or closed, objects fell off tables, and drawers rattled and opened. Other than the apparition and phantom door, everything seemed to happen consistently in each room.

"Does this stuff happen on the main floor too?" Eric asked curiously.

The young man nodded. "It's more pronounced up here, but we get the same disturbances. The room at the end of the hall on the third floor...that one has the most activity."

Declan looked intrigued. "The one by the attic?" At the owner's nod, Declan said, "I'll take that room then."

Ryan's face lit up with excitement. "I'll take one on the third floor too!"

Trey let out a dramatic sigh. "I'd better stay on the third floor to babysit these two."

Skye patted his arm sympathetically. "Don't have too much fun with that. I'll take one of the rooms by the bathroom on the second floor." Something about the door appearing intrigued her. And, for some reason, it reminded her of the derelict space station with the broken doors.

Ian's expression was getting more worried by the minute. She gave him a reassuring smile. "Ian, you can take the room next to mine, and Eric can take the one across the hall."

Eric grinned companionably. "If Skye gets scared in the night, we can save her." He winked at Ian, getting the laugh he was expecting.

"More like if we get scared in the night, she'll save us," Ian said dryly.

"Exactly." It wasn't believable that anything could scare Eric, but Ian understood what he was saying. They wouldn't let anything happen to him.

The owner was confused by their exchange. "Don't you guys believe in ghosts?"

Skye said, "Kind of depends, I guess. We're mostly here because Ryan," she pointed at their excitable friend, "really wanted to check it out. I'll be honest, I'm a bit skeptical, but staying in a haunted house is still a fun idea." She wasn't lying. Staying in a haunted house, ghost deficient or not, was a bit of an adventure.

The owner's façade of pleasantness faded. Exhaustion was clear in his voice as he said, "You won't be skeptical after tonight. Everything starts happening around midnight and doesn't stop until the sun comes up."

Declan glanced sharply at him and asked, "Have you considered trying to get rid of what's haunting this place? At some point in time, you and your wife are going to need to get some solid sleep before it starts causing serious health concerns." At the owner's startled look, he shrugged, and boldface lied. "My parents are both doctors. You pick up a lot."

His face crumpled. "The money seemed worth it at first. A few things here and there, but it's been happening more and more frequently. It started a couple of weeks ago after the door started appearing. It got worse on the third floor, and it spread down here. We can't get any sleep."

Declan said seriously, "You might want to think about doing something. I can't say I know what that something is, but money isn't worth your health or sanity. Of course, I say that, and here we are, staying in a haunted house. But you never know, my tiny friend over there might scare away your ghosts by being annoyed they woke her up and challenged her skepticism." He got the expected, if strained, laugh his joke warranted.

The owner rallied and said, "Breakfast is at eight down in the dining room. If you need anything, don't hesitate to let us know."

Declan gazed at him somberly and said, "Try and get some rest."

The owner left them on the second floor, a thoughtful expression on his face as he mulled over what Declan had said.

Trey asked Declan, "What was that all about?"

He shrugged and said bluntly, "They're both exhausted, and it's taking a toll on them. If they don't get a break from the stress and exhaustion, they're going to have some serious issues." He was a true healer at heart.

Trey couldn't argue with his logic, so he picked the easier target to tease him about. "Your parents are doctors?"

Declan's grin was smug. "He believed it, didn't he?"

Skye shook her head at their bantering. "You're both impossible. But that being said, I haven't sensed a single thing out of the ordinary since we walked in here. How about you?"

The other three guardians shook their heads, and Ian said, "It feels kind of creepy and uncomfortable. I'm not sure if that's actually me feeling something, or if I'm just freaking myself out."

Ryan shook his head. "It's not only you, I'm feeling it too, and I was excited about being here. Can you guys sense other monsters if you don't use your powers?"

Eric said, "Yeah, we'd know if something that isn't allowed here was here. But it could be something allowed that isn't breaking any laws of creation. We can't look too seriously, because if it is a haunting, we'll scare the ghosts away before they start."

Ian nodded as if Eric's answer had been clear. "So, at this point, it could be haunted or not. We don't know. Maybe there's a monster, but we're not sure."

Skye pressed her lips together to fight off a laugh. "Don't worry, if it *is* ghosts, we can make them go away in an instant. If it isn't ghosts, it's easier for us. So far, nothing has hurt anyone, only scared people. And despite how horror movies portray things, ghosts generally aren't malevolent forces from a nightmare."

Ian took a deep breath. "Generally, aren't. But not completely. That's the kind of thing you say before we end up in a house full of ghosts or monsters trying to kill us. If I get killed tonight, I'm haunting you for the rest of your days and making your coffee cold."

"Duly noted. I will not let you die because I like hot coffee in winter."

Eric smiled at Ian and offered, "If you're that worried, we can bunk together."

"I might have to take you up on that. I thought I was going to be okay until we got here."

Ryan turned expectantly to Declan and Trey and got zero sympathy from both of them. Trey shook his head. "You're too excitable, Ryan. I don't think I can handle it."

They headed to their rooms, Ian and Eric investigating to see which one was the easiest for them both to stay in. Skye couldn't help but wonder what it was like to not be a guardian and to feel the creepiness of a haunted house.

It wasn't that she didn't feel fear, but that cold in the pit of your stomach, hair on the back of your neck standing up feeling wasn't something she had ever experienced. Being a guardian desensitized you in some ways. There wasn't much of a fear of the unknown when you knew so much about all of creation. Although considering the trade-off, she wasn't sure it was a bad thing.

Sarah Eriksen

Chapter Five

Skye's eyes snapped open as she heard squeaky door hinges. She pushed herself up on her elbows, her eyes adjusting to the darkness. Her closet door was open. Not wanting to give anything away to the ghosts, she put on a show of fumbling for the light and turned it on. Sure enough, the closet door had opened.

She got up with a hint of a sigh and closed it, making sure it was latched and not loose enough to open on its own. It was closed tight. She crawled back into bed and shut off the light, closing her eyes. A few seconds later, the hinges squeaked again as the door opened.

"What woke you up?" Trey's mental voice sounded oddly alert for the time of night.

"Something has decided to open my closet door. So, I closed it, and as soon as I shut off the light and got comfy...it opened again."

"Sounds like a real ghost then, did you—?"

"Check to make sure the door latches shut? Of course, I did." She managed to sound only slightly annoyed. *"Guess I'll start messing around with the ghost and give it something to do."*

"Keep closing the door and trying to make sure it can't open?" He said with a hint of a laugh.

"Pretty much. At least until I give up and leave it open. How are things upstairs? You seem awfully awake." Skye closed the closet again and wedged the desk chair under the doorknob this time.

Chaotic Haunts

"I'm just keeping an eye on things up here so the other two can sleep. I haven't noticed anything yet, but that doesn't mean that there's not some floating apparition in the hallway or something."

"Well, if there is, hopefully Ryan will give it a thrill by seeing it."

"Seriously, how do ghosts not know we're guardians when we can't see them and don't react?"

"The same reason so many people are skeptical of ghosts to begin with. Some people simply ignore things like that." The chair made an audible thud and scraping sound as it was moved out of the way enough for the door to open again.

She said out loud, "Okay, you win. I'll leave the door open, but it'll just let dust get on everything in the closet and require more cleaning."

Skye snuggled into her covers again and heard the door close softly. Her shoulders shook with silent laughter. Apparently, the ghost didn't care for dusty closets.

Ian woke up to an urge he couldn't ignore. He stayed still for a moment, then silently cursed. He wasn't going to be able to fall back to sleep. He listened carefully. There were no weird noises, no creepy sounds. He could do it. He could make it to the bathroom and back without seeing any ghosts. He wasn't going to wake up Eric for this.

After a good few minutes of a mental pep talk, he slipped out of his pile of blankets on the floor and snuck out of the room. The hallway had a faint, dim hint of light, but he could sort of make out the outline of the bathroom door. He hesitated, then made a silent dash for it, the hair on the back of his neck standing on end as he felt the dark hall looming behind him.

He grabbed the doorknob, thinking it was strange how it felt warm, before opening it and stepping inside. The door slammed shut behind him, and he forgot about his full bladder as he stared in horror at the scene in front of him that was most certainly not a bathroom.

Skye was drying her hands on a towel when Ryan let out a deafening scream upstairs. The man had a set of lungs on him. No wonder he was such a good singer for a variety of musical genres.

"I take it Ryan got to see his ghost? Or did you play a prank on him, Declan?"

Sarah Eriksen

Declan protested, *"I was going to wait to do that until closer to morning, after the normal ghosts and ghouls made their appearance. And that being said, apparently, there is a horrifying shadowy thing in the hallway in front of my door. I got nothing. Well, other than a drawer in the nightstand opening and closing all night."*

Eric's voice chimed in as Skye opened the bathroom door. *"Have you seen Ian? He's not in the room with me."*

"He's not up here either." There was a bit of an echo as Trey talked to Ryan, trying to calm him down so he could explain what was in front of Declan's room.

Skye waved at Eric as he opened his door down the hall. Something caught her attention out of the corner of her eye, and her head snapped to her left. The mysterious appearing door was there.

She glanced back at Eric and jerked her thumb and chin at the door. "I think I have a clue where Ian might have gone. I thought I heard a door open in the hallway while I was in the bathroom."

Eric headed her way as she grabbed the doorknob and then let go, looking at her hand. She looked at him in surprise. "It's warm. That's not too typical of ghosts. Usually, they do cold."

He tested the doorknob too. "That is strange." A loud crash at the end of the hallway made both of them jump and turn. A stack of books had been shoved off an end table. Loud knocking sounded upstairs as the haunting got more active.

Skye shook her head in disgust. "Those poor books. The owners weren't joking about this place. We'd better see if Ian went through the magic door."

The knob turned easily, and the door opened without a sound. Eric and Skye found themselves facing a distorted black and white image. She did a quick check with her mind and found Ian's presence immediately.

"Well, that's clearly a door to another dimension of some kind," Eric said blandly.

"Yep," Skye said, biting her lip in thought. "That raises an awful lot of questions, doesn't it?"

More crashing sounded upstairs, and a running dialogue in the back of her mind told her the boys had their hands full.

"You better go help. It looks like they have some exciting poltergeist stuff going on involving books being lobbed at them. I'll rescue Ian and investigate."

"Be careful."

"You know me!" She winked cheerfully, choosing to not think too hard about her control issues and the possible difficulties of being in another dimension. She needed to save Ian, and flashy sparks aside, she did have plenty of power to protect him.

"Exactly." Eric gave her a pointed look with a grin.

"Why does everyone say that?" She stuck her tongue out at him and stepped through the doorway.

Eric called, "Shoes, Skye!"

He heard her laugh as the door closed behind her on its own and faded from sight. Eric shook his head and ran to the stairs, nimbly leaping over a chair that moved in front of him at the last minute.

Skye spotted Ian hiding only a few feet away. He had his back to a brick wall and was crouched down, trying to make himself as small as possible behind a stack of wooden crates.

Her voice was a whisper. "Ian."

He flinched, then sighed in obvious relief as he recognized her. "Can you explain...all this?" He gestured around him with his arms.

Skye took in their surroundings. They were in some kind of an alleyway with towering soot-streaked brick buildings. The ground was rough cobblestones with a single gutter in the middle full of things she didn't want to think about since it was bad enough that she could smell it. The air was damp and redolent of the smoke from coal and a general sense of filth. Everything was also very much in black and white.

"Well, if I didn't know any better, I'd say we're in an old black and white monster movie. Or someone decided to recreate a black and white version of London from about 130 years ago."

Ian's expression was bewildered. "So, are we actually in either of those things? Because if the past is in black and white, I have some questions."

While she had been talking and looking around, she had been searching with her mind. "It's hard to say. I mean, we aren't inside a movie, but it has the feel of one. And we haven't time traveled that I can tell, and I should be able to tell. All I know is this appears to be another dimension, but something about it is odd."

"Is there a standard for other dimensions?"

Skye shook her head. "Not really. They're all pretty weird from the ones I've had the joy of seeing or hearing about. And unfortunately, we have to find another way out. Our entrance closed behind us." She waved her hand in a vague gesture.

Ian's worried gaze followed her hand. "Can't you teleport us out?"

Skye's nose wrinkled with her apologetic expression. "Well, dimensional travel is a little bit more difficult when we don't know the exact make-up of the creation energy used for it. That, and I tried to manipulate a bit of energy already to re-open the door, and it didn't work. Teleporting could be really dangerous at this stage."

"You're saying you're broken?" Ian's voice cracked as his panic built.

She shook her head vehemently. "Not by a long shot. I still have my mad skills and powers, but I'd rather be a tad careful since we might not want to attract too much attention at this stage." Her caution wasn't only because of her current problems with glowing. Dimensions had to be created by a god, and the last thing they needed was to anger a god.

"Shouldn't your magical mind database be giving you information on this?" He managed to sound calm again.

She wasn't getting any information in her mind about the location yet. "It could be a new dimension. These things happen all the time. There might not be any info on it. If Amonir was concerned, I'd have heard from him. Normal procedures for random interdimensional travel are straightforward. Try to blend in, don't draw attention, and observe for others."

"You aren't inspiring much confidence. But how do you propose we get out of here if you can't teleport?"

"I'm going to see if I can find another door back to our world." She had been searching for one from the second she made sure he wasn't hurt.

"So, we're going to wander around a black and white version of Victorian London in our modern and colorful clothes and open doors until we find one that takes us home? That's a lot of doors."

"Of course not. I'm getting lost in your questions. I have a general sense of something around here that feels like our world, so we should head there and see if there's a door or something. And as far as clothes, if we stay hidden, we should be fine. Just let me get my bearing on where we need to go and let the others know what's going on."

She was projecting more confidence than she felt at the moment. Traveling to other dimensions wasn't rare or unusual for a guardian, but they normally went to ones Amonir sent them to, well prepared and informed beforehand. The worst things they dealt with were atmospheres and environments that would kill a normal human. You simply had to plan accordingly. New dimensions were always creative in their designs, even though this one seemed oddly specific.

She hadn't been entirely joking about someone recreating London. Time travel was interesting, and she had visited London in 1887. Apart from the total black and white film appearance, it was a perfect replica down to the smell and feel. While she felt confident she could keep them safe, she was worried about the unknown aspects. She was also a bit excited.

Trey seemed to be distracted by something. She reached her mind out politely to Eric instead and asked, *"Did you guys save Ryan from the big bad ghost?"* She could feel Trey and Declan connected loosely to Eric's mind and a weird echo effect with her own connection to her twin.

"Yeah, we did. We went into Trey's room and closed the door. It contented itself with knocking for a while and then left. Did you find Ian? And where did you two go?"

"I've got Ian. We appear to be in a black and white version of Victorian London, complete with the horrific smells of the era. The door closed behind us, but I can feel something like our world somewhere around here."

"So one-way doors in and out?" He sounded intrigued.

"I'm thinking so. Dimensions you can only access through doors aren't that uncommon. I could probably teleport if I tried, but I don't know enough to want to punch through. We don't know who made this place, and it could be a bad idea to piss them off."

"Makes sense."

Declan jumped in with his usual lack of politeness. *"Ryan finally let us in to see what he saw. I don't blame him for screaming. Get ready for this."*

Sarah Eriksen

An image of a shadowy figure floating in the hall of the bed and breakfast popped into their minds. It appeared to be a woman in a long dress. Tattered shreds of a skirt floated a good foot above the ground. Everything was shadowy except its pale face, which was straight out of a nightmare. A halo of snarled long hair surrounded the ghastly visage with black sunken eyes. Its arms were almost exaggeratedly long with claw-like fingers.

Trey chimed in, *"I give that ghost credit. It did a great job of making itself terrifying. But we never found the poltergeist."*

"Well, you have fun. I think getting out of other dimension Victorian London is going to take a bit of time."

Trey spoke again, *"Eric said the door disappeared after you went through, so we won't be able to help."*

"Pretty sure she can handle it, Trey." Declan mocked with acidic sarcasm.

"Pretty sure I don't need your help defending my abilities, Declan." Skye mimicked his tone flawlessly. *"Keep me updated on your haunted house if anything else fun happens."* She left before she could hear any replies, ignoring the faint echo of her brother talking to the others.

She nodded at Ian and said, "Let's go find the magic door back to our world."

Skye headed down the alleyway, with Ian following close behind. She tried getting a feel for the dimension they were in but couldn't come up with anything other than it was weird. She slowed as she neared the street ahead, listening with her ears and her mind for sounds of people or anything kind of trouble. Nothing of note, but it seemed to be late at night.

She popped her head around the corner. There was still nothing unusual other than the black and white color scheme. A gust of wind stirred up the disgusting smells and rustled a bit of newspaper stuck in the mud.

Ian, curious as ever and not caring too much about what else might be in the mud, grabbed it. She was still scanning the area when she felt Ian tap her shoulder with the back of his hand. "I think we might have another problem on our hands."

Skye studied the paper. "Of course. Why couldn't it just be Victorian London? It has to be the White Chapel murders edition. Guess we better avoid any serial killers, prostitutes, and law enforcement."

"So, we're in another dimension—"

Skye cut him off. "That is a black and white version of Jack the Ripper's London? Yep. Let's get moving and get out of here. One fun thing about alternate dimensions…the creators generally take some serious poetic license to their creations."

"So, we might not be dealing with Jack the Ripper?"

"Or we might. Either way, it probably won't be good. Let's hope we don't find out." She didn't want to have to fight her way out of an unknown dimension for a number of reasons. The last thing they needed was her power surging while she tried to defend them. She'd end up blowing a hole in the dimension or something and pissing off a god. But she'd do whatever was necessary to keep Ian safe.

Ian looked like he was going to argue, but something in her tone sunk in. "You're right. Let's just get out of here."

It didn't matter who was behind the stories in this dimension, there was a murderous something on the loose, and they needed to get out. Even if it was an accurate rendition of the murders, there was nothing that said the murderer was going to be a normal, average human.

Skye and Ian hurried down the main road, sticking to the shadows as much as possible. It was almost ridiculously easy at times. They avoided the areas with people, skirting alleys that were occupied for various reasons, dodging tavern doors, and popular locations for prostitutes. Thankfully she could feel the connection to their world getting closer despite the twists and turns they had to take.

She slowed down, trying to pinpoint the best route through the small lanes and alleys they were currently in. "We're pretty close." She turned into a small alleyway and headed down a few stairs.

Ian managed a relieved smile. "You were right. It wasn't too bad."

Skye shook her head as a scream of absolute terror sounded a fraction of a second after he spoke. "Word of advice, never say anything like that when stuck in nightmare murder dimensions. It's like a magic trigger for 'bad thing will happen'."

Sarah Eriksen

The scream had come from the general direction they were headed. Skye scowled. This was going to get tricky. "Stay close. We don't know what we're up against."

They snuck the rest of the way down the alley, and Skye got her bearings again. She didn't dare take a peek with her mind in case the creator of the dimension was watching the scene, but she could sense the door in a closed-off courtyard. It also happened to be where the screaming had come from.

They had two options. Try to run past the murder or hide until it was over. And either way, hope they could get to the door before something terrible happened to them. Skye debated. The longer they stayed, the worse their odds were of getting caught up in the mess.

"Ian, you're going to hate this."

"That's not a promising start." He was scared but holding himself together admirably.

"We have to get past the murder that is currently taking place around the corner up here to get to the door. If we wait, we could get caught up in the story and arrested or something worse. We're going to have to make a run for it."

"Right. Run past a Jack the Ripper murder happening." He had stayed calm and focused as they snuck through the streets, but this was pushing his limits.

"It's easy. I want you to stay to the left, the door is on that side, and I'll stay between you and whatever it is." She projected confidence into her voice to try to reassure him.

"I don't want to overthink this. Stay to the left, run. I can do this."

Skye frowned faintly. "And…be prepared for anything when we run around that corner. I mean anything."

Ian steadied himself, curiosity at war with fear on his face. Skye flashed an encouraging smile and opened her mind up, preparing to gather a tightly controlled trickle of creation energy in case she needed it. She nodded at Ian. They burst into a run at the same time, turning the corner and finally seeing the other dimension's version of one of the White Chapel murders taking place.

Ian stuck to the wall as close as possible without giving up the ability to run. He spared a glance for the nightmarish scene in front of him, stumbling over a cobblestone as he saw the disturbing sight.

Chaotic Haunts

Skye shook her head in amazement. Alternate dimensions never disappointed. The partially mutilated body of a prostitute was sprawled on the cobblestones. The ceramic garden gnome that was in the process of causing the mutilation glared at them as they burst into the alley, screaming as it brandished blood-covered surgical tools. Skye threw a small explosive ball of energy at the gnome as she leaped over the body. It tumbled and crashed against the ground.

She grabbed Ian's arm, and they slid to stop in front of a rather innocuous door that leaked telltale traces of their world. She grabbed the handle and pulled it open as the garden gnome started to run toward them, its ceramic feet clattering on the cobblestones.

She felt an odd flicker in her mind, a sense of something or someone inside the dimension that didn't fit, but she didn't have time to find out what it was. She shoved Ian through the opening ahead of her.

The gnome leaped toward them, its bloody scalpel held aloft, and she slammed the door shut, leaning against it. She had expected a crash as the gnome collided with the door, but the connection to the dimension was severed as soon as it was closed.

Skye shook her head in amazement and said, "Well, that was pretty fucked up." She glanced at Ian, and they both started laughing.

"Jack the Ripper is a garden gnome?" His laughter was relieved, with only a hint of hysteria remaining.

Skye's laughter died to intermittent giggles, and she managed to say, "Not the real one, but in that dimension, apparently so."

"You warned me, but I couldn't have imagined that."

"Me either." She glanced around. "Now, where are we?"

Ian caught his breath and started studying their surroundings. "I don't think this is the bed and breakfast." They were in a small dark room in a basement judging from the high windows that were so filthy it was impossible to see anything out of them. There was a rusty antique wheelchair sitting in the corner, along with the general detritus of an old abandoned building.

Skye pinpointed their location instantly, another guardian trick. "We appear to be in an abandoned psychiatric hospital in England."

Ian blinked his eyes in confusion. "England?"

"Yep."

"Psychiatric hospital?"

Sarah Eriksen

"You got it."

Ian shook his head. "Nope. I don't like it."

Skye said, "Well, we're back in our world. I can teleport us to the bed and breakfast at least. There's still a couple of hours left before we have to check out." They had only been in the dimension for an hour or so.

"I'm not altogether sure that's a great thing either, but I'll take poltergeists and whatever made Ryan scream over being in an old insane asylum."

"What, you don't want to stay and check it out?" She teased.

"I'm the one who can actually see ghosts, and you're seriously asking me that?"

Skye smiled. "I need to study the door over here for a bit before we go. Don't worry. This is our world and normal ghosts. I can summon some energy, and they will leave us alone." She held up a hand, and a tiny white swirl of blue and white flame popped up with only a faint hint of sparks. "There, no ghosts will bother us now."

"I don't understand why that would work, but I'll take it. And, please hurry."

"Of course."

Chapter Six

Skye studied what appeared to be an ordinary door. She reached her hand out and tried the knob. It wouldn't turn. A mental glance showed a small storage room crammed full of junk. Not a single hint that it was ever connected to another dimension. A one-way exit door had overlaid itself on a regular door.

A fleeting feeling of similarity with the dead doors on the space station crossed her mind again. There wasn't anything that gave her a concrete connection, but it was an odd coincidence. Of course, odd coincidences were part of everyday life for guardians. She should reach out to Kya and see if they had solved the mystery of their doors that weren't doors.

She turned back to Ian. "It's a normal locked door now."

"That's good, isn't it?"

"I suppose so. It's weird that we have a one-way door into another dimension, and a one-way door out. And both are in very different locations. I guess it's better than doors letting things go in and out of the other world." She shuddered at the idea of Jack the Ripper garden gnome crossing into this world even if the exit was in an abandoned location.

"Except the door that let me into the other dimension showed up out of nowhere and let both of us in, but closed behind me, and then you." The door had stayed open on the bed and breakfast side of things after Ian had gone through.

"Yeah, that part isn't very good. But it's fairly recent, not like it's been doing this for years. We should probably warn the owners to block off the area where the door shows up, so no one else wanders through." She was confident Amonir would make sure nothing like that happened, but it didn't hurt to try to get them to take some precautions. "Let's head back."

"Before the boys start worrying about us?" Ian asked wryly.

"Oh, Trey's been keeping an eye on us the whole time, so I'm sure he's relaying every detail. I've been ignoring them as much as possible because the overprotective eavesdropping gets old fast."

"I don't know how you do it."

"Me either. One of these days, I'm going to disappear and cut myself off from all of them for a month or two." She winked to show she was joking.

She didn't truly mean it. She was grateful to have people in her life who cared, but sometimes she needed to deal with things herself and not have them constantly worrying about her. It was even more difficult to deal with right now. If they knew of her struggles, they wouldn't give her a moment's peace as they tried to help.

She teleported them back to the bed and breakfast. The boys were in the sitting room area on the second floor, drinking an assortment of beverages. Trey and Eric both looked worried and relieved, triggering more of the same feelings she had shared with Ian. Declan merely raised one eyebrow with a challenging stare. He grinned when she gazed impassively back.

It was worse since coming back from Meriten. Her brother was being far more protective of her, and at the same time, trying to be way too nice to make up for being a jerk. They had mended the rift between them, but things hadn't gone back to how they were before. Things were changing, and it scared him more than he wanted to let on.

He relied on her to be the strong and stable one, and despite her best efforts, he was picking up on some of her emotions, and it was making him worry more. He struggled when he couldn't fix things, especially where she was concerned.

Eric managed to be more subtle with his concerns. He was always supportive in a quiet way, but his worry was as clear as Trey's. He seemed to be torn between staying in the background, there if she needed him, and wanting to step in and protect her.

Declan was the same as always, a complete and utter pain in the ass…to the outside world. He was far more observant and intuitive than most people realized. He had always been able to see past whatever walls she put up, right to the heart of what was wrong. And he always knew the exact things to do to help her without her having to ask. It was why he was her closest friend.

Declan gave her a dubious look and said, "I thought you couldn't teleport out of there."

Skye sat down, smiling gratefully at Eric, who passed her a mug of her favorite tea. Leave it to him to know she'd want tea and to keep it warm for her. "You're correct. We didn't teleport out of there. We found a door back to Earth and ran through it before ceramic garden gnome Jack the Ripper stabbed me with the scalpel that he used to murder a prostitute."

Declan opened and closed his mouth a few times as he tried to come up with a suitable retort to her response and finally gave up. "I've got nothing. I literally can't think of anything to say in response to that."

Skye smirked and took a sip of her tea. "When we ran through the door, we came out in the basement of an abandoned psychiatric hospital in England."

Ryan shuddered. "I was going to say I was jealous of your dimensional trip, but I'm glad you got to go to a creepy abandoned hospital and not me. This place has been enough fun for one night."

Ian said, "The other dimension was almost more terrifying than the hospital. That was creepy, but Skye used her powers to make sure if there were ghosts, they'd leave us alone while she studied the one-way door."

Eric mused, "One-way door into an alternate dimension, and one-way door out. That's bizarre. A bed and breakfast here, and an abandoned hospital in England. That's a lot of random things."

Skye agreed. "Well, the other dimension was a black and white version of Victorian London smack in the middle of the White Chapel murders, which still doesn't explain the two locations for those doors. Guess we'll have to dig into it a bit more or let Amonir tell us what to do." The guardians all had sudden expectant looks on their faces that quickly faded to disappointment. "Guess it's not critical."

Sarah Eriksen

She finished her tea in one long gulp. "Well, I'm going to head back to bed. It's nothing that can't wait until tomorrow."

Ian asked incredulously, "You can sleep after all that?"

"Trust me, weird dimensions, murders, monsters, scalpel-wielding garden gnomes... that's not the stuff that makes me lose sleep."

Declan asked, "What *does* make you lose sleep, Skye?"

She simply smiled and said goodnight.

Ian frowned into his mug of tea and glanced at Eric. "I hate to even ask it, but I really need to wash this nasty 'mud' off from London. And I do not want to accidentally walk through another dimensional door again or meet a ghost."

Eric smiled sympathetically. "I'll make sure you survive a bathroom trip, and no ghosts will bother us." He held up his hand, and a pale blue ball of lightning appeared.

Ian and Ryan both relaxed, tension visibly dissipating from their bodies. Ryan shook his head in wonder. "It's amazing how I can't tell how freaked out I am by whatever is here until you do that, and suddenly I don't feel it anymore."

Trey said with a hint of wistfulness, "It's amazing to us how much of an impact ghosts can have on atmospheres and emotions. Let's head back upstairs, Ryan. No ghosts guaranteed." A small ball of pale golden fire appeared in his hand.

The rest of the night was quiet, just as the guardians promised. The owners seemed surprised that the ghost activity had died down a few times before sunrise. Declan suggested they do something to make sure no one walked through the phantom door. They seemed unsure about it until he pointed out they would be liable if something happened to one of their guests. The fact they didn't question that the ghostly door posed a danger hinted at a degree of divine intervention smoothing things over.

They chatted with the owners about the history of the house and the hauntings, taking the time to learn what they could. The location had always had minor poltergeist activity, but nothing more than doors opening, or things being knocked off a table.

The haunting activity had increased around the same time a guest mentioned the strange door. The connection between the haunting and the dimensional portal was clear, but nothing about it made sense.

Chaotic Haunts

Skye was quiet on the drive back the next morning, while her mind ran in circles trying to piece together anything about the other dimension that was consistent. The doors leading to and from Earth and the likeness of old London indicated some kind of connection to their world. Unfortunately, the more she thought about it and tried to put the pieces together, the less sense it made. She hated things that didn't make sense.

Trey glanced over when she sighed. "Want to talk about it?" He managed to sound polite instead of pushy. He did have his moments where he could read her emotions right.

Skye glanced at Ian, who was sleeping in the back seat. It was clear he hadn't slept much the rest of the night and was making up for it.

She shook her head. "It's nothing, really. I mean, it was definitely bizarre, but that's not unusual for alternate dimensions. It doesn't make any sense."

"So, it's going to bug you because you can't figure it out." It was a statement and not a question.

She let out a breath. "Pretty much. Maybe one of these days, I'll learn how to let things go when they don't make sense."

"I wouldn't worry about that too much, guardian. I need you to investigate the dimension and its connections to your world. There are most likely other doors." As usual, Amonir barged into the conversation as though he was a part of it from the start.

Skye and Trey exchanged looks, and Skye replied, "Is there anything I should know? And am I the only one working on this?"

"You are the only guardian I have with the strength to pull significant creation energy to protect yourself in an alternate dimension no matter the make-up and energy of it. Your friends can help you, but I do not want anyone other than you going in there at this point."

Another job assignment because of her unlocked powers. She pushed away the unpleasant emotions triggered by the thought.

She said, "Alrighty. I guess I'll be heading back to the jolly old weird ass alternate dimension London sometime soon." Amonir didn't reply, taking a typical exit by abruptly leaving the conversation.

Ian sleepily chimed in, "For the record, I'm not going back to creepy-ass alternate dimension London."

Sarah Eriksen

Skye was curled up on the couch with a blanket, a cup of tea, a plateful of cookies, her laptop, and a purring grimalkin sprawled against her hip. Her tea and cookies floated in the air on either side of her as she logged into the guardians' online site. She absently rubbed Mr. Grimm's fluffy belly with one hand and snagged a cookie with the other as she waited for the page to load.

She scrolled through the main feed, reading a lot of interesting things about various creatures and situations, some hilarious, some serious, but nothing that sounded like a dimensional door. She sighed. It had been wishful thinking on her part. She clicked on her own status update and typed a new post.

"I found a one-way dimensional door in a haunted local bed and breakfast that took me to a black and white version of Victorian London. The exit took me to the basement of an abandoned asylum in England. I'm supposed to investigate this dimension. Has anyone heard of anything going on around the world with phantom doors that have just started appearing recently?"

She wasn't sure if she'd get any replies any time soon, but with the number of guardians around, she might get a few promising leads. She grabbed her tea and another cookie and settled back, watching a movie and paying half attention to her laptop. A few minutes later, her computer chimed with a notification.

"There's a rumor here in Queensland of a door that appears at random in an abandoned amusement park. The haunting stories have been around for a long time though, so I'm not sure if it's what you're after."

Skye read the comment with interest. Another door in a haunted location. It had potential. She tapped out a quick thanks and did a fast mental check on the location along with the time.

It was mid-morning here, so it would be really early morning there. She would be less likely to run into people at that time, and the door in the bed and breakfast liked late night hours too. She finished her tea and cookies and scratched Mr. Grimm's chin, sending her dishes to the kitchen with a touch of energy, and putting her laptop on the table.

She reached out to Trey. *"Hey, I'm headed to Australia to check out a haunted amusement park."*

"Want any company?"

Chaotic Haunts

"I think I should be fine, but can you watch the shop for me today? I'll let you know if I find a door to the other dimension."

"Don't forget your shoes."

She couldn't even be annoyed at his reminder as she pulled her sneakers onto her feet and gave Mr. Grimm a few more chin scratches.

She was kind of relieved to do a job on her own. She needed to figure out how to restrict creation energy down to acceptable levels again. At least on her own, she wasn't putting anyone else at risk if the energy surged while she tried to control it. She wasn't worried about using her powers. That wasn't an issue. In an unknown dimension, at least she knew she could wield enough energy to pack a punch, even if she burst into sparks and fire in the process.

She appeared right outside the amusement park and took a moment to adjust to the change. Early fall at home was early spring in Australia. The temperatures were comparable, but it was a bit more humid. She laughed at her whimsical comparison of locations. Being able to teleport pretty much anywhere never got old.

She walked silently to the fence surrounding the amusement park, searching with her eyes and mind for any possible witnesses. There was nothing living, apart from a lot of wildlife, in the park at this precise moment since it was so late, or early. Of course, she couldn't tell if any ghosts were in the park either.

She grimaced. She hadn't thought this through very well. The door in the bed and breakfast had appeared at the same time the ghost activity started acting up. She only had one instance to go on, but it stood to reason that the two things were somehow related. She would either have to search the entire amusement park, trusting to luck to find the door, or bring in a hapless bystander.

She grabbed her phone. "Hey Ian, want to help me out?"

"I almost dread asking what kind of help you want on my day off."

"Well, I kind of need someone who can see ghosts to help me for a minute."

"I'm not going back to the bed and breakfast." His tone was firm.

"Don't worry. I'm in Australia. But same difference." She was multitasking while talking on the phone with Ian, mentally asking Eric if he could bring Ian to her location if Ian was willing.

Sarah Eriksen

"You're tempting me with a free trip to Australia? Why are we hunting ghosts in Australia? And more importantly, how many other deadly things are there that could kill me? Also, how are you calling me from Australia?" His curiosity could always defeat any other emotion he might have.

"You don't have to worry about too much wildlife that will kill you in an abandoned amusement park. I think we can protect you against that much. As far as ghost hunting, I'm checking out another possible door to the dimension. And before you freak out too much, I just need your help here. I'm the only one going through the door this time. Eric will take you home when, or if, we find it. And do you really need to ask about how I'm calling you from Australia?"

"Fair point on the phone. I guess I can do this for you. But you owe me big time. And if there are any clowns, I'll never forgive you."

"If there are clowns and I can see them, I promise I'll obliterate them for you."

"Alright, what—" his voice cut off with a strangled shriek. "Eric, maybe you could try *not* appearing out of nowhere after all the ghost stuff last night." His phone disconnected, and Skye giggled.

Eric and Ian appeared a moment later. Ian's outrage was still clear on his face. Eric spoke in her mind, *"The look on his face was priceless, but I genuinely didn't mean to scare him. You didn't tell me you hadn't told him I was coming over to get him yet."*

"I'll take the blame for that." Skye knew Eric wouldn't have deliberately tried to scare Ian.

Ian was losing his disgruntled expression as his eyes took in everything around him.

Skye said, "As much as I'd love to let you enjoy the scenery for as long as you'd like, they use parts of this park during the day, so we should get moving. Let us know if you get creeped out, see strange stuff, or hear things."

He shook his head in disbelief. "First time out of the country, and I get to be a bloodhound for my haunting deficient friends."

Eric chuckled. "After we get Skye to her magic door, want me to show you around for a bit?"

Ian's eyes lit up. "Alright, let's go find a door so I can have a mini vacation!"

Skye forced herself to channel the barest trickle of energy and waved her hand at the fence. It disappeared in a small section so they could walk through. She ran the risk of warning the ghosts, but the park was large enough that her energy shouldn't have scared them away. At least not for long.

Ian watched the fence reappear behind them. "Aren't you ever worried about security cameras and technology catching things like that?"

Skye and Eric exchanged smiles. Eric replied, "With the number of cameras and tech around don't you think you'd have seen some of it by now? Amonir takes care of that stuff for us, so we don't have to worry too often. We're still careful, but it's not an issue for us."

"That feels a lot like cheating." He sounded disappointed.

Skye laughed and said, "It totally is, but then I could disable the cameras from here, so it just saves us the effort."

They walked past old booths and rusting rides, vegetation taking over wherever cracks in the pavement provided an opportunity. It was enormous, and they were covering a large amount of ground, walking on pathways through what was once a scenic park, passing old buildings and rides.

Skye had always liked abandoned buildings and places like this. There was something melancholy and beautiful about it. It was haunting in an emotional instead of a ghostly way.

She kept her senses open, hoping to feel the other dimensional door as they wandered through the park. She turned her head, feeling a faint hint of something like she was being watched. It flickered away so quickly that she wondered if she imagined it.

She was distracted enough that she almost walked into Ian, who had slowed down as they neared the old picnic and concession area. She could feel rising tension and anxiety rolling off him. They were in a large open space full of booths and old buildings with chairs and tables scattered haphazardly.

He peered around, his shoulders hunching up. "Can you guys hear that?"

The guardians looked at him expectantly, and he clarified, "It sounds like a kid talking. I can't hear what they're saying though."

Skye shook her head. "I can't hear it. Eric?"

"Nothing. But do you see fog?" He pointed at a fine mist rising from the ground and filling the entire area. It stopped after a bit, not rising much above mid-thigh on Skye.

Ian raised his eyebrows in surprise. "You can see the fog but can't hear anything? It's getting louder." He inched closer to the guardians.

Eric said, "If ghosts interact with the environment, we can see the effect, but we can't see or hear them directly. That or the fog is normal, but I don't think so based on the kid you can hear."

Skye asked Ian, "Can you pinpoint a direction the ghost is coming from?"

"I can't tell where it's coming from. It sounds like it's everywhere. And I can't see anything." He turned around, trying to see something…anything. "I don't know if it's the creepy kid voice and fog, but I'm totally feeling freaked out right now."

"Well, we can safely say this park is probably haunted then. But where is the door?" Skye scrunched her eyes closed, trying to sense the dimensional energy without using her powers to enhance her reach. She hadn't paid attention to how it felt in the bed and breakfast, but she had a good hour to get a sense of the feel of the energy while inside it.

Ian pointed toward the largest building across the picnic area. "There's something over there."

They turned to follow his direction, and Skye shook her head. She said apologetically, "I'm not seeing anything. If it starts coming toward us and you get uncomfortable, let us know and we'll scare it away. If my theory is correct, ghost activity is getting stronger, so the door should show up."

Eric was fascinated. "That makes a lot of sense. The energy from the other dimension is riling up the ghosts, and they're more active because of it."

Skye shrugged. "It seemed likely based on what the owners at the bed and breakfast said."

A strange tingling sensation tickled the back of her neck. She could feel the energy from the other dimension. She turned away from where Ian had seen the ghost, and sure enough, there was a door in the middle of what had been a blank cinderblock wall.

"There's my door, so it seems my theory might be correct. You two go have some fun while I explore the other dimension."

Ian shuddered. "Have fun in creepy Victorian London without me."

"Be careful, Skye."

She made a face at him and teased, "You keep saying that. It's like you think I'm reckless or something."

Eric smiled and didn't say a word.

"Um. The creepy ghost kid is headed this way, and it's angry." Ian said urgently.

Skye gave them a wave and jogged to the door, feeling Eric summoning creation energy to scare away the ghost for their friend.

Sarah Eriksen

Chapter Seven

Skye gave the creator of the dimension some credit. Traveling through the door was as smooth as if she had teleported herself. A split second later and she took a deep breath of cool air full of the scent of crushed pine needles and damp forest.

Dark pine trees dipped their heavy, needle-laden branches toward the ground. She was in a forest, and it was not black and white. It was dark, green, cool, and full of mist. It was beautiful, in a danger was most likely lurking somewhere kind of way. The portal was in a decrepit old shack with a solid oak door that closed firmly behind her.

"Well, it's not White Chapel." Her voice sounded too loud in the misty woods. A wolf howled somewhere in the distance. "And it still feels like a movie." She headed down the path as the fleeting connection to her world disappeared behind her.

She studied the scenery as she walked, feeling a vague impression of the door back to her world somewhere ahead. The forest reminded her of a video game she enjoyed playing in her downtime. Tall, dark pines, dark scrubby undergrowth with glowing eyes blinking now and then. She was glad for the hoodie she had been wearing, and she was enjoying the walk in the woods. But then, she'd always had a thing for gloomy scenery with trees and mist.

She could feel the glimmer of the door getting stronger as she walked along the packed dirt trail. Everything seemed like a typical forest, even with the eyes in the bushes, but she kept her guard up and used her guardian senses to get a feel for her surroundings.

Chaotic Haunts

The energy was the same as the White Chapel location. It was part of the same dimension, despite the obvious visual differences. She could see a faint hint of light ahead as the trees thinned out. Caution seemed like the best idea, so she slowed down. She didn't know what bizarre things she would encounter here after the garden gnome Jack the Ripper.

She crouched down behind a bush that didn't have any glowing eyes blinking at her. She hadn't sensed any presence of life, so she wasn't too worried that the eyes were dangerous but better safe than sorry. There was a small cluster of buildings ahead, abandoned and more than a little decrepit. A cemetery with a large monument in the middle was nestled on a hill beyond the buildings.

There was still nothing out of the ordinary, except a few wisps of misty shapes that she would call ghosts, except she could see them. She tested them with her senses and only ended up more confused. They were nothing more than little bits of energy meant to look like ghosts. It was an almost perfect replica of a creepy haunted cemetery straight out of a video game or movie.

First black and white Victorian London, now a haunted cemetery. There had to be a connection, but it wasn't clear what it was. The dimension appeared to be recreating actual or fictitious locations from her world, or a similar world, but in slightly skewed ways.

The locations of the doors didn't make a lot of sense either. Abandoned amusement park and a haunted forest cemetery? Bed and breakfast and Victorian London? She couldn't sense any hint of presence that indicated who the higher power was who created this world. It would have to be a god or an exceptionally gifted demi-god with a knack for creation. And that would be far less likely.

Skye studied the misty apparitions while she tried to reach out her mind to find the other part of the dimension that she had previously been in. No matter which direction she sent her mind, it seemed to be an endless forest with very little to be excited about other than the buildings and cemetery in front of her.

A few abandoned and ruined houses were scattered around, along with rocks, trees, more trees, and mist. There were a couple of paths in and out of the cemetery. But none of them seemed to lead anywhere, except the one that went up a hill to a large crypt. And that was the location of her exit back to Earth.

Sarah Eriksen

"Alright, I guess it's time to see what it's like to interact with fake ghosts in an alternate dimension." She stood up and stepped out of the shadows under the trees. She paused long enough to give them time to notice her, and there were no reactions.

She strolled toward the buildings, preparing to defend herself if something happened. The fake ghosts didn't seem to notice or care what she was doing. She veered toward the monument to take a closer look. It was a figure of a young woman carved from something reminiscent of white marble.

She tried to make out the name carved on the plaque at the base, but the misty ghosts suddenly started freaking out. They started flitting around faster and pulsating with light before rushing away to the buildings like they were afraid. Skye frowned, she hadn't done anything differently, and it seemed far too delayed to be a reaction to her.

A faint pink glow through the trees caught her attention. It grew brighter as it moved toward the clearing. Skye's pulse sped up, and she edged closer to the crypt that was her only escape, keeping her eyes on the glow.

A bright pink basketball-sized ball floated out of the woods. Skye stared at it in consternation. It gave off a menacing aura so intense that it was almost tangible to her senses. A normal person would be paralyzed in fear. She had no clue what context a highly dangerous pink bubble in a haunted forest and cemetery could be, but she knew she didn't want it to get near her.

She bolted toward the crypt, glancing back. The ball moved faster toward her, glowing brighter. She jumped over a small stone ledge and slid around a corner inside the door of the crypt. She leaped down the stairs and turned another corner, searching frantically for her exit as a bright pink light filled the stairwell behind her.

The exit wasn't a door this time, but it was fitting for the location. She grabbed the wooden edge of an upright coffin and yanked it open, knocking a toppling skeleton out of her way. She jumped through the murky portal as the pink ball reached the bottom of the stairs.

She crashed out of a broom closet into a pitch black room that smelled of old musty paper and leather. She knew that smell. Books. Old books.

She was in upstate New York in the basement of a library. She wondered if this location was haunted too. She hadn't had a chance to explore the asylum and hadn't wanted to torture Ian after everything he had been through. She wished, not for the first time in the last day or so, that guardians had some way to sense ghosts, at least enough to know if they were there or not.

A book flew across the room inches in front of her nose. She let out a tiny growl of irritation. Then again, some ghosts had no problem making themselves known to anyone.

"Nice try, but I don't want concussion by book tonight." She summoned a tiny ball of light that flared up brightly as creation energy fought against her control. She crushed down the surge of power as a book dropped to the floor a few feet in front of her.

"Honestly, one would think a ghost in a library would take better care of old books." She picked them up and set them carefully on a shelf before teleporting herself home.

She dropped onto her favorite chair with a sigh. She wasn't sure what to make of any of it, so she headed to the shop.

Trey handed her a coffee and dropped down into a chair across from her. "Any luck in the other world?"

"Well, I'm more confused now than I was before. Going to an alternate dimension with a black and white version of London was different, but whatever. This time it was a dark forest with a ghost town and a cemetery. And by ghost town, I mean wispy ghosts were floating around the cemetery."

"You could see them?" He was surprised.

"They weren't real ghosts, but they were created to resemble ghosts. They didn't react to me at all. The whole thing was extremely strange. Endless forest and not much else." She quickly described the scenery to her twin.

"It sounds interesting. Same deal? One door in and one out?"

"Yep, the door dropped me on a path in the forest, and the exit was a coffin inside the lower level of a burial crypt."

"I find it hard to believe that it was that simple. You said the London version had a garden gnome murdering and dismembering prostitutes. A haunted forest with ghosts that don't care about intruders seems pretty tame."

"Sure, until a floating pink ball showed up and scared the ghosts away." She grinned to herself as she waited for his reaction.

It was obvious he wasn't sure he believed her. He asked cautiously, "A pink ball?"

"Yep. Bright pink, basketball-sized, and incredibly dangerous. With menacing terror that you could physically feel coming off of it. It came after me. I didn't want to let it get close enough to see what it would or could do, so I ran to the exit. Ended up in the basement of a library in upstate New York with a friendly ghost that likes to lob books at people's faces."

"Good thing for the ghost that you can't actually hurt it. You almost murdered Ryan when he dog-eared a page in one of your books. I'd hate to see what you'd do to someone that deliberately damaged them." He laughed.

She protested, "They were old books. Fragile. That ghost was clearly not a librarian. And murder is justifiable when you dog-ear book pages. That's just evil on a level that cannot be comprehended."

"There's a reason why I don't ever touch any of your books and always buy my own copies. It's safer that way."

"Smart man." Skye laughed at her brother's silly bantering and grabbed her laptop to check the message board for any other haunted houses and doors while the shop was quiet.

"Any luck?"

"Only a handful of posts about haunted locations, but nothing about doors. I might have to give it a day or two to see if anything else pops up. Worst case scenario, I guess I could go back to the first door and take some time studying the location a bit more."

"I'm sure you'll have no issue getting another reservation."

She bit her lip absently. "Or I could go to the forest again and see if the evil pink ball of doom was there because of me. Maybe it's part of the dimension. And when it saw me, it wanted to attack. I might be able to explore more if I only have to avoid it."

"Still sounds kind of dangerous."

"You're not wrong, but it seems a bit easier to navigate than old London with a murderous garden gnome on the loose."

Chaotic Haunts

Trey snorted. "The conversations we get to have. Murderous garden gnomes. Pink ball of doom. I'm almost afraid of what other doors might have to offer."

"You're telling me. We see some weird shit, but this is definitely up there."

"So, how did you find the door in Australia?"

"Someone posted a tip in response to my question that directed me there. I had a theory, and Eric and Ian helped me out."

"Eric and Ian?" Trey sounded put out.

"Ian was already off, and you had agreed to cover me at the shop. That left me with Eric and Declan to help out. And quite frankly, if you had to pick between them to be a responsible adult who won't aid in scaring Ian to death, who would you pick?"

"Fair enough. But then you came into the shop anyway, because you don't seem to understand how to take advantage of me working so you could slack off." He dodged her well-aimed attack with a throw pillow. "So, you brought Ian along to sense ghosts and Eric to take him home?"

"You got it. My theory seems to be correct. The ghosts get more active before the door shows up. I wonder if the other dimensional energy irritates them."

"So maybe you should ask if anyone has heard of haunted houses getting suddenly more…well haunted, I guess?" He made an excellent point.

"It's as good of a start as anything, I suppose. It's not like I can investigate every haunted house in the world, and it *is* getting closer to Halloween. That will make it harder to filter out actual claims from people who think every drafty hallway and speck of dust on a camera is a ghost."

"And it's not like any of us will have first-hand experiences with it."

She let out another sigh as she typed a new message, clarifying the haunting activity. At the very least, guardians wouldn't post a bunch of nonsense, so she wouldn't have to filter through too much.

Skye stared blankly at the front window of her shop, lost in thought and absently stirring her coffee. Try as she might, she couldn't piece together any connections that made any kind of sense.

Sarah Eriksen

"Good thing I'm not Vincent. I totally snuck up on you," Ian spoke from right next to her.
She replied absently, "He never comes in the side door. It's not as dramatic as the front door. So, I would have seen him." She turned to him and asked archly, "Who says I didn't notice you anyway?"
"Spoilsport."
She gave him an innocent grin and asked, "How did your mini vacation go yesterday?"
"Well, apart from starting off with a crazy haunted amusement park, it was a lot of fun. Eric promised to take me around to a few other places around the world in the future. Without ghosts, though. How did your trip to the other dimension go?"
"It was...other dimensional." Skye grinned mischievously.
Ian's eyes narrowed behind his glasses. He knew she was teasing him. He fought the urge to ask a million questions. Curiosity was his besetting sin. He caved. "Was it black and white? Did you end up back in London? Were there more murdered prostitutes and evil garden gnomes?"
"It was full color and a haunted forest with a cemetery, fake ghosts, and a creepy pink ball of doom."
"Fake ghosts? You can't see real ghosts, but you can see fake ghosts? What's the point of fake ghosts?"
"You're more worried about fake ghosts than the creepy pink ball of doom?"
"Honestly, I'm not sure I want to know about that."
Skye laughed and was saved from having to reply by the arrival of a handful of customers that needed assistance.

Ian ventured, "So, pink ball of doom."
Skye replied, "Yep. It was bright pink, floating, evil, and going to kill me. So, I ran away from it."
"I would say that was a logical and sound thing to do."
"I'm pretty sure I could have fought it off, but I have no clue what it was or what it intended to do. Exploring another dimension is different in that sense. I don't have the answers or knowledge on how to kill the things that are there. I mean, enough energy and power would probably have done something, but it's odd not knowing."
"So, you get to feel like the rest of us do all the time?"

Skye stuck her tongue out at him. "Maybe."

His eyes glinted in amusement, "Sucks, doesn't it?"

She leveled a mock glare at him, "Yes. Yes, it does."

The door opened, and Eric waved at them. "I wanted to let you know that I asked my family to look into some of the hauntings around where they live to see if anything sounds like your phantom doors."

Skye said, "Oh yeah, you said their castle was haunted. I fully expect some ghost stories about the haunted castle full of guardians someday."

Eric chuckled. "Any time you want. But they haven't had anything out of the ordinary happening. At least, nothing different from what they're used to, and no dimensional doors. But there are lots of haunted places in that area of the country, and they're well known, so they can at least eliminate the possibilities if not find one for you."

"That's great! At this point, I could use all the help I can get."

"Your investigation didn't go well, I take it?"

"Depends on what you mean by that. If making less sense was the goal, it went extremely well. If I don't get another lead, I'll have to go back to the first door and see if I can spend some more time there."

Ian said, "I'm not going back to that place with you."

Skye smiled reassuringly. "I know where the door is there now. I think you're safe."

"Next time, you can drag Ryan along to play ghost detector for you."

She shrugged nonchalantly and teased, "Fine. No more trips around the world for you."

He protested, "That's not remotely fair."

Skye was in the middle of cooking dinner when her phone rang. That was unusual enough for her to interrupt what she was doing and see who was calling. It was her friend Shali.

"Hey, girl. I saw your post about haunted houses with doors and unusual activity, and I think I have something for you."

"Something up by you in Seattle? Sounds like I should go there anyway. Even if there isn't a dimensional door." Skye had always had a love for the Pacific Northwest and Seattle in particular.

"One of these days, you'll figure it out and move up here already."

"Downside to owning a business here. Kind of hard to pack up and leave." Skye felt a wistful touch of longing. She loved the shop and

Sarah Eriksen

loved her life. But she was starting to feel like she was getting pulled in multiple directions balancing her regular job, her life, and her guardian job. Maybe her current mental state could be blamed for changing the usual casual desire to move to something more serious.

"You and your irritating logic. Well, there is a house up here outside of the city that has done ghost tours for a long time. Sort of a murder house kind of thing. Reputed to be haunted. People who have stayed there for investigations catch hit-or-miss little things."

"The typical doors and sounds and dust balls kind of stuff?"

"Pretty much. Enough to keep people interested, but not stuff that happens daily. The only downside to this one is that you'll have to register for one of the tours. The activity has been picking up, so they've been doing them nightly, rather than only weekends."

"Sounds promising. Want to send me the contact info so I can sign up for the next available one?"

"Can do! Now. Business is done. Let's catch up on the usual."

Skye spent the next hour or so catching up with her friend and finishing her meal. Mr. Grimm made a pointed appearance next to his food bowl. He finished his meal and rubbed against Skye's legs with a purr of thanks, then promptly disappeared outside on some important business of his own.

Trey was conspicuously absent, but a quick check in the back of her head explained why. He was away helping with a migration that was passing through. It was nothing complicated. But it was time-consuming as the magical glowing creatures were very slow-moving. She got a mental image of a beautiful winding path of light full of glowing fish-like creatures. And a sense of her brother reading a book while he kept an eye on everything.

Skye pulled up the website Shali had sent to her and scheduled herself on the next available tour, which wasn't until two nights from now. Not as fast as she could have hoped for, but with Halloween coming up, haunted houses were a big thing. Especially ones with full-blown apparitions.

If Amonir was worried, he would have made it easier for her to get in faster. That or he couldn't contend with the Halloween insanity. Even gods had limits at times. She wouldn't have to drag Ian or Ryan along if

Chaotic Haunts

she was on a tour since there would be plenty of other hapless victims freaking out over all the ghost activity.

She passed her time the following day working in the shop, keeping tabs on any leads she could find about prospective hauntings while trying to come up with the best way to show up at a haunted house in another state.

Ian interrupted her train of thought. "You're thinking entirely too hard. Working on the alternate dimension conundrum?"

"Nope. Thinking of the best way to show up at a haunted house that is sort of located by itself on the coast in Washington without just appearing in front of a bunch of people."

He nodded knowingly. "Sounds tough."

"I'd rather fight a goblin horde, to be honest." She joked.

"I guess walking up is out of the question?"

"I could teleport my car to some back road and drive, I guess. But since I plan on jumping through a door, I'd have to go back and get it."

"I don't envy you on this job."

Skye made a face at him.

Sarah Eriksen

Chapter Eight

She finally decided the easiest way to get there would be to teleport into the woods and walk up. If anyone asked, she was dropped off and would get picked up later. A rather spurious reason, but as believable as anything else. And more convenient than having to deal with teleporting a car.

"I'm heading out. See you when I get back." She stopped long enough to zip up her hoodie. She was headed to Washington and was prepared for rain.

Trey didn't look up from his laptop. "Try not to have too much fun. I can't wait to hear what weird ass shit you find this time."

"Maybe it'll be totally normal. You don't know."

He turned to her and asked in disbelief, "Do you seriously think that's going to be the case?"

"No. But it would be a surprise." She stuck her tongue out at him and teleported to a small path close to the road leading up to the house.

A drop of rain splatted onto the top of her head, and she flipped her hood up. "Good thing I love walking in the rain."

She bumped into a tall man as she exited the woods. He jumped at her sudden appearance, almost dropping his phone that he was using to light the semi-dark road. Cars were parked further down the hill where there was more space. The road was too narrow to drive up to the house, let alone park.

"I'm so sorry!" She exclaimed.

He let out a hint of a laugh. "Nothing to apologize for. Although if I'm this jumpy at someone appearing out of thin air, then I've probably already ruined any chance I have of acting like ghosts aren't going to scare me to death."

Skye could see better in the dim light than he could. She liked his humorous, self-deprecating expression. She said, "Don't worry. Your secret's safe with me."

"I knew I could count on you. But what on earth were you doing in the woods?" Small groups of people were moving toward the house or back to their cars on the dark road.

"My friend dropped me off on the other side to avoid the parking down there." She waved at the congestion of cars. "It was easier to cut across than go around." She wasn't lying too much, and he seemed to accept her explanation.

"That makes sense. I'm Ben. And I promise I'm not normally as jumpy as I seem."

"I'm Skye. I'll try harder next time I'm sneaking through the woods to make more noises and forewarn anyone walking by. Of course, then they'll think I'm a wild animal or something, which might be worse."

"You could try not taking shortcuts through dark woods at night? For your own safety if nothing else." He was teasing her and playing along with her banter.

"That's probably the smarter choice. But I like to take chances sometimes. Like going on a haunted house tour by myself."

"I wasn't going to say anything. I didn't want to come across as a creep. But I did notice you are alone. And you don't have any equipment or anything with you." He patted the strap of a camera bag on his shoulder.

Skye shrugged. "I guess you could say I'm here for the experience itself. Not really for the ghost hunter aspect of it."

"I can respect that. I like at least filming a bit. You never know what you might see."

"Please tell me you aren't one of those people who freaks out over every speck of dust that shows up on a camera?" Her voice had a touch of dry sarcasm.

"Oh no. Nothing like that. In fact, I've gone to a few of these before and never caught anything. But I figure I might as well record it for fun. Even if there are no ghosts, there's always the avid ghost hunters to laugh at." His sense of humor made Skye smile. The night might not end up being too bad after all.

They neared the top of the rise, and the house loomed into view on the bluff. It was everything a haunted house should be. It stood alone in a bunch of dead grass with one completely dead tree on the perimeter and more enormous moss-covered trees in the distance. The ocean and rain together made for a lovely sound. A flash of lightning lit up the sky, illuminating the house for a moment, followed by a rumble of thunder.

Ben whistled softly. "That was picture perfect for a movie or something."

"You're not kidding." It was almost perfect enough that Skye wondered about tampering here, but her guardian senses didn't pick up anything.

They walked up the driveway to a cluster of gaudy bright awnings at odds with the atmosphere of the haunted house. Skye caught Ben casting a few surreptitious looks her way as they walked into the brighter light near the house.

A large handful of people were already scattered around the lawn, chatting and waiting. The tour was close to two hours long, and they started them at 5 pm, keeping it going until dawn. Skye had booked the 11 pm one, hoping she had guessed a decent time for her investigation.

The website hadn't mentioned any phantom doors, but that didn't mean there wasn't one. If the door didn't appear when she was inside, then she would probably have to resort to ruining the ghost tours by turning invisible and lurking. It would scare away the ghosts, and make the ghost hunters mad, but she could live with it.

She accepted the pamphlet the host handed to her and walked over to the refreshment table laden with bottled water, granola bars, and fruit. She grabbed water and a granola bar, perfectly willing to snack while waiting. Ben followed her, opting for the same snacks.

Her senses told her he wasn't a creep; he was a genuinely nice guy, so she didn't mind. He was taller than her with a medium build. He had dark wavy hair, a nicely trimmed beard, and dark eyes behind a pair of glasses. He was dressed practically in jeans and a hoodie like her.

He awkwardly cleared his throat. "I hope you don't mind if I hang out with you while we're waiting. I came by myself too. If you'd rather be alone, I'd totally understand." He seemed more nervous now that he could see the strange woman who had run into him in the dark.

"I don't mind at all." She glanced at the others gathered around. It was a good mix of people seeking the thrill of being scared and a few serious ghost hunters with their fancy handheld EMF detectors and expensive cameras.

Skye turned her gaze back to Ben and asked, "So why are you here? Camera aside, you don't seem to be a serious ghost hunter. You also don't seem to be someone who would actively search out a not-so-cheap scare for fun." She winked and grinned.

He winced in mock pain as she teased him about jumping earlier. "You're right on both counts. I'm not here to get scared on purpose, and I'm definitely not a serious ghost hunter. I like the idea that there's more to the world than we normally see or know. So, a haunted house that is suddenly more active right before Halloween? It sounds super gimmicky, but at the same time, if I pay a little money to spend time in a legitimately creepy house and maybe see a ghost? I think it's worth it. How about you?"

"Honestly? I don't expect to see or hear any ghosts myself. But I'm curious about the history and the stories about the new happenings and goings on."

He gave her a puzzled look and asked, "Why would you pay for a haunted house tour if you don't expect to see ghosts?"

Her expression was whimsical, and she said, "Maybe I hope I'll be surprised by seeing something unexpected sometime." She grinned impishly. "Or maybe I'm secretly terrified of ghosts and trying to act like I don't believe in them." She was having fun talking to him. It was a nice break from everything going on in her life. A hint of normalcy she didn't get to experience too often.

He fought back a smile. "I'd love to say I'll protect you from any scary ghosts that pop up, but I don't think you'd take me seriously after you already scared me to death."

Her burst of laughter made more than a few people turn around. She asked, "How about I protect you from the scary ghosts? I have it on good authority that I am absolutely terrifying. Of course, that authority is my brother, so make of it what you will."

Sarah Eriksen

"This is where I should act offended at the idea of a girl protecting me from ghosts that may or may not exist, right? But hey, if you want to protect me from ghosts, I'm totally fine with that."

"So, what makes you feel like there's more to the world than what we normally see? And if I'm prying, you don't have to tell me." She was sincerely interested. Sometimes people with curiosity about the unknown had previous encounters with a guardian or the creatures they dealt with.

He shrugged and said, "I don't mind telling you. I was walking home from a late-night D&D game with some friends when I was twelve, and I swear I saw a strange shadow following me. Of course, at first, I thought it was a trick of the street lights. But then I saw it in the light, so I started to run. I heard a loud crash behind me. When I turned, I swear I saw someone tackling the shadow. It happened so fast...I don't really know what happened. I know it sounds pretty crazy."

Skye smiled and said, "I believe you."

He asked, "Really? I've told that story to a few people before—"

"And let me guess, it was just your imagination after hyping up your brain with D&D?" She mocked the typical reaction his story would have gotten.

"That pretty much covers it. You're not one to blame the world of D&D for overactive imaginations or worse?" He mimicked her tone but couldn't hold in a laugh.

"There's a lot of weird stuff in the world that can't be explained. You experienced something you couldn't explain, but it doesn't have to be a product of an overactive imagination."

"Have you had any weird unexplainable stuff happen to you?"

The host was waving them over to start the tour. Skye smiled enigmatically and said, "Oh yeah. All the time."

Skye tuned out the words of the tour guide. It was a typical opening. Don't use flash photography. Turn off your phones to not ruin the experience. She double-checked her phone and slipped it back into her back pocket.

So far, she didn't sense any of the telltale signs of other-dimensional energy, but that didn't necessarily mean anything definitive. There was still a while before midnight. If this door was the same, she had some time before it would show up.

Chaotic Haunts

She hung back and let the rest of the group head in first, smiling and saying she didn't have any camera equipment, so she'd rather stay in the back. The avid ghost hunters were grateful, and the thrill seekers were happy to get inside faster.

Ben grinned enthusiastically at her and hefted his camera. "Shall we?"

Skye followed him up the slippery rain-covered stairs and held in a laugh as they walked inside the house. Dark peeling wallpaper, threadbare carpet, dimly lit corridor, cobweb-filled corners. It was a perfect haunted house from appearances alone.

She had to fight with herself to not say her cynical and sarcastic observations out loud. Instead, she reached out to her twin. *"This haunted house is pretty spectacularly staged. I'm almost ashamed any ghosts are stooping low enough to haunt it. It's too obvious."*

He gave life to the reaction she needed by laughing hysterically. *"Maybe we should make a fake haunted house. We could make a fortune pretending to be ghosts."*

"Not a bad idea. But probably not something to mess with just the same."

The guide led them down the hallway to a large open room with a wide staircase to the upper floors. The house was old but had been remodeled with an open floor plan on the main level. They were encouraged to explore the room and take pictures or videos if they wanted.

Their guide started animatedly telling a story about a family dispute that ended with a murder-suicide. She was a great storyteller, and it was clear why she had been picked up to do the tours.

Skye moved toward the fireplace, on the opposite side from where the crime had taken place, giving the others an unobstructed view of the room. Ben followed her, snapping a few pictures here and there. She watched how he staged his camera, wondering if he was focused more on capturing the house instead of hoping for ghosts.

She asked, a curious expression on her face, "Feeling creeped out yet?"

He shook his head. "Nope. How about you?"

"Nothing. But I think I'm broken when it comes to feeling creeped out in a haunted house."

"Does this go hand in hand with the belief that you won't be seeing any ghosts?"

A crash from the other side of the room stopped her from having to reply. They joined the rest of the tour, where the pair of ghost hunters were chatting excitedly and holding up their cameras.

Skye hung back and listened as Ben asked, "What happened?"

The older ghost hunter replied, "Something threw that book. We're seeing if we caught it on camera." He pointed at a book lying on the floor near a chair.

Skye shook her head, scowling in the direction the book had been thrown from. Ghosts seriously had no respect for books. They always threw them. She was tempted for a moment to summon creation energy and scare them away, but she didn't want to ruin the fun the others were having.

"Skye, come check this out!" Ben waved her over excitedly.

Everyone was crowded around the camera. The ghost hunters started the video again. The footage was wobbly, but they managed to catch the tail end of the book flying through the air.

Skye had to give it to the ghosts. They were good. The footage was real, but anyone a bit skeptical would be able to tear it apart as staged. She hoped she managed to fake excitement for the others.

The tour guide waved them over to the basement door, and they headed downstairs. Ben whispered to her, "So you got to see a ghost after all, and you don't seem excited."

"That was more of a poltergeist, if anything. And we didn't see any of it. We heard the aftermath." She spoke quietly enough so the others wouldn't hear.

"That's true. You don't think they faked it do you?" He sounded disappointed.

"I don't think so. But you have to admit the video footage is hardly conclusive for a haunting."

"Maybe the ghosts are smart enough not to get caught in the act?" He was teasing, but he certainly hit the nail on the head with his observation.

Skye's grin was full of mischief. She said, "If I were a ghost, I sure would want to make it more difficult to prove, wouldn't you?"

The basement wasn't much more than a jumbled-up converted root cellar, cramped with shelves and the remains of an old coal heating system. Cobwebs covered every possible nook and cranny. The owners had left a bunch of random junk on the shelves. There were a million empty jars for canning, some old toys, and tools. Pretty typical of what you would find in most garages or basement storage spaces.

The guide was now telling a story of a strange man who had broken into the cellar ages ago. He had planned to steal something when the family went to sleep but ended up being discovered and then killed by the owner of the house instead.

Skye rolled her eyes and said sarcastically, "They call this a murder house. It sounds more like a thief who didn't understand the finer points of stealth."

Ben couldn't hold in a chuckle, getting a dirty glare from the younger couple who were there for the thrill. He mumbled an apology, looking embarrassed at the attention.

Skye grinned winningly at them, and they turned away in irritation, going back to exclaiming over their camera footage.

She whispered to Ben, "They must have a lot of dust on camera. They are way too excited."

He covered his mouth this time as he laughed, muffling the sound.

She gave him an apologetic look. "Sorry. I hope I'm not ruining the ghost tour for you with my less than enthusiastic reactions to this stuff."

"Not at all. You're making it a lot more fun. And you're not wrong. They are definitely excited over dust." He grinned at her as she held back a laugh.

Footsteps sounded above them, making all of them jump, except for Skye. It sounded like someone was pacing on the floor upstairs. The girl in the young couple glanced at Skye in annoyance and said, "I suppose you think that's someone up there trying to scare us."

She said wryly, "Not at all. If an actual person is walking up there, we'd have a lot more dust falling from the rafters. I'd say it's a real ghost. I bet if you go upstairs, there won't be anyone." She already knew there wasn't anyone above them. She might not be able to sense ghosts, but she could sense if a person was up there.

She stepped back as the couple rushed to the stairs, the others following quickly. Skye noticed the guide was showing signs of stress. She placed a gentle hand on the woman's arm and asked, "Everything

Sarah Eriksen

alright? Don't worry. I'm not going to be dramatic and excitable like the rest of them."

She gave Skye a strained smile. "The footsteps just started tonight. It's been getting a lot more active every day. But I'm sure we have nothing to worry about."

Skye did her best to reassure her. "I'm sure you don't have anything to worry about. But if you start getting too stressed out doing this, it would be good to take a break. Ghosts tend to interact more with people when they start to show stress. Or, if you're doing this for the pay, maybe start pairing up."

The girl gave her a bewildered look. "You didn't seem to believe in ghosts like the rest of them, but now you're talking like you're an expert on hauntings?"

"Let's just say I know a lot more about this than I let on. There's a reason why I'm a lot calmer than the rest of them. I've had plenty of experience with this kind of stuff. And whether or not you believe what I'm saying is true, at the very least, you have to admit you'd probably feel a lot better if you had someone with you who knows the history of this place."

"You're probably right." Skye wasn't using her powers, but guardians could project a bit of calm in situations like this to help with emotional stress. Of course, with her questionably stable control at the moment, adding her powers might well be less a projection of calm and more of a hammer-like sedative.

Skye let the guide go up the stairs ahead of her and felt a playful tug on her hair. She turned around and raised one eyebrow. "If you know what's good for you, you'll save your tricks for someone else." She started to walk up the stairs again and turned back, saying sternly, "And stop throwing books. Seriously."

Chapter Nine

Ben was waiting for her at the top of the stairs. "I was about to come looking for you. I think the passionate ghost hunters are no longer mad at you since the room is cold and no one is here."

"Ah yes. Cold spots. That aren't possibly related to the fact that this house is ancient, drafty, located on the coast, and it's late night in autumn?" The basement had been damp but warmer with all of their bodies, so the first floor felt noticeably colder. Skye would be able to feel temperature fluctuations caused by ghosts, and she wasn't picking up anything unusual.

"I didn't think it was any colder either. See any ghosts down there?" He teased.

"Something pulled my hair, and I told it to bother someone else and stop throwing books." Her tone was matter-of-fact.

"You're joking, right?" His voice was hesitant.

She smiled, winked, and joined the rest of the group. The guide appeared less stressed, or at least she had it under better control again. They were about to head upstairs, where a gruesome bunch of murders had happened over the years.

The first story was about a family that had all been killed in their beds. No one was ever caught, and the deaths remained a mystery. There were still no stories about any phantom doors, however. Skye wouldn't be upset if it turned out to be a total bust. She was enjoying herself.

The second floor hadn't been remodeled to be more modern. A long stretch of hallway wound around with rooms scattered along either side of it. Most of the rooms were connected with doorways giving them more than one option to move around. It would make it easier for Skye to slip away if she needed to.

The guide took them into the first room to the left, which proved to be a good-sized library in the round, tower-shaped part of the house. There was no record of any murders taking place there, but it was known to have poltergeist activity, with books being knocked down or thrown.

Skye sighed, and when Ben gave her a questioning look, she answered, "Poltergeists are obsessed with books. It's always books being thrown. I own a bookstore, and I love books. Seriously, they need to have a bit more respect and stop damaging antiques." The library was full of old, well-preserved tomes. She could have happily spent days in there looking at them.

He chuckled as silently as he could manage. "That's pretty awesome you own a bookstore. Any chance it's nearby so I could stop and visit sometime? If that's not too presumptuous of me."

She gave him a reassuring grin and said, "It's not close by. It's more like a few hundred miles east of here. I was here visiting a friend and thought this would be fun. Not to say you wouldn't be welcome to visit if you happened to be traveling that way."

A book flew across the room in front of them and slammed into the door. Skye leveled a frosty glare in the direction the book had come from and muttered, "I told you. Obsessed with books."

She stepped back as the others hurried over to take pictures of the book and wave their equipment over it. A few faint flickers on their EMF detectors gave them the thrill they wanted. They had all seemed to come to the conclusion that Skye wasn't that into the haunting but wasn't going to get in their way.

"Are you really more bothered by the fact a book was thrown, rather than the fact that a poltergeist literally threw the book a few inches in front of your face?" Ben asked doubtfully.

She shrugged. "I have unique priorities."

No one caught that activity on camera, and Skye had a sneaking impression that the ghosts were deliberately trying to mess with her now. After a few more silent minutes with nothing else happening, the guide prompted them to move into the next room.

It was the first of many bedrooms on the upper floor where a murder had taken place. It was a very active room for hauntings and ghost activity. The guide opened the door to a large bathroom and led them across to the other bedroom.

"If you set up your cameras in this direction, you might catch one of the ghosts. A misty figure of a woman in white has been known to show up in the doorways to the bathroom. We think that it was the lady of the house who was murdered in this room. The records were destroyed in a fire, so we haven't uncovered the full story, but her appearance suggests it happened a long time ago."

The ghost hunters suddenly raised their equipment in excitement while the young girl clung to her partner, terrified of something. Skye raised an eyebrow and whispered to Ben, "What's going on?"

He blinked in surprise and blurted out, "You can't hear it?"

She shook her head, raising her hand in a vague gesture with a shrug.

"It sounds like a woman screaming and crying." He was disturbed by the sound. His expression was tense and apprehensive.

One of the ghost hunters exclaimed, "Oh my god! Are you guys seeing this?" He pointed frantically at the bathroom. The ghost hunters aimed their cameras and handheld voice recorders toward the door while the girl buried her face against her boyfriend's chest. He was staring at the door, his expression starting to look like he regretted coming along.

"Is there something there?" Skye asked Ben. When he gave her a look of utter disbelief, she sighed. "I know it seems weird. But I told you I wasn't going to see any ghosts tonight. I want you to tell me what you see."

"There's some definite mist in the doorway. I've never seen anything like this." He had his camera raised and was filming avidly. Skye was more than a bit envious.

The room let out a disappointed sound in unison, and Skye guessed the mist had disappeared. Ben beat her to her question. "It dropped to the floor and was gone. And it's quiet now." He frowned. "How is it you can't see ghosts? It doesn't make any sense that you are the only person in the room who couldn't see it."

She shifted her feet, uncomfortable by the question. "I can't really explain it. But I can't see or hear them. If I could tell you why I would. But it wouldn't make an awful lot of sense." She hated when she had to provide half-ass explanations for things.

Sarah Eriksen

He seemed to accept her response, although curiosity was rolling off him. "Alright. Why would you come to a haunted house if you aren't going to be able to experience the fun?"

She figured there wasn't harm in answering truthfully at this point and said, "I'm looking for a door."

"Like architecturally speaking?" The group slowly moved into the other bedroom, taking pictures of everything as they went.

Skye tilted her head back and forth thoughtfully, and said, "That's not entirely inaccurate, but not quite true." So far, the doors she'd found hadn't been consistently tied to real doors on Earth.

She slipped through the ghost hunters to stand off to the side out of their way. Ben kept glancing at her, his expression part confusion and part curiosity. Humans who had close encounters with guardians and their world either ignored it, came up with logical explanations, or kept their curiosity. Ben was clearly the latter.

She finally said, "Go ahead and ask. I don't mind." He had politely not pried, but his silence, coupled with strong emotions, had been just as loud to her.

He looked grateful for the invitation. "How did you hear the footsteps but not the screaming and crying?"

"Those are two very different sources for those sounds. One was caused by something impacting the floor, and the other was caused by something I can't see or hear. Technically I didn't hear the ghost walking. I heard the floor reacting to the ghost's steps."

As if on cue, a loud thump sounded above them. The tour guide jumped as much as the others. Skye watched her while the rest stared at the ceiling. She was terrified, so this must be something unexpected. Skye walked over and whispered, "Is that new too?"

The girl locked eyes with her. "There has never been anything upstairs. No rumors, no sounds, nothing. All of the ghost activity has been here or downstairs. We never go up into the attic."

Skye said, "You said the activity has been picking up. Where has it been getting the most active?"

"This floor first, and a little bit on the main floor the last few days. It always seems to be around midnight or right after when it gets more noticeable. I can't let them go upstairs, and they are going to want to go." She sounded more terrified of confronting the ghost hunters than of the haunting.

"Tell them there are raccoons in the attic, and we can't go up there because of safety and liability reasons." Boring and ordinary explanations were the best way to deter the overly curious. It was a skill every guardian learned at a young age.

The girl gazed at her as if she had just performed a miracle. Skye gave her an encouraging smile. "You got this."

Skye stared at the ceiling while the guide explained to the others that the attic was off-limits. She was trying to reach out her senses without using her powers. She couldn't get the same range without a boost of energy, but it still worked. She couldn't feel anything resembling the other dimension. But then, the door might not be open yet.

She was confident she'd be able to sense it as long as she was in the house when it appeared. She had been able to sense the doors back to Earth from a good distance away. But she still didn't have enough answers. At the very least, it was clear the ghost activity was picking up, judging from the reactions of the others.

The guide managed to convince them to move to the nursery and playroom across the hall. She was animatedly telling them about the horrific things that had happened there. Her enthusiasm seemed a little over the top as she tried to keep the focus away from the noises above them.

Skye lingered back by the door. She wanted to get up to the attic. Her gust was telling her that if there was going to be a door, it would be up there. With all the other activity, a phantom door anywhere else in the house would have been a big topic. She had to wait for the right moment to slip away. She just hoped the ghosts would provide the distraction she needed to make her escape.

The ghost hunters were clustered around the door leading from the playroom into the nursery. They all seemed uncomfortable, so Skye guessed something was playing around.

"Can you hear crying?" the young girl exclaimed.

One of the ghost hunters pointed into the nursery. Everyone stared at the door, seeming paralyzed with varying emotions from fear to excitement. Skye didn't know what had their attention but now was her chance. She slipped out into the hall and snuck to the attic door.

Sarah Eriksen

"Didn't she just tell us the attic is off limits?" Ben whispered right behind her.

"I should have known I wouldn't be able to slip away without you noticing. And yes, she did, so you should probably go back."

"If it's not safe, we should both go back, or let me come with you in case it is a deadly pack of raccoons."

Skye kept her face neutral, even though she wanted to let out an exasperated sigh. She knew a determined man when she saw one. And sometimes, it wasn't worth the breath arguing, especially when she didn't want to get caught. She pointed a stern finger at him. "Fine. But no heroics."

He nodded, and Skye tested the door, fully expecting it to be locked. She was surprised when it opened under her hand. She pushed Ben inside ahead of her and closed the door quietly behind them. The stairway was narrow and more than a bit of a squeeze as she apologized and slipped past him.

"I'm all for equal rights and everything, but I would feel better if you let me go first."

"I'm not offended, but I promise you, it's far safer with me going first. I'm more than a match for a raccoon, or a ghost, or whatever else we might encounter up here. You'll have to let me know if you see a ghost, though."

"We're not going to see much without a light up here." He turned on the flashlight on his phone and aimed it over her head. They reached the top of the stairs and glanced around the attic. It had a solid wooden floor with a few boxes and old steamer trunks in jumbled piles tucked in where they fit. A hint of light came in through the gabled windows, but not enough to see by without guardian senses.

They both jumped as they heard a scream from below. Skye shook her head. "I'm guessing the ghosts are having a grand old time down there."

"It was pretty crazy before you slipped away. Crying, and a rocking chair moving on its own."

A loud thump sounded from the opposite side of the attic around a corner.

Skye started to walk toward the noise, and Ben said, "You do know this is how bad things happen in haunted houses in movies, right? As soon as someone leaves the group, they end up getting killed or something."

Skye shrugged. "I can safely say any ghosts in this house would disappear faster than you can blink if I wanted them to." They turned the corner, and Skye felt the telltale tingle of the other dimension.

"Well, that's good because that's one of the most terrifying ghosts I could have ever imagined seeing." Ben's voice held the first hint of panic she had heard all night.

Skye stared in consternation at the figure in front of them. She could see it too, which meant it wasn't an actual ghost. It was a tall figure wrapped in shadows, with a tiny glint of metal at its throat. The blurry portal of the door to the other dimension was behind the shadowy figure.

Skye pushed Ben behind her. "That's not a ghost."

"Maybe you can't see it, but— "

She cut him off. "That's just it. I *can* see it. It's not a ghost. You should go back to the group. I need to deal with this." She stepped back, pushing him further behind her and toward the stairs.

"Is that the door you were looking for?" The creature started to shamble toward them slowly, and there was a faint hint of shadowy movement on the other side of the portal.

"Yep. Cover for me. Tell them I got scared and left or something."

"You're not going through the door, are you?" He was terrified, but his concern for her was sweet.

She turned and smiled at him. "Don't worry. I'll be fine. I'm trained for this stuff. And what's more important, you'll be fine."

He didn't argue even though it was clear he didn't believe her. Instead, he said, "I know it's not great timing, but maybe we could meet for coffee sometime." He slipped a piece of paper into her hand.

She glanced down in surprise and smiled, slipping it into her pocket. The shuffling footsteps were getting closer, and she said, "You better go."

She ran toward the shadowy mummy monster and coated herself in a light layer of creation energy with only a hint of faint sparks. She slammed into the creature, tackling it through the doorway into the other shadow.

Sarah Eriksen

Ben stared as the door closed, and all the creepy feelings from the haunted house slipped away. This was, by far, the strangest night he had had since he was a kid walking home from a D&D party. A beautiful and witty woman had tackled a shadowy monster through a door that disappeared. He smiled, happy he had managed to slip her his number. He just hoped she would call him, even if it was only to explain what the hell had just happened.

Chapter Ten

Skye hit warm, sand-covered stone, a cloud of black dust encompassing her as the ghostly shadow figures exploded under her body. She coughed and pushed herself up, brushing sand and mummy dust off her clothes as she took in her new surroundings. She had fallen out of an opening in a decorative wall into a small burial chamber. The walls and panels were intricately decorated, and there was only one hallway leading out.

"Great. An Egyptian-style tomb." It would be a total maze designed to confuse grave robbers. If the last two parts of this dimension had given her any idea, the scenery would be accurate, but something else would be off about it.

She reached out with her mind to get the layout of the tomb and was met with a shadowy distortion the further she tried to see. She couldn't feel anything blocking her. It was as though the dimension itself wanted this location to be mysterious.

At least the mummies had been easy to kill. They had turned to dust when they landed against a rough block of stone. She turned to study where she had come in. The phantom door had disappeared, leaving a decorative stone panel that looked like a fake door.

There was an open sarcophagus leaning against the wall, its lid on the ground in front of it. The shadowy being must have been a mummy that escaped its coffin and ended up in the haunted house. The second shadow must have wandered in behind it.

Sarah Eriksen

It was the first time something from the other dimension had crossed over that she knew of. The doors to White Chapel and the forest had closed behind her after she entered them. But if something escaped this dimension, then it meant that the door had to have been open inside for something to pass through it.

The doors weren't necessarily one way. Hopefully, it was unique to this one and not a sign of something getting worse. The last thing she wanted was the pink ball of doom to wreak havoc at the amusement park or anywhere else.

"Amonir, we thought these doors were only one way, but a mummy came through one to Earth. The girl at the haunted house said she had never heard anything from the attic where the door was before tonight, but it might be a problem."

"I'll keep an eye on it to ensure no one gets hurt. Thank you for the update."

The god left abruptly, making Skye frown as touches of anxiety threatened to bubble up. She felt like she was failing at getting her powers under control. It was her responsibility to figure things out since he had already given her guidance. But this mummy situation was not personal. This was the job he had told her to do.

It wasn't unusual for him to leave his guardians alone to figure things out. He had an entire universe to pay attention to, and the level of independence he granted them for doing their job only helped them. But his distracted absence when she already felt so disconnected and alone made her worry more about her failure to control her powers.

She felt Trey's flicker of concern and locked her emotions back up in an iron-clad grip, sending him wordless reassurance. She had a job to do, and she needed to stay focused.

"Guess I'd better find a way out of here." She moved to the door, her senses on alert for any possible dangers. The corridor was lined with cobwebby torches flickering with bright flames. Skye shook her head in disbelief, just like a video game, torches burning in an underground tomb with no signs of people around. Maybe she'd find some fresh produce in barrels while she was at it.

She rounded a sharp corner, and the hall angled downward. Her feet scrabbled on the sand-dusted stone, forcing her to proceed with more care.

Chaotic Haunts

A strange wind caused the torches to flicker as she neared the next corner. The stone floor dropped at a steep angle that would be impossible to walk down. The torches left feeble spots of light that didn't illuminate the very bottom.

A sensible person would sit down and slide carefully. Skye stepped onto the steep slope and slid down on her feet, sinking knee-deep into a pile of sand at the bottom. She slogged her way to the cleared stones nearby, paying for her reckless descent with effort.

The next hall had a slight upward incline. She could see a brighter light at the end of it. As she neared the end of the corridor, a shadow passed across the well-lit opening, and a shuffling sound of something dragging through sand echoed out.

A quick mental peek showed a mummy. A real mummy. One far less shadowy and much more substantial, covered in tattered rags. The room was a mess of large slabs of stone in various states of falling or fallen, giving her plenty of cover.

She entered the room without making a sound, using a large block to hide from the mummy. She hoped this one would turn out as easy to kill as the other one. She searched for a weapon, knowing full well she could summon a sword if she needed to. But she wanted to keep a low profile to be safe. A hilt jutted out of the sand in the shadow of a tipped over slab of stone.

"That's conveniently placed." She thought to herself as she waited for an opportune moment to move without being seen. She could only sense the one mummy, but that didn't mean there weren't more of them. And there could be plenty of other currently unknown dangers.

She hefted the sword, it was a little heavier than she was used to, but she swiftly adjusted to the weight. She ducked behind another stone block where she had a slightly better view.

The mummy was shuffling aimlessly in the middle of the room, and there were multiple exits visible. Her guardian senses didn't give her any hints that it was anything other than a real mummy, albeit a mobile one.

So far, every pocket of this dimension she had been in had a movie or video game kind of vibe. At least the mummy wasn't giving off feelings of inexplicable and terrifying doom like the pink ball. She decided to chance it and attacked, swinging the heavy blade and cutting it in half. It fell to the ground in two pieces, both of which were still trying to move.

Sarah Eriksen

The torso flipped over and started dragging itself toward her. She grabbed a spear from a half crumbling statute and stabbed it through its chest, using a touch of power to imbed the tip in the stone floor. She crouched down and studied the still wiggling corpse. It was an authentic, ancient mummy. It wouldn't have been out of place in any old monster movie or an ancient Egyptian tomb.

She gripped the sword and headed toward the four openings on the far side of the room, closing her eyes and trying to see with her mind past each door. She could see the areas she where had already been with no issue, but she couldn't see far ahead.

There was no choice but to physically explore them and hope she found the right path. She jogged down the left corridor; it ended in a burial chamber and appeared to be a dead end. The next one was also a dead end unless she wanted to climb up a narrow air shaft.

She moved into the third opening. It didn't end immediately like the first two. She turned and studied the fourth opening in case it was more promising. It headed down in a slow spiral. The third one seemed promising as far as distance, but the fourth one could be just as good or bad. She wasn't getting much of a sense of the exit door yet, and she could always backtrack if her first choice didn't pan out. She hoped.

She debated her two options and finally settled on door number three.

"How's it going?" Trey popped into her mind.

She wasn't sure if he was asking about the emotions he felt earlier or the dimension. She opted to answer the one she was comfortable with. *"I've got real mummies in what appears to be an Egyptian tomb."*

Trey responded immediately, *"Seriously? Are you—?"*

"If you are about to ask me if I'm sure, I might give you a mental slap that will knock you out for a week."

"Are you going to be able to find the exit?" Trey changed tracks quickly.

"It's going to take a minute, I think. But I get to explore a perfect replica of an Egyptian tomb right out of a monster movie or a video game." The narrow hall turned a corner and suddenly widened into a torch-lit corridor covered in detailed symbols. *"It's pretty impressive."*

She moved to study the murals more closely, raising her eyebrows in surprise and disbelief at the content. They depicted a story in detail. The first panel showed a group of people, possibly explorers. The next panel showed the same group discovering a room full of large eggs. The third panel showed the eggs bursting open, with creatures leaping out of them onto the explorers.

"Okay, found the weird part of the tomb." Skye let Trey take a peek through her eyes, enjoying his reaction. *"Mummies, garden gnome serial killer, zombies I can handle. But if a xenomorph shows up, I quit."*

"I wouldn't blame you."

The entire wall of the corridor was full of a detailed depiction of the movies. She glanced at the other wall covered in a collection of internet memes centered on cats. Egyptian tomb, internet cat worship. It kind of worked.

Skye headed into a narrow corridor, her senses on high alert for potential new threats, hoping it was an unnecessary precaution.

The tomb was fairly linear for a maze. Her current route had no path but forward. The halls were getting narrower with each turn. They would be impossible to pass through if they got much smaller. She rounded the next corner, turning sideways and squeezing through the narrow gap toward a promising pool of light ahead.

She slipped out of the tight space and scowled. The room appeared to be a dead end with two large statues and a pedestal with a heavy urn on it. She had been walking through these halls for a good few minutes and was not remotely in the mood to backtrack.

She felt her brother's inquisitive non-verbal question at her obvious irritation and blocked him out. She needed to focus. There was an empty shaft underneath the stone floor that dropped a long way to a far more open chamber below. The twisting corridors had unveiled enough of her mental map to show the fourth corridor had a nice smooth descent to the same lower level.

Her frustrated sigh echoed in the small room. She turned to go back when a glint of light on the urn caught her eye and made her pause. The empty shaft was right in front of it. The flash of light had been far too well-timed not to be deliberate.

Skye stood in front of the decorative piece of pottery, contemplating the possible ramifications of triggering such an obvious trap. She shrugged and pushed the heavy urn off the pedestal. The floor underneath her immediately collapsed, and she fell, surrounded by a shower of sand.

Sarah Eriksen

The shaft wasn't wide, but she was falling fast. She kicked both feet out, dropped her sword, and pushed her hands against the wall. The rough stone scraped her palms, and she hastily covered her hands in a small protective shield.

Her descent slowed, and she dropped nimbly to the sandy floor at the bottom. She inspected her injured hands. They were scraped up with a few deeper cuts that stung and bled. At least she had been wearing shoes, so the bottoms of her feet were intact for a change.

Self-healing was not one of her strengths, but she was able to pull the sand and debris out of the scrapes to clean them. She placed a tiny invisible bandage of energy over her palms to slow the bleeding. She managed to keep her energy usage as small and muffled as possible and hadn't noticed anyone noticing her. Deities tended to have pretty obvious presences when they noticed things invading their space.

She picked up her sword, ignoring the stinging in her palm, and surveyed the next room. It was beautiful in a gloomy, creepy tomb way that wouldn't have been out of place in Skyrim. Dark ceremonial caskets lined the circular chamber. This dimension took some serious liberties with genre mixing.

There was an opening on the far side, and a mental peek told her it was the other path from above. She was finally getting a faint glimmer of the way back, and it was through a barred and locked door. She had to admit she was relieved she could finally feel the way out.

The barred door had no handle and no obvious way of opening it. She searched for a switch or trigger. A large explosion of cracking stone broke the silence. She spun around and raised her sword as a large mummy pushed the lid of the sarcophagus out of the way. More cracks sounded as mummies broke the seals and forced their way upright.

Skye played more than enough video games to know when to use a scene like this to her advantage. She ran toward the first mummy before it had a chance to sit up, swinging the heavy sword with both hands and decapitating it.

She spun and kicked the second one hard in the stomach, knocking it back and cutting it in half. Unlike the mummy in the upper chamber, these stopped moving after being slightly dismembered.

A rag-covered hand grabbed her shoulder. She twisted the sword in a tight spin, slicing through the arm. She shifted as the mummy fell back and stabbed it through its torso. Luckily for her, the sword was sharp enough to cut through mummified flesh.

She mentally snorted at how ridiculously powerful the sword was. It was cutting through mummified flesh as easily as, if not better than, her glowing creation energy swords. Despite the obvious carnage around her, this sword was just a normal sword.

She cut another mummy in half from shoulder to hip and reached her mind out to her brother. *"It's like I'm in a damn video game, monster movie, pop culture mashup."*

Trey wordlessly shared her mayhem for a moment. *"From what you're showing me, this entire dimension is a bizarre mashup of a lot of things from our world."*

"And it still makes no sense." She cut the head off the last mummy, and a loud clunky noise sounded, and the barred door swung open. *"Huh. Cleared the mummies out of the room, and the locked door opened."*

"Think you'll have to fight an end boss?" He joked.

"I hope not. Considering all of the murals in this place, I can't even begin to fathom what would be deemed an end boss."

"Good luck."

Skye made a face and headed into another corridor covered with memes, and thankfully no mummies. She could feel Trey was worried about her going off into the weird dimension alone, but he was managing to keep it mostly to himself. She appreciated his effort to not be overbearingly protective. She had enough going on in her own head that she needed to figure out.

The end of the hall had two openings. They both appeared to run parallel to each other, straight to a large room at the end. Two corridors would suggest two separate paths and destinations, but she didn't have to worry about losing a companion since she was alone. She picked the one on the right and moved through the short hall toward another bright light.

She stared at the ridiculous treasure room she was in. The creator of this dimension had mostly stuck to the Egyptian tomb theme with the statutes, jewelry, and general piles of loot. She wasn't the least bit tempted to steal anything. And something told her that touching the treasure would be a bad idea. She picked her way delicately across the sandy floor, avoiding coins and spilled gems.

Sarah Eriksen

Halfway across, a loud rumbling sounded ahead of her from the wall where the next exit was. She let out a resigned sigh as she watched the entire stone slab start to sink.

"Of course." She said to herself as she bolted toward the exit, no longer caring about being cautious. The wall was dropping at a steady pace and was already halfway down. She threw herself into a slide, using a touch of energy to boost her body across the distance without worrying about being crushed.

The stone thudded softly against the floor behind her, and she flinched. She turned and glared at it, waving away a cloud of dust. She had had plenty of clearance when she slid, so it shouldn't have closed that quickly behind her. It was another perfect movie moment, barely getting to safety before being crushed to death.

She was in another large room, this one a long rectangle, with more coffins lining it. She could see the exit on the far side behind a very ornate sarcophagus. It was an obvious end-boss setup. She hefted the heavy sword and started forward, preparing to take out more mummies with each step.

She was halfway across the room, and no mummies had dramatically burst out of their tombs to attack her. She made it to the fancy sarcophagus, and it was still quiet. She couldn't help but feel like something else was supposed to happen in this room, but there was nothing.

She studied the carving on the top of the sarcophagus, it was a rather innocuous-looking woman, but the placement and detail implied it was someone important.

A loud crash resounded in the room, and a shadowy figure appeared at the far end of the hall. It was another mummy like the one in the haunted house, only much larger. Skye watched it as it stomped its way toward her.

The other mummy had died when she tackled it, so this one shouldn't be any different. She threw the heavy sword with all her strength and watched it spin through the air, slamming into the mummy's chest. It exploded in a dark cloud of dust.

Skye shook her head at the overpowered weapon straight out of a video game. She glanced at the sarcophagus one more time, still as mystified as she had been since this started.

Chaotic Haunts

She walked through the door, teleporting back to her world, and screamed as a horrifying visage appeared in front of her face. She reacted on pure instinct and sent an explosive blast of power into the monstrosity, blowing it up while sparks flurried wildly around her.

Her brain finally caught up with what her eyes had seen, and she realized she had blown up a ventriloquist dummy. She was surrounded by props and clothing packed into a small space. Her mind pinpointed her location. She was in a prop closet in a theater in New York City. It was surely haunted as every other location seemed to be, but anything that might have been around would have run away after her show of power.

"Haunted theater and a creepy doll. I'm glad I can scare away ghosts so easily." She shuddered and teleported herself to an alley outside. It had been a long night of exploring, and she needed something to eat.

Sarah Eriksen

Chapter Eleven

She sat on the kitchen counter eating a delicious pastrami sandwich she had grabbed from a deli in New York. She was waiting for the boys to arrive for an early morning discussion. Having a pastrami sandwich at breakfast time when she hadn't slept all night should have seemed wrong, but she took it in stride. Declan appeared first and joined her on the counter, stealing her bag of chips and eyeing her sandwich.

Skye turned away, holding her sandwich closer to her body. "You can go get your own damn sandwich."

"You seriously didn't bring back enough sandwiches for all of us?" He pouted.

"Of course, I did. They're on the table." She nodded her chin at them.

"I knew there was a reason I liked you. Even if pastrami sandwiches for breakfast, is a weird choice."

"I wasn't about to risk getting murdered for not bringing enough awesome New York deli sandwiches home with me. I don't know why I bother being so nice. It's not like you guys can't go get your own food from wherever you want, whenever you want. And are you telling me you haven't been up all night too? So, it's not breakfast for you either." She could tell he was tired.

"You're not wrong. But sandwiches always taste better when someone else pays for them." Declan grinned winningly at her, ignoring her unimpressed stare. "Hey!" he exclaimed as Trey stole the sandwich he had unwrapped off the plate in front of him.

"What?" Trey mimicked Declan's mannerisms flawlessly.

Chaotic Haunts

Eric snagged the pickle spear Declan was about to throw at Trey out of the air and took a bite. "Don't go wasting perfectly good pickles on Trey."

Trey looked affronted. "Did you take Declan's side?"

Eric's lips twitched into a faint smile, and he unwrapped a sandwich, thanking Skye politely and ignoring Trey. "Did you invite Ian and Ryan too? Or just brought extra sandwiches in the hopes that it would keep these two quiet longer?"

Skye replied, "As lovely as the thought is, I invited the other two since they have been in on this and might have some different insight. I bought a cheesecake to keep these two quiet longer."

"Oh...cheesecake? Now you're talking my language." Declan's eyes lit up. "Where is it?" His gaze followed her finger to the fridge, and he leaped into action.

"What kind of cheesecake?" Ryan asked with a yawn. He had just arrived with Ian. They were both disheveled and looked tired.

"The tasty kind I bought in New York. Sorry, I woke you both up. I figured you'd want to be part of things."

Ian waved off her apology and eyed the food with curiosity. "Did you end up in New York after wherever you went? Or was this a tasty detour? You were in Washington last night, weren't you?"

"Yes, I was in Washington, then I was in an Egyptian tomb full of real mummies and pop culture references, and I ended up blowing up a ventriloquist dummy in a prop room in a theater in New York City. And since you can get delicious pastrami sandwiches from awesome delis at all hours...I figured I should indulge."

"You've been in an alternate dimension since last night?" Ryan looked horrified.

"Well, the ghost tour started pretty late, and it was a little over an hour before I finally found the door to the alternate dimension. And I'd guess I was in the other dimension, maybe two hours? Give or take." She hadn't been paying attention to the time while she was inside.

Eric studied her face, concern clear in his gaze. "Does time move differently there?"

She said, "I don't think it does. I mean, it kind of felt like I was lost in a video game, and you know how many hours can pass when you dive into a good RPG. I wasn't paying attention to the flow of time, but it didn't feel unusual or off, so I'd guess no."

As a guardian who could time travel, she knew where and when she was as soon as she thought about it. She had always been very sensitive and aware of the intricacies of time movement, so time moving differently would have stood out to her.

Ryan asked, "So the alternate dimension is mirroring our world and video games and pop culture in general? What's the point?" Ian nodded in agreement, his mouth full of food.

Skye shrugged. "Maybe the god who created it just likes Earth pop culture?"

"It could be that simple. But the fact that doors are opening where innocent people could go through them makes it a bit more concerning." Eric reminded them.

She agreed with him. "That's the main concern. The haunted house I was in seemed mostly safe since the door was in the attic, and it was not part of their tour. Although, the ghosts apparently get way more agitated when the doors open, so that could be dangerous. And, there was a mummy thing in the attic from the other dimension."

Ian asked, "Do you think the ghosts could start hurting people? I don't want to think about things from the other dimension coming here."

Declan said thoughtfully, "It's a distinct possibility. Ghosts harming the living isn't totally unheard of, but not usually on a large scale. Have you asked Amonir about watching the doors if mummies are coming through?"

Skye grumbled, "I told him about it. But I'm not getting much from the boss on this one. I'm assuming it's still up to me to investigate, and if the danger escalates, I'm sure we'll be called in to make the big bad ghosts disappear. Or mummies. Or pink balls of doom."

She watched Declan's face as he fought the desire to comment on her last statement. It was impressive that he didn't hurt himself by holding it inside.

Trey had been abnormally silent throughout most of the discussion. He asked, "So, any idea on new leads?"

Ian jumped in excitedly, "I was googling haunted houses and stuff for you while you were gone. There are a lot of haunted locations with creepy things, although I couldn't find anything recent about doors. But some of them are places no one is allowed to go to, so I have to wonder if there are doors in them, but since no one is allowed, there's nothing online."

Skye said thoughtfully, "It's a solid possibility that I could investigate. Did you have somewhere specific in mind?"

"Well, I was reading up on this place in Utah, Skinwalker Ranch?"

"That's way too far above my pay grade," Skye said, raising both hands and shaking her head.

Ian frowned, his face comically confused. "Wait…you guys get paid?" His question managed to set Declan off laughing.

Skye explained, "No, we don't get paid for this job. But that place isn't somewhere we're concerned with."

Ian's curiosity was visibly building. "So, the crazy things there are real? I mean, you deal with weird things all the time, but I didn't know about those before this year. That means you have to know the truth about what goes on there."

Skye shook her head. "Even if we did, it's not our business. There are a few places like that around the world. There's a reason for it, and we don't mess with it. If whoever is behind this put a door there, they have a far bigger problem on their hands."

Ian said to Ryan, "I don't know about you, but I have no desire to ever go near there now."

"Now? I didn't want to go there before this. Haunted houses are one thing, but that place is another."

Skye laughed at their banter. "I think I'm going to check out the bed and breakfast again tomorrow. I have three doors I know of, and they all go to different parts of the same dimension. This time I want to take my time and see if I can learn anything. Someplace where I'm at least familiar with the danger." She felt confident she could handle the ceramic garden gnome.

She paused and regarded her two non-guardian friends, saying hesitantly, "I hate to ask this, but it'd be really helpful if one of you could tag along to see if the haunting stuff is the same as it was last time. No going into the other dimension. Ghost detector duty only."

They both looked dubious, and Ian sighed, caving in. "Fine. I'll do it, but I'm not going into garden gnome murderville, and one of you has to come with to scare away the ghosts if they get too ghosty."

Eric offered, "I'd be happy to tag along."

"Good. Now, one of you call them up and get me set up to go tomorrow. In the meantime, I need to shower off mummy dust and sand, and go to bed." She paused and asked, "Who's covering the shop?"

Ian raised his hand. "Gwen wanted to get a few extra hours in to save up for the grandkids' birthdays next month, so she's staying a little later today. But I could use some help before lunchtime."

Skye gave Trey an expectant look, and he slowly caught the hint. "Let me get a couple of hours of sleep in, and I'll be there."

Declan lingered while the rest left. Skye asked, "Yes, Declan?"

"How have you been ignoring your hands this entire time?" He dropped his usual snarky demeanor since they were alone.

She glanced down. Her scraped hands started stinging as she remembered she had injured them. "I honestly forgot." Some of the smaller scrapes had healed, but the deeper ones were still noticeable.

"Well, at least it's not the bottom of your feet this time. You seriously walked around New York with your hands sliced up like this?" Gentle waves of bright green energy soothed her palms and healed away the cuts. "One of these days, we'll figure out why you're so terrible at self-healing. It's not that hard."

"Says the man who can heal anything. Besides, it's not uncommon to struggle with it. And I was hardly the weirdest thing in New York City." She laughed.

"Fair point. People probably didn't notice your sliced up hands with all the sand covering you. Now go get some sleep. You're so tired it's making me tired."

"Yes, Mr. Bossy, sir."

He smiled and patted the top of her head. She scowled at him and slapped his hand away. "You'd better get some sleep too. And thanks for the heal."

Skye woke up at an odd hour in the evening and seriously debated going back to sleep. The guardian job could give you jet lag when you bounced around various time zones and kept weird hours. She wanted to sleep more but knew it would be better if she got up for a while and went to bed at a more normal hour later.

Chaotic Haunts

She sat up, crossing her legs and summoning her laptop from downstairs to settle on her lap. Mr. Grimm muttered softly at the disruption to his comfy sleeping spot by her feet and spent a few minutes rearranging the blanket into a fort for himself.

Skye's hands flew across the keyboard as she started searching for haunted locations around the world. She made a few notes of places that sounded promising, but nothing screamed randomly appearing door that was a brand-new part of a haunting.

Thinking about the doors reminded her of the strange coincidence. She reached her mind out to Kya. *"Hey, cousin."*

Kya sounded tired. *"Hi, Skye. You sound tired."*

"So do you." Skye pointed out. *"I was up all night exploring a strange new dimension. It's a whole big thing."*

"That sounds exciting, although I'm guessing it's not why you reached out?"

"You're right. I'm having a gut feeling of coincidence. It's probably nothing, but I'm running out of ideas." She paused then asked, *"Did you ever figure out the not actual doors on your space station?"*

"Not yet. Unfortunately, more pirates showed up not long after you left, and we've been dealing with that situation."

"Korbin lied about how many other pirates there were?" Skye was surprised. He hadn't seemed like the dishonest type.

"No. He didn't actually know how big the operation was. There were enough of them that it took some time to get everything handled. And then, on top of it, the aliens got out." Kya was frustrated, which spoke volumes about how bad things were.

"That sounds terrible."

"It really is. We've barely settled down enough to get back to the original objective of the mysterious not doors. I'm sorry I don't have anything more to tell you."

"It's okay. I can't see the connection between haunted houses and doors to another dimension here and doors that aren't doors on the other side of the universe. It's probably just my brain grasping at straws while I try to make sense of things."

"I understand—" Kya's voice cut off, and there was an echo as she spoke out loud, "What do you mean one got out again?" She said to

Sarah Eriksen

Skye, *"I have to go and take care of an alien again. I'll let you know if anything comes up that might help you."*

"Good luck, cousin."

She hadn't expected to get any answers to the whole dimensional door situation. But one thing she had learned as a guardian was to always follow up on leads or instincts, no matter how unlikely.

She sighed and logged onto the guardian website, scanning to see if she had any updates on alternate dimensional doors. Nothing new, but she spent a few minutes browsing the newsfeed for entertaining stories from other guardians. Sometimes when she let her mind wander, pieces of her current puzzle would fall into place.

No luck this time. Nothing made sense other than the dimension being something like a skewed tribute to Earth pop culture. She eventually gave up and logged into her game to get lost in something with logical quest objectives until she was tired enough to sleep.

She dozed off again at a more normal time for bed and woke up to an interesting tangled pile of laptop, grimalkin, and blankets. It was much earlier in the morning than she was used to getting up, but she had finally slept herself out. As much as she wanted to linger in bed, it was probably a good idea to go to the shop early. She'd been missing work so much lately that even the normal excuses would stop sounding believable.

It was difficult owning the shop while fighting monsters and saving the world. She wasn't unique when it came to juggling her guardian duties and having a normal job. But the last few months, the guardian job had taken a lot more time than it used to. For the first time in her life, she honestly wondered if she would be able to continue doing both.

The hint of uncertainty set off the other feelings she had been having lately. She felt like her life was spiraling out of control, and she didn't know how to fix any of it. She could feel a glimmer of worry in the back of her mind as Trey noticed her emotions. She took a deep breath and shoved everything far away from his senses. She didn't know what to do, but that never stopped her.

She walked into the shop and shook her head, laughing as Ian did a double take at her. She slid behind the counter and started to help him with an order. "Are you that surprised I came in? I mean, I do own the place."

"I figured you'd be sleeping still. You never come in this early."

"Believe me, I slept enough." It was the truth. She had slept longer than she was used to, even if it had been broken up a bit.

"Then I guess you don't need me to make you a caramel macchiato?"

"What does sufficient sleep have to do with me needing coffee?" She asked in confusion.

"That's fair." He started pulling shots to make her favorite iced coffee. "Eric made the arrangements to go visit haunted house land later. He said he'd swing by and pick us up when the shop closes. Since the haunting stuff happens so late, he didn't think we'd have to rush over."

He handed her the coffee, and she took a sip, sighing in bliss. A bliss that quickly faded as the door slammed open and a high-pitched shrill voice sounded in the shop, saying her name dramatically. At least Vincent probably thought it was dramatic. It was a bit more on the asthmatic and grating side.

In a rare moment of visible irritation at him, Skye snapped. "No. Whatever it is, no. You need to leave."

Her anger took the wind out of his sails. Quite literally. He had on a cape that might have been white at one point in time but was discolored and large enough that it could have been used as a sail. He was visibly regrouping, confusion racing around his face.

She uttered a colorful curse under her breath that made Ian almost choke on his coffee and stormed into the storage room, closing the door behind her with a definitive click of the lock. She felt a little guilty for leaving Ian to deal with him, but she couldn't handle it at the moment.

She felt bad for Vincent. He had always been a socially awkward kid who had been picked on by bullies growing up. Even Declan and Trey picked on him to try to get him to leave her alone, but they were careful not to be cruel.

She wished she could figure out how to make him realize his behavior was not appropriate. She wasn't interested, and he needed to learn that no meant no. He had a lot of issues, and she honestly felt bad for him. She just wished he'd get the help he needed.

Skye jumped as someone knocked on the door. It was Ian. "He's gone."

She slipped cautiously out of the storage room. "How did you get rid of—?" Her voice trailed off as she saw a very guilty Ryan and Trey.

"What did you do?" Her tone was deadly enough to make both men flinch.

Ryan shifted uncomfortably under her gaze and admitted, "It was my fault. Not Trey's. He was trying to get Vincent to leave so you could come out of the storage room. I said you had to get ready since you and Eric were staying at the haunted bed and breakfast. I thought it would scare him away. You know...the idea of you and Eric going to a hotel together. And then there's the ghosts. He's afraid of so many things, I kind of thought it would freak him out."

Trey said, "It did get him out of here, so it wasn't the worst thing in the world."

Skye stared at him in disbelief. "Until he decides to follow us there to try and sabotage my date that he thinks I'm on and ends up following me into an alternate dimension? You know damn well he didn't hear anything other than me and Eric going to a bed and breakfast together."

"I mean, I would totally be fine with him getting stuck in an alternate dimension for a while. Or at least terrified by real ghosts enough to stay away from you. We could rig it, so it's like you're haunted after being there, and then he'd run away all the time." Trey grinned winningly. He wouldn't let Vincent get stuck in another dimension, but it didn't mean he wouldn't think about it.

"While I admire your ability to overthink your evil plots against Vincent, it wouldn't be okay to do that to him."

"Not even the ghosts?" He said coaxingly.

She couldn't stay mad at her twin for things like this. "Okay fine, but if he shows up and tries to save me or hide behind me, I'm trading places with you, and you can deal with it."

Ian's eyes widened in excitement. "Is this one of those weird twin things you guys do?"

Trey traded thoughtful looks with Skye. He said slowly, "I don't think so. I mean, we did it one time, and it wasn't too difficult. But it was in a battle, and there was a lot going on, and it sort of just happened. In theory, I think any guardian with a solid grasp of spatial relations could do it. We probably just have a bit of an edge."

Ian seemed disappointed that Trey didn't give a lengthier explanation but surprisingly didn't dig further.

Skye couldn't resist teasing him, "What, you aren't going to ask twenty questions trying to figure out how we do what we do?"

He sighed dramatically. "I've given up on trying to understand any of it. I've come to the conclusion that I don't really want to know how. I mean, sure, you get the energy, and then you do stuff with it that looks like magic. So, I've convinced myself you are using magic, and that's good enough for me."

Skye winked. "I mean, magic is basically some kind of energy, so it's true enough."

Sarah Eriksen

Chapter Twelve

Skye slid into the back seat of Eric's car, fully intending to get a nap on the drive over. She wasn't too tired, but it was going to be a long night. She glanced up in surprise as the other back door opened, and Declan dropped in.

He said, "I was bored and figured I'd tag along." His answer was more than a little dodgy.

Skye asked, "So Trey asked you to help with something unspecified and boring, and this was your excuse to get out of it?"

"Actually, it was Ryan. But you're not wrong." He grinned.

"You're impossible."

Eric glanced back and said, "I only booked two rooms this time, so you get to sleep on the floor."

Declan clasped his hand to his heart and said tragically, "And here I thought you were finally going to confess your undying love for me. But floor it is."

Skye had a strong feeling he wasn't tagging along because of boredom or because of some kind-hearted desire to keep Ian safe from ghosts. Not that he wouldn't arbitrarily do things when he was bored. And he would absolutely protect Ian without hesitating.

He was up to something. He turned his head toward her, winking and smiling before leaning back against the seat and closing his eyes. She'd figure it out later. He had the right idea. She closed her eyes and did her best to doze off while listening to Eric and Ian talking in the front seats.

Chaotic Haunts

Skye woke up to Declan's hand lightly patting her shoulder. She had needed the nap more than she realized. They clambered out of the car and walked to the bed and breakfast.

Ian asked, "Aren't they going to be suspicious that we came back?"

It hadn't crossed her mind, but it was October, and the place was haunted. They'd probably assume the group of them were really into ghosts and being scared. She wasn't used to thinking up cover stories unless she was time traveling or on another world.

Eric answered, "They're probably happy for the business and think we're crazy ghost fanatics."

"I'm slightly disappointed that you don't have convoluted and clever backstories to make the weird shenanigans make sense." Ian's chatting was his way of coping with stress.

Skye felt guilty for asking him to help. Until she could figure out how everything connected, she had to know as much as possible. Which meant knowing what the ghosts were up to in each location.

She needed to find another way to track the ghost activity and not have to constantly put Ian through this. He was a good sport and he trusted them, but she didn't want to keep putting him in stressful situations. Sure, they could take care of ghosts in the split second it took to summon creation energy, but there had to be a better choice.

They were greeted by only one of the owners this time. He said, "You guys must really like haunted houses." His voice was strained.

Declan smirked. "It's the season, and we don't live too far away. How have you been?" His gray eyes studied the owner shrewdly as he sent a touch of invisible creation energy flowing out to check on his health and stress levels.

The young man replied, "We took your advice, and my wife went to stay with her parents for a few days to get away. It's been tense. The business is nice, but I'm not sure it's worth it anymore."

He was remarkably forthcoming, and Skye gave Declan an inquisitive look. He shook his head slightly. He wasn't nudging the man into talking more. It was stress and anxiety overflowing and coming out since they were familiar from visiting before.

The young man shook himself and asked, "Did you want the same rooms as before? We're not full tonight since it's the middle of the week. Your other friend is going to join you later, right?"

Skye felt a sinking feeling of dread in the pit of her stomach. Trey and Ryan wouldn't be coming later. They both had things they were doing. There was only one person it could be.

Eric asked, "Did this so-called friend of ours call to book a room after me?"

Declan added, "And did he have a very shrill and painful to listen to voice?"

The man nodded, his face full of confusion at their reactions. "He said he had friends who were going to be here tonight."

Skye let out a soft noise of irritation and said, "He's not one of our friends. But, can we have the rooms on the second floor at the end of the hall? And if you can put him on the third floor, that would be enormously helpful."

"I could try and cancel his reservation if it's going to be trouble." He sounded worried.

Skye shook her head. "Don't worry about it. He'll be annoying, but he's mostly harmless."

Declan scoffed, speaking in her mind. *"Mostly harmless?"*

"We both know he's completely harmless and pretty irritating. But we need to keep him away from the interdimensional door."

He pointed out. *"You know he won't stay on the third floor. He'll go knocking on all of the doors until he finds you."*

"Not if he can't get out of his room." She sent him a mental impression of a wink.

Declan coughed and covered his mouth to hide the laugh he couldn't contain at her diabolical plan.

"I'll put him on the third floor, no problem." He checked them in and showed them to their rooms. Skye watched in bemusement as Declan casually walked into the room she was planning on staying in and flopped onto the bed. She threw her hands up in a shrug at Eric and Ian, who both looked as confused as she felt.

Eric smiled at her gesture, and they both winced as Vincent announced himself with a shrill and dramatic monologue. Skye shivered in disgust and backed into the room, closing the door. It would have been a lot easier if Ryan hadn't let it slip that they were having a night away. They could have hung out in the sitting area together until the ghosts made their appearance.

She put her hands on her hips and asked Declan, "What are you doing?"

"Lying on the bed." He cracked his eyes open, seeing her irritation. "Or did you mean in a broader sense? Do any of us really know what we are doing?"

She kicked his foot lightly, where it hung above the floor. "You know what I mean. Why are you here? And don't give me the whole 'I was bored' excuse. Even if it's true, you're here for a reason."

He laughed. "Maybe I wanted to save you from your stalker."

It was slightly more believable as excuses went, but she was sure it wasn't the reason. She waited patiently for him to finally cave and tell her what he was up to.

He grumbled, "How can you not say a word, and it's just as loud as if you were speaking?"

"It's a gift." She flashed him a cheeky grin.

"Fine. I wanted to check on the owners and make sure they were doing okay. And this alternate dimension has me curious and worried. The ghosts acting up, and the poltergeist activity getting serious. That stuff can hurt the living. A little fear, it's not the worst thing for most people. But…" His voice trailed off.

"But getting hit with flying objects being thrown by a poltergeist can do some serious damage." She dropped onto the edge of the bed next to him.

"Yep. And, from what you told me, the haunting activity seems to be acting up in correlation with the doors. And, we both know there are very nasty things that are attracted to active hauntings. Things that are extremely dangerous to everyone."

She nodded in agreement. There were many creatures, such as wraiths and liches, among others, which were often mistaken for ghosts but were extremely dangerous entities. They were drawn to the energy projected by ghosts when they were actively haunting places.

She wasn't too worried yet. If a wraith or a lich showed up, a guardian would take care of it. But he was right. Increased ghost activity meant the danger was real.

Declan continued, "And if ghosts are acting up more in response to these doors, it means someone has to figure out why. And I get that that someone is you. And no one has been told to help you, which means Amonir has probably told you to handle it on your own."

He had always been good at reading between the lines. She asked, "And if that's true, you decided to come along on your own anyway?"

He shrugged and simply said, "I don't like how this feels, and I'm not okay with you having to handle everything on your own, capable as you are. Eric will be protecting Ian, so I'm here to back you up if you need me."

Skye could feel his sincerity. As off balance and out of sorts as she had felt lately, she was glad he had decided to come along. She had done her best to hide her fears and uncertainties from everyone, but she had never been able to conceal anything from him. He always understood her better than anyone, including her twin. It was why he was one of her best friends.

She knew she was one of the few people who got to see the serious and caring side he kept hidden under his carefully constructed mask of 'difficult pain in the ass'. The moments were rare, and he did appreciate humor to balance out overly serious moods before he felt too uncomfortable, so she teased him. "You just want to make sure I remember to put on shoes before I go into the other dimension."

The mask slipped back on, and he smirked at her. "Someone has to remind you, and it might as well be me. I mean, you did see what you were walking through last time, right?"

"Fine. But you're not sleeping in the bed with me."

"Of course not. You're going to sleep on the floor so I can have the bed." He grinned and laughed as she walloped him with a pillow.

Skye relinquished the pillow and asked, "How long before Vincent tries to come down here?" She had mostly joked about locking him in his room. If anything, that would have to happen later for his own safety, to keep him from roaming the halls when the ghosts started acting up.

"I could always open the door naked and scare him away." He offered with a wink and a laugh.

Skye rubbed her hand over her face and said, "Declan."

"What? He thinks you're here with Eric. The confusion alone would be priceless."

"Or we could ignore him?"

"You're no fun." He pouted.

"Maybe I just don't need to see your naked ass tonight." She said reasonably.

He smirked, mischief sparkling in his eyes, and she cut him off, holding her hands up in the air and closing her eyes. "Or any other night, for that matter. Or day, or at all."

"Fine. Your loss."

Skye glared at him. "Maybe Vincent will fall in love with you at the sight of you in all your naked glory, and then he won't be my problem anymore." A brilliant idea crossed her mind. "I could muck with his head and make him obsessed with *you*." She'd never mess with anyone's mind; that was truly evil.

"You are a cruel, cruel woman Skye." He shook his head in disappointment.

They both turned their heads as a loud banging sounded across the hall. Seconds later, Vincent's shrill voice demanded to see his beloved. Declan and Skye winced at the tones of his voice grating their ears.

Eric's voice was clear and easier to understand. "She didn't come with us, Vincent."

"I know my beloved Skye is here! Ryan said as much!"

"Well, Ryan must have been messing with you. She's not here."

Declan gave Skye a positively evil smile. *"Disappear, please."* She ducked down between the bed and the wall, out of sight. She didn't want to take a chance on invisibility making the ghosts behave for the night. But she could still watch the dramatic scene unfold with her mind without a power boost in such close quarters.

Declan grinned at where she was hiding and pulled his shirt off, dropping it on the floor before opening the door and saying dramatically, "I thought I heard the dulcet tones of my darling Vincent." He leaned against the door frame in a provocative pose.

Vincent spun around, tripping over his cape and righting himself with an asthmatic huff. He faltered as he stared at Declan.

Skye clasped her hands over her mouth to hold in her laughter. Vincent definitely was heterosexual, but he had not expected to turn around to a half-naked Declan. And as much as she teased him and had zero interest in him herself, he was a very well-put-together man.

Any confidence, as misplaced as it was, that Vincent had brought with him, dwindled to nothing as he stared at Declan, who was positively smoldering at him. Declan tilted his head toward the room and raised one eyebrow with a sexy smile and a slight nod at the bed.

Confused thoughts chased around Vincent's face comically as he stared and peered into the empty room behind him. A look of horror crept into the confusion, and his face flushed a strange, sickly shade of red.

"Don't worry, Vincent. You're not my type." Declan smiled wickedly and closed the door, flashing one last smoldering gaze before it latched shut.

Skye fell back on the floor, shaking with laughter she tried to stifle. She always felt bad for Vincent whenever she dealt with him. But Declan's outrageous flirting was by far the best way he had ever handled the sad little man.

Declan peeked into Skye's hiding spot and grinned as he watched her laughing. "Imagine how much more awesome that would have been if I had been completely naked."

"I think full nudity would have actually killed him. The look on his face when he realized you were hitting on him was priceless." She took a shaky breath as she tried to get her laughter under control. "Thank you, though. He'll probably avoid this area for the rest of the night."

He grinned and picked his shirt off the floor, pulling it back on. "It would have been better if you had been in the bed acting delicate and shocked at the interruption. Although come to think of it, he might have come in even with the idea of me being in the equation. To save you, of course."

She giggled at the image. "I'm not sure I could have pulled that off. And I shudder to think of how determined he would be to save me from your dastardly seduction. Besides, that would probably actually break him completely." Declan understood her compassion despite the situation.

"Well, at the very least, he'll probably avoid me like the plague for a while. I can hang out at the shop and be a serious Vincent repellent." He smirked.

"I'm going to sneak to the bathroom really quick while he's upstairs." She kept a mental eye on Vincent's location and rushed down the hall. She hurriedly washed her face and changed into some comfy capris and a tank top to sleep in until it was time to jump into the other dimension.

Chaotic Haunts

She could hear Declan, Eric, and Ian laughing in the hall. Vincent was still upstairs, hiding in his room. His emotions were a chaotic mess after his encounter with Declan.

She felt Eric's polite mental nudge before he spoke. *"I never imagined Vincent could beat a hasty retreat for any reason. But he was out of here so fast after Declan closed the door. Even the zombie that chased him didn't make him move like that."*

"It's probably the first time anyone has ever run from the sight of Declan's naked chest." Skye joked.

Eric chuckled. *"It doesn't appear to have damaged Declan's ego, but I'm not sure Vincent will ever recover from the flirting."* He had checked on Vincent too.

"All joking aside, he seems to be okay up there. Confused for sure, but not broken."

Eric said seriously, *"I'll keep an eye on him. The ghost activity upstairs was pretty intense last time too."* None of them wanted Vincent to get hurt.

"I thought about locking him in his room. It seemed like the activity was worse in the hallway. And thanks, he is a horrible little pain in the ass, but he doesn't need to be terrified and traumatized from scary ghosts tonight. He's already had a rough night."

"I don't think Declan would let him suffer that much, and that's saying something."

Skye smiled. *"He's not that mean."* Eric knew Declan had a far more caring heart than he let on. But they both respected his preference to not have that aspect of his personality acknowledged in any significant way.

"Time to try and sleep and see what the ghosts are up to tonight. Good night, Skye."

"Night, and thanks, Eric." She slipped back into the room she was sharing with Declan. True to his word, he had taken the bed, sprawling across the entire surface. She considered the situation for a moment, then planted one foot on his hip and a hand on his shoulder, shoving him to the far side of the bed.

"Hey!" He glared at her over his shoulder before dissolving into laughter at her determined expression.

She slid into the bed, shoving one of the extra pillows between them and rolling onto her side hugging it. "Good night, Declan."

Sarah Eriksen

He asked, "What if you sleep through the haunting hour and miss the door?"

"I'm not going to sleep, but it doesn't mean I can't be comfy in bed while I wait."

"Oh good, then I'm going to sleep."

Chapter Thirteen

Skye slipped into a resting state that wasn't quite sleeping. She was still aware of what was going on, but her body and mind were able to relax. It wasn't too long before the closet door started opening and closing. She felt Declan shift restlessly on the bed as the sound woke him up.

"That's annoying." He grumbled.

"Yep. The ghost in this room loves opening the closet door. Last time I told it off and said it was going to let dust get in there and make more work for the owners, and that stopped it. But last time, it wasn't opening and closing the door repeatedly."

"More active? Or a different ghost?"

She said, "I have no idea. I'm guessing we'll find out soon enough if things are acting up more. It seemed to pick up pretty fast last time."

"What time is it?" He asked and answered himself, "A little after midnight."

A shrill scream echoed down from the third floor. Skye's eyelids popped open. "Guess that's my clue to take a peek in the hallway."

Eric politely reached out to her. *"I locked Vincent in his room for the time being. He won't be able to bolt down here. But I'll head up to check on him as soon as you're clear."*

"Thanks, Eric."

Skye slid out of the bed and walked to the door.

"Shoes, Skye," Declan said with a yawn as he got up, pulling on his jeans and grabbing his shirt.

Sarah Eriksen

She turned and slid her feet into her sneakers. "Thank you."

Eric opened the door across from them, looking cautiously out into the hall and nodding at Skye. Ian stood behind him in the room, shoulders hunched with tension.

Skye asked, "Are the ghost being extra ghosty?" She used humor to try and ease some of his anxiety.

A faint smile flashed across Ian's face, and he said, "Yeah, it's pretty freaky feeling, same as before. But I disappeared through the door before I noticed too much."

She turned toward the wall where the door was last time. It hadn't appeared yet. She felt Declan's hand on her shoulder and moved into the hall so he could also see. They all looked up as they heard a loud thud overhead.

"Guess the poltergeist is back," Declan said. A book flew down the hallway toward them. They ducked back, and it thudded harmlessly against the bathroom door.

Skye felt the warning tingle as more loud thuds were heard from upstairs. "Can you guys feel that?"

Eric shook his head, and Ian said, "Nothing other than what I'm feeling already."

Declan said thoughtfully, "I can feel something faint, but not sure what it is."

The door materialized in front of them, and she shared her impression of the energy that she could feel with Declan and Eric.

Skye said, "Guess it's time to go explore jolly old black and white, White Chapel. Make sure Vincent doesn't have a heart attack. It'd be a hassle for the owner to deal with." His confusion had changed to fear with the poltergeist activity, and he wasn't in any kind of shape to handle that level of anxiety.

She grabbed the warm doorknob and pulled, revealing the blurry black and white image. She grinned at them and stepped through the portal, landing in the same monochromatic alleyway she had been in before.

Declan stumbled into her a second later, and she turned around, staring at him in shock. "What are you doing here?"

"Helping?"

She stated the obvious. "Amonir said no one was supposed to come into this place other than me."

"Since when has that ever stopped me?" He asked pointedly.

He was right. He frequently disobeyed direct orders and didn't care. And somehow, he always got away with it without getting into trouble. She hadn't realized when he tagged along that he meant to follow her into the other dimension.

The portal disappeared behind them. "Well, there's no going back now anyway." She didn't say it, but she was glad he had followed her. She hated admitting it, even to herself, but she had felt a strange separation and distance ever since returning from Meriten. On the surface, nothing had changed between her and her friends and brother. It wasn't anything they were doing, it was just how she felt, and it was unsettling.

Declan walked around, studying the alleyway. "This place is weird."

"That sums it up pretty well." Skye stretched out her senses, trying to get a clearer feel for the strange new dimension. Same kind of feelings as the last time, and a general sense of the door back to their world.

"It's odd, I can feel people here, but they don't feel like real people." Declan was doing the same as her, trying to pick up what he could.

Skye hadn't looked in depth at the people last time, other than to avoid them. Her goal had mostly been to get Ian out and to safety. And the other two parts she had been in hadn't had people, only fake ghosts and mummies.

She was curious about his take on it. "What are you sensing?"

"It's their minds. Their bodies seem to be real human bodies with normal functioning systems and organs. But their minds are...odd. I'm not sure how to describe it. Take a look." He tapped the side of his head, and she linked with him.

The information flowed into her mind. The people in this dimension had limited thoughts. Their conversations were structured, with no inner dialogue or feelings behind them.

Declan's mind voice said, *"They're like NPCs in a video game or something. Most people, even monsters and creatures from other worlds, as long as they have the ability for thought, will have a constant jumble in their head with words or images. But these people seem...scripted."*

He nailed it on the head. The people felt like video game characters with limited dialogue options, even though they had living bodies.

"So, it's a black and white version of White Chapel, with NPCs to get the story going, and Jack the Ripper is a ceramic garden gnome." Skye rubbed her hand across her forehead. This place was more and more confusing.

"Did you interact with any of the people last time?"

"Nope. It seemed more prudent to find the exit and get Ian out safely. He might not have been in any danger, but I couldn't risk it."

"That makes sense. Maybe we should try some limited interactions and see what happens."

Skye nodded in agreement. "We should try to see if there's an edge to this space too. It's hard to read, but the other two places I was in are nothing like this, but also clearly part of the same dimension."

"Do you think you'd recognize those other locations if they somehow connected here?"

"Possibly, but I couldn't say for sure unless we find a door into them from here. On that note, can you sense the door to our world?" Skye asked him.

He frowned as he concentrated, then pointed in the same general direction she could feel. "It seems to be over there."

"Oh good. If we get separated, I won't have to worry about you getting stuck here too."

"You're assuming the door stays open after one person goes through it?"

"I went through the exit right behind Ian, and it closed on our side right after. I wonder…" They both shook their heads at the notion of getting stuck there.

Declan said, "Let's not get separated."

Skye agreed emphatically. She felt confident she could teleport out the more time she spent in the weird dimension but didn't want to piss off whatever god created it. Not that she had felt the presence of a god in any of the locations she had been in. She was reasonably sure Declan would be able to teleport out too, but neither one of them wanted to get stuck here.

He asked, "Okay, time traveler. Do you think we should change into more period-appropriate clothes?"

Chaotic Haunts

Skye thought about it and said, "We're in full color and not black and white. I don't know if clothes will matter. Maybe we can approach one of the people here and see if we freak them out too much and worry about it then."

It was standard procedure to appear period appropriate when you time traveled as a rule, but this was hardly a normal circumstance, and it certainly wasn't actual time travel.

They walked cautiously out of the dead-end alley and headed in the general direction of the door back to Earth. Declan paused frequently to study the world they were in. Every little aspect was perfect: the bricks, the cobblestones, the filth, even the sooty, muggy, cold air.

Declan said, "The attention to detail is certainly impressive." He stepped over a questionable trail of something foul in the center of the street.

Skye followed him and said, "The smell is certainly accurate for the time." She had plenty of experiences time traveling, and the past was not always pleasant smelling.

"Why would you make a replica of the past and add the bad smells? I mean, points for accuracy, but why would you do that to yourself?" Declan grimaced.

Skye shrugged. "I'll add it to my list of questions to ask the creator of this place if we ever meet them."

He pointed up. "We should check out the rooftops, maybe see some distance and find an edge?"

"Not sure how far we'll be able to see with the pollution, but worth a shot. Give me a boost?"

"Yep." He leaned against the wall behind him, bracing his legs and cupping his hands. She leaped nimbly into his grasp, and he lifted at the same time, launching her upward. She grabbed a brick ledge and pulled herself up, feet scrabbling against the wall as she clambered to the roof.

She took careful steps to the peak and gazed out at the city. The air was smoky, and the sky was dark. Dim glowing spots showed the lights dotting the town. Brighter spots revealed the more popular late-night districts that were full of people. It looked like London, with no obvious edges in sight.

She stretched out her mind, not sensing any presence that felt like a god, only her, Declan, and the oddly scripted minds of the people below.

Sarah Eriksen

Eventually, at the extreme edge of the city, she felt like she bumped up against a wall.

"I think I found the edge." She showed Declan what she was seeing.

"Weird, so it's just London. Nothing outside that you can tell?"

"I'll follow it left if you want to go right and look for...an exit? Something else?"

"Look for something weird...in all the weird. Got it." His mind shifted away as he tested the edge of the odd pocket of the alternate dimension.

They quickly met back up on the opposite side of the city.

"Nothing, you?" Skye asked.

"It seemed pretty solid. I got a hint of something in the city back that way." He mentally gestured off to the south. *"It wasn't our world, it was something else, but it disappeared before I could lock onto it."* He shared the odd sensation with her.

She scowled. *"That's not the first time I've felt something like that. Whatever it is, it disappears fast. I'll keep an eye out next time and see if I figure out what, or who, it is."*

"Oh goodie, we get to come back for more exploring?" He was equally sarcastic and excited.

"You weren't even supposed to be here now…" her voice trailed off. It was pointless to even argue with him. She jumped down from the roof, landing without making a noise. "Shall we go find some people and see how they react to us?"

"Sure. Is the door back to our world still there?"

"Yep. Can't you feel it?"

"I can." He grinned and then laughed as she leveled a glare at him.

"It'd serve you right if I left you here."

"You'd never do that, you're too nice, and you'd feel bad."

"Don't push your luck." She muttered, picking up a clean newspaper from the top of a stack of wooden crates. It was the same one Ian had read. Only it wasn't covered in mud and filth. She felt Declan's curiosity and held up the newspaper so he could read it over her shoulder.

"Jack the Ripper strikes again." He read out loud. "Who is Mary Ann Randall?"

"One of the victims? I don't know all of them off the top of my head. There were a lot."

"It sounds sort of right, but slightly off. I'll do some digging later." It was safer not to do too much with their powers, even accessing information. Besides, it wasn't exactly mission-critical to know at the moment.

"Considering Jack the Ripper is a ceramic garden gnome, not sure if everything in this place will be historically accurate."

"That's fair, but it doesn't hurt to check." He smirked.

He wasn't wrong. Even if things here didn't add up, it was still an extremely good copy, and maybe there was something to it that would help explain things. Or it would end up adding to the confusion.

They heard voices as they neared a corner. It was a casual sounding conversation, even if it was hollow, with no feelings clouding the words. It was an interesting comparison. They were used to feeling emotions underlying words and giving more meaning to them. It was odd to not feel any at all.

She raised her eyebrows and looked inquisitively at Declan. He tilted his head and shrugged. They rounded the corner, walking past the two men who were drunkenly chatting. They took no notice of the guardians as they passed. They stopped by the other corner, giving it a moment to see if anything would happen at all.

Declan said thoughtfully, "This is weird."

"That's the word of the day for sure. They don't seem to realize we're here." The conversation hadn't been interrupted at all. It was like they had been invisible. Jack the Ripper garden gnome had seen her the last time, though, so that wasn't likely.

"I wonder if we talked to them if they would react. Like an actual NPC in a game."

Skye said, "You can try it if you want. I don't think it'll cause any serious problems."

A scream ripped through the night. Jack the Ripper had found his next victim. The two men jumped and then ran down the alley and away.

Declan said, "Maybe not."

Skye tilted her head, pinpointing their location. They had taken a different route than she had with Ian, exploring as they went. They were near the courtyard where the door to their world was. "I'm almost positive that scream came from the exact same spot where the murder was last time."

"That's odd. Well, relatively speaking. Everything is odd here. But, why would the murder happen in the same spot?" He looked thoughtful. "Unless it resets itself?"

"Only one way to find out." She grinned and took off toward the door, and he ran after her. They dodged past a few people who were running away from the scream. Declan deliberately bumped into one, turning his head to watch how they'd react. They didn't even acknowledge him.

Skye skidded to a halt at the corner of the building. The sounds coming from the alley were disturbing as Jack the Ripper completed his murder. Declan made a disgusted face. They had both seen horrific things and inflicted massive injuries themselves, but a recreated murder was still unpleasant.

"Ready?" Skye asked, and he nodded. They both knew they could risk using creation energy at this point since they were right by the exit back to their world. Caution wasn't as necessary, and if it didn't work, they could jump through the door.

They stepped into the alley and stared at the sight in front of them. The garden gnome wielded its surgical knife with precision, blood splattering its ceramic body and face.

Skye said, "Well, it's the same as it was last time. You were right. It's resetting."

"That's one of the most disturbing things I've seen in a while, and that's saying something."

The gnome's head lifted, rage on its smiling face. It rushed at them, ceramic feet clattering on the cobblestones. They dodged the maniacal garden statuary, and Declan kicked it with enough force to launch it across the alley. It somersaulted and landed on its feet, running back at them.

Declan exclaimed, "Nope. I do not like that."

Skye agreed with him and raised her hands, creation energy blazing and sparking around them. She gestured forward, and a contained blast of blue and white fire slammed into the gnome, shattering it into a cloud of dust as it leaped toward them, blade extended.

She grimaced. "I didn't like that either." Shouts sounded with the thudding of boots on cobblestones. They had been ignored up to this point, but Skye didn't think it was a good idea to be caught at the scene of the crime. They ran to the door, jumping through and back into their world, slamming it shut behind them.

Skye stood up, brushing ceramic dust off her clothes. That had been a close call, but they had escaped the dimension in one piece. The same couldn't be said for the garden gnome that had tried to kill them with a surgical knife.

Declan asked, his voice comically confused, "Skye, I *was* wearing pants this entire time, right?"

Skye answered, "Yes, you were. Why are you asking?" She turned and blinked in surprise. "What happened to your pants?"

He shook his head, his eyebrows raised in surprise. "I have no idea. And you didn't lose your pants."

Skye glanced down to confirm that she still had hers on. "Nope. I am not without my pants."

He shook his head, at a loss for words, and summoned a pair of shorts to pull on.

It was the same creepy basement in an abandoned psychiatric hospital in England. Other than Declan's oddly disappearing pants, there was nothing unusual about it.

"Well, this place certainly looks like it should be haunted," Declan said, eyeing the old wheelchair.

"Ian didn't like it when we were here either." She tried the doorknob. "And the door is solidly locked, same as last time."

A scraping noise sounded behind them, and they both spun, seeing the wheelchair turn and slide forward a few inches. Skye raised her hand, a small ball of coldfire glowing in her palm. She glanced over at Declan. He was similarly posed, with a bright green ball of fire in his hand. They traded glances and then laughed.

Declan said, "We almost get murdered by a ceramic garden gnome, and then almost kill a wheelchair. We should ask Ian to do some research on this place to see what kind of hauntings it's known for."

Skye laughed and said, "He'd probably enjoy that. As long as we don't ask him to come back here."

"He's been a good sport about it so far."

"He really has, but I'm not going to keep putting him through this. I know he doesn't like it, even if he trusts us to be able to scare away the ghosts."

"Ryan would probably like it more. He enjoys being scared by everything."

"Even after his close encounter in the bed and breakfast last time?" She asked.

"Possibly. You could always ask him. Not sure who else you could drag along if you need someone who can see ghosts."

"True. Well, the haunted house tour has plenty of people already. I might have to try that one again." Her words reminded her that she should reach out to Ben and see how the rest of the tour had gone.

"I want in on that one too." He pointed his finger and added seriously. "I'll even book the tour for us." He pulled out his phone, connecting himself to his own internet signal. "Shocker, they miraculously have an opening for two later tonight at 11 pm."

"Guess Amonir doesn't care that you're tagging along." Skye sighed. He always got away with things. She didn't know how he did it, but he always did.

He flashed a charming smirk. "It's a gift. And we better get back and get what little sleep we can get." They teleported back to the bed and breakfast and crawled into the bed. Skye shoved a pillow between them again, getting a laugh from Declan.

"It's pretty quiet." He said with a yawn.

"It is." She reached out to Eric feeling him respond far too quickly to have been asleep. *"How are things going?"*

"Vincent had a full-blown meltdown, and we had to call an ambulance to take him away. I tried to make the ghosts go away before it got worse. Like right after you and Declan left, but it was too late."

"Ouch. I'm sorry. Is he alright?" She felt bad for Eric having to handle everything, and a touch guilty if Vincent had been hurt.

"He's fine. Just a panic attack, thankfully. I've been staying awake to make sure the hauntings didn't pick back up again so Ian could sleep. How did it go this time?"

"Well, the dimension seems to reset itself, and it appears to be a faithful recreation of the whole of London. We're going to go back to the haunted house in Washington tonight to check out that theory."

"*I like how Declan has inserted himself into the investigation.*" Eric laughed.

"*You know how he is. It's not bad having another set of eyes and a different perspective. Even though I was told no one else was supposed to come along.*"

"*Well, I'm happy to help. But I'd probably end up asking permission first. I don't think I can get away with things like Declan.*"

"*Can anyone?*" Skye laughed.

"*You better get some sleep.*"

"*Yes, mom.*" Skye smiled as Eric chuckled at her sarcastic reply.

Sarah Eriksen

Chapter Fourteen

Skye stared out the front windows of the shop, absently stirring her latte as she leaned against the counter.

Ian asked, "Did you get any sleep?"

She blinked, bringing her focus back, and turned her head toward him. "Not a lot. We got back at like 4 am."

"Want me to stay and close up tonight?"

She thought about it for a minute, then shook her head. "Nah. I should be able to get a nap before Declan and I head to Washington. We have a later tour, so we can get in when the door opens."

"I'm glad you're going there. You don't need me for ghost detecting." He laughed.

"That was part of my reasoning behind it. But don't worry, I'm not going to ask you to come sense ghosts for me anymore. I know you don't like it." She smiled.

He looked relieved. "I don't like it, but I don't mind helping either. If you need someone to sense ghosts, I can do it." He was too good of a friend to not help if she needed him.

"I appreciate it. I'll ask Ryan, though. Or see if Amonir has any ideas on anyone. You've been a great help, but at this point, I don't want to cause you more unnecessary stress."

He grinned. "You could always ask Vincent to come along. He certainly would be willing."

She winced, still feeling a bit guilty about Vincent's panic attack. Not that it was her fault he obsessively followed her to a haunted house.

Chaotic Haunts

She said, "He might actually die from fright. Eric told me how he lost his mind over what? Footsteps in the hall?"

"Yeah, it wasn't even that bad compared to the first time we went. And he was screaming in absolute terror. Eric was pretty fast with the whole magic making ghosts disappear thing, but it got a little too exciting for everyone." He shook his head in sympathy.

Skye knew how he felt. She couldn't stand Vincent, but no one should have to go through that much terror, even if he did bring it on himself.

Ian grinned. "Good news, he probably won't try to follow you to any more haunted houses. You could just say you're going to one, and he'll run away."

"You're terrible. But if it works as well as Rhaeadr standing around and glaring at him. I might have a newfound love for going to haunted houses." She had a sudden brilliant idea. "Maybe the shop should be haunted."

Ian shook his head. "No, we don't need ghosts here."

She waved her hand dismissively. "Not real ones. I can totally fake a haunting."

Ian considered it. "I can handle a fake haunting. Just promise you'll warn me first."

Skye and Declan teleported near the haunted house and made their way through the rainy woods to the path leading up to it. She remembered she needed to call Ben. She had so much going on that she kept forgetting. He was open to the ideas of magic, monsters, and ghosts, but tackling a mummy through a magic door that disappears might have stretched his worldview. It was a conversation for another day, however.

"Why did we trek through the rainy woods again?" Declan grumbled, his hood pulled up over his head and rain still splattering his face.

Skye rolled her eyes. "A little rain won't kill you. And it's easier to use the lame excuse of being dropped off on the road instead of coming up with a way for a car to be here that we'd only have to teleport back after."

"You and your annoying logic."

"You didn't have to come, you know." She gave him a pointed look as they exited the woods and walked up to the haunted house. It was as busy as it had been the last time.

Sarah Eriksen

"And miss out on the video game mummy dimension? Not on your life." He grinned. His tone was joking, but underneath was a glimpse of his more serious side. He wasn't always easy to read, but he also never did anything without reason. She believed him when he said he wanted to make sure someone had her back, but there was more to it he wasn't saying. She knew him well enough to know that whatever it was, he'd tell her eventually.

They stepped under one of the awnings scattered around the lawn. More interest meant more people, and more people lingering to talk about the crazy haunted house after the experience. They picked a spot with the least amount of people to wait for their tour to start.

Skye felt something she hadn't really felt, or paid attention to, in years. A powerful ripple of temporal resonance fluttered around her. It was a side effect of being a time traveler, ripples that connected you to people, places, and things. The downside was that when you felt temporal resonance, it was usually well before you ever met who, or what, you connected with. It was an echo that brought your attention to something important to you and would someday make sense once you figured out what caused it.

It was interesting to feel it now and more intensely than she was used to feeling. The normal things that triggered the resonance around her had been around for as long as she could remember. She was so used to it that she didn't notice it anymore. It had become background noise. But this was significantly stronger than she had ever felt.

She placed her hand lightly against her chest as she felt the ripples, catching Declan watching her curiously. The resonance around her was strong enough for him to notice it too. She shook her head and shrugged in confusion at his silent question. She had no clue what would be causing it.

Skye absently watched the people leaving the house, and her eyes widened as she recognized two of them. One was a big man who wouldn't have looked out of place on a Viking ship with his long blond hair and braided beard. The other had a more average build with neatly styled dark hair and a goatee.

She excitedly smacked Declan's arm to get his attention.

"Ow, what?" He asked in irritation.

She whispered, "Look at who that is." She pointed toward the two men. The dark-haired guy's eyes widened, and he repeated her same gesture to his friend.

Declan said, "Holy shit. That's Stefan Anderson and Morgan Smith."

Skye nodded speechlessly as Stefan followed Morgan's pointing finger, and a massive grin lit up his face. Stefan was the lead guitar player, and Morgan was the bass player, of her favorite band, Origins of the Lost.

"Are they walking over here? Why are they walking over here?" She asked in a surprised voice. She was freaking out more on the inside but keeping a mostly calm exterior. It wasn't easy, since the temporal resonance wasn't fading. It was getting stronger as the two men approached.

Declan was as surprised as her. He might not have been as big of a fan as she was, but he wasn't too far behind. "I'd say the temporal resonance freaking out around you may have something to do with why they're coming over here. Maybe they know you."

"If they do, I haven't met them yet." She'd seen them perform live a few times over the years, but she had never spoken to them.

Stefan's grin was huge as they got close enough to talk. He exclaimed, "I always wondered if we'd ever bump into you two in your own time."

The two guardians traded shocked looks, and Skye waved her finger comically back and forth between her and Declan. "Both of us?"

Declan gave Skye a smug smirk. "About time you start dragging me along in your time travel shenanigans, especially if it involves meeting these guys. And hopefully getting into some concerts for free."

She covered her face with her palm and sighed. "It hasn't happened yet. And don't think because they've already met you, but not yet really, doesn't mean that some unspecified thing couldn't happen that would change the past that already happened, but hasn't happened yet."

Confusion washed over Declan's face as he tried to follow her convoluted time travel logic. "Did you just…threaten to kill future me in the future, or future me in the past, or both somehow? Can you actually kill me in two different times?"

She ignored him and turned to Stefan and Morgan, who were both chuckling at their banter. "I'm guessing I, or we, meet you sometime in the past but not yet? And I'm sure future me has told you not to tell past me anything because Time is a nitpicky bitch about that shit."

Stefan burst out laughing and said, "Future you may have said something like that. But, it's only a couple more years for you. It's been a while since we first met you, though." He was comfortable talking about time travel, which was surprising.

Morgan said, "I'm guessing you two are here because of whatever is stomping and dragging its feet around in the attic that is barred off from, and not part of, the tour."

Stefan chuckled again. "It's not like they're here for the ghosts they can't see."

Skye and Declan both laughed, and she answered, "You are correct. There's a door to another dimension in the attic, and if there's footsteps still, then there's another mummy up there from the other world."

Stefan said, "I remember you once told me about weird doors and dimensions. I forgot about it. It's so awesome to see you guys again, even if you don't know why yet." His excitement was delightful.

The tour guides were signaling the start of their group and interrupted any potential conversation into questionable spoiler-ridden territory. Skye said with a grin, "Looks like it's time for us to go be annoyingly boring in a ghost tour of a haunted house and sneak away to jump into another dimension."

"Stay safe, you two," Morgan said with a smile.

Stefan surprised them with a massive bear hug. He whispered, "Stay safe and take care of each other."

They both smiled and said goodbye, heading to the door of the haunted house.

Declan asked, "So what the hell does that mean?"

"Which part? The part where the guitar player from Origins of the Lost tells us to take care of each other, which feels like a hint of some kind. Or the part where they know both of us, which implies that we meet them in the past and spend enough time with them, so they know us really well?"

"All of it. But more notably, the temporal resonance that was popping around you the entire time. It was so damn strong I'm surprised they couldn't feel it." He said seriously. "I know their music always causes it, but it's clearly not only the music."

She bit her lip as she thought. She finally shrugged and said, "Sounds like, in a few years, I might finally have an answer."

"You aren't even going to be curious about it?" He gave her an incredulous look.

"Nope." She lied, her mind awash with a million possibilities.

"You're no fun." He said, but he knew she was lying.

"I'm more worried about mummies in an attic. The White Chapel place had reset, so if the doors open and close and mummies are getting out, does it disappear when the door does? Does it stay? Do we have a horde of mummies crowding the attic as new ones pop out?"

Declan nodded sagely. "Those are some very valid questions. Along with, how do we sneak into the attic and not get noticed when we aren't with the rest of the group?"

She shrugged and grinned impishly. "Magic?"

He shook his head in mock disappointment.

"What? We could totally avoid the tour and sneak in. Or we could go on the tour and annoy the shit out of everyone who is super excited about the ghosts and then sneak in later. Either way, we have some time to kill before the door appears."

"I vote we annoy the tour. At least it'll be fun."

They lined up behind the group of people holding ghost-hunting equipment. They were serious with a variety of handheld cameras, EMF detectors, and a handful of voice recorders.

"Oh good, serious *ghost hunters. We'll be extra annoying."* Declan's voice laughed in her mind.

"That's better than the ones here for the thrill of getting scared. They get pissed off when you don't notice anything or react at all."

"We could summon a tiny bit of creation energy to make the ghosts go away and piss them off even more."

"Let's not ruin their tour." She said it seriously, but she was also tempted.

"Oh, come on." He wheedled. *"It'd be fun, and it's not like it would ruin their reputation after the last few weeks."*

"No, Declan."

They followed the tour inside, hanging out at the back and trying to appear interested as the tour guides told the story about the murders in the house. Skye was thankful it was a different guide and that there was no one around to recognize her from before. She wasn't in the mood to answer questions about why she was back. Especially after her abrupt disappearance last time.

She reached out with her mind, not feeling the telltale tingle of the door. She caught a faint sensation of being watched again that quickly disappeared.

"Did you feel that?" She asked Declan.

"I got a hint of something, but it disappeared too fast to make out what it was."

At least he confirmed that what she had felt was real. She changed the subject. *"It doesn't feel like the door is open yet."*

"That's not promising if there's a mummy up there," Declan said. *"I hope the door is locked with something strong."*

"The mummy burst into dust with minimal impact last time. It was on the other side of the door, which might explain it, but they might not do well against solid objects."

The ghost enthusiasts gasped as their various equipment flashed, picking up some kind of reading. Cameras snapped pictures in the direction that seemed to be the most active.

Declan watched them with a wistful expression. *"I wonder what it's like to sense ghosts. I mean, we deal with strange things all the time, but this seems so different."*

"I know what you mean. They can go through life not knowing even a fraction of what we know, but we can't get creeped out in a haunted house." Skye was curious too. It's not that they were immune to fear or didn't get freaked out by things. They'd just never know what it was like to be so afraid of the unknown like this.

Skye yawned, watching the ghost hunters jabbering excitedly about things in the main room. Declan wandered around, doing his own study of the house. The guides started gathering them up to head to the basement when Skye's senses screamed at her. She spun and snatched the heavy book out of the air right before it crashed into the face of one of the ghost hunters.

She turned in the direction it had been thrown from, snarling through clenched teeth. "This is an antique book. What is *wrong* with you?" She set it down carefully on a chair before noticing everyone was staring at her. The guides and ghost hunters were shocked and impressed, while Declan bent over, shaking with silent laughter.

She lifted her hands with a shrug. "I hate when people damage books. A poltergeist is no exception."

The ghost hunter, whose face had almost had a close encounter with the book, said, "I'm very grateful for your fast reflexes. Thank you."

"You're welcome." She was uncomfortable with the attention. The guides rallied and started talking again, directing the attention to the basement. The ghost hunters were immediately focused on the haunting again. Skye turned and glared at the book that was lifting up off the chair. It dropped back down with a small thump and cloud of dust.

"It's going to be hard to sneak away without someone noticing," Declan said, his mental voice hinting at the laughter he was holding in.

"You're not wrong. But I can't sense the door yet."

They turned to head down the stairs and saw one of the guides waiting for them. He glanced at them, dropping his gaze and shifting his feet nervously.

Skye didn't need to feel his emotions to know he was worried. Judging from his uneasy reaction, it probably had more to do with the attic than the basement.

He said in a rush, "This might sound strange, but one of my friends was doing this a few nights ago, and she had said something about a woman on the tour who wasn't scared by the ghosts. Kind of like you two don't seem to notice anything about this place." He amended, "Other than the poltergeist stuff."

Skye and Declan both nodded and waited for him to continue.

"She also said the woman disappeared, and the freaky noises from the attic stopped a little bit later. And I'm kind of wondering if maybe that's why you're here? Or I'm totally misreading things and losing my mind because this place is getting more and more terrifying to work in."

Declan snorted, and Skye said, "Well, you're not misreading things. We're kind of here for what's in the attic." At this point, she wasn't sure it was worth the bother trying to come up with a plausible story. The guides were stressed out enough as it was, and they'd come up with logical explanations for their own peace of mind once things settled down.

The man let out a relieved sigh. "Oh, thank god. The owner of the house went to see what was going on up there and bolted out in a panic. Then he had the door locked up. I don't know what's up there, and I don't think I want to know."

Skye asked, "Has the haunting stuff been getting worse lately? Specifically, later at night, and when you start hearing footsteps in the attic?"

He seemed surprised by her specific questions. "I've done this tour for a few years, and the ghost stuff has never freaked me out. I mean, it's creepy, the feelings, the noises. But it's never felt dangerous to me because nothing ever happened. The poltergeist stuff is new, and everything feels…I don't know, angrier? I can't really explain it. But a few nights ago, I heard the footsteps in the attic, and then everything got more intense. So yeah, I think it's been getting worse. What is it?"

Declan patted him on the shoulder, sending a nudge of calming energy into the man to reduce the heightened anxiety away from a panic attack. "I hope you'll understand that we can't say too much about it. But suffice it to say, we're trying to figure out what is going on and stop it."

Skye felt a prompting from Amonir and said, "Don't be too surprised if a lot more people who can't seem to see or sense ghosts start popping up on tours more often." She looked up as she felt the tingle of energy telling her the door had opened. "Keep people out of the attic, and probably warn them about books getting thrown at faces."

Declan followed her gaze, trying to sense what she was sensing. "If you don't mind, we're going to disappear and take care of the attic problem for tonight."

Skye said blandly, "If anyone asks what happened to us, say he got lightheaded and freaked out, and I had to get him out of here before he fainted."

Declan protested with a laugh. "Why am I the one who has to be freaked out?"

"Because they won't believe the girl who grabbed a book out of the air and yelled at a poltergeist would suddenly be a delicate fainting flower."

The guide let out a surprised and slightly hysterical laugh at their antics. "Thank you. I don't understand any of this but thank you." He left to rejoin the tour and make sure they had time to make their escape to the attic.

Declan said, "It's kind of nice when people accept that weird shit happens and don't question everything about it."

"Especially when it means it's easier for us to do our jobs?" She was happy about it too. It wasn't that common in their everyday guardian lives. "Maybe because the people running these tours already believe in something more than ordinary, it makes them a bit less skeptical to the idea of more things existing."

"Or they're so freaked out by the scary ghosts they're desperate enough to accept the idea that someone else can take care of it?" Declan laughed.

"That too. It's serious enough that Amonir is going to send guardians to hang out on the tours to protect people. I have to wonder. In this one, a mummy crossed over to our world, but there was a sarcophagus right inside the door. The bed and breakfast doesn't have anything near their door, so is that why nothing has come through it?"

"That makes sense. What about the other place you went to?"

"It was an empty forest by the entrance, so same kind of thing." She didn't want to think about the pink ball of doom escaping the dimension. But she was sure Amonir was keeping an eye out for things at the other places.

"Guardians babysitting haunted houses is kind of hilarious when you think about it." Declan's humor was not misplaced.

Sarah Eriksen

Chapter Fifteen

They reached the locked and bolted attic door. They could hear the shuffling thumping steps from inside the space. Declan tilted his head closer so he could listen. "I get why this freaks them out so much. It's like the perfect horror movie sound."

Skye agreed with him. "I'm starting to wonder if the god who created this dimension was really into movies and video games. Other than all the weird shit that makes no sense."

"Poetic license?" He studied the lock. "Guess we're going to ruin the haunting since we didn't ask for a key."

A handful of terrified screams erupted from the floor below them, along with a solid thud of a body hitting the floor.

Declan glanced back toward the stairs and said, "Sounds like that might be a good thing." He touched his finger to the lock, sending a lance of green energy into it and opening the door. He gestured grandly for Skye to enter first.

"So chivalrous." She mocked him with a laugh.

"Yes, chivalry, the art of politely letting you enter the potentially dangerous attic first." He flashed a charming grin and bowed before turning to close the door, locking it with another touch of energy.

She sent a small ball of light into the attic above them and headed up the narrow stairs. The shuffling thumping footsteps paused as the light flared into the room, then resumed with a staggering gait as the two mummies bumped into each other to turn around and face the threat.

Skye said, "There was only the one mummy that came through the door last time and a shadowy mummy inside the dimension. Nothing had come through before then."

"These two make it seem like one a night?" He thought about it and said, "Maybe it took time for the door to…I don't know…be powerful enough to let them cross? I'm just throwing out ideas here."

"I'll add it to the list of things we don't understand. But I better tell the boss."

"Amonir, it looks like one mummy has come out of the door each night since I was here. Whomever you send to babysit this place will have to have access to the attic to clear it up before they fill the space to capacity." Skye chuckled to herself at the image of the attic space crammed full of the large mummies. She felt his brief mental acknowledgment.

Declan watched the shadowy figures shuffle toward them. "Those are some pretty detailed mummies."

"The last time, it was vaguer and more shadowy. But at least they're pretty fragile." She punched one in the chest, and it dissolved into dust. The new sharper detail gave credence to Declan's suggestion.

"These ones? How many types of mummies are there in this place?"

"Well, this kind, and then others that are sort of monster movie mummy style, and then there's the video game ones. Oh, and there's the boss."

Declan punched and disintegrated the second mummy. "That didn't narrow it down at all you know. What kind of movie mummies?"

"The kind where you cut off an arm, and the arm starts crawling toward you." They reached the open door that gave a murky glimpse into the torch-lit tomb on the other side and the shadowy mummy walking toward it.

"Dismembered body parts that can move on their own. I like it. No logic, no reasoning. And solidly freaky for horror movies." He loved old monster movies as much as she did.

Skye laughed and jumped through the door, kicking her foot out at the same time and killing the mummy on the other side. For all that Declan was deliberately a pain in the ass most days, she truly was grateful he was tagging along. And she was starting to think it was the main reason he was doing it.

Sarah Eriksen

She had a bad habit of isolating herself when she was struggling. Not that it was easy to isolate herself with a twin prone to excessive worrying lurking in the back of her mind.

Declan had figured out a long time ago that she tended to set aside her problems to prevent Trey from falling into a dark depression. Over the years, he had developed tactics to deliberately distract Trey from focusing on her troubles, to give her time to figure things out. And when it was bad enough, he inserted himself more obviously into her life to make sure she knew she wasn't alone.

She turned and watched as the dimensional door closed behind them, turning back into a decorative wall panel. "That's strange. The bed and breakfast door doesn't open on its own, that I'm aware of. I guess the one at the amusement park could, but I went through it as soon as it showed up. This one is open almost immediately from the time it shows up. But they closed behind us as soon as we come through it."

Declan studied the intricately carved panel and the sarcophagus. "The one in the bed and breakfast didn't close behind Ian on the outside but closed behind you, right? Was it closed to him from the inside?"

"Yeah, it closed behind him after he went through it. Then it closed behind me once I was in, and Eric said it had closed on the other side."

"So, it seems to let more than one person in, but not back out. I followed right behind you both times I've been here. I wonder if it closed on the outside."

Skye said, "Even if it does close on the outside after a certain time, it doesn't explain why it closes behind us, but mummies are getting out."

"Maybe they stay open on our world longer if no one goes through?" It was a simple answer.

She didn't have a better idea. "Well, we know how the White Chapel door closed on the outside. And we have no clue about this one, but—" Her voice trailed off.

She had an idea and reached out her mind to Eric, feeling that he was still awake, and gave him a polite mental nudge. Trey was asleep, and since he was watching the shop for her, she didn't want to bug him.

"Hey, Skye, what's up?"

"We're trying to figure out these doors and why this one is letting out mummies. As near as we can tell, the doors close on the inside after someone goes through. And, you said the bed and breakfast door closed

Chaotic Haunts

right after me. Declan has a theory that the doors stay open on our world for a set time if no one goes through. We can't tell if the door on the inside stays open until someone goes through, but I think they might."

"That would make sense. The doors are triggered by people crossing into the dimension, so they could, in theory, stay open and let things out. But I'm guessing there's another reason you reached out." His mental voice had a hint of a grin and a laugh.

"Did you happen to notice if the door at the amusement park closed behind me?"

"We left right after you jumped through, and I don't remember if it was open or not." He sounded apologetic.

"Don't worry about it. I'm wondering that if the doors stay open on both sides unless someone goes through, that's how the mummies get out." It wouldn't explain how the door opened on the inside, but half of it making sense was better than none. She asked hesitantly, *"Do you think you could go to Australia and see how long the door stays open?"*

"You're worried that things might spill into our world if the door is open on both sides."

"Yeah, the place was pretty abandoned, but I don't want to think what would happen if the pink ball of doom could wander through a door that opens by itself. I told Amonir about this one, and he's going to send a guardian or guardians to keep an eye on things. But—" her mind voice trailed off.

"You want someone who has been around the phantom doors to other dimensions to check it out and see what's going on and report back?" He laughed.

"If you can, that would be great. I don't know how long we'll be in this place, so I'm not sure if I'll be able to get there the next time it opens."

"Well, it's a few hours after midnight, and I'm awake anyway. It's not a problem." His voice went quiet for a minute, and then he said, *"You don't have to feel bad about asking me to help. I'm happy to help. This is some unusual stuff going on, and while I might not insert myself into your business like Declan, I genuinely don't mind helping."*

"I know. It's bothering me that I can't figure this place out. Well, the connections to our world. The weird dimension could just be a weird dimension. But the fact that it has at least one place spilling into our world, and I can't tie it together...it's worrying me."

"Because there could be other locations spilling into our world that you haven't found yet? I'd think Amonir would be able to notice that much and tell us."

"He's been remarkably silent lately, but I'm sure you're right." He tended to leave them alone a lot, but it didn't mean he wasn't aware of things.

"It's around 8 pm there. I'll head over once it's a bit closer to the haunting hour. And I'll let you know what the door does. Even if it doesn't help us figure it out, it'd probably be good to know how long it stays open." He made a good point.

"Watch out for poltergeists while you're there. They seem to be acting up more with this stuff."

Declan walked around, studying the room and waiting patiently for her to finish. She hated having to bother Eric to help with things. He had had a lot on his plate with training his cousin and dealing with the emotions during their reunion. She mentally slapped herself. She was probably projecting her issues out and worried she was bothering everyone.

"Eric is going to watch the door in the amusement park to see how long it stays open if no one goes through it."

"Sounds super exciting." He said dryly. He pointed at the sarcophagus, "I think I figured out how your mummies are getting out."

"What did you find?"

He crouched down and brushed some sand lightly off a textured stone that stood out from the rest of the floor. "It's a pressure plate." He pushed it, and the decorative panel rumbled and slid into the floor, revealing a small room.

Understanding dawned on Skye's face. "The mummy steps on the damn floor when it pops out of the sarcophagus and opens the portal."

"That would be my guess. And maybe it's opening the door on our side when it does that."

"There's nothing near the door inside White Chapel and the forest place. You might be onto something."

He said, "Unfortunately, it doesn't mean things can't get out of those doors."

"But it doesn't seem as likely." She reached out to Eric again and relayed the information they had just uncovered.

Declan waited for her attention to return, then said, "So. Care to show me around the creepy mummy tomb?"

"Do me a favor first. Tell me if you can see very far with your mind." Last time she hadn't been able to map out the area with her mind. But now, the areas she had previously discovered were clear in her mind.

He raised his eyebrows in surprise but then closed his eyes and concentrated. A few seconds later, he frowned. "Huh. It gets murky if I try to see too far away."

"That's what happened to me last time, but the areas I explored before...I can see clearly now."

"It's like a dungeon map in a video game. All blocked out until you explore it." He smirked. "I wonder if there's a map somewhere that will reveal the entire place."

Skye opened her mouth and then closed it with a thoughtful grimace. "That makes sense. Everything else about this part of the dimension has been like a video game. There's even a room where the door opens once you've cleared the monsters."

There wasn't any information available for this new dimension other than what she uncovered herself, but she still had access to everything that existed on Earth. The information was slow to show up in her mind, but she could still search through it. She checked for anything that would match this pocket, or the other two, but nothing specific came up. Not even a small indie game or random programming someone had made when they were bored or in school.

"Well, it's not based on any games that exist." She said.

He asked sarcastically, "Because you know every game that has existed enough to know that?"

She gave him an expectant look and waited for him to figure it out. He scowled briefly, then laughed as it clicked. He tapped the side of his head. "You looked it up."

She patted his shoulder sympathetically. "There you go. Let's go find some mummies. And while we're at it, see if we can find a dungeon map."

Sarah Eriksen

Eric had waited before going to the amusement park. He wanted to make sure it was dark before he headed in. He checked with his mind to see if any other guardians had been sent to keep an eye on things, but it was quiet in the park portion. There was no one around.

He understood Skye's worries that Amonir was being so silent on the situation where it was now bleeding out into their world. The fact that it was spilling over in even one location was concerning. Especially when people loved investigating hauntings around autumn and Halloween.

He was glad Skye had asked him to help out. He was worried about her after everything that had happened. She was always incredibly capable and independent, and he admired that about her. But he also knew she tended to isolate herself when she needed to work things out.

He could see there was a loneliness in her that she tried to conceal from everyone. With her new powers setting her so far apart from any other guardian, he could guess what her current struggle was. Declan was clearly worried too, judging from how he started inviting himself along on her missions. He was making sure she wasn't alone, and Eric was glad Declan was with her.

He hadn't been surprised things hadn't lasted between her and his cousin. They were from two very different worlds. Rhaeadr had given him a few pointed suggestions about being too stupid to make his feelings known. But all he could offer her was friendship. No matter what his feelings were. And like her, he kept a lot of his feelings hidden deep down away from everyone.

He turned a corner and almost crashed into the man who was standing there. They both jumped back, startled. Eric knew he had been lost in his thoughts, but not enough that someone should have been able to surprise him.

"Holy shit. You scared me to death." The man gasped with a laugh. He was tall and handsome with dark brown hair and dark brown eyes in a pale face.

Eric forced a smile and apologized. "I'm sorry. I wasn't paying attention to where I was going. I didn't expect anyone else to be here."

"Yeah, I snuck away from the set on the other side of the park to check out the haunted side of things. The guards have been going on about how crazy it is over here lately." He shrugged and flashed a charming smile. "Not going to lie, I was curious. But it's kind of freaking me out too. It feels so uncomfortable over here."

Eric nodded, cautiously trying to get an impression of the man in front of him and figure out how he had surprised him. He seemed normal enough, freaked out for sure, heart racing from being startled. But there was something off about him, a hint of something dark and unnerving.

The man asked, "I guess you're here for the ghosts too?"

"You got me. I heard it gets pretty crazy around here, and since I was in the area, I figured I should check it out." Eric smiled faintly, pasting a nervous expression on his face as he glanced around apprehensively. Easier to act like he was sneaking into some place he shouldn't.

"More power to you. I'm not sure I can handle it. I thought I could, but…I'm man enough to admit I'm kind of terrified." The man flashed his charming and disturbing smile again. "Don't worry. I won't breathe a word about you being here."

"I appreciate it. Not sure how long I'll make it either. It's pretty intense." He lied.

"Well, good luck, and sorry for scaring you."

"Sorry about that too."

"No worries, man." The man sauntered off, not looking for a second like the terrified person he had claimed to be.

Eric watched him leave, troubled by something but not able to figure out exactly what it was. He could sense the man's presence clearly now, so it made even less sense that he hadn't noticed him. He'd have to be more careful and warn the others. He just wished he knew what he was going to be warning them about.

He made it to where the door had opened and found a place with a good view of the area. He tucked himself into a spot where no one would see him. He didn't want to get surprised again tonight. Fog rose from the ground, and the door appeared across the concession area. He wasn't sure if it was the unsettling encounter that was getting to him, but he felt a little creeped out.

Chapter Sixteen

Declan handed her the sword he had used to kill the mummy and grabbed a spear with a long blade on one end from a statue nearby. It was similar to his usual choice of magical weaponry.

Skye said, "So last time I went down that hall, and it goes on for a long time, and eventually you get to a dead end with an obvious trigger and fall down a shaft to the lower level."

"Which explains the scraped and bloody hands." He said pointedly.

Skye ignored the comment and said, "Once I got to the lower level, it was apparent this hall," she pointed to the fourth corridor, "also takes you down there."

He glanced toward the other two openings, quirking his eyebrow inquisitively.

"Those are dead ends."

"Probably worth exploring that one then?" He turned back to the fourth opening.

"Unless you want to see the weird as fuck murals first." She grinned and jerked her thumb at the third door.

He glanced at her, then at the door, and then tilted his head back, giving in. "Okay fine. I do want to see them."

Skye couldn't help but laugh. It was fun sharing this experience with a friend. All the dangers and worries aside, this part at least was a lot like playing a video game. The distraction, along with not having to use creation energy for much of anything, gave her a much needed break from her troubles.

Declan's mouth dropped open as he stared at the murals in amazement. "The amount of detail covering all the movies is impressive."

"Right? And the cat memes are—"

"Fitting? Egyptian-style tomb and cats. It really does work."

They headed back to the other door, pausing and sending their minds as far out as they could. Skye had a clearer picture, but there were still some murky spots she hadn't explored.

She said, "This ramp looks very clean and wide open, and this is a tomb, so it *has* to have booby traps."

Declan said, "Maybe the deadly shaft drop would be a better option than a trap-riddled death ramp."

"Well, we should be able to figure out the traps, so you tell me." She shrugged.

He debated for a minute. "Let's play with the traps. Something tells me it might not be a bad idea to know as much as possible about the paths in this place."

He voiced what she had been feeling. The strangeness, the things that didn't add up, and the inability to see everything quickly and easily made her want to know as much as possible too.

They entered the corridor, laughing as torches burst into flame in sequence down the ramp. The first trap was easy to figure out. The floor was full of different colored stones scattered around with no apparent pattern.

Declan sighed with disappointment. "Pressure plates, a little too obvious."

"Easy enough to get across." She bounced down the hall, leaping across the stable and solid stone blocks. Declan followed a few steps behind, giving her room in case she needed to backtrack.

The hallway took a sharp downward curve. It was lined with narrow gaps that would obviously shoot something out of them. Skye crouched down, placing her hand on the floor and sending her mind out. "Not pressure plates this time. Something must trigger them when we go. I'm guessing it's a timing thing."

"So run as fast as we can and be prepared to stop or leap spectacularly if we can't outrun it?"

"Might as well." They both took off as fast as possible down the curved ramp. Declan's longer legs gave him the lead in seconds as they sprinted down the incline. Mechanisms started to trigger behind them, and Skye caught a glimpse of metal blades slashing out into the hall.

The traps moved a lot quicker than she had anticipated. Declan reached safety and turned as she moved toward the wall and used her momentum to run up it and flip herself over the last blade that slid out, landing gracefully next to him.

"Nice job, short stuff." He had to tease even though he meant the compliment.

"Good thing you could outrun it. Not sure your gigantic frame could have dodged that blade."

"Stairs for this next section, how much you want to bet it'll turn into a slide with something bad at the bottom?" He asked.

"Sounds about right." They both grinned and stepped confidently onto the stairs. Two steps down and the stones shifted into a steep ramp. They both leaned back, controlling their sliding bodies with ease. A dark gaping hole appeared with disturbing abruptness as they descended.

Skye shifted her weight as she neared the bottom of the ramp and launched herself across the spike-filled pit, landing in a controlled somersault, sensing Declan do the same next to her. She glanced back and said, "Well, the drop shaft was slightly less dangerous, but I think this one is faster, even with the traps."

Declan was staring into the pit. "There's a dead body down there."

Skye asked, "Like a nice touch part of the scenery dead body or an actual dead body?"

"I mean a real one. But...it doesn't seem to be human."

Skye peered over the edge. The dead body was surprisingly familiar and definitely not human. She pressed her lips together and gave Declan a confused look. "That's a dead space pirate."

"Space pirate? Why is there a dead space pirate in an Egyptian tomb in another dimension?"

She threw her hands up in the air. "Fuck if I know." It seemed the feeling of similarity between the phantom doors and the not doors on the space station was a lot more than a bizarre coincidence. Although how it could be connected was beyond her comprehension at the moment.

She reached her mind out to her cousin, pulling Declan's mind along for the ride.

"Kya, did you lose some space pirates?" She recognized this one because she had poked him in the chest before scaring him and his two friends into a small storage room on a space station on the other side of the universe a couple of weeks before.

"Hello, Skye. Hello Declan. Hold on one moment, please." They heard the faint echo of her mind voice as she spoke out loud, "Well, where is the third one? Can we get it locked down?" She paused. "Okay, I'll head there next. I might also have a lead on where those three pirates ended up."

"Sorry about that. Our alien friends got loose and are rampaging around the station. Again."

Skye smothered a mental laugh at the frustration in her cousin's voice. *"I take it things haven't improved since the last time we talked?"*

"This place is a mess, and it's only gotten worse since we talked. Doors opening and closing without any controls, aliens breaking loose because of it, and three missing pirates. But you seem to have found one of them, and that is making me curious."

"Take a look. I'm positive it's one of the ones I trapped in the docking bay. And he's quite dead." Skye linked with her cousin to let her see.

"That most certainly is one of them, and where are you? It looks like a tomb."

Declan smirked. *"It's a fairly accurate depiction of one, with some serious liberties taken on the details. And it's in a different dimension."*

"The dimension you've been investigating, Skye? Can you give me the details this time?"

Skye said, *"I'll give you the short story, but we have three haunted locations on Earth, that we know of, with doors to this weird ass dimension and doors that exit to a different place on Earth. Each part of the dimension seems to be its own bubble, and there is no obvious connection between any of them. And now we have at least one dead space pirate in this one. So how the fuck did he get here?"* She knew the answer to her question, but still felt a desire to ask it if only to give voice to how improbable it sounded.

Declan said, *"You have doors that open and close randomly on your space station and a bunch of doors that aren't actually doors? And we*

Sarah Eriksen

have phantom doors appearing in haunted houses and a dead space pirate from the other side of the universe. Seems pretty obvious your space station has a door to this dimension."

"*I can't say you're wrong, but that is the strangest thing I've ever heard.*" Kya was stunned.

Skye knew how she felt. They dealt with the bizarre and improbable all the time, but this place was getting stranger by the second. "*We'll have to meet and see if we can figure out what the connection is. But first things first. You are missing* three *pirates?*"

"*Yes, the three you locked up in the small room in the cargo bay. It was a perfect holding cell. We just had to make sure they had rations. But then the other pirates came back, and the aliens got loose. Once we finally got everything settled, I went to check on the pirates, and those three were gone. Tate figured out the doors were opening on their own, which is probably how they got out. We assumed they escaped in the chaos since we haven't been able to find them...until now, apparently.*"

Declan said, "*Great, we have two more pirates in a freaky-ass video game style Egyptian tomb with doors that open into our world. Let's hope they didn't find the exit.*"

Kya's mind focused on something closer to her, and she cursed eloquently with a string of words that made Declan raise his eyebrows in impressed surprise. "*I have to get this situation under control. I'll be in touch. Let me know if you find the other two pirates.*"

"*Good luck, cousin,*" Skye said and withdrew her mind. She asked Declan, "Shall we find the other space pirates?"

"Yeah. But can you ask Kya to teach me how to curse? Because that was some of the most descriptive and amazing language I have ever heard in my life."

"You can ask her yourself." She laughed as he shook his head, changing his mind. "Let's see if I can find them...if they're still alive." She sent out her mind, feeling Declan's brush against hers briefly as he also started to search for telltale signs of two living presences in the weird dimension.

"I'm not sensing anything alive in here."

He agreed. "Me either. But let me see if I can find any dead bodies."

She nodded, then, on a slight inner prompting, walked over to where the shaft she had dropped down the last time was. She called out, "Found one of them." Skye was kind of impressed that the tiny pirate had moved the heavy urn above. Unfortunately, she hadn't been expecting the floor to give way.

Declan said, "I found the other one, I think. It's kind of murky ahead for me, but I'm guessing it's the room with the mummies you have to kill to open the door."

Skye said, "Might as well move on and get out of here."

"I wonder where they came into this place. Not the whole door on a space station bit that makes no sense. But where in the tomb."

"Maybe one of the two dead ends up there? We know for a fact the third and fourth door lead down here, and we have two very dead pirates at the bottom of both of those. So, maybe the first or second one was the entry point from the space station."

"And maybe the one that isn't the entrance drops down to the mummy room?"

Skye frowned and sent her mind searching out and up. "You're right. There's a trigger and a trap door to a slide that ends in that room."

"So, they divided up and died. I kind of feel bad for them."

She felt bad for them too. She had locked them up, to begin with. They had escaped only to end up in a far more dangerous place.

Declan echoed her thoughts, "There's no way you could have known they'd end up here. They were safe where you locked them up."

"True. But how the hell did they end up here?" They walked into the room full of open coffins and shuffling mummies. The dead space pirate was visible in the middle. He had triggered the fight and hadn't lasted long.

They moved to opposite sides and cleared the chamber. Declan deliberately lobbed off a few hands to see if they would move on their own. "Well, these mummies aren't as much fun as the one upstairs." He sulked.

"Declan, stop dismembering the mummies just to see if the body parts will crawl around."

"I can't help it." He laughed again as the door opened. "Is the boss in the room with the exit?"

"Yep. But we have to get through the treasure room with the dropping wall first. I did take out the boss by throwing my sword into it, so it wasn't too bad. You can kill it if you want."

Sarah Eriksen

The wall did its timed drop to perfection this time too. She pointed down the hall, "If we walk to the fancy sarcophagus, the boss will appear behind us. She shook her head as he ran excitedly ahead of her. She moved off to the side and out of the way as she followed him, watching as he engaged the boss mummy with his spear.

After a few parried attacks, he said, "I thought you said this thing went down easily." He wasn't struggling, but his spear wasn't doing the trick.

"Catch." She tossed him the sword, and he grabbed it, spinning and cutting the large mummy in half in one easy blow. She shrugged. "Apparently, it's the sword. Good to know."

"Magic sword needed to finish the level. Huh." He walked over to the sarcophagus and studied it. "This looks like the woman in the paper in White Chapel."

He was right. The carving was simple on the sarcophagus, and the newspaper had been blotchy ink printing, but there was a resemblance. "We finally found something that connects two of the locations."

"How did you miss that?" He asked her.

"I didn't see the picture on the newspaper. Ian had grabbed a sheet, but it was filthy, and we could only see the headline about Jack the Ripper." They stepped through the exit into the prop room in New York, and she managed not to jump at the site of the dummy this time.

She brushed sand off her clothes and said, "The creepy forest place had a monument in the graveyard with an inscription. I didn't get a chance to look at it because the pink ball of doom showed up, but how much do you want to bet it's probably the same woman?"

"I think it's a good educated guess. We should probably check that one out next to confirm it."

"Do you seriously want to see the evil pink ball of doom that bad?" She asked as they did their best to clean the dust off their clothes.

"I mean...I kind of do, and I kind of don't. But for the sake of research, we should probably confirm the name. But there's something far more important to take care of first."

Skye glanced at him as they appeared in an alley outside the theater, blinking in the early morning light. She asked, "Get some awesome sandwiches?"

"I mean, we kind of earned it."

Chaotic Haunts

She couldn't argue with his logic. "As long as we can find some coffee on the way." Food and caffeine were a necessity since it didn't seem likely they would be getting sleep any time soon. Figuring out the connection between the weird dimension and a derelict space station on the other side of the universe was going to take some time.

They were standing in line, close to the deli entrance, sipping coffee they had grabbed from a less busy shop on the way.

Skye said, "Eric just left to head to the amusement park and see how long the weird door stays open and if anything crosses over. We'll have to meet up with him later tonight since we're all going to need some sleep eventually.

"Hey, neither one of us was going to be able to sleep with an empty stomach. Besides, there can't be that much excitement watching a dimensional door in an abandoned park."

The person in front of them inched a bit further away from them, and she held in a laugh. They had cleaned off the dust and sand from the tomb, but their conversation was still strange enough to warrant concern.

Declan had caught the movement too and opted for the usual plausible conversation turning point. "At some point, we'll get too old to spend all night playing around in video games." They both felt the tension ease in the person in front of them.

Skye had to wonder how other guardians had managed conversations in the past before video games provided a good explanation. Logically, they probably talked mind to mind more often, but it wasn't as fun as hiding obvious conversations in innocuous pastimes.

Skye yawned. "We should really try to get some sleep today. Kya is still busy rounding up pirates and rampaging aliens, but we'll want to meet with her once that's settled to figure out how the hell three of her space pirates ended up in the weird dimension."

"We should bring Eric and Trey along, for backup."

Skye nodded absently. He was right. Even though Amonir hadn't wanted all of them going into the other dimension, he had certainly not bothered to stop Declan from coming along. The other world didn't seem to be too dangerous in any way they couldn't handle so far, but that didn't mean it would stay that way. And having more eyes and minds trying to figure things out wouldn't be a bad idea.

She sighed and said, "We could probably ask Ryan and Ian for some input too. Not sure if they can go with us on a space mission, but they might think of something we wouldn't."
"You should ask Ian to research the name and see if anything comes up. There has to be some sort of a back story there. It could be interesting to know why little Easter eggs are popping up everywhere."
They grabbed their sandwiches and teleported back to her house. They ate in companionable silence, and Declan followed her up the stairs to crash in the guest room. It would have been almost as fast for him to teleport home, but he didn't want to risk picking up a hitchhiker creature when he needed sleep more than anything.
Skye crawled in her bed, checking with Trey briefly and letting him know she had bought him a sandwich. He reassured her that he and Ian had the shop covered. She could feel he was still concerned about the emotions she was trying to hide from him. He hated when he couldn't help her, but at least he was trying to give her space.
It was starting to bother her that everyone was so worried about her when she didn't know how to fix it.
She rolled onto her side, feeling Mr. Grimm snuggle up against her back, purring and kneading the blanket. Her mind raced with the things she had to get done, not giving her rest.
She needed to get with Eric to find out how things went babysitting the door. She should go back to the amusement park and check out the forest again to confirm if the monument was connected to this Mary Ann Randall person. She should also ask Ian to dig into the name and see if there was a connection to their world.
And she had almost forgotten, but she wanted to call Ben. She felt bad for not reaching out to him before. He had seemed like a nice enough guy, and he had been extremely helpful. The least she could do was explain some of what was going on. Or at least provide a more plausible explanation for diving through a phantom door.
Her mind was a muddled mess. She took a deep breath and tried to clear the spiral of chaotic thoughts. It took a few minutes before her brain calmed down enough that the exhaustion in her body was able to drag her into sleep.

Chapter Seventeen

Skye groaned as she felt Amonir's less than subtle mental wake-up call. She cracked her eyes open, deliberately ignoring him as much as she could. Her room was full of late evening light, which meant the sun was setting, and she hadn't slept remotely long enough.

"What?" She snapped.

"You should call the young man you met in Washington and meet up with him tonight."

"Did you seriously wake me up to tell me to set up a date?" She knew she was still half asleep, but that seemed strange, even for her boss.

"More to explain things to him before he does something dangerous, like try and sneak into the attic and go through the door himself. Kya still has her hands full at the moment, and the doors we know about are as secure as I am able to make them."

"Wouldn't one of the guardians assigned to stop people from doing that...stop him?" She could feel his exasperation and slapped her hand around her nightstand to find her phone. *"Okay. Fine. Is this typical diffuse the situation talk? Or full-blown, this is what we are, talk? Or a gray area in the middle?"*

"Probably not every last little detail, but I'm sure you'll figure it out." Amonir could do sarcasm better than any of them.

"Can I ask why you're so grumpy? I know I'm being difficult right now, but I'm sleep-deprived."

His mental presence felt contrite. *"I'm sorry, guardian. Cosmic politics and things that would bore you to tears. But you are right. I am being grumpy, and it's not your fault. Once you talk to this man and get things settled, take Declan and Eric to Kya, and figure out what this connection is. I'll try to help where I can, but this situation I'm dealing with...is messy."* He left a lot unsaid, but it was still more than a bit concerning.

"You got it." She felt his abrupt departure and shook her head. When the boss was acting distracted and weird and irritated, it meant the cosmic politics were a nightmare. She was glad that it was well above her pay grade.

She raised her hand, and the slip of paper with Ben's phone number flew into her grasp. She tapped the number into her phone and held it up to her ear, hoping she didn't sound as asleep as she felt.

"Hello?" Ben answered.

"Hey, Ben? This is Skye, the ghost deficient girl from the haunted house."

"Oh, hi!" He sounded pleasantly surprised and laughed at her dry description of herself. "I was hoping you'd call."

"Yeah, sorry it took so long. Things have been kind of hectic. I was wondering if you would like to meet for some coffee or something...tonight. If you're free."

"Um...well, it's already sort of tonight, and I'm in Seattle, so not sure when and where would work for you." He paused awkwardly, then blurted out, "I mean, I *am* free tonight."

"Great." It was a little after seven where she was, and it was going to take a minute to get ready. "I'm in dire need of caffeine, and Seattle is full of good coffee. Think you can meet me in an hour?" She rattled off the location of one of her favorite coffee shops in downtown Seattle.

"Yeah, I can do that. I'll see you soon."

"See you in a bit." She hung up and dropped her phone onto the mattress, narrowly missing Mr. Grimm. She rolled onto her side, scratching the fluffy ruff around the grimalkin's neck and feeling his purr vibrate the air in the room.

"How have you been, Mr. Grimm? I feel like I'm not around a lot. Is Trey taking care of you? And more importantly, are you protecting him from the pixies still?"

He let out a coughing chuckle sound and stretched with a yawn. "Garrd'an safe." He nuzzled her hand, letting her know he wasn't mad at her for not being around as much. Grimalkins were notoriously self-sufficient, and he was more than content to be a spoiled domestic house cat with some magic perks.

She reached her mind out to Trey as she tapped on her phone to check and see if there were any more haunted locations or doors popping up on the guardian social media page.

"How's everything at the shop? I'm starting to feel guilty for not being there." It was the closest she could come to admitting how terrible she felt about not being able to balance things.

"It's all good. Had a near run-in with Vincent earlier. It took him a solid minute to realize I wasn't you. I think he needs new glasses."

Her mind voice was full of laughter as she asked, *"Were you like...crouched down to take off a solid ten inches of your height?"*

"I was leaning on the counter, but that's a good point. Maybe I need to grow a beard."

"I'd be okay if he transfers his undying, eternal love to you."

"I don't think I'm his type." Trey joked.

"I can safely say Declan is definitely not his type." Skye giggled and shared Declan's dramatic half-naked flirting that had eviscerated Vincent.

"Oh my god. I knew he had done something, but not that." He paused and then asked, *"Why were you and Declan sharing a room?"*

Skye rolled her eyes at the misguided protective streak her brother had. *"He tagged along, and Eric had only booked two rooms. And while there were plenty of empty ones available, I was planning on jumping into an alternate dimension as soon as the door opened. So, it was stupid to pay for another room."* None of them were hard up for money, but there was no point in wasting it either.

Skye couldn't resist teasing her brother. *"Besides, if Declan and I want to have a romantic fling, it's none of your business."*

"I don't even want to think about that. Any of it." His voice held a laugh and a good dose of disgust.

"Then stop it." She sent a mental wink to take the sting out of her words. *"I have to run off for a coffee date in Seattle, per the boss. The guy I met at the haunted house up there needs some things answered and explained. Then it sounds like Declan, Eric, and I have to go talk to Kya about some weird stuff going on in her derelict space station."*

Sarah Eriksen

"What about the magic doors?" She hadn't had a chance to relay any information.

"Well, we found three awfully dead space pirates from her space station...in the Egyptian tomb video game world."

"How the fuck—"

She finished his sentence, *"Did they get there? Exactly. But apparently, Kya is still rounding up rampaging aliens, and Declan gets to sleep things off. While in the meantime, I get to go explain about me jumping through an interdimensional door and killing a mummy in a haunted house."*

"I don't envy you. And I don't get to come see the space station?" He sounded put out.

"I'm sure you could pop over after you close the shop. As long as you don't mind not getting any sleep tonight." She didn't like leaving him out either, but they both knew Amonir would put a serious foot down if there was a reason for him not to go.

She could feel the hesitation that he did his best to squash down as he replied, *"I'd really like to see it. Although, from your explanations and reactions that I can feel while you're in the alternate dimension, Declan can keep having fun with that part."*

Skye laughed. *"I think you'd like the tomb one. It's totally a video game dungeon."*

"You better go, so you're not late for your date. And don't feel bad about not being able to be at the shop. I don't mind helping out at all." There was a lot he didn't say, and Skye appreciated that he was trying his best to give her the space she needed. It wasn't easy with their connection, but the effort meant a lot.

"Not a date. But thanks."

Skye popped into a dark alley near the coffee shop, a faint flicker of temporal resonance giving her pause. She looked around the dirty alley, wondering what the hell could or would happen there to cause it. Whatever it was, her future sure seemed to have some interesting things going on.

She pulled her hood up against the rain, running lightly to the coffee shop. She stepped inside, checking with her mind and her eyes to see if

Ben was there yet. She had beat him, despite her late start on getting ready.

Minutes later, she was settled into a comfy booth with a view of the café, a massive coffee, and a delicious Italian pastry in front of her. One of the biggest perks of being a guardian was getting away with eating things like this all the time. Between the physical side of the job and the energy burned using her powers, her body craved the fuel.

She had downed half of the pastry by the time he entered the shop. He smiled and waved at her. He walked over and sat down, eyeing her pastry. "I was going to ask if you wanted to grab some dinner, but I see you already have dessert."

She laughed and shrugged. "It's a bit of both at the moment. It might be breakfast, honestly. I'm not entirely sure what meal my body currently wants. But it's tasty."

He ordered himself a chai and a bagel with cream cheese. "Nothing so fancy, but I'm not sure I can have dessert for dinner and not regret it later."

Skye said, "I had a pastrami sandwich at about 11 am today and then went to bed, so I'm not going to judge." She knew Amonir trusted her to figure it out. The way Ben had taken things in stride in the haunted house, she figured she wouldn't have to dance around the issues too much.

He seemed surprised. "You went to bed at 11 am? You have some interesting hours."

"Well, I spent all night fighting mummies and ended up in New York after that, and we were starved, so deli sandwiches sounded like a win."

"You were in New York this morning?" His confusion was a little comical.

Skye took pity on him and said, "I know you have a lot of questions, and I'm going to try to answer what I can. But yes, I was in New York this morning. And last night, I was in the haunted house we met in. And in between those two places, I was in an Egyptian-style tomb killing mummies with my friend Declan." She felt it was prudent, and less confusing, to leave out the space pirates.

"So, the shadowy ghost you tackled through the door in the haunted house was a mummy?" He asked carefully, the words sounding strange out loud.

Sarah Eriksen

She tilted her head back and forth. "More or less. Not a real mummy. More like a construct designed to look like a real mummy." She cradled her coffee in her hands, carefully directing a touch of creation energy around them to make their conversation unclear to anyone who might hear it.

She spoke before he could ask any more questions, "Let me try and explain what I can. The world is full of people like me who take care of weird things that go bump in the night. Or go bump in the day. Weird things in general that go bump."

"Like mummies and magic doors in haunted houses?" He asked cautiously. He was curious and not panicking, which was promising.

"Like doors in haunted houses connected to an alternate dimension. The one in the house happens to be something of a replica of a tomb with mummies." She didn't go into details. "And I'm trying to figure out why these doors are appearing. Because it's not good. Especially where that mummy came through the door into our world."

He stirred his chai, taking in her words and processing them. He finally said, "So the scary shadow I saw when I was a kid was real."

"It was probably some kind of a creature from another world that doesn't belong here. And if you remember someone tackling it, it was probably someone like me getting rid of it." She kept her tone calm and matter-of-fact.

"So, you're a monster hunter?" He asked, perplexed at their strange conversation.

She wrinkled her nose with a laugh. "Well, that's kind of true. It's much more detailed and convoluted, but more or less."

"Other dimensions exist, and monsters come from them?"

It was a logical leap. She explained, "Sometimes. They come from lots of places. The universe is vast. The haunted house and dimension thing is a little different."

He laughed softly. "I feel kind of stupid for not being able to process this. I mean, I believe what you're saying. It's just kind of crazy."

"I understand. It's one thing to want to believe there's more to the world than what we can see. Especially when you want to believe in it. But it's another thing to find out that it's real." She smiled ruefully. "I know a lot of stuff, more than I can even hope to explain, and I still get surprised and confused by things."

"I'm guessing you can't explain too much anyway. But what can you tell me?" He smiled, curiosity warring with stunned disbelief.

She thought about it. "Well, how about what is real? Gods are real, and I won't go into details on who created us, but there are a lot of gods that exist across the universe. And because of that, there's an impossible to describe variety of life out there." She frowned into her coffee. "Although gods are always stealing each other's ideas, so not as much variety as you might expect sometimes."

A startled laugh burst out of him. "Are you criticizing higher powers?"

"I do it all the time." She shrugged and grinned. She had wanted to make him laugh. "Let's see, what else is real? Well, magic is real, and plenty of variety there too."

"I don't know why, but it makes me happy to know magic is real."

"If you want to know if it can be learned, I'm sorry, not usually. The few ways to learn how to use magic generally involve bad deals you'd regret later. The rest of us that can use it have been trained for years."

"So, you can use magic?"

"More or less." She felt Kya's mind and heard her politely say the station was under control when she had a minute to talk.

She said apologetically, "I'm going to have to go soon. There's a whole situation going on with the phantom doors, and I need to meet up with some friends to discuss recent developments."

"Can you answer one thing for me?" He asked.

"Of course." She had an idea what was coming.

"Why can't you see ghosts?" His confusion was clear on his face.

Her laughter exploded out of her. "Not one person like me, at least not that I know of, can see ghosts…unless we use our powers. As soon as I do, I could see a ghost, but then they run away." She flipped her hands up in a shrug. "Ghost deficient."

He chuckled. "I guess I get why you were so calm in the haunted house then."

She stood up and tilted her head toward the door. "Walk with me for a minute." She needed to get someplace where she could teleport, and it wouldn't hurt for him to see some proof of her powers.

Sarah Eriksen

They walked out into the rain, and he said, "I know there's a lot you didn't tell me, and I'm guessing it's because you can't. I hope you know that I'm not going to go tell anyone. Your secret is safe."

"Oh, I know. I wouldn't be here if you couldn't be trusted."

"I feel honored you think I'm that trustworthy." He glanced at her in confusion as she paused by the same dark alley she had popped into earlier.

She smiled, but said somberly, "Please don't go looking for danger. I know for a fact you were tempted to go back to the haunted house to check out the door in the attic."

His abashed expression only confirmed what Amonir had told her. She continued, "The curiosity is great, and odds are someone like me would protect you. But three people died in that dimension last night because they were unprepared to deal with it. Knowing more about these things can be dangerous."

"From the haunted house?" He sounded horrified.

She corrected him. "Sorry, no, I should have specified that. They were three space pirates from the other side of the universe. But the end result was the same."

"How did space pirates from the other side of the universe end up there?"

"That, my friend, is an excellent question. And why I'm leaving to go and try to figure it out." She gave him a stern look. "Now. No seeking out crazy stuff because it could get you hurt. I joke about a lot of things, but I do live a dangerous life. The difference is, I'm trained to handle it."

"And I'm not." He sounded disappointed. She could feel his desire to know more, the curiosity still strong in him, but he also was afraid. It was what she wanted him to feel. Not terrified but scared enough not to be stupid.

She had an idea pop into her head. "Hey, you're really into haunted houses and ghosts, right? Like you don't mind being in scary haunted places."

"No, I don't mind. It's fun, even when it gets crazy like that house."

She grinned at him. "Don't be surprised if I call you and ask for help. My friend Ian could use a break from being our ghost detector when we're hunting for doors."

"I would love to help if I can." He was earnest, but then he said, "But maybe not the other dimension stuff."

"Nope, ghost duty only." She felt Declan nudging her mind this time, impatient. "And now I'm going to use this convenient alleyway to make my dramatic exit." The temporal resonance flickered again as she walked into the alley.

"I didn't know filthy alleys were good for dramatic exits."

"Well, dark alleys are great when you need to teleport to the opposite side of the universe. Take care of yourself, Ben." She smiled and disappeared with a faint hint of white and dark blue sparks drifting to the ground and fading from sight. The wonder on his face more than made up for the concerning flare of her powers sparking uncontrollably.

Sarah Eriksen

Chapter Eighteen

"They both disappeared sometime in the madness of the aliens breaking loose." Kya's ordinarily calm voice was agitated and full of worry.

They were standing in the center of the middle ring of the space station. It was a little worse for the wear after the latest rampage. Declan, Trey, and Eric were still wide-eyed and excited at being on a real space station, even a weird one full of pirates and aliens locked up everywhere.

Skye asked, "Can't you reach them with your mind?"

Kya shook her head. "I haven't been able to find them. Wes is used to the guardian job, so I'm not as worried about him. Korbin has turned out to be incredibly talented and versatile, but this is probably out of his depth."

Declan surprised them by saying, "If they disappeared into the other dimension, it shouldn't be too surprising you can't reach them."

Everyone's eyes turned to him, and he said, "Skye's the only one who's been communicating across dimensions from the inside. I tried reaching out to Trey while we were in there, and it was dead air, so to speak. Maybe her fancy powers are giving her an edge?"

He was right. She had been the one reaching across the dimensional barrier to talk to them. "But mind powers are separate from creation energy unless we use it for a boost to like to look around. I wouldn't think my new powers would change that much. It's not like I'm using creation energy to talk to people, even with the distance."

Chaotic Haunts

Kya said, "Maybe not. But you and Trey have always had stronger mind magic because of your connection. You might not notice it, but it's apparent with how easily you both communicate with emotions and expressions coloring your mind voice. And the people you talk to more often pick up your tricks."

Skye and Trey gave each other considering looks. Kya was right. When they talked to other guardians, they could feel emotions. It was a normal part of mind magic, but it was subtly different than when she spoke to Declan or Eric.

Skye forced the conversation back on track. "We can figure it out later. Let me see if I can find them." She had talked mind-to-mind with Wes before, so he would be easier to connect to. She felt Kya link her mind to hers, adding the sense of familiarity she had with Wes to give Skye a boost.

Finding someone wasn't necessarily hard with mind magic. But it was a lot faster when you knew the person. She was trying to find Wes in a new dimension that existed somewhere in creation but with no obvious connections. Even the doors on the space station felt dead without a hint of any other reality. She needed all the help she could get.

She had a good sense of the areas in the dimension she had been to and started there. It would have been easier from inside, but it still existed somewhere and apparently was connected to the space station. It took her a few minutes, but she finally caught a glimmer of him and homed in, lightly touching his mind and making him jump.

"*Wes, what happened?*" Kya asked, using the link from Skye to talk to him.

"*Kya! I ducked into a door to get away from one of those damn things, and the next thing I knew, I was in a forest.*"

Skye felt a sinking sense of dread. "*Is it full of large pine trees, kind of dark, a little eerie but pretty? Gray and misty clouds and a lot of blinking eyes in bushes?*"

"*Skye? Have you been here before?*" He sounded surprised. He might not have known exactly what pine trees were, but the description must have been clear enough.

"*Yeah, and it's not great. I'm going to come and get you out.*" She did her best to get a sense of where he was in the forest while she calculated how to get to him. It was mid-afternoon in Australia. She wasn't sure she could justify time travel to bounce back to the night before to go in, and if she did, she'd be there before him, which could be dangerous too.

"*Skye, what are you not saying?*" Kya asked in concern.

"*Wes, if you see a pink floating ball anywhere. Run. I'm not sure exactly where you are in relation to the exit to our world. But the floating pink ball is bad.*"

"*What exactly is it?*" He was an experienced mercenary from a high-tech world. He remained calm despite the situation and wanted any information that could help him.

"*I have no idea, but it's not good.*" Skye's tone shook his confidence. "*I'll maintain a light touch on your mind since I'm apparently the only one who can connect across dimensions at the moment. So, if you need something, yell.*"

She opened her eyes as Tate returned. "What door did Wes disappear through? Do we know?"

Tate nodded. "I was able to find it finally."

"Take me there." Skye's face was determined.

"This is ridiculous." Skye scowled at the metal panel in front of her. It did look a lot like a door but was not currently a working one. There wasn't even a hint of energy from the other dimension on it. She turned to Tate and Kya. "So, it opened by itself? Did you notice anything? A power surge?"

Tate shook their head. "It just opened. Nothing unusual, at least not on any of our equipment."

Eric asked, "Can you time travel to get to him?"

Skye shook her head. "Time travel to when the door opens would put me too far back or too far ahead from when he went in. I'm not sure I can time travel inside the dimension, and I can't risk it. I'm going to have to try and navigate him out."

Deeper mind links weren't too different from normal mind-to-mind communication. Emotions were more noticeable, and sometimes a few jumbled stray thoughts drifted to the surface. She could do it as long as he was okay with the closer connection.

Kya said, "He has enough mind magic himself that a deeper link shouldn't be too hard. Now that I have a better idea of what you were looking for, I'll keep trying to find Korbin."

Declan offered, "I've been inside the other two of the three parts Skye has been in. I'll see if I can help." Kya nodded her thanks.

Skye dropped down to the floor in a graceful movement, sitting with her legs tucked under her, and reached out her mind.

"Wes."

"Still here. And I'm guessing you don't have good news."

"That's debatable. As far as me coming to get you, the door on the space station seems to be back to not a door. And the door I know of from my world won't open for hours. So, I'm going to try and guide you out."

"What do you need me to do?" He was calm.

"I'm going to form a deeper link with your mind that will let me feel and see what's going on around you so I can get you to the exit. It's not much different than what we're doing right now. You'll just notice a lot more emotions."

"I'm assuming it goes both ways?" He caught on quickly.

"Yep. Don't worry. I won't be able to see your deepest, darkest thoughts and secrets. Minds don't work that way. I'll only hear what you want me to, same as talking out loud."

"If it'll help get me out of here, let's do it."

Skye appreciated how pragmatic he was. She took a deep breath and linked her mind closer to his, feeling a slight hint of resistance from the weird dimension before she settled in. His emotions became sharper in her mind. He was as calm inside as he was outside. She felt his surprise as he became more aware of her.

"This is different. But you're right, not too much." A burst of surprise came from his mind. *"Is there someone else here?"* His confusion was obvious as he felt the part of her mind that was tied to Trey.

"Oh yeah. That's my brother Trey. It's a whole weird twin thing. He's always sort of there." She focused slightly and said, *"Now, let's see if I can figure out where you are. I'm going to try and reach out with my mind through our connection. It'll feel kind of strange. You just watch out for floating pink balls of doom."*

Sarah Eriksen

She felt his acceptance and quiet curiosity. His mind was a very peaceful place. She could see why Kya got along so well with him. She reached out her mind, relieved she could sense things despite not being there herself. It wasn't as strong or as clear, but it was better than nothing.

He was watching the woods from a sheltered position near a fallen log. It was well hidden, but he wasn't blocked in. He was already covering the immediate area with his eyes, so she didn't have to tell him to look around so she could see.

"I'm glad whatever I'm doing seems to be helping you." He laughed as he felt her emotions. *"I apologize. It might take some getting used to being able to feel what you're feeling."*

"Don't apologize. I'm used to having someone else constantly in my emotional business. You're not going to offend me. The good news is that you aren't too far away from where I entered this place, from what I can tell. More parallel to the location. Head down the path in front of you." She gave him a little mental direction since she couldn't physically point.

Wes moved from his hiding place without making a sound on the forest floor. He scanned the woods around him, alert for any signs of danger. *"The blinking eyes in the bushes are so strange. You'd think a predator would move or attack. Or if something was hiding, it would run away."*

"I'm not entirely sure they're animals. The way the three parts of this dimension have been so far, it would track for it to be background scenery."

"How do you mean?"

"It's like a video game or a movie. It's a set...a stage. Basically, it's creating a mood for the entire place. I'm not sure if I can explain it much better than that."

"I get the idea of what you're saying. We do have theater and entertainment in my fancy high-tech world, as you call it. And Kya has shared some things she enjoys too." He stopped where the path split in two.

Skye sent her mind out, not getting as far as she'd like, and said, *"Go to the left. The other path seems to loop back."* She hoped the left path would connect to the one she had been on originally.

"This is a rather pretty place. Even though it feels wrong." Wes noted.

Skye was curious about his impression of it. He wasn't a guardian, so he might feel or see things in a different way. *"Elaborate on it if you can. We're trying to figure this dimension out, and you are a fresh set of eyes and senses."*

"I'm not sure how to describe it. I can smell the air and feel the humidity and the ground. There are even sounds, like insects and rustling. It feels like I'm in a forest somewhere, but it feels empty."

It was similar to how Declan described the people in White Chapel, alive but empty. This forest was real and felt real, but something was missing.

"It's like someone recreated an existing place but didn't quite get it right," Skye said.

"That's a good way of putting it."

Skye directed him along a parallel path for a few minutes when she suddenly felt the faint hint of the door back to her world. *"Finally. I can sense the direction of the door. I'm going to do something slightly strange to point you at it."*

"Alright." His voice was hesitant, but his emotions weren't worried.

She felt his surprise as she turned his body and aimed his head toward the sensation. She let go as fast as she took control. She didn't like using a mind link like that. *"Sorry, I know that's disconcerting. But now you know the direction the exit is in. Not that there's an awful lot of light, or sun, or shadows or anything to help."*

"No, but I have a pretty good sense of direction even without that. You're not going anywhere, are you?"

"Nope. But I like to take precautions where I can."

"I'm glad you feel that way. I tend to over plan every step of a mission myself."

"Well, I don't know that I ever plan *that much. I do have a bad habit of flying by the seat of my pants and hoping my reckless choices work out. But in this kind of situation, I can try to be a bit more tactical. Do you see the small game trail? It should get you to where I was last time."*

He followed her direction and broke onto a slightly wider path. One that was thankfully familiar.

Sarah Eriksen

Skye said, *"Oh good, this is a direct shot to the exit. And on the topic of planning things out, I'm going to give you clear directions to take to the exit since I now know where you are in relation to it."* She sent the mental map she had of her prior route to his mind.

"Got it. And thank you."

"Well, as long as the pink ball of doom doesn't cut things short, I do need you to take a look at something for me in the cemetery by the exit." She hoped she didn't curse herself by saying that. She was hoping that if the dimension had reset itself, the ball would be off in the same direction it had been earlier.

"Should I hurry?" He was able to pick up her emotions and interpret them.

"Might as well." She reached out to her brother, *"Hey can you go to the library basement to pick up Wes and bring him back to the space station? We found the exit. It'll be a couple of minutes before he gets there."* She sent him the location.

"But I might as well go make the book-throwing poltergeists behave, so he doesn't get clocked in the face when he arrives?" Trey finished her thought.

Skye laughed, *"Exactly."*

"On it."

Wes had observed the twin's exchange with fascination. *"That was different. I mean, I have spoken to Kya and her twin before, but it was nothing like that."*

Skye smiled. Kya and Kyleeria also had a strong twin connection, and it was slightly amplified through their elven heritage and goddess-given powers. *"I know how their minds feel in a link, so I know what you mean. There's something different with Trey and me since we're both guardians. It's usually very obvious to anyone who links with us."*

"There's a clearing ahead."

"Yeah, slow down before you head into the cemetery and ruins so we can take a look. I can't sense the pink ball of doom, but I didn't sense it last time until I saw it. The fake ghosts didn't like it either, so that'll be a good indication if it's near."

Wes crouched in the shadow of a scrubby bush and peered at the dilapidated buildings and floating ghosts. *"I've never seen a ghost before. Are those accurate?"*

Chaotic Haunts

"I've never seen one either, so your guess is as good as mine. But they seem calm, so head to the statue in the middle of the cemetery. The ghosts ignored me last time, so it should be fine if you want to run."

"Got it." He bolted from his hiding spot toward the statue, moving fast and leaping over the small rusty iron fence. He skidded to a halt on the gravel path. *"What am I looking at?"*

"The inscription." Skye followed his gaze as he found it. *"Mary Ann Randall. That name seems to be the connection."*

Wes caught a glimpse of one of the ghosts flickering past him and turned his head. *"They are acting differently."*

"Yep, the pink ball is probably coming." Sure enough, it loomed through the trees on the far side of the cemetery.

"I see what you were talking about." Wes could feel the sense of doom and wrongness about the ball. His calm façade gave way to hints of panic.

"Go." Skye could feel the pink ball of doom through their link more clearly than anything else in the dimension.

Wes ran to the crypt, fear giving him a boost of speed. He jumped down the stairs in a few controlled leaps and burst across the open space to the coffin. He pulled the door open, shoving the remains aside, and stared at the murky and watery image in front of him.

"Leap through, and you'll be on my world."

He glanced back, seeing a faint pink glow on the stairs behind him, and jumped through the portal, crashing into Trey, who was waiting on the other side. They both turned as the door closed behind him, sealing firmly shut.

Wes stared at him, startled at the resemblance to Skye. "You must be Trey."

"Yep. I know. It's freaky how much alike we look," he said dryly. "We get that a lot."

"Not as freaky as that pink ball." Wes felt Skye's mind pull away from his.

"Yeah, I got a hint of that from Skye. It's...not good. Let's get you back to the derelict space station full of space pirates and aliens." The fact that it sounded like a better option said a lot about the pink ball of doom.

174

Chapter Nineteen

Skye blinked as her mind settled back where it belonged. It wasn't quite the soul split from her body feeling she got when she jumped into her twin's body, but deep mind connections still took a lot of focus. She said out loud, "They should be back shortly."

She turned her head toward the others, the words she was about to speak dissipating from her mind in a disorganized rush. She pressed her lips together in consternation and asked, "Declan, is it a little drafty on the bottom half of your body?" She waved her hand in a vague gesture at his bare legs.

His brows furrowed in confusion, and he looked down. "What the actual fuck?"

Eric asked, "What happened to your pants?"

"I don't know!" he exclaimed. "That's the *second* time this has happened." He summoned a new pair of jeans onto his body and glared suspiciously at Skye. "Are you stealing my pants?"

Skye asked, "Why on earth would I steal your pants?"

He stared at her, his eyes narrowed, and finally said, "That's a fair point."

Trey and Wes appeared, and Trey gave Declan a puzzled look. "Did you change clothes?"

"I don't want to talk about it."

Skye changed the subject. "Welcome back. And what I was going to say a minute ago before I was distracted by Declan's disappearing pants...the monument in the freaky pink ball of doom place had Mary

Ann Randall on it. We have a picture with her name on a White Chapel newspaper, a statute with it engraved in the spooky woods, and a sarcophagus with the same person."

"I knew there was something there," Declan said.

"Yes, and we should check it out. But first, we have to find Korbin. Unfortunately, I wasn't able to reach far through the mind link with Wes." Skye glanced at her cousin, who was mirroring her cross-legged position nearby. "Any luck?"

"Nothing so far." The fact that Kya's voice held a trace of concern said she was truly worried about him.

Skye said, "Let me send Ian a text so he can start digging into a possible connection. Then I'll link with you and see if we can find him."

It wasn't the best solution, but it was a start. Luckily, the other two parts of the dimension they knew of weren't as dangerous. She didn't know Korbin that well, but from her only interactions with him, he seemed smart enough to stay put and not blunder around without knowing what was going on.

She pulled her phone out of her pocket, distracted by the pile of notifications on her screen. She had a handful of texts from Ben, and the content caught her attention. All thoughts of texting Ian fled her mind as she read through the messages, excitement building in her.

He'd been fascinated by what she had told him and was a member of a number of ghost hunter groups online. Some of them were closed groups for members only. He had heard of three locations that had been hot topics because of increased activity and doors supposedly appearing out of nowhere.

She said, "Korbin is still the top priority. But my new friend Ben is a ghost hunter and has some information on three potential doors to our weird little dimension."

Kya glanced sharply at her. "Korbin could well be in any of them."

"Exactly. We can link up and search the two places I'm familiar with. He wasn't in the forest with Wes. If I can find Wes in the other dimension, then we should be able to find Korbin in the places I know at least."

Kya said, "And if we can't find him, we can split up and search the new locations."

Eric asked, "How do we stay in touch while we're in there?" It was a good question.

Declan answered, "Easy. Trey goes to one, and one of us goes with him. Skye goes on her own...because it's her. And then someone else goes with Kya." He turned to her. "You have a twin connection of your own, right? So, in theory, you'd be able to reach out to her even with the weird dimensional shit."

Kya appeared mildly impressed. "It's more that we know if something is wrong with each other, nothing so in-depth as Skye and Trey, but she'd know if I was in trouble. I'll let her know what's going on. She'd have no issue talking to our mother to get in touch with Amonir." She gave Declan a calculating look. "It's possible that with your close connection to these two, you might be able to reach them even in a different part of the dimension."

Skye said, "We haven't all been inside in different parts at the same time. We might be able to talk to each other. But, having a solid connection outside is a good contingency plan." They should still be able to reach out to Amonir if it was an emergency. Speaking to a god was not the same as talking to other guardians, but they didn't usually bother him unless they had no other choice.

Declan grinned at Kya. "Guess it's you and me then." Her expression didn't change, but she somehow managed to look resigned.

Skye sent Ben a text back asking him for the locations and thanking him profusely. When he asked if they needed any ghost detecting skills, she let him know it was a time-sensitive rescue mission but thanked him again and reassured him she'd be in touch.

She linked with her cousin, and they searched for Korbin in the other two familiar pockets of the dimension. It didn't take long for them to determine he wasn't in the White Chapel dimension or the Egyptian tomb.

Skye said, "Okay. We have a haunted lighthouse, a crypt, and an old hospital that have solid leads on random appearing doors with increased ghost activity."

Declan raised his hand and said, "I call lighthouse." Everyone stared at him, and he said, "What? I like beaches."

"Okay, Declan and Kya, you get the lighthouse." Her grin was full of mischief as she said, "On lake Michigan."

"Dammit." He crossed his arms with a sulky sigh.

Trey offered, "Maybe your alternate dimension will have some exciting beaches."

Declan shook his head in disbelief. "Why would you say that? Now we're going to have beach horror movie world."

Kya interjected, "Where are the other two? We want to get to them while the door is still open."

"The cemetery crypt is in Rome." She frowned and checked with Amonir before saying, "I'll take that one. Worse case, I can jump back a couple of hours and go into it. It'll be morning there, but it's a small enough jump I should overlap in the time since Korbin disappeared."

Eric said, "Then Trey and I will take the hospital."

"It's in Maine." It was faster for her to send the details Ben had shared with her mind. "I'll see if I can pull all of you into a mind link while we're there. And if I can't get all of us in one link, I can keep channels open to each of you. And Korbin is the priority, but if you see anything about this Mary Ann Randall person, make a note. Or anything else weird that stands out."

Declan said, "Right, anything weird that stands out in all the weird."

Wes laughed at Declan's snarky joking. "We'll try to keep the aliens and pirates contained. Which has been ridiculously difficult from the minute we landed."

Declan asked, "Why don't you just kill the aliens?" It seemed like an obvious solution to eliminate one of the more significant problems.

Kya said, "There are several reasons, but mostly it's that they're damn hard to kill. Even if I cheat and use magic." She amended, "Either kind of magic." She was a guardian but also a formidable elven battle mage.

Declan smirked. "You could always just blow them out an airlock? Problem solved?"

Wes' jaw dropped in surprise. He had clearly not thought of that. "They aren't currently in a spot to try it, but when they break out again, I'll keep that in mind."

Trey laughed. "I like how you said when not if."

"This place has destroyed any sense of optimism I might have had."

Declan and Kya approached the lighthouse in the darkness. The glow of lights at the base and the faint hint of chattering voices told them they

Sarah Eriksen

weren't going to be able to sneak in. They paused in the darkness, where they had a clear view of the small crowd of people by the lighthouse.

Kya asked, "Any ideas?"

"I'm guessing it's a ghost tour." A scream sounded from inside the lighthouse. "And either there's an overly dramatic person inside, or something bad is happening. I'd say we only have a couple of options. If the information from Skye's friend is reliable, the door will be somewhere on a landing in the middle. So, we try to get in on a tour and hope the door is there and sneak away. Or we go invisible, ruin their tour and sneak in."

More screams sounded from inside, and a handful of people burst out, shoving and tumbling as they bottlenecked at the small door.

Declan watched the panic unfold and said, "Or we go into the chaos of whatever terrified them, and you know…help." If this place was like the rest, then the ghost activity was getting worse, and who knows what scared them. Regardless, he was going to make sure no one had any serious injuries.

They jogged up to the lighthouse, Kya's tall stature, and half-elven perfection drawing more than a few stares. Declan grabbed the arm of one of the tour guides who was gasping for breath in the midst of a panic attack.

Kya assessed the situation lightning quick and started directing people with a tone of authority that made things happen without questions. It bought Declan some time to work his literal magic. And also got the handful of people who had been knocked about in the mad rush out of the lighthouse some much needed help.

Declan sent a delicate touch of soothing energy into the man, easing his racing heart and diffusing the adrenaline kicking through his system. "Focus on me. Now take a deep breath with me." The man took a deep breath, and when that worked, he repeated it a few more times. He drew out the shock as the man started relaxing.

Declan maintained the calming touch of energy and asked, "What happened in there?"

"It was a ghost, but nothing like I've ever seen before. This place has always been freaky, and it's been much worse the last couple of days. It's usually random touches, noise, or shadows. But this was straight out of a nightmare." His fear tried to spike again but couldn't compete with Declan's healing touch.

"Any chance there's a door that's been appearing late at night, and things get much worse when it shows up?" Declan asked, his usual sarcasm toned down to a dry and blunt delivery.

The man was bewildered. "How did you know?"

Declan managed to not say anything snarky in reply to the obvious ghost tours generating a lot of excitement. He could also feel a hint of something inside the lighthouse, and it was not a ghost.

"Kya, I think there's a lich in there." He was close enough to the entrance that even his minor healing should have scared away any ghosts.

She shifted her focus to the lighthouse, chin dipping in a brief nod. *"It's a nasty one too, and it seems to be mad that the ghosts have disappeared. We're going to need to take care of it quickly."*

Declan told the guide, "It's not safe in there right now. You should make sure the people who were in there with you are okay, and then maybe call it a night." He had done a quick check for any serious injuries, but other than some bruises and a lot of panic, everyone was going to be okay.

The man seemed to collect himself and challenged Declan. "Who are you?"

Kya turned the full weight of her gaze on him and smiled. The man's cheeks flushed bright red, and he got flustered as she said, "We were passing by and stopped to help. But I think they really do require *your* help and guidance." She smiled again as a breeze from the lake shifted a few strands of hair from her crown of braids, and they fell becomingly around her face.

"Right." The man moved to go take charge of the situation.

"Was the breeze necessary, Declan?" She asked with a sigh. The elves of Arborea had hair that always managed to be perfect, no matter what happened to it. She was only half-elven, but her hair had that fully elven trait. It would somehow look beautiful in the middle of a hurricane.

They wrapped themselves in a swirl of energy to discourage attention, and he said, "I mean, the whole gorgeous elf girl smile thing was probably enough, but the fancy magic hair just made it that much better."

Sarah Eriksen

He flashed her his most charming smile and gestured grandly for her to enter before him. He said, "I know the smile isn't actual magic, but it's seriously impressive how well you can wield it with such devastating effect."

"Considering you are more than capable of laying on the charm that thick yourself, I'm surprised you're so impressed." She stepped into the shadowy interior of the lighthouse, allowing herself a brief smile as he clasped his hand to his heart at her fatal insult.

Declan straightened up from his dramatic pose and followed her inside, closing the door behind them with a small gesture. The air was unnaturally cold, and their breath puffed out in clouds of mist. They both peered up into the darkness, finding the tattered shadowy shape of the lich floating above the grating on the first landing.

Kya reached out politely to Declan to link their minds. They weren't used to fighting together, and it was a small enclosed space. They'd need the extra edge.

"I'll shield you from its draining spells if you want to do the dirty work." Declan offered. A lich wasn't necessarily hard to defeat for a single guardian, but this would allow them to focus on taking it out without getting in each other's way.

"Sounds good to me. Thank you."

He raised his hands, bright green energy blazing around them. He gestured the palm of his right hand toward Kya, his left turning in front of his chest. They both glowed with a green flowing energy that swirled in constant motion as it covered them, fading until only hints of green flashed with the movement, like light on water.

Kya waited for his spell to finish and then crouched down, leaping in one powerful movement to the landing, a hint of violet flame trailing under her feet. She slashed out with a black dagger, held so the blade was parallel to her forearm. The inky black of the metal glowed with a shimmering hint of dark purple fire along the edge.

The lich screamed in agony as the blade ripped through the twisting tatters of its shadowy outer layers. The ragged tendrils weren't clothing. They were tentacles of power, floating around it to absorb energy and emotions.

Kya spun, another black dagger in her left hand. She stabbed downward into the chest of the creature. Her right hand rose and sliced the tendril reaching for her. The flowing shield surrounding her flashed and flickered as the tattered energy brushed against it and then recoiled as if it was in pain.

"That's a neat trick with the shield." She commented as she hacked off more pieces from the lich.

"The movement makes it hard for it to latch onto, and if it does, the shield gives it a piece of its own medicine." Declan's healer mind was good at coming up with small variations that used someone's strengths and turned them into weaknesses.

Kya stepped back in a sudden move and crossed her arms in front of her, daggers disappearing. She thrust her left hand out with her palm forward. The faint symbols tattooed on her arms blazed bright with elven magic, and a ball of fire launched out of her hand, blasting a hole through the shadowy layers into the lich's ghostly core.

She twisted her hands and pulled them in front of her, the tattoos fading back as dark violet fire formed a concentrated ball that disappeared as she gestured. It reappeared inside the hole left by her other magic and exploded outward, burning through the weakened remnants of energy.

The lich screamed as the fragile bones holding it together shattered and burnt into dust. Wisps of energy drifted upward and out, fading into nothing.

"I don't think I'll ever get tired of your combo magic stuff. It's amazing." Declan stomped up the stairs to where she was standing. She was dangerous enough using her powers separately, but she had figured out how to use both in a deadly combination.

Kya said nonchalantly, "It works well enough. Can you sense the door?" Her brow furrowed as she reached out with her mind.

"I don't notice it as well as Skye can, but it has a faint tingle feeling." He shared the sensation with her as they moved up the round set of stairs inside the lighthouse. The next landing had the odd shimmering door that led to the weird dimension. It was closed like the one in the bed and breakfast.

Declan said, "Well, at least it's not like the one in the other haunted house that's letting mummies out into our world."

He grinned as he opened the door and asked gallantly, "Shall we?"

Sarah Eriksen

Kya bowed her head politely, and they stepped through the watery portal into the other dimension.

Chapter Twenty

Trey and Eric stood in a scrubby tangle of overgrown weeds and bushes in the darkness outside the hospital in Maine. Trey studied the massive old structure, feeling an unpleasant and heavy sensation in the air.

He glanced at Eric and asked, "Can you feel that?"

"The people in the building? Or the creepy, uncomfortable feeling? Or something else?" Eric replied with his own questions.

"I didn't even think to look for people in the building. I meant the creepy feeling. It's kind of heavy and stifling, and it's not just the east coast humidity." He reached out with his mind and felt the presence of a handful of people inside.

Eric closed his eyes, a faint line appearing between his eyebrows. "I think there's something else in there with them."

"Something that's causing the heavy feeling," Trey said. There were a handful of creatures that could be the source behind it, and none of them were good. It was probably the closest the guardians would ever come to knowing what a haunting felt like.

Eric found the source. There was a cold and dark presence lurking deep within the hospital. "It's a wraith." He withdrew his mind quickly. Wraiths were vile creatures often mistaken for evil spirits, which is why they liked to frequent haunted locations.

"Oh great. This is going to be fun. I'm guessing the people inside are ghost hunters since there's no one else around, and they seem curious and excited to be in there."

Sarah Eriksen

"You're probably right. And we're going to have to get the wraith neutralized before we try to find the door."

Trey agreed. "Any chance you've been able to sense the doors at the places you've gone to? I didn't notice much the first night since we were busy upstairs."

Eric shook one hand back and forth. "I got a good feel for the one I was babysitting in Australia. But I was pretty close to it and knew where it was going to be. I think I can recognize the energy, but I don't know if I'll notice it unless I'm close."

"Too bad this isn't a smaller old creepy abandoned hospital," Trey said dryly, looking at the tall, sprawling building. It was in remarkably good shape, which only meant they had more places to search.

"Maybe we'll luck out, and the wraith will be by the door." Eric did his best to sound optimistic.

"Maybe we'll luck out, and it'll also banish itself before anyone sees it." He shrugged with a hint of a grin. "If we're being optimistic, we might as well hope for the best."

Eric shook his head. "I think Declan is starting to wear off on you. Are we going to ruin their haunting so we can move faster?" They had a lot of ground to cover and people to dodge.

"Might as well." They wrapped creation energy around their bodies, making themselves invisible.

They had barely made it into the lobby when it became clear that the people inside were more than just a ghost hunting group. They were also recording everything for their podcast. They had cameras and equipment covering every inch of the place. The guardians didn't have to worry about being caught on camera. But if there was equipment set up where the wraith was, or the door, things just got a lot more complicated.

"We're going to have to short-out their cameras they've staged," Trey said.

They walked past the first two ghost hunters who were standing still, looking around in confusion, their handheld cameras forgotten. One of them said, "That's so weird. It's like it disappeared."

Trey held in his laugh even though they were wrapped in silence as well as invisibility. He felt a little bad for ruining their haunted hospital experience, but it was still funny seeing their confusion.

Eric said, *"They have a base set up near here that's streaming all the places where they set up the cameras. We should see if any of their hard work shows us our door before we take out the equipment."*

"Smart idea." Trey was always impressed with Eric's skill at analyzing situations and finding simple solutions. It was entirely possible they would have a camera where the magic door was appearing. *"The wraith seems to be staying put, at least. And none of these guys are close to it yet."*

"That's kind of odd behavior for a wraith," Eric said.

"Right? You'd think it would be going after the ghost hunters."

"They do like to feed off fear, and ghost hunters aren't exactly here for the thrill and the scary aspect of things."

"You have a point. They're mostly more excited than afraid."

"Something feels kind of off about this whole thing. More so than usual." He had to correct himself. Everything felt off about these situations.

They snuck into the room where the screens were set up and listened to two of the ghost hunters talking.

"It's so strange. It's like the readings just stopped and reverted to normal." The girl said.

"Maybe they're onto us and don't want to put on a show?"

"But then why all the activity up till now? We've had readings off the charts, temperature fluctuations everywhere, noises, and shadows. This has been an insane haunting, so why would they stop?" She picked up a radio and spoke into it, "Check back, team one. What's the status on the activity by you?"

The walkie crackled with static, and the person on the other end replied, "It seems to have died down."

The girl repeated the same check-in with the other two teams and got the same types of responses. Trey hovered near her and studied the screens. *"Do you think the door will show up on a camera feed?"*

Eric replied, *"That's a good question."* He thought about it for a minute and said, *"It shows up fine for regular eyes, so I would think it should. But it* is *a door to an alternate dimension, so hard to say."*

"Shit. The wraith found a camera." Trey had hoped the creature wouldn't be smart enough to use the cameras to try and lure people to it. This one must have gotten away with attacks at haunted houses before.

Sarah Eriksen

"Do you see that?" The girl exclaimed in excitement. "It's a full apparition." The wraith's body was covered in a pale mist twisting and wrapping around it. On the camera, it looked like fog had condensed into a vaguely human shape. The girl started calling to her teams. She wanted the closest group to head to where the wraith was and the rest to come back so she could investigate herself.

Eric sighed and tapped the side of the monitor with the wraith on it, a tiny spark of electricity leaping from his finger and shorting the circuits. He repeated the motion with all the monitors, wiping the feed and the recordings.

He nodded at Trey and said, *"Let's go."*

Trey jogged from the room with him, the breeze of their passing going unnoticed as the two ghost hunters tried to figure out what had shorted their systems. Eric sent small sparks at the equipment they passed, guaranteeing they wouldn't be able to catch anything on camera.

"That's going to be expensive for them to replace," Trey said with a laugh.

"The monitors will have to be replaced, but I'm only shorting out the power source for the cameras. I'm not a monster." Eric laughed too.

"You mean you're not Declan."

"I don't think he'd be that mean either." Eric had always tried to give Declan the benefit of the doubt.

Trey knew Eric was right. Declan did tend to be a total pain in the ass and didn't take much of anything seriously, but he wasn't a mean person.

Eric changed the subject as they dashed along filthy hallways and up a set of creaking stairs to the second floor. *"Something strange happened at the amusement park when I was babysitting the door for Skye."*

"Strange how?" Trey paused to get his bearings. The second floor branched off to the separate wings, and the wraith was still above them to the right.

"I bumped into a man. But I hadn't sensed him at all. I was trying to keep an eye out for security, and I didn't sense him."

"That's really weird. Was he a ghost?" Trey's voice teased, but his mental tone said he wasn't taking it as lightly as he sounded.

"Definitely real. But something about him felt off." He slowed as they turned a corner and came across two of the ghost hunters who were headed in the same direction. *"This could get awkward."*

"Can we lock them in a room?" Trey asked, mostly serious.

"I don't think that's the best idea in this place."

The atmosphere in the hall changed, growing heavy and oppressive as the temperature dropped and the air became chilly.

One of the ghost hunters exclaimed, "Did you hear that?"

"Sounds like someone crying." They hurried toward the sound, handheld cameras raised.

"Trey, are you doing that?" Eric asked, hearing a faint hint of crying.

"It's not me." His eyes widened in surprise. It was muted, but they could hear the crying sound the two ghost hunters were investigating. They both reached out with their guardian senses, sharing a shocked look. It was an actual ghost, and it wasn't hiding from them.

Eric reached out. *"Amonir, we can hear a ghost, and we're using creation energy."*

"That's interesting," He replied to both of them.

Trey asked sarcastically, *"Anything we need to worry about if ghosts aren't hiding from us?"*

"I'd avoid killing any of them," Amonir replied dryly. *"It's not like you can confuse a ghost with something else. Be careful. Odds are they are riled up because of the wraith."*

"Maybe they're riled up because of the dimension," Eric said. *"The haunted houses have been more active since these doors have been appearing."*

"Do you think things are escalating, guardian?"

"I'd have to run it by Skye, or Declan, for their observations, but I'm inclined to think so."

"Be careful, guardians." Amonir's presence disappeared.

Trey let out a frustrated groan. *"That wasn't very encouraging."*

"Hey, on the bright side. We get to experience a haunting." Eric grinned.

"Probably should tell the others." By unspoken agreement, Eric reached out to Declan, and Trey talked to Skye.

Eric connected easily to Declan and said, *"Hey, either the dimension or a grumpy wraith is agitating the ghosts in this hospital so much we can hear and feel one of them."*

"You're shitting me?" Declan said. "Nothing like that here. Just a pissy lich that Kya is destroying so we can jump through our door. Thanks for the head's up."

"Of course. Good luck." Eric could feel the lingering echo of Trey talking to Skye and smiled at her response which was almost identical to Declan's. The two were a lot more alike than most people realized. He felt a faint hint of a tingling sensation that was probably the door.

"I think the door opened." He said to Trey.

One of the ghost hunters exclaimed in excitement at something from their radio. "The door opened! Let's get moving."

Trey mirrored Eric's sigh. "We broke their cameras. How the hell did they know it opened? And more importantly, where is it?"

"By the wraith, I think. I must have missed something else they had hooked up if they could see it still."

"Of course." They sprinted past the ghost hunters to the end of the hall and the staircase that was tucked around the corner leading to the top floor. "A normal door would be super helpful about now to keep them down here."

"I have something better." Eric turned and faced the hallway behind them. The other two ghost hunters had caught up, and they were headed toward the guardians.

Eric held his hands in front of his chest, palm out, and closed his eyes. Shadowy dark energy surrounded his hands and his fingers crackled with hints of blue lightning. He exhaled, and the lightning disappeared as a wave of energy washed down the hallway, neutralizing their electronics and filling the corridor with impenetrable darkness.

He moved his hands in a circular motion, silvery energy glowing faintly around them in complicated strands. They wove together in a complex knot invisible to the ghost hunters in the unnatural darkness. As the twisting convoluted strands of his energy grew, he finally released it into the space in front of him. The tangled energy faded out of sight but still twisted around in a spell of redirection.

"Okay, that is an awesome trick." Trey was impressed. Eric's skills with creation energy and spells were always awe-inspiring.

Eric smiled faintly at the compliment. *"They'll think the darkness is normal since none of their equipment is working now, and if they do happen to get to the end of the hallway here, they'll get turned around and head back."*

He gestured one more time, and a faint glow of light appeared at the other set of stairs leading back down. If they moved in the right direction in the dark hallway, they'd see a faint glow and be drawn to it. *"It's not perfect, but it should buy us enough time to take care of things."*

"Where did you learn to do that?"

"My uncles. Family vacations in the castle usually wound up as guardian training sessions. I figured out how to manipulate things so I could get away and take a break."

Eric smiled at the memory, keeping the deeper meaning to himself. His uncles had spent all their time training him to use creation energy in every conceivable way possible. They wanted to make sure he'd never have to be afraid if he ever found himself in a situation with impossible odds again. They were the reason why he was so skilled with using creation energy as magic.

Eric said, *"I'll take point against the wraith."*

"I was hoping you'd say that. Your fancy magic will be much more effective. I'll play defense." Trey took the stairs two at a time, Eric close behind him.

"There's the door at the end of the hall." Eric pointed to the oddly glowing door that was thankfully closed.

"And there's the wraith."

The misty figure was far more ethereal and detailed to their guardian senses. Like a real ghost, any image caught on the equipment would be blurry and easy to be skeptical about. But the reality was disturbing.

A core of darkness flickered with cold, pale energy. Wisps of glowing vapor coalesced into a shape that appeared spectral and human. A vaguely hand-like shape reached forward in a pleading gesture as the temperature in the room plummeted with its spell.

Trey raised his hands and drew the cold energy toward him, his own body glowing faintly with a shield of energy resembling sun sparkling on snow. The wraith's cold magic encountered frosty creation energy and compacted down into a concentrated ball as he pulled it toward him.

Eric swung his right hand out to the side in a throwing motion, and a ball of bright blue lightning flew into the wraith, exploding and crackling across its outer vaporous protective layer. He pulled his left hand down, fingers clenching into a fist, and a bolt of lightning blasted down. The crackling lightning suddenly ignited into silvery-blue flames that raced around the wraith's body, making it scream in agony.

"You going to do anything with all that frosty energy?" Eric asked as he held out his hands, directing the energy around the wraith and feeding the flames and lightning.

"Maybe make a snowman? Do you have something else in mind?" Trey quipped as he continued to draw in the cold energy, keeping the harmful magic away from both of them.

"I'll give you an opening." Eric sent his idea to Trey and pulled his hands together. The lightning and fire condensed in a small spot on the misty layers. He flicked his hands forward, ring and index fingers pointing at the wraith, and the energy ripped through its last layer of protective magic. A sharp spear of ice made from its own deadly energy slammed into the opening and exploded outward, shards of frozen magic ripping through the dark core.

Eric gestured one last time and the remnants of the wraith dissolved into harmless motes of energy that dissipated into nothing. He walked over to the camera and touched it lightly, wiping out the images it had recorded of the wraith. It hadn't been hooked to the main screens. The ghost hunters had been smart and put multiple cameras in this room.

Trey was standing with his eyes closed and a frown on his face as he scanned the hospital with his mind. "Nothing left here that we have to concern ourselves with. Shall we?" He jerked his chin at the door.

"Let's do it." Eric dropped his hands to his sides, fingers spread wide, dissolving his redirection spell and setting the darkness to fade out naturally.

Trey opened the door to the murky portal, and they ducked through.

Chapter Twenty-One

Skye pulled her hood over her head and tugged the zipper up higher. Rain that was more like a gently falling mist filled the old lich-yard behind a church in Rome. Crumbling tombstones packed the grounds with a few larger burial crypts scattered around. And there was no hint of the door. She got a mental nod from Amonir and teleported again, this time back a few hours.

The tingling sensation of the door was clear now that it was night. It was somewhere underneath the buildings around the church. There was a mass of tunnels and crypts spreading out below her. The door was further away from the ones connected to the main church. She trudged through the mist, her sneakers crunching on the wet gravel.

It was a little disappointing to be here to find a door and jump through it into who knows what. It would have been far more fun to explore the area. Autumn was her favorite season. There was something about the leaves, the rain, and the old tombs that she found beautiful, in a somber way.

She reached her mind out, looking for signs of people while she tried to find an entrance to the crypts below. After all the other doors, she half expected to find ghost hunters lurking. But the only presences she sensed belonged to a few security guards.

The entrance she needed had a single guard standing at the door to the crypt. She lightly felt for his emotions and was surprised at the amount of anxiety present. She sent her mind further and sighed when she found the cause. There was a revenant inside the crypt.

Sarah Eriksen

That made things more than a little inconvenient. Unlike a zombie, a revenant had a mind that worked and a lot of power. They could only be brought back to life with serious magic that far outstripped a necromancer's skills. This was serious.

"Amonir, there's a revenant here."

"I don't like what these doors seem to be attracting, but that is extremely concerning. Please get rid of it and keep me posted." His presence left abruptly.

"Well, I was going to just leave it there, but since you asked so nicely, I guess I'll have to do my job or something." She muttered under her breath, kicking a twig off into the darkness. She felt her brother's wordless inquiry at her annoyance and reassured him it wasn't anything serious. Sometimes it was exceedingly irritating having him so aware of her emotions.

She could sneak in, but something told her it wasn't going to be necessary. Besides, she had teleported twice with no hitchhikers, and with her luck, a third time would attract something. The last thing she needed was a fast entrance bringing who knows what else with a revenant inside an ancient historical crypt.

The guard heard her coming and put his hand on the baton in his belt. She stopped as soon as she was visible to him and waited. He studied her briefly and then asked, "Are you here because of what's been disturbing the ghosts?"

She loved being able to understand every spoken language. She also loved being able to immediately know enough to reply. "Yes, and I'm also going to take care of whatever is causing that racket in there."

Relief washed over his face, and he sighed. "Then I have to thank you. The ghosts aren't bad enough. Now there's something else moving in there." He turned and pulled a key ring off his belt, waving her over.

"You don't seem surprised."

He understood what she meant. "I've met people like you before. I was hoping one of your kind would show up once this started." He gestured at the crypt and the eerie sounds coming from inside. "I don't mind the ghosts. They play and make noise. But something has been stirring them up, and now there's something else."

"I'll take care of the creature in there. And we are working on the other situation. I'd appreciate it if you could leave things locked up like this."

"Of course. Are you going to be coming back out?"

"Not through here. You can lock up behind me." Even if the dimension somehow let her back out in the same location, she didn't have to worry about being locked in a crypt. She gave him a reassuring smile. "Don't worry. We'll be watching things and hopefully get it back to normal soon."

"That's good to hear." He opened the door, and she slipped inside. The heavy wood and metal door thudded shut behind her, chains rattling as the guard locked it back up.

As she neared the bottom of the stairs, she saw the intricate designs made out of human bones lining the hall. Human remains didn't bother her, but they certainly gave the crypt a disturbing feel.

She paused as her brother reached out to her and shared that he and Eric could hear a ghost in the hospital they were in. *"Are you fucking kidding me?"*

"No, I'm not. It's kind of cool and freaky. Did you have to jump back to get to the door?" He could tell she was out of sync with the time he was in. Their timelines were constantly locked together, and they moved at the same speed forward no matter where, or when, they were.

"Yeah, a couple of hours. There's a revenant in the creepy bone crypt."

"And I thought a wraith was bad."

"Because alternate dimension shit isn't terrible enough, we get to have all the monsters in haunted houses too." It had only been a matter of time with the increasing ghost activity.

"Well, good luck, we'd better get moving before these ghost hunters get themselves killed."

"Good luck with that."

She felt Eric's presence focus back on Trey's mind as her brother faded into the back of her head. She hoped she'd be able to talk to all of them once they were inside the other dimension. She was worried they'd get into trouble, and she wouldn't know. She smiled wryly, her brother's overly protective attitude drove her insane, and here she was worrying about them.

Sarah Eriksen

The logical part of her brain knew they would be able to call out to Amonir. The god would have no reason not to be able to hear his guardians no matter where they were. They were all extremely talented, but it didn't stop her from worrying about them. This dimension didn't play by normal rules.

The crypt was small, and it wasn't connected to the bigger catacombs that drew the tourists. A small corridor at the bottom of the stairs led into a larger room with two chambers on either side. Human bones decorated every inch of the rooms in intricate designs.

A large platform with a carved marble coffin was in the center of the large room. She could feel the dark presence of the revenant as it shuffled around the crypt, periodically letting out a mournful cry.

She rolled her eyes, unimpressed with its theatrics. It was doing it on purpose. Revenants were intelligent and usually had some memories of their previous life, depending on who or what brought them back. But even with memories, they were dark, cold, unfeeling creatures capable of thought.

And this one was making ghostly sounds to scare people away with cheap theatrics. She would love to know why it felt the need. The crypts were supposedly haunted, so it seemed unnecessary.

She drew on creation energy, trying to control the stream of power, sparks flashing around her wildly before settling into a faint glow that she forced away with a grunt of effort. She stepped into the crypt, an incandescent sword appearing in her right hand, her left hand glowing with coldfire, and her head throbbing with the effort to contain it all.

The revenant came to a stop, its back to her. It was covered in armor with a tattered red cloak hanging from its shoulders. Either it had been a human with a penchant for LARPing, or it wasn't from this world. It turned to her, its eyes glowing faintly with pale energy.

"How lucky you showed up." Its voice was hollow and raspy.

"You're going to have to elaborate on that," Skye replied dryly as she walked into the room, keeping her body facing the revenant as she scanned for the door.

The revenant coughed out a dusty laugh. "I was told you were incapable of respecting your betters."

Skye nodded and then shrugged. "I suppose it would depend on who you consider are my betters. A dusty reanimated corpse in a tomb on a world it doesn't belong on? I'm not entirely sure you would classify as better." She tilted her head to the side and gave it a considering look. "I mean if we're going to compare...I at least belong here, and I'm still alive, so I think I'm ahead of the game."

She could sense the door in the middle of the room, and since it wasn't visible, which meant it was inside the coffin. She wondered who had figured out a door was appearing inside a heavy stone coffin that a normal person wouldn't be able to open. Unless the ghost hunter groups had used deduction to guess a door was in the crypt based on the activity. However, they had managed it, they had figured it out. The door was definitely inside the coffin.

"Foolish mortal, you have no idea of the forces you are messing with." The revenant snarled. They were easy to anger, and taunting was a skill guardians were encouraged to become proficient at.

Skye sighed dramatically. "I guess you'll just have to tell me then."

The revenant drew in another raspy breath and pointed a gaunt hand at her, opening its rotting mouth to speak. A powerful force hit the revenant, and its body arched, a scream ripping from its throat as it threw its head back in agony.

Skye stared in surprise. She had not been expecting that. She couldn't recognize the energy either. The revenant's eyes glowed brighter, and a snarl of blind rage spread across its face. Whatever the spell was, it had done two things. It stopped the revenant from revealing something important and turned it into a berserk monster.

She waited until the last second and then dodged to the side as the creature rushed toward her. Its heavy sword dripped with dark energy as it swung down in a powerful blow. The blade cracked the stone of the floor as it struck.

She was done playing games. Sparks flared around her in a frenzied rush as she let go of her tight mental grip holding everything back. Creation energy surged violently into her, and her body erupted with coldfire.

She blocked the next blow with her sword, pushing its blade back toward it effortlessly. She thrust her left hand forward and struck its chest. Energy exploded out of her palm, igniting the revenant's armor with vibrant flames that were no longer cold but burned with the heat of a sun.

Sarah Eriksen

The revenant shrieked as the flames ate at its armor, weakening the protective spells that were layered and built into it. It staggered back, cold misty energy enveloping it in an attempt to combat the damage.

Skye pressed her advantage, summoning her second sword and launching a flurry of attacks that it desperately tried to parry. She drew it off balance as it attempted to block each stroke of her blades.

It teetered, arms flailing as it tried to regain its footing. She ducked into the sudden opening and slammed her foot into the side of its knee, feeling the crunch as bones shattered and dislocated.

The revenant screamed in rage and dropped to the ground on its undamaged leg. She swatted its next reckless swing away with careless ease. She held up her left hand, sword reforming into a compact ball of incandescent coldfire.

"Anything left in there with a mind?" She asked it. It lunged toward her with a wordless snarl, and she kicked it in the face, knocking it back once more. "I guess not." The ball of fire exploded into its chest, fed by more energy she directed into it. The revenant was reduced to a pile of dark ashes within seconds.

She studied the ashy remains, releasing the creation energy swirling through and around her. She had fought this creature like she always would. Disable the protective spells while dodging attacks, and eventually take it out once you weakened their defenses. But she had managed to destroy it without the usual effort.

She was starting to wonder if she needed to rethink some of her tactics. There were reasons to handle things certain ways, and she certainly wasn't going to be able to solve every encounter by using insane amounts of energy and disintegrating creatures. But maybe trying to use the normal tactics she had used for the last fifteen or so years wasn't working anymore.

The pile of ashes disappeared with a flash of blue and white sparks as she gestured at them. She shook her hand to wave away the sparks floating around it. Changing her tactics might be a good idea, but she wasn't sure how it would help with her other, more concerning issue with controlling her powers.

It was time to find the door. She turned to the elaborate marble coffin, inspecting it closely; the portal was inside. She raised her hands and lifted the heavy marble top into the air. There was no way any normal ghost hunter had found it. She added it to the list of mysteries. The murky, watery portal filled the inside of the coffin.

"This is only going to be slightly awkward." She couldn't leave the coffin open. The heavy marble lid rose higher, and she jumped into the air above the portal, her body flickering with sparks of energy. She held herself aloft and then dropped through the door, the heavy lid falling slowly in a trickle of sparking energy that controlled its descent.

She tumbled feet first through a door and landed with a splash in musty water. She kicked her feet, finding the bottom under her, and stood up in a scant two feet of water. She glanced around. She was in a cell of some kind with thick stone walls. The water she had landed in appeared to be moderately clean, with only a few traces of slimy algae.

First things first, she needed to find the others. *"Did you two make it into your part of the dimension?"* She asked Trey and Eric.

"Safe and sound. And we can hear you loud and clear." Trey replied.

"I couldn't find you from the second we entered, though," Eric said.

"I could feel you the whole time but didn't try to reach you since you were distracted with your revenant. You're not going to believe this place, Skye." Trey laughed.

"You'll have to tell me all about it in a minute. Any sign of Korbin?"

"Nothing that we can tell. Can you reach the others?" Eric was more pragmatic than Trey, as always.

"Yes, I can. I was going to check on them next. I'll keep a light touch with you." She couldn't sense a direction for their location, but she could find their minds with no issue. She had felt Trey's presence the entire time too, so it seemed likely he would have been able to reach out to her at least.

"Hey, you two." She reached out to Kya and Declan.

"Hello, Skye," Kya replied instantly. *"No sign of Korbin here. And I wasn't able to call out to you or Trey. But I can still sense Kyleeria."*

"I'll look for Korbin now." Skye closed her eyes and reached out of the space she was in. She felt a faint presence nearby that flitted away and disappeared. She frowned. It had to be the same something or someone. She really should try to figure out who or what it was. But this was a rescue mission, and it was very much not Korbin. She stretched her mind out further and had better success.

She breathed a sigh of relief. *"He's in this one. And seems to be okay."*

"That's good to hear." Kya's voice was relieved.

"I do not like that damn music." Declan's voice sounded annoyed. *"I'm glad you found Korbin."*

"At least the music seems to give us an idea of when it gets dangerous," Kya said calmly.

Skye bit back a laugh and said, *"So Trey is laughing at the place they're in, and you guys have a soundtrack? I'm in a damn dungeon with stagnant water that I fell in after jumping inside a coffin."*

"I'd almost prefer the dungeon over this weird-ass creepy forest," Declan said.

"I'll stay in touch." She had kept her mind lightly on Korbin in case he needed something while she sorted out the communication barriers.

"Back away for a bit and let me see if I can find you," Declan said.

Skye was a little surprised but gave him the go-ahead and then drew away from him. A few seconds later, he barreled into her mind with remarkably little finesse.

"Good lord Declan. You haven't been that awkward since we were kids." She rubbed her temple.

"Sorry about that. I thought I could still feel you when we got here, but I wasn't sure until you reached out. There's a thin barrier, or like dense fog or something in the way, which makes it harder to sense you. I might have used more force than I had to get through it. But at least I can scream at you if I need to."

"Is that the only reason you decided it was so important to be able to reach me while we're in here?" Skye asked.

"The rest of us have buddies. If something happens, I want to make sure more than one person can find you." He meant it, and it must have been along the same line of reasoning that had made him follow her into the dimension before this.

"Thanks, Declan."

"Of course." He knew she was thanking him for more than that. He always tended to look out for her when she didn't even know she needed someone to be there.

She pulled back, keeping a light touch on her friends' minds in case they needed her. She was pretty good at having group conversations with multiple people in her head, but to have four separate connections at the same time took a bit more effort.

"*Hey, space pirate.*" She spoke in Korbin's mind, feeling bad when he jumped.

"*Skye?*" His mental tone wasn't quite as strong as Wes' had been, but it was obvious Kya had been working with him since he was able to reply easily. She could feel hints of panic and fear along with relief at finally hearing from someone he knew.

"*The one and only. Are you okay?*"

"*I'm unharmed if that's what you mean. How'd you find me?*" He seemed more confused that she was there instead of Kya.

She walked around the room she was in, studying it while she chatted with him. "*Well, I was exploring a weird dimension with one of my friends, and we stumbled across some dead pirates from your space station. I asked Kya if she was missing some space pirates. A couple of hours, later we find out you and Wes were missing. I found Wes since he was in a place I'd been before. But it was total dumb luck we found you this fast.*"

"*If you're trying to be reassuring, you might be missing the mark.*" His emotions were calming down, and his humor was returning.

"*There's five of us in three very different parts of this dimension. We couldn't find you from the outside. But thanks to a new friend of mine, we found some new doors that seemed promising and jumped through them. And you happened to be in the one I jumped into…so…luck.*" She pushed at the thick metal bars blocking the entrance. There wasn't a door or a lock, only floor-to-ceiling bars.

"*I'll take lucky.*" His mind voice hesitated for a second before he said, "*I'm glad you're here. I was starting to get worried.*"

"*Well, we found you, so no more worrying. Now stay put, this dimension has a lot of strange things, and some are dangerous.*" She searched for something that would get rid of the bars without her having to use her powers.

"*Oh, I'm not going anywhere. I'm stuck in a room with a door that won't open and a sword that is impossibly useless.*"

Skye's mind voice was bright with laughter. "*How exactly is a sword 'impossibly useless'?*"

Sarah Eriksen

"Well, I popped into this room I can't get out of, and there's this shiny pretty sword. Seemed like a good idea to grab another weapon since none of mine are working. But you can't hit anything with it. And I do mean anything. I couldn't even hit the wall with it if I tried. And believe me...I tried."

"Okay, that does sound pretty impossible and extremely useless. Well, sit tight. I'm on my way."

He asked hesitantly, *"Can you stay in touch with me while you head here?"*

Skye could tell he was uncomfortable asking her that but simply replied, *"Of course."* His relief at her words was clear. He might be safe, but he had been trapped by himself for several hours.

An odd shape in the wall caught her eye. There was a small lever neatly hidden in the blocks of stone. She pushed it upward, and the bars slid down into the floor.

"Oh, goodie. Another video game style dungeon."

Chapter Twenty-Two

"I'm just saying. We're in a creepy forest with a covered bridge, and the background music is totally building up. I guarantee if we go that way, something bad is going to happen." Declan said.

The music had started out as subtle, pretty, and haunting. It shifted to something more intense and had been building as the small footpath they followed took them to a larger road. Kya hadn't been able to find Korbin in this part of the pocket dimension either.

Declan could feel her worry, even though she did a good job keeping it to herself. And neither one of them could reach out to the others. It might have been wishful thinking on his part, but he was pretty sure he could still sense Skye's mind. Only it was like something was in the way.

They both studied the woods around them. The trees were massive but twisted and dark. The leafy canopy overhead let in the barest strands of gloomy light. Faint will-o-wisps appeared here and there in the distance, glowing with an eerie pale light. The ambience reminded Kya of the dark forest on her home world.

"I don't disagree with you, Declan. I can't figure out where the music is coming from. Everything you have encountered before has been like a movie or a video game, right?"

"Pretty much. Like someone tried to recreate things with some serious creative license." He had explained how the people in White Chapel had felt incomplete in their minds.

Sarah Eriksen

"So, we're in a dark, scary forest with a soundtrack. I don't see how else to cross the river, and I'm not sure I want to chance swimming." She glanced at the murky water. As if on cue, a strange fin briefly breached the surface and disappeared back under.

Declan scoffed. "Good timing. I wonder if the creepy river monster will show up whenever someone thinks of swimming." As he said the last word, another strange fin appeared. He flashed a mischievous grin at Kya and said, "Swimming." He laughed as the river monster made another appearance.

Kya fought a smile and said, "Let's stop taunting the river monsters and be prepared for whatever is going to happen when we cross the bridge."

"How does one prepare for a situation like this?" He asked but still walked forward. The music intensified, and he said, "I think the answer is to be ready to run."

They stopped at the entrance to the covered bridge, and a wolf howled in the distance. Kya said, "That's a nice touch."

"You say that now, but when we get chased by a werewolf, it's all your fault."

Kya tilted her head, accepting the pre-emptive blame. "I want to try something before we do this. Stay there for a moment." She backed up slowly on the road, head tilted to one side, listening. She stopped a few paces back and said, "The music hasn't changed."

Declan walked toward her at her beckoning gesture, the music stayed the same until he reached her, and then it subsided slightly. "Oh good. We can use it to avoid potentially stressful situations."

"Maybe. At least we know it's somehow tied to both of us."

"Sure, until we get separated and find our own terrible, scary movie scenarios." He said wryly.

She had watched movies before and understood his meaning. Her mother was human, after all, but she hadn't watched a scary movie in a long time. "Let's not get separated then if we can avoid it."

He nodded, surprisingly serious for a change. The danger in this dimension was real, even if they were more than capable of handling things. The mummies in the crypt hadn't been too difficult to kill, other than the final boss that had required a magic weapon from inside the dimension. The only truly terrifying thing Skye had talked about had been the pink ball of doom. The rest of it was just odd.

He looked at Kya and asked, "Shall we?"

"Might as well." They walked back to the bridge, stopping when Skye reached out to them. Thankfully, Skye had found Korbin where she had ended up. Declan muttered something about hating the music, making sure they could both hear him, before asking Skye to help him try something.

He used the connection she had created to talk to them to pinpoint her mind. He hadn't been mistaken. He could feel her presence. It was just hard to find and even harder to get through the strange fog blocking things. Kya waited patiently for him to finish what he was doing.

His focus returned, and he grinned. "I wanted to see if I could find Skye after she connected with us. It's different, but I can do it."

"How is it different?" Kya asked curiously. She could feel his mind clearly and had heard and felt Skye with no issue when she had reached out. But as soon as Skye had left, she couldn't sense her anymore.

"It's murky. Normally your mind kind of homes in on the person's mind since you know it. But it's like there's something in the way that makes it harder to see and feel. Like if you were trying to find something in thick fog in the dark." It was the best analogy he could come up with.

She closed her eyes, trying to follow the path Skye had taken to speak to them, and felt a muted version of her cousin's mind. "I see what you're saying now. It takes a lot more effort. I wonder how Skye has managed it without any difficulties."

"It's Skye. Something got in her way. She got annoyed and then just did what she was trying to do anyway, blatantly ignoring whatever is blocking her like it isn't there. She does that. A lot."

Kya's laugh was musical and bright, creating an odd counterpoint to the scary forest. "You're right. She does tend to be like that." She gestured at the bridge and repeated Declan's question from earlier. "Shall we?"

They stepped onto the bridge, and the music intensified again. A few more steps in and the air felt heavy. Everything darkened as the music continued to build up. They picked up their pace without even thinking about it. Halfway across the bridge, the music peaked, and lightning flashed.

Declan scowled. "You know if we look behind us, something is going to be there, and it's going to chase us, right?"

She said, "Might as well get it over with." They turned at the same time.

Lightning flashed again, providing the perfect silhouette of the dark figure on a dark horse that reared up on its hind legs.

"Nice touch," Declan said as the horse's front hooves hit the bridge, and it started to charge toward them. The two guardians bolted the remaining distance, exiting the unnaturally dark bridge as intense chase scene music filled the air.

The sound of hooves pounding on the boards of the bridge seemed unnaturally loud. They ran down the path into the dense woods. It curved abruptly, turning into a steep hill. They lost sight of the horseman as they flew down the slope. The ground leveled out, and a large dead tree stump that was tall enough to hide them both caught their attention.

"That's ridiculously obvious." Declan laughed. They pushed through the scrubby brush, finding the opening on the side opposite the road. He grinned and gestured for Kya to go inside first.

She sighed and moved past him, pressing her back against the damp and crumbling wood. Declan followed her, shifting to the other side and trying his best to be polite and not crowd her. The space was roomy enough for the two of them to fit comfortably.

"Why are we hiding?" Kya asked. It was a good question. They were more than capable of taking out a single rider on a horse.

"It seems to be playing out like a movie or a game. We could challenge the rules and reality of this dimension or play along and hide in the obvious dead tree hiding spot?"

"I suppose you're right. If we don't play along, it might get dangerous. As it is, we outran a horse with no issue, so we were meant to get away."

"Or at least get here." The music had slowed down but was picking up again with suspenseful intensity. They heard the slow clomping of the horse's hooves on the dirt path. Kya rolled her eyes at the drama, and Declan covered his mouth to hold in his laugh.

"What movie or show is this from? A scary dark rider on a horse." Kya asked to distract him from his laughter.

Chaotic Haunts

"Take your pick. The number of books, movies, and stories that start with a scary rider on a dark horse is ridiculous. It seemed kind of generic. At least, it wasn't anything I've seen before."

"Well, hopefully, the hiding spot works." Another feeling of oppressive and heavy air surrounded them. *"This would probably be terrifying if you didn't know what was going on."*

Declan agreed with her. He didn't feel afraid himself. He knew he was more than capable of surviving most things. But this dimension was crafted perfectly for suspense and fear. A loud snap of a twig breaking sounded in the distance, and the rider took off in the opposite direction of where they were hiding.

Declan said, "Well, that was convenient." He followed with his mind and didn't sense any presence that indicated another person was alive in there with them. "I think it was a planned sound. I can't find any people. Even fake people."

"I didn't feel anyone either."

Declan slipped carefully out of the tree as the music eased up and returned to the pretty background theme. "Guess we follow the road?"

"I don't see any other paths to take."

"I can feel the door back to my world in the same general direction now too." He gave her a curious look. "Can you feel anything leading back to your space station?"

A flash of surprise crossed her face but quickly disappeared. She closed her eyes to concentrate as she sent her mind out, feeling for hints of her part of the universe. She finally shook her head. "Nothing that's jumping out at me."

He shrugged. "It was worth a shot."

"You're not wrong. As many dead doors as we have on the station, with three at least that are linked to this place, it stands to reason one of them would connect here. But if it's the same as the ones to your world, then it might be a one-way door as well."

"Doesn't mean we can't go out the door. We have at least one with a mummy constantly popping across onto Earth. It doesn't hurt to keep an eye out while we're exploring." His charming grin flashed across his face.

Kya simply smiled in return and turned to walk down the path. He was incorrigible, but she had to admit, to herself at least, that he kept things entertaining.

"This is insane." Trey laughed.

Eric agreed, "Of all the things Skye has told us about so far, I don't think I could have ever imagined this. Can you still feel her? I can't seem to reach out of this place."

"Yeah, she's still there in the back of my brain." He tapped the side of his head. "She had to jump back a few hours to get to the open door, so she's a little out of sync with the rest of us. That's probably why you can't find her. On top of the block the dimension seems to have on mind to mind talking."

"That would do it. We should be able to sense a door back to our world somewhere in all of that." He gestured at the massive labyrinth sprawled in front of them at the base of the hill they were on. The walls were a mix of dark gray stone and vibrant green hedges. Trees could be spotted here and there, some in larger clusters and others standing alone. Mist hovered in spots suggesting the presence of water.

"Yep. I'm going to take a look." Trey closed his eyes, sending out his mind and feeling for the presence of people and the door back to their world.

"I'll see if I can feel anything that might link back to the space station." Eric saw Trey nod, and he closed his eyes, sending his mind out. Nothing obvious jumped out at him, but he did feel the sensation of their world smack in the middle of the tangled maze. "I think I found the door back, but nothing else."

"Same. There seems to be some hints of minds, but they seem kind of empty. Probably the same thing as the people in White Chapel Declan told us about. And I can't feel Korbin's mind either. How about you?"

"Nothing. I checked for life signs as well as his mind in case he was unconscious."

Trey let out a disappointed sigh. "I didn't even think to do that."

Eric gave him a reassuring smile. "This is new territory for both of us. Alternate dimensions, ghosts, rescue missions for people from the other side of the universe? It's a first."

"Thanks. That makes me feel a tiny bit better." Trey laughed as they headed down the hill to the entrance to the labyrinth.

Trey's thoughts turned inward as they navigated the steep incline. This was a very different situation, and it was certainly out of his comfort zone. He liked his objectives to be clear and straightforward. He had to be honest with himself. The rift between him and Skye after everything that had happened, had taken a toll and left him feeling unsure of a lot of things.

He was a little envious of his twin sometimes. She always held it together no matter what the universe threw at her. She saw what was going on and what needed to be done, and she did it. It didn't matter what obstacles or dangers. She always made it work.

He tried to understand how she could piece things together, but it was where they had always differed. Deep down, he knew they had different strengths and ways of seeing the universe. Their differences were just more noticeable now that she was so much more powerful.

He was happy she had forgiven him for his stupid reaction to everything. He had been so angry he couldn't keep up. It wasn't her fault he struggled with self-worth and confidence in himself. He locked down the spiral of thoughts that would lead his mind to dark places. He could hide some of it from her, but not all of it when it got bad.

His own feelings of uncertainty drew his attention to the spot in the back of his mind that was his twin. He knew she had been struggling with something, but he didn't know how to help. He wasn't entirely sure he understood what was going on either. She had always been much better at concealing her emotions away from him. He was doing his best not to pry. One thing he did know was that she wouldn't appreciate him trying to fix things.

Trey shifted his attention away from his inner musings and watched Eric for a moment. "I think we're starting to wear off on you."

"How's that?"

"You're way too excited to explore a weird labyrinth in an alternate dimension. I wouldn't have ever pictured you being excited about this."

He smiled crookedly. "Why not? A new unexplored dimension no one knows the details about doesn't happen that often. It's genuinely exciting. We rarely get to experience things in life without being able to know what we have to know to survive. This is kind of scary and nerve-wracking. I'm not a thrill seeker by any means, but it's kind of fun. Might as well enjoy it."

"Okay, you make a good point."

Eric continued, "Besides, is it a bad thing for my overly serious self to enjoy the little things more?" He grinned as Trey laughed at his joke. Eric didn't mind making fun of himself. His traumatic childhood experience had given him a pretty serious outlook. His uncles had done their best to give him and his sister a normal life after everything, but some wounds never fully healed.

He was happy to be able to have these experiences with his friends. He had been envious of their close camaraderie when he first met them, but they dragged him right into their group without any hesitation. Their friendship was truly the best thing that had ever happened to him.

They stopped at the wall to the labyrinth, and both burst out laughing. The door was intricately carved out of heavy, dark gray stone. The walls stretched so far to either side that they disappeared in a haze of distance with no other visible entrances. And the entire thing was just over three feet tall.

"It's even worse up close." Trey reached his hand up, feeling for an invisible magic wall and finding nothing. He leaned over and looked at the first part of the maze. He felt a nudge of a spell, but it wasn't connected to the wall, and he brushed it aside.

"It certainly is scaled down a bit." Eric's shoulders shook with laughter. "I can't sense anything dangerous, though." He studied every bit of energy and power down into the deep layers underneath, and nothing was unusual about it. There was a hint of some kind of spell near the door, but it faded away after brushing against him.

"Well, here goes nothing." Trey went to step over the wall, and Eric grabbed his arming, stopping him.

"Let me. If something goes wrong, you'll be able to reach Skye." The serious side of him was back.

"I don't like that you're right but okay." Trey grudgingly agreed.

Eric stepped over the labyrinth wall, his tall frame clearing it without any struggles. He stood on the stone path and turned around. Nothing bad had happened. "That was underwhelming. But it seems fine."

Trey stepped over the wall just as easily. "It really seemed like something was going to happen, didn't it?"

Eric agreed. "I was positive it was going to be more than just a short wall."

"And now we can spend the rest of this trip worrying about why it's so normal if small scaled."

Eric laughed with him. Trey was right. With all the other weirdness, it seemed even more bizarre that size was the only thing off about this place. "At least we can step over the walls with no issue."

Trey's face lit up with a smirk reminiscent of Declan at his most mischievous. "Well, *we* can. Skye would struggle a little bit with them."

Eric smothered a laugh. The walls were probably an inch or two too high for Skye to be able to step over easily. "I'm sure she'd find her own way."

"Of course, she would," Trey said without a hint of irritation. "Guess we walk our way over the walls to the door?" It seemed too easy somehow.

"I guess so." Eric stepped over the next well, avoiding a fancy, spiky finial on top. The labyrinth was on a smaller scale, but it was still vast. It was going to take them some time.

Sarah Eriksen

Chapter Twenty-Three

So far, everything had been straightforward in the dungeon Skye had fallen into. The room outside where she had entered appeared to be a guard station. She grabbed one of the swords from a nearby rack, taking a few swings to get used to the weight. She was getting tired of not being able to use her own weapons.

"Amonir, how long do we play along and go incognito in this alternate dimension? I have yet to sense the presence of the god who created this place, and it's starting to seem a little odd."

He surprised her by answering immediately, *"It is unusual not to sense anything with the amount of time you have spent there. But, from what you and the others have relayed, it seems to have some fairly specific dynamics. While I'm sure your powers would work, it also seems to be as easy, if not easier, for you to use what is available that seems to be programmed into it."*

"It's way too much like a video game."

"Have you had any luck with the name you keep finding?"

"Shit. I forgot about that. The rescue mission sort of took over." She had been sidetracked by Ben's texts about haunted houses and doors and had forgotten to reach out to Ian.

"Well, that is far more important. But I think the name might give you a clue." He faded away.

"Nice and cryptic as usual, boss man." She pulled her phone out of her pocket, chancing the energy required to connect it back to her time and world. She tapped out a quick text to Ian and asked him to do some digging into the name Mary Ann Randall and see if he could come up with anything. She gave him the context that she had seen so far. He replied immediately with two words, "on it."

"Skye, are you still there?" Korbin asked.

"Yes, I am. Sorry. I had to follow up on something."

"Just making sure you hadn't disappeared on me." His fear had lessened, but he was still trapped in a room in another dimension. A little anxiety was understandable.

"Nope, just multi-tasking. So, tell me more about your useless sword?" It would help distract him while she navigated her way out of the dungeon. There was a set of stairs that curved upward ahead of her. She had one path so far. She sent her mind out to search for hidden areas, but nothing was coming up yet.

"Well, when I appeared in this place, I immediately checked my weapons, and they seem to have no power. Then I saw the sword and thought it was better than nothing. I've had some experience fighting with a stun baton, and figured I'd be able to defend myself with a sword at least."

"That makes sense." They didn't utilize the exact same fighting techniques, but he'd be able to do damage and block, at least.

"So, I took a few practice swings at some candles in here. And I couldn't hit them. I tried quite a few times and got the same result. Which is odd, to say the least."

Skye bit her lip to hold in a laugh at his frustration. *"Is it the sword or the candles?"* She knew it wasn't him. Even if he couldn't use a sword, he'd have hit something with it after a few swings, at the very least.

"I wondered that too. So, I tried to hit the door frame, and it swung wide and knocked me on my ass. You can't hit anything with it."

Skye glanced at the sword in her hand and gave it an experimental swing before slashing through a candle in a sconce on the wall. *"The sword I picked up seems to work. I murdered a candle with it."*

"Well, at least one of us has a working weapon." His frustration was real, but he immediately apologized. *"Sorry. I know I'm being less than gracious at the moment."*

"I think you're allowed. You're stuck in an alternate dimension with a sword that doesn't know how to be a normal sword. What's going on with your other weapons? You said they weren't working?"

Sarah Eriksen

She didn't know what type of weapons he was carrying and had no clue how they would even work anyway. She hadn't brought weapons with her since she could make her own, in theory at least. She had yet to try and summon her swords inside the dimension.

"Well, I use energy pistols, and they have no power. I'm not sure how. I maintain them constantly, and they don't appear to be damaged."

"They don't have a charge or anything to stay powered up? That sounds like a stupid question, but I don't know how your weapons work in your part of the universe."

"No, they have a single power source that lasts pretty much forever unless it gets damaged, and I checked that already. The ammunition portion has to be replaced periodically, but I had just done that before I headed to the space station, and I haven't used them. They should be good for a few years. It's like they stopped working."

"Got it." The information trickled into her mind sluggishly as he explained it. That part of guardian stuff was still working, with a touch of a lag. It was like her high-speed mental internet had downgraded back to dial-up. "I'm guessing something about this place has rendered them useless. I doubt they're broken. I'd also guess they'll be fine as soon as we leave here."

"That would be nice. I mean, it'd be better if they worked now, but I'll take what I can get."

She finally reached the top of the stairs and encountered another door. This one opened easily and led into a larger hallway lined with cells covered in barred doors. Two guards were walking up and down the hall. They turned as she stepped into the room.

"Hold on, Korbin, looks like I have to fight some guards." She scanned with her mind. They were oddly blank, like the townspeople in White Chapel. More NPC-type characters.

"How did you get in here?" One of them asked.

"Through the door," Skye answered.

"She must have escaped her cell." The second guard exclaimed. "Get her!"

"This is a boring script, you guys." She stepped back, settling comfortably into a fighting stance with the sword held up defensively. She parried the first guard's attack and kicked her foot into his gut, knocking the wind out of him. He collapsed to the ground, gasping. She stomped on his hand and kicked his sword away as he screamed in agony.

She blocked the next guard's two-handed attack, forcing his blade off to one side. She used her momentum to spin in front of him, sliding her sword around and thrusting it back through his chest while his arm flailed out and away from her. She stepped forward to the first guard, kicking him onto his back and planting her foot against his chest.

"You won't escape alive!" He gasped at her.

"What else can I expect to find in here?"

"You won't escape alive!" He repeated.

She tried a few more questions, getting the same response, and finally stabbed her sword through his heart, putting an end to the repetitious answers. "Useless NPCs." She muttered to herself.

"Okay, guards are not helpful."

"I'm glad you're alright," Korbin said, relief in his voice.

"Come on, I was playing chicken with a bunch of giant rampaging aliens, and you're worried I couldn't handle two guards?" She teased while she pulled a key ring off one of the bodies.

"For all I knew, the two guards were worse than rampaging aliens." He teased right back.

Skye laughed. He was surprisingly charming. The first time they had met, he had been under a lot of stress. *"They were boring guards with limited dialogue. So, you're in a room with candlesticks. I'm guessing it's not a prison cell?"*

"No, it's some kind of waiting room? A few chairs and tables, candles. A couple of shelves with decorations on them. It's quite comfortable and elegant. And there are two locked doors on either side of the room. One of them is the one I came through."

"You didn't try to leave?" She wasn't judging. It was a sound call to stay put.

"I tried the door, but it's locked. And it seemed more prudent to stay put since none of my weapons work, including the sword. That and the other door is also locked. I don't have a choice about staying put."

She fought back a laugh as she made her way out of the dungeon. There had thankfully only been a couple of keys on the key ring, and she had found the right one on her second try. *"Smart man. Apparently, the* door from the space station goes to a nicer place than the door from the coffin in a crypt in my world."

"That sounds unpleasant." He chuckled ruefully. *"I'm still trying to wrap my head around the fact you live on the other side of the universe and have strange powers."*

"Kya filled you in on all of the wonders of the universe then?" Skye teased.

"She did. And offered me a job on her crew."

"I'm assuming you took her up on the offer?"

"Of course. Good pay, a badass boss who has powers? Easy choice. Although, I'm not loving the whole aliens breaking out constantly on the space station thing. But she assures me it'll get better."

"I don't know as much about her job, but if it's anything like mine, then expect everything to never go as planned and always be weird." She followed another long hallway full of locked cells to a staircase leading up a short distance.

"Considering my current situation, I won't argue."

She was getting closer to where Korbin was. She went through a large wooden door and entered a clean hall with a bright blue carpet running down the middle. Beeswax candles flickered cheerfully in evenly spaced sconces along the wall.

"Well, I appear to be out of the dungeon, and I'm getting closer. It's annoying. I can't see that far around me until I've been there." She could feel his confusion and explained, "I have a way of seeing with my mind and mapping out places around me almost instantly. It's a guardian thing. We don't get lost easily."

"That sounds convenient."

"Yep. But the dimension seems to prevent that in different areas. I can sense the general area where you are, but I can't see the path straight to you, let alone anything else here."

"If I could send up a flare for you, I would." He chuckled.

"Well, since we're in a castle or something, it probably wouldn't help too much. But I do appreciate the thought." She headed down the hall in the direction of his presence.

"So, how do we get out of here? After you come and save me, of course." He didn't sound bothered in the least at being saved by her.

Chaotic Haunts

"Well, if this place tracks like every other part I've been in, there should be a door back to my world somewhere. As soon as I find it, I can take you back to the space station."

"As much as I hate the space station, I'll be happy to get out of here. I don't love this place."

"Anything in particular that you don't love about it other than being stuck in a room with locked doors and broken weapons?" She asked.

"I think that's mostly it."

"I had to ask. Sometimes people who aren't guardians pick up on things we don't."

"You mean you aren't perfect?" He teased.

"Far from it. I leave perfection to Kya." Her cousin's half-elf blood certainly made her seem perfect. Skye had good self-esteem most days but had to admit she was jealous of her cousin's elven hair. Hair that looked great no matter what happened to it would be very useful if you were in a hurry. Or if you fell into a pond full of algae after leaping through a coffin. She had used a touch of energy to get rid of most of the filth, but she wasn't going to spend any time or effort primping.

"I won't disagree with you there."

"It's even worse when you're in a room with all her siblings. And the rest of the elven court." Her five cousins somehow managed to get the best aspects of mixing human and elven blood.

"If they're anything like her, that would be intimidating. Although, I'm sure you can hold your own."

Skye smiled as she realized he was flirting with her. She had to tease and chose to deliberately misunderstand him. "I'm pretty sure Kya could kick my ass in a fight. Then again, I'm actually more powerful than her now. I might stand a chance of winning."

Skye slowed down as she neared a wider hallway. She could feel his presence further down and to the side. No NPCs were around other than a set of guards at the opposite end.

"I'm in the hallway outside the room you're in. But I'm going to see if the guards will pay any attention to me before I start trying to get you out."

"I'm not going anywhere." He said with a laugh.

Sarah Eriksen

Skye rounded the corner and walked down the hall. The guards seemed uninterested in her, but she walked closer to make sure. They didn't move or react, so she returned to Korbin's prison.

She turned to the door and studied it. Nothing seemed unusual about it. She grabbed the doorknob, and it refused to turn.

"That is you, right?" He asked as he heard the door rattling.

"Yep. And there's no keyhole." She sent her mind into the room, searching for something that would unlock the door. Korbin was lounging in one of the chairs, his long legs stretched out in front of him with his ankles crossed. His posture was far too casual and comfortable for someone waiting to be rescued.

She said, *"Try moving one of the candlesticks on either side of the door. Pick up the candle and see if they bend or turn or something. There has to be a trigger that will unlock it."*

"Alright." He moved to the candlestick to the left of the door and pulled on it. It immediately shifted forward and down. A mechanism whirred, and a loud click sounded inside.

Skye pushed the now unlocked handle, stepping inside after taking a cautious glance at the guards. She turned to Korbin, who looked no worse for the wear.

She grinned impishly and said, "Hey, space pirate."

"Smuggler." He said firmly before a charming crooked grin cracked his face. He clasped her shoulder. "Thank you for rescuing me."

"You're welcome. Although I don't think you can say I've rescued you until we're back on the space station."

"Well, thank you for rescuing me from the locked room. And I will thank you again, more profusely, when you deem me fully rescued."

"I'll allow it. Let's take a look at where you came through." She crossed her arms as she studied the decorative locked door. It was a mirror image of the one to the hall. She tilted her head to the side and then placed her hand on the smooth wood. "It's a door. And it goes nowhere. Same as the ones from my world. They turn into a dead door the second you come through them."

"So, they're one way? That sounds so odd." He laughed.

"Yeah. But when the door from my world closes, then another one opens to exit from. You'd think this would be the same."

"So, how do you find the exit?"

"I can sense my world when the door is open. It gets stronger the closer I get to it. I've barely picked up a hint of it since I got up here from the dungeon."

"Would you be able to feel if there was another door to the space station?"

She liked how he asked the right questions. "I mean, I've been there before, so I would think I could sense it. But I'm not feeling it right now." Her brow furrowed in thought. "I haven't felt anything like it in any of the parts of this dimension I've been in. But, until the last few hours, I hadn't tried. We didn't know the space station was connected to it. And that is the part that makes no sense."

"So, it's possible you haven't felt any connection to the space station because no one had come through a door from there to this place before." He smiled at her surprised expression. "If the exit opens when someone enters…then you might not have had anything to sense. I'm not an expert, but it would be logical if they acted the same way."

"You could be right. It could also be bad timing." It was her turn to smile at him. "You're good at coming up with ideas. If you can figure out the connection between random as hell haunted locations on Earth, a weird dimension full of things from Earth, and a derelict space station on the other side of the universe, I'd be happy to hear it."

"That's a lot of information that doesn't seem to add up." He laughed again.

"Exactly." She sounded discouraged.

"I'll see if I can come up with something. If only to prevent another sigh of frustration." He smiled warmly at her.

She had to laugh. "Well, if that's the motivation you need, I'll sigh in frustration every five minutes or less. I better let Kya know I've partially rescued you now."

"Kya, I'm with Korbin, and he's fine. The door he came through is as dead as any of the other doors on the space station."

"That's good to hear. I'm glad he's safe." Her mind voice was full of relief.

"He seems to have settled into your crew."

"He's turning out to be quite an asset. Although I fully expect his excessively charming personality to get him in trouble at some point." It was obvious she enjoyed his personality.

Sarah Eriksen

"Declan has the same kind of charm, and he hasn't been murdered. Yet." Skye pointed out.

"I don't think there is a force in this universe that will ever stop Declan from being Declan."

"I'm grateful for that." She said it honestly. He drove her crazy, but she'd never want him to change.

"I am too. He has some deep layers hiding underneath his very carefully crafted masks. I worry about him sometimes. But I'm glad you have each other."

"Me too." It was interesting that Kya could see through Declan's public personality. He only let a select few people see those deeper parts of himself. Skye wasn't entirely sure Trey saw anything other than what Declan wanted him to see.

She opened her eyes, her humor bubbling to the surface with a half-smile that revealed the hint of a dimple in her cheek. "Show me this lame-ass sword that can't hit anything."

He grinned and pulled the sword out of a fancy inscribed scabbard, turning it and handing it to her hilt first. She picked it up, noticing the lightness of the blade. It was quite shiny, with pretty designs etched into the metal. It also appeared to be enchanted. She swung it at the candles on the table and laughed as her whole body shifted, and she missed. She tried a few more swings with a similar result.

She gasped with laughter. "That's hilarious."

"I'm relieved you can't hit anything with it either. My dignity has been restored." Her laughter was contagious, and he couldn't help but join her.

Skye pulled out the sword she had picked up and sliced through the candles with ease, traces of laughter lingering in her voice. "It's definitely the sword. I don't know what it's for, but I think it's supposed to be enchanted."

"Like magic?" He didn't sound skeptical, just curious.

"I'm guessing it has a purpose that's not obvious yet."

She thought about how to explain it. "This place seems to be a made-up world with set stories you get to immerse yourself in. You enter this room and immediately find an enchanted sword that is worthless for anything obvious. It's like a quest item you're going to need later. I hope that made some sort of sense."

"I followed well enough. So, we hang on to the magic sword that is currently worthless in case we need it later, as we try to find our way out?"

"Pretty much. You can have the sword that works if you want. I'm okay fighting without a weapon and can always grab another one from one of the guards."

He looked like he wanted to protest and leave her with the weapon, but pragmatism won over chivalry, and he accepted her offer. "It feels so wrong to leave you with the useless weapon, but then I have to remember you are not a normal woman."

She said, "Don't worry, I'll be fine with the broken sword as long as I don't try to hit someone with it. Although, it could be useful for dodging. If you try hard enough to hit something, it'll move you out of the way." She felt for the vague sense of the door back to her world. "It's going to be a bit of a trek to get to the door. Shall we?"

"I'm more than ready to get out of here."

Chapter Twenty-Four

"I told you we were going to get chased by a werewolf." Declan managed to spit out as they bolted through the woods.

Kya merely shook her head, impressed he could speak while they ran. A large half-man half-wolf creature in ripped pants was loping after them.

The dimension had played the scene like an old horror movie. They had come across an injured man, his arm wrapped in a torn piece of cloth saturated with blood. The music hadn't given anything away until the last moment when he suddenly turned into a werewolf.

Declan pointed down the road. There was an abandoned cart with a lit lantern on it. "I think we can use that to light it on fire?"

"Good idea. It was another of those incomplete people, right?"

"Yes, definitely a product of this world." He grabbed the lantern and threw it. It shattered too easily, the oil igniting and splattering over the werewolf. It screamed and bolted back the way it had come before collapsing into a motionless heap.

Declan said sarcastically, "I get the impression you could have thrown the lantern the wrong way, and it would've somehow still hit it."

Kya asked with a hint of a laugh, "You mean it's programmed to kill the werewolf?"

"It gave that impression when I checked to make sure the oil was combustible."

"That's specific. But everything about this place has had a linear feel. One path to follow, easy to find hiding spots, now a lantern designed to always hit the werewolf who chases you?"

"Right. It's like you're meant to be scared but easily survive?" His lips curled in a disgusted sneer. "It's like playing a video game on story mode. You might struggle, but odds are you won't die unless you stand still and let the bad guy kill you."

"I've never played video games, but I understand. This place is designed to frighten you without any real danger. But why would anyone want to deliberately be scared?"

"I get it," Declan replied, pushing a low-hanging branch aside so Kya could move through the narrow path. "We deal with monsters all the time. But we have knowledge, power, and skills to stay alive. Fear for people like us is different. For someone who doesn't know the things we know, going someplace where you can be scared without the danger gives you a thrill and a rush."

"Thrill seeking?"

"Basically. People who go to haunted houses to get scared enjoy the excitement. But most of them wouldn't seek out situations that are actually dangerous. The fact that the 'monsters' in a staged haunted house can't hurt you makes it fun. I guess."

"I see what you're saying, even if I can't imagine wanting to be afraid for fun." Her world had been embroiled in a war for most of her life. Fear was not something she would ever consider enjoyable.

Declan's smile was charming, but he toned down his over-the-top flirting with her. "Are you telling me you aren't having fun running from horror movie monsters?"

She smiled back. "I actually am. It's a nice break from hunting down intergalactic bounties."

"Okay, I'm a little jealous because that kind of sounds fun to me."

Kya stopped and pointed ahead. "There's a town down there. I can feel the door back to your world nearby."

The tangled path they were on connected to a broader road that went straight to the gates. The town huddled against a rocky outcropping. There was a steep hillside full of tall, twisted trees on one side and a raging river of death on the other. The path was still linear from the point they had entered. They had no choice but to go into the town.

Sarah Eriksen

"Oh great, what could possibly go wrong?"

"Do you want me to list that alphabetically?" Kya asked as she stepped onto the main road, and the music took on a mildly suspenseful tone.

"Tate, they had to have something that made them open," Wes said.

"I know, but I'm telling you, there was no measurable power surge. Nothing. Every bit of equipment I have shows that nothing changed. All I can see is they opened."

"Play it again," Wes said softly. He wanted to figure out how the hell the doors kept opening.

The footage was remarkably clear, thanks to Tate's manipulation. They could see where the three pirates had been locked up. Then something opened the hangar door along with the large upstairs hall, releasing the aliens.

Wes asked, "Was there a surge anywhere at all, even something unrelated?"

"Sorry, there was nothing. It's odd. The doors opened down there and on the upper level at the same time." There was no logical reason for them to open on two separate levels simultaneously.

"It's alright, Tate. I'm just frustrated. This makes no sense."

The pirates escaped at the same time the alien had broken out. The ships had been disabled, so they went in search of their companions, only to catch up to the alien running loose.

Wes made a note of the door they had gone through. It was exactly what happened to him and Korbin. The aliens had surprised them, and they had ducked into a room to hide.

"There has to be something that made them open."

Rachel spoke up. "Maybe it's creation magic? I mean, everything Kya told us sounded like a big mess. And it sounded like a lot of the whacky dimension stuff is connected to Kya's cousins' world? So, we won't find something normal."

Wes said, "You're right. I'm going to go take a closer look at those doors."

Tate said, "I'll stay here and keep an eye on things. I'll call out if our alien friends break loose."

Chaotic Haunts

Rachel jumped down from her perch on one of the consoles. "I'll come with you since I missed out on the whole exciting rescue. You might need me to see things you don't." She grinned and sauntered out of the room ahead of Wes.

He smiled at her back. She had a point.

They stopped at the door he had disappeared into. It was a solid panel. Rachel held a small diagnostic tool out and ran a scan. "Nothing there and nothing unusual."

"So, what was different? The aliens were loose. I didn't notice any open doors when Skye was helping us trap them, but I don't know that any of us were paying attention."

"I don't think it's a good idea to set even one of those things loose to see if they're making doors open." Rachel said dryly.

"Wasn't even thinking of it." Wes shuddered at the idea. The crew was more than capable of handling themselves in dangerous situations, but he didn't want to risk it.

Rachel was studying a panel in the middle of the door. "What do you make of this? It's some kind of symbol."

Wes glanced down, bending his head to get a better look. "It's trees in a forest."

"You're seriously getting that from those scribbles?"

"This door took me to a forest full of tall trees. There was also a graveyard." He pointed at some more symbols.

"Okay, I can see it now. None of them noticed that when they were here?"

"It's low enough that you can mistake it for scratches or scuff marks." Considering the state of the space station, it didn't stand out.

Rachel shifted to stand on her tiptoes. "You're right."

"I don't know if I would have made the connection without having been inside. I wonder if all the doors have something like this. The pirates were in some sort of a tomb. Let's go find that one."

They jogged around the curving corridor and found the door. Sure enough, there was a sketched design of a large triangle with odd lines underneath it, and a strange, stylized figure standing in profile.

Rachel shrugged. "It could be a tomb? Do they have large pyramid-shaped tombs on Earth?"

"I think we need an expert to figure that out. And they're all inside the other dimension."

"Can you reach Kya?"

"I can try, but there is something different about communicating into the dimension." Wes closed his eyes and concentrated on reaching his mind out. He clenched his hand into a fist and pounded it against the wall next to the door panel. "Dammit, I need to be able to talk to them."

The door panel flickered faintly at his words.

Rachel exclaimed. "Did you see that?" They exchanged looks, and Wes thumped his fist against the wall. Nothing happened.

Rachel asked, "Maybe it's the words?"

Wes repeated them, hit the wall again, and still nothing.

Rachel tucked a strand of curly blond hair behind her ear. "So, it's not the words or hitting it. Maybe it's the emotion? We've both seen Kya's magic when she's pissed off. Emotions do seem to amplify things."

"You could be onto something. Let me think about it. The aliens saw me, so I wasn't able to turn on my cloaking shield. I needed a place to hide, and then there was an open door."

"The pirates would have needed a hiding spot too."

"Maybe it's the need for a door to be open?" He frowned at the panel in front of him, trying to force a need for it to open, and it flickered. "You're brilliant, Rachel."

"I know." She shrugged nonchalantly. "But we don't want to go jumping into a tomb that killed pirates."

"I don't think we want to jump into any of them." He shuddered at the thought of the pink ball of doom. "We don't want anything from there coming out to us. We're going to have to wait until they get back."

"Why don't we get some pictures of the images on all the doors? Mark off the ones we know with something a bit more visible?"

"Good idea. At least then we'll know which ones to avoid if the aliens break out. Again."

Rachel said archly, "I think you mean when."

"I'm getting tired of these stupid walls. Why don't we follow the maze for a while?" Trey grumbled. They were both tall enough to step over them, but it wasn't easy.

"I'm good with that." Eric sighed in agreement. They had made progress stepping over the walls, but it was getting old. "Watch out for traps."

They had encountered their fair share of pits full of spikes, trip wires, and dangerous tricks. The entire thing would have been horrible to navigate if they were the size the labyrinth had been designed for.

They both studied the layout of the labyrinth, and Trey headed to the left, turning along the paths that continued forward. Worse case, if they ended up with a tricky dead end, they would just step over the wall again. The labyrinth may have been smaller in scale, but it was expansive. It was taking a lot longer than they would have guessed to navigate it to where the door was.

Trey said, "I've been meaning to ask if you've been doing okay after everything that happened on Meriten."

Eric hopped over a section of pressure plates. "Why wouldn't I be okay?" He smiled to himself. There had been some eye-opening revelations with meeting his cousin, but he always took things in stride. And if Trey wanted to pry, it meant he had good intentions but no clue how to express them. He was the clumsier of the twins when it came to emotions.

"I mean, long lost cousin dredging up some horrible shit that happened in your past and having to come to terms with it." And there it was. Trey did not know how to do subtle.

Eric slid around a bushy tree that came up to his chest. "It might come as a surprise to you, but all that horrible shit from my past happened a long time ago, and I have come to terms with it. My family is big on processing trauma and therapy and things like that."

He wasn't lying. His family had helped him deal with what had happened that night. It had been a lot of work to come to terms with it and even more work to learn how to move forward for himself, but he had managed it.

Trey looked surprised. "Oh, well, that's good." It sounded lame as he said it.

Eric said, "I always wanted to meet my cousin, but I didn't know how to find him. And even if I had known where he was, I wouldn't have had a clue how to have a conversation about why he was abandoned by his father and how it tied to me. But it worked out." It had been nice finally meeting him. And he was happy he could fulfill his uncle's wish and help resolve some things for his cousin Rhaeadr.

Trey's awkward discomfort was almost tangible. He clearly wanted to say more but wasn't sure how to approach it.

Eric was too nice to let the uncomfortable silence drag on too long. "Spit it out, Trey. Whatever it is." He could guess the direction it was going to go. Trey had dropped plenty of not-so-subtle hints over the last few years.

"I guess, I was wondering if you were okay since Skye and Rhaeadr were…" his voice trailed off uncomfortably. He didn't like talking about his sister and her personal relationships at all.

Eric chuckled. "I know you have some strange romantic notion in your head with wanting the two of us to hit it off. But, no, it didn't bother me. It was nice to see her happy." He held up a hand before Trey could continue toward conversational territory Eric didn't want to dive into. "Look, I understand where this is coming from, but please stop."

He knew his feelings were hidden and masked better than most guardians. He had asked Amonir for help with that. Whether his choices were right or wrong, they were his. And he knew Skye would quite possibly murder, or at the very least, maim her brother if he tried to interfere in her personal life.

"Okay." Trey gave in grudgingly and changed the subject to a safer topic, pointing at a statue in an open area ahead of them. "I get the feeling the name Skye wanted us to look for will be over there."

Eric watched him jog ahead. He was happy he had successfully diffused Trey's attempt at drawing him out. He appreciated that Trey cared enough to want to help, but he had his reasons for keeping things the way they were. He wished it could be different, but it was better this way. And he valued the friendship he had with the three of them more than he could ever hope to express.

"Ha! Mary Ann Randall," Trey said triumphantly.

The statue was beautifully carved with flowering vines growing up and around in an artful way. Eric had the impression that the vines would always be in a perfect state and never become overgrown. Even with the dimensions seeming to reset, the feel of the statue was more timeless.

"It's beautiful, but it seems sad," Eric said.

"I agree. It's like a memorial." He reached out to Skye. *"We found your mystery name in this labyrinth."* He shared the image of the location with her.

"Interesting. It's starting to feel like a memorial for someone."

"I said the same thing."

"I asked Ian to check out the name. Everything seems to connect to our world somehow, so maybe he'll have some luck."

Eric said, *"I think he will, but who knows what it'll mean."*

Skye laughed. *"At this point, I doubt I'll be surprised with anything we find out."*

"Unless it ends up being something boring and ordinary after all the crazy," Eric said dryly.

"It probably will be because that would be weird in comparison."

Trey said out loud, "Do you feel that?"

Eric turned his head in the direction of the exit point. Something was happening there, and the dimension didn't like it.

"We'll talk later, Skye. Something is happening here," Trey said.

"Be careful, guys."

"What the hell is going on?" Trey exclaimed as he ran toward the exit. There was a loud and angry noise coming from it.

"I think something is trying to come through." Eric placed his hand on top of the wall in front of him to jump over more easily.

"That's not great." Trey loved pointing out the obvious.

"No, it's not. And what the hell would be coming through?"

Trey said, "I'm guessing a pissed off ghost, or a lich, or a wraith, or a revenant."

"I'm not sure which of those would be the worst thing. They're all bad."

"I'm going to hope it's not a ghost. The rest we can do something with at least." He leaped over another wall. "I have a sudden desire to start yelling parkour."

"You'll never live it down if you do."

"If anyone found out, I'd know you told them."

"Exactly. Are you going to take the risk I'd keep that to myself?" Eric laughed.

"When did you become so evil?"

"Maybe Skye is wearing off on me."

Sarah Eriksen

"I would have said Declan."

"Maybe it's you." Eric teased, leaping over the last wall and grabbing Trey's arm to prevent him from tipping into a pit full of sharp spikes.

"Thanks." He looked around as he regained his balance. "So, where's the exit?"

Eric pointed down to a carved panel at the end of the maze corridor they were standing in. It was a little over two feet square. "I think that's it." The panel seemed innocuous but was glowing with angry energy as something pounded on it from the other side.

"Are you fucking kidding me?" Trey said as he eyed the small door. They'd have no problem fitting through it one at a time, but it was going to be awkward.

"I don't know what you're complaining about. You're skinnier than I am." Eric pointed out.

"I guess a run then slide would be the best option to get through it fast and safe." Trey ignored Eric's comment about his wiry build.

Eric stopped him. "Let me go through first."

Trey raised his eyebrows in a silent question, not arguing but wanting to know the reason.

"Skye is still in her part of the dimension. The last thing she needs is you getting hurt by whatever might be on the other side of that door." He made a good point. If it was something they weren't prepared for and Trey got injured, Skye would feel it. If it was bad enough, it could end up getting her hurt as well.

Trey said grudgingly. "You're right. But don't go getting yourself hurt, either. My healing skills are getting a lot better, but you don't want to take a chance on me having to deal with a critical injury."

"Good thing I'm more than capable of healing myself." Eric teased. All guardians could re-distribute energy to speed up their natural healing processes when they had downtime. But being able to fully self-heal an injury in seconds was surprisingly difficult for most guardians. And neither one of the twins could self-heal worth a damn.

"Rub it in, why don't you." Trey laughed. "Let me know what to expect on the other side, so I can be useful as fast as possible, please."

"Of course." Eric took Trey's suggested exit idea and ran toward the small panel watching it open as he neared. He dropped into a slide at the last minute, pulling his arms tightly against his chest, trying to make himself as narrow as possible as he slid through the opening.

He flew through the dimensional door, and his body met with no resistance on the other side as he sunk into frigid ocean water. Instinct kicked in, and he shoved the water away from his face, wrapping it in a small bubble that was suddenly full of air. His body adjusted to the cold as he channeled energy to counterbalance the temperature.

His mind scrambled to find what was on the other side, and he was shocked to find nothing. There was a pocket of air above him. He broke the surface, letting go of his air bubble and raking his wet hair out of his eyes. A heavy board was banging against the portal back to the other dimension.

"It's fine. Just be prepared for a refreshing plunge in the cold ocean." He called to Trey.

Seconds later, the other guardian burst through and fell in a less than graceful plunge into the icy water. The door closed behind Trey as he popped up and took a breath, dipping his head back to get his hair out of his face.

"I guess we know the door doesn't close behind the first person that goes through it. What was trying to get in?"

"A board." Eric pointed to the heavy flotsam banging into the side of the ship where the door had been. "We appear to be in an old, crashed ship somewhere in the Atlantic."

Trey scowled. "You mean *under* the Atlantic."

"In…under…basically the same." Eric shrugged, turning in the water and swimming toward the angled floorboards on the other side of the cabin.

"Other than the whole crushing weight of the ocean over our heads and unexplained pocket of air?" He followed, climbing onto the boards using a touch of energy to dry himself off and warm up. His breath formed a cloud in the chilly air.

"Well, there's that part of it, but we can teleport out." Eric laughed, drying himself off too.

Trey replied to Skye's concerned reaction to his emotions. *"We're fine, Skye, nothing but a ghost ship under the ocean."*

"Is that why you're freaking out?" She asked.

Sarah Eriksen

"I don't want to talk about it." Trey didn't like closed-in spaces much, but for some reason, the idea of being trapped underwater had terrified him as a child. He had learned how to swim, including doing a ton of diving lessons and things to help him overcome his fear. But it didn't mean that he liked it.

"Eric don't let the ocean murder my brother," Skye said.

"I promise I'll protect him from the big bad ocean."

"Knock it off, you two." He looked at Eric. "Let's get back to the space station and see if they could use any help."

"You don't want to explore? There could be treasure. This might have been a pirate ship." Eric was only teasing him a little.

Interest flashed across Trey's face, but then he shook his head. "Nope. We have to be responsible."

Eric laughed. "Can't handle being on a ship under the ocean, but has no problem being on a space station on the other side of the universe. You do keep the mystery alive, Trey."

"If I understood it, I probably wouldn't have these issues anymore."

Chapter Twenty-Five

Skye examined the wand in front of them. It didn't have any magical properties she could see, but it had to be a quest item. They had fought the guards at the end of the hall without any mishaps. Korbin was more than competent with a sword that wasn't defective. The knight inside the room had taken a bit more effort, but they managed to take him down.

The battle revealed a door hidden in an alcove. One of the keys she had looted from the guards in the dungeon unlocked it. They followed a short hallway and ended up in a room with a wand displayed on a pedestal under a beam of light from a stained-glass window.

Korbin said, "It looks like a trap."

Skye agreed. "It does, but I'm not seeing anything that screams trap. No mechanisms, no apparent openings for things to get us. But it's obviously a trap." She crossed her arms over her chest and tapped her foot in irritation.

She was annoyed since this was the last direction they could head in. The rest of the castle had been remarkably small, only the dungeon and a few halls upstairs. This was the only room left, and it was obvious that the wand was going to do something.

She let out a resigned sigh. "Since there aren't any physical traps, it must be magical. Or at least whatever passes for magic in this weird place. And unfortunately, I got nothing."

"So, what's the plan?"

"We grab it at the same time and see what happens?"

Korbin chuckled. "Your sense of adventure is truly inspiring."

"Most people call me reckless." She winked at him as they grabbed the wand together.

Light exploded in the room, and she felt the tug of a teleportation spell. Skye reached her mind out, making sure Korbin stayed with her as the spell dumped them on dew-covered grass in a corridor lined with hedges.

The spell had been fundamentally sound but lacked some pertinent details, making their arrival a lot rougher than it should have been. Skye landed awkwardly, stumbling into Korbin as he fell forward. He wrapped his arms around her reflexively, regaining his balance and keeping both of them on their feet.

"Thanks."

"You're most welcome." He bowed his head and grinned as she stepped back.

The magic wand sparked and crackled on the ground, disintegrating into a handful of wooden splinters. Skye said wryly, "I guess we don't need that anymore. And there's only one way to go."

The dewy lawn stretched in front of them, lined with tall hedges. Small orbs of shimmery blue magic floated in the air, lighting the way.

"I'd love to gallantly take the lead, but from a tactical standpoint, I feel that you are the logical one to go first." Korbin teased.

She reassured him. "Don't worry. If anyone asks, I'll make sure to tell them you heroically led the way."

He said sardonically, "The only people who would hear this story would already know better."

They hadn't made it far when she felt something odd. She stopped abruptly, barely noticing Korbin bumping into her. She held up her hand, gesturing for him to give her a moment. "There's something strange going on."

She closed her eyes to concentrate, sensing Korbin move next to her in a defensive position. She felt it again, a strange flicker coming from the dimension itself. It seemed angry. She wasn't sure she wanted to know how a location could have emotions, but it was a good sign to get out of there.

"I don't know what's going on, but let's move." She didn't want him to panic, but the urgency was clear in her voice. Korbin nodded grimly, hefting the functional sword in his hand and running with her down the path.

Skye's instincts screamed at her. She shoved Korbin back with a push of energy. The ground bucked under her feet, and she launched herself forward into a somersault, turning and sliding across the ground. She regained her footing and lifted her hands, ready to fight.

A rotting hand burst through the ground and clawed at the wet grass, scrabbling to pull the rest of its body through. Guttural snarls filled the air as the zombie forced its way out of the earth. More moans sounded up and down the lawn.

Korbin stepped back as another hand broke out of the ground. "What the hell is this?"

Skye was floored. These were real zombies. This wasn't a product of the dimension. They didn't belong here. No wonder the entire place was reacting the way it was.

"Well fuck." She threw caution to the wind and summoned her swords. Unsteady cascades of sparks and flames flashed around her body as she tried to control her power. She sent a careful flow over Korbin's sword, giving it a magical edge that would work against the zombies.

She thrust her arm down, sliding a blade through the skull of the zombie in front of her that was half out of the ground. It slumped forward briefly and then started clawing at her legs. She stomped down on one decomposing hand, her shoe slipping as the rotting flesh slid off the bones. The ground was too soft, and the zombie's hand sunk into the damp soil instead of breaking.

She let go of the sword and sent a lance of energy into its head. It flared out into a bright halo as it deactivated the reanimation spell. Thankfully, the quick burst of energy hadn't been unstable.

"Skye!" Korbin yelled as he hacked at the zombie pulling its way out of the ground in front of him. He had cut off both hands, but it was still trying to crawl its way out of the damp earth. He swung his sword and took its head off, cursing as the body kept moving.

She watched with consternation and admiration in equal measure. Korbin had some seriously creative and descriptive cursing, but also, the zombie's dismembered bits were still animated.

"Well, that's new." She flicked her hand toward the zombie's head and shot another lance of energy into its skull, disabling the spell with a flash. The body parts slumped to the ground, immobile.

"Sorry about the push." Skye apologized as she crouched down to study the undead remains, ignoring the other reanimated corpses pushing themselves out of the ground around them.

"It's quite alright. I realized what you were doing," Korbin said as he nervously eyed the other zombies that were snarling as they fought the grass and dirt to get out.

"Don't worry, I won't let them get close," Skye said as she held her hand out, getting a feel for the spell. She raised her eyebrows in surprise. "Well, someone a lot more powerful than your run-of-the-mill necromancers reanimated these things."

"What does that mean?"

"I have no clue, but it's probably not good." Skye stood up, glancing at the sword still in her hand and the other stuck in a skull. They hadn't done a lot of good, but she felt better having her normal weapons available. The one in the zombie's head disappeared in a scattering of sparks with a single thought.

Korbin stared at her, his eyes begging her to give a better explanation.

"I honestly don't know what it means. But the good news is, I used my powers and didn't piss off a god. The bad news is that these zombies aren't part of this dimension. They're from outside it. So now we have someone sending zombies into an already dangerous place. On top of everything else."

"You're remarkably calm, considering how bad that sounds."

Her shoulders lifted with a resigned shrug. "After everything I've been through the last few months, a few inexplicable zombies seem pretty minor." She pointed her hand at the corpse behind him that had managed to get most of its body out of the ground, killing it with a blast of energy. "And, since I can use my powers, I'm not too worried about them at the moment." She was more worried about who or what was behind it.

"I guess I can understand that." He stared at the now dead zombie.

Skye reassured him. "Don't worry. I'll get you out of here in one piece. But we should get moving."

"I appreciate it. I never would've imagined returning to a space station full of aliens that refuse to stay locked up would sound so good."

"But it does?" Skye asked with a laugh, turning and sending multiple lances of energy out, killing the zombies in front of them.

"In comparison, yes." He rallied a smile and said, "Not that I'm not enjoying spending this time with you."

Skye admired his ability to flirt while surrounded by reanimated corpses popping out of the ground. She asked, "It's the zombies, right? Too much?"

"I've seen plenty of dead bodies in my time, and I much prefer them when they stay dead."

"You and me both. I've had about enough fun with zombies for a lifetime or five."

The path ended and opened into a large courtyard with flickering colorful lights floating under the branches of an enormous tree. A fountain with a carved figure was centered with multiple-colored lights floating around it.

"I bet that's the statue for this Mary Ann Randall person." Skye pointed.

"And I'm guessing *that* is whatever the useless sword is for." Korbin pointed at a strange dark figure standing in front of an elaborate door on the other side of the courtyard.

Skye followed his hand and nodded. "I think you might be right." She turned her head to the left. The door back to her world was off to the side and not behind the shadowy figure. But then, Korbin had come through from the space station and not Earth. It was possible that following the story in this dimension would lead them to the exit to the station.

"Give me the useless sword, please." She held out her hand. "I'll feel better if I'm the one attacking whatever that is with this worthless piece of pretty metal. We don't know what's going to happen, and I should be able to protect myself at least."

"I really want to argue with you again, but you're right."

Skye held in a laugh at his disgruntled expression. "You have no idea how much I love that you don't argue with me about everything."

He grinned and asked, "Do you get a lot of arguments when it comes to who gets to fight big bad monsters?"

She sighed and stalked forward. "Far more often than I should, and almost exclusively from my brother."

"He's protective, I take it? That seems like it would be an admirable trait in most siblings. My own brother has tried to kill me on more than one occasion. I think I'd like having a brother who didn't want me to die."

"That sounds like a fascinating story I really want to hear someday. And, when you put it that way, I guess an annoying overprotective brother who isn't trying to murder me isn't so bad." As if on cue, she felt a flicker in the back of her mind as something triggered a fear response in Trey.

She sent out a wordless question and felt his reassuring response along with a brief explanation. They were on a ghost ship under the ocean. No wonder he was afraid.

They paused by the fountain. The name was engraved on a silver plaque at the base of the statue. Korbin said quietly, "It's a memorial, isn't it?"

"It's starting to look that way." Skye knew it was right as she said it. Every tribute was done in painstaking and lovely detail. It paid tribute to someone who meant a lot to whoever had created it. The statue was the clearest depiction she had seen so far. It was a young woman, maybe a teenager, and it was clear that it was the same person in each place.

"Do you know what it means?" Korbin asked curiously.

"I don't. And I'm not sure finding out will explain the other things going on. I'm starting to wonder if there's a reason none of this makes sense. We keep trying to find connections, and the only common factor seems to be memorials for this girl." She knew she was talking right now to try and work her way through a tentative and fleeting idea in her mind.

"I agree the connection between your world, this one, and the space station doesn't make any sense to me." Korbin offered helpfully.

Skye studied the shadowy figure on the other side of the courtyard, watching for zombies while she spoke. "That's exactly it. But for the first time, I'm seeing a linear path through a story in this place. If we ignore the fact that I got dumped into a random dungeon that was a dead end, then the point where you entered was the start."

The guards she had encountered had tried to capture her. She wondered if they would have locked her in the dungeon if they had caught her. It would explain the hidden lever to escape from it.

Korbin listened to her and didn't say anything, letting her put her thoughts into words.

"If we assume the door from the space station was the start. The logical path would have been to either avoid the guards at the end of the hall and explore or go immediately to them."

"Right, because after we explored, there was no place else to go except there." He frowned thoughtfully and asked, "Where did you get the key for the door?"

Her eyes lit up. "You're brilliant! The key was on one of the guards in the dungeon. Logical story path, we left the room, had to explore and find a key, then fought the guards and found the next step."

He was caught up in her excitement. "The wand that teleported us here."

"If we ignore the zombies that don't belong, we are now at a courtyard with a creepy figure and a possible exit." She smiled triumphantly at him. "And I can feel the door back to my world, off in that direction." She pointed at a small break in the shrubs off to the side.

Understanding dawned on his face. "If we're following a story, we wouldn't be pushing our way through a hedge into the woods when there's something guarding an obvious door."

"Yep. I guess the only way to test our theory would be to go fight the shadow monster with the useless sword and see what happens."

"Is this what you do all the time? As a guardian, I mean." His voice was tentative as if he hadn't had to say those words out loud before. Kya had told him about everything, but now he was living in a new kind of reality that was vastly different than what he was used to.

"Nope. I can safely say this is not remotely normal compared to anything I've dealt with. And I've seen and handled some weird shit. Of course, what I consider normal might be kind of out there." One thing about being a guardian, your life was guaranteed to never be dull.

She gestured for him to stay back and moved toward the shadowy figure, holding the magic sword in her right hand, and her own sword in her left. She spared a mental laugh at the difference. Her sword sparked and flashed, glowing with true power. The other blade was dull in comparison, even though it passed for magic in this dimension.

The shadowy figure expanded and grew, and a deep voice bellowed out, "You will not pass."

"I think you'll find that I will too pass," Skye said, rolling her eyes at the rather obvious dialogue choice.

A blast of darkness flew at her, and she raised the useless sword. It exploded with light, glowing a vibrant pure white with rainbow flashes in the brightness. The darkness burnt away as the light glowing around the blade hit it.

Skye had to admit it was an impressive display, even though to her guardian senses, it was not much more than a light show. She swung the bright blade forward as the darkness dissipated, and a beam of light flew out and pierced the shadowy figure. Light built inside of it, and it cracked, exploding with the force of the energy.

She blinked as the light dissipated and the sword returned to its useless if pretty form.

Korbin said, "That was incredibly impressive."

Skye turned to him with an unimpressed frown. "It was certainly a light show."

"You didn't think much of it, I take it?" He asked with a laugh.

She shook her head and said, "It felt kind of contrived and underwhelming." She was used to some spectacular magic, so maybe she was being overly critical.

He gestured to the incandescent sword in her hand. "I suppose in comparison to that, it's rather unimpressive."

Skye couldn't help but smile at his wry comment. "I guess if you aren't used to seeing guardian powers, this would have been pretty spectacular."

"The little I've seen of your powers has been impressive for certain. But to me, and I don't mean this as an insult, that light show was easily as remarkable." He grimaced apologetically, worried he might have offended her with his comparison.

Skye considered what he said. Everything seemed staged, like a video game or a movie. This was a magic battle, and it made sense that it was more for show. It would also explain why everything was so easy to kill. Or at least why the things from inside the dimension were easy to kill.

Chaotic Haunts

"You're frowning again, and that was not my intention. I'm sorry if I offended you."

She hurried to reassure him. "You don't have anything to apologize for, I'm not offended. There are too many thoughts in my mind trying to figure this place out. And that being said…we killed the bad guy, so I guess we try the door?"

Korbin gestured for her to go ahead, grinning and bowing slightly. She shook her head with another smile and placed her hand on the door. It warmed up, and a new sensation that was both familiar and different appeared. The carved panels slid outward, revealing a murky portal and a clear feeling of the space station, as well as the presence of her twin and Eric close to it.

She froze in confusion as her mind pinpointed the location and time. She had traveled back a few hours, and it hadn't been long enough to make up for the jump and the normal forward flow of time. And yet, she had caught up to when she would have ended without the time jump.

"Amonir?" Her mind voice was concerned enough to get his immediate attention.

He quickly assessed the situation. *"It's nothing to worry about. It appears that Time was concerned with you being out of sync with the others when you talked to them, so the dimension adjusted the flow of time to get you back."*

"I didn't feel a thing." That was more than a bit odd. She had always been exceptionally aware of the flow of time.

"Don't worry about it. It seems to be built into the time flow of this dimension. It's fairly complicated but would account for the time resetting each day."

Skye rubbed her forehead, feeling the start of a headache as she tried to wrap her mind around messed-up dimensional time. She gave up and filed it away under 'it is what it is' in her mind.

She turned to Korbin, pointing at the portal. "That goes back to your space station. I told you I'd get you back in one piece."

"Thank you, Skye. I mean it." He lifted her hand, placing a gentle kiss on the back of it and gazing up at her with a charming, flirtatious smile.

"You're welcome, space pirate." Her mischievous grin had a charm that was all her own.

Sarah Eriksen

He straightened up and shook his head in resignation, smiling at her impudent teasing. "I believe it's former smuggler turned mercenary."

"Still sounds like a space pirate to me."

A loud rumble of raw, angry emotion raged in the distance from the direction of the door back to Earth. Skye scowled as she turned her head toward it.

"Guess I'd better go see what's pissing off the dimension over there. I'm sure I'll see you again soon." She winked at him.

His smile faded as he followed her gaze to the angry red sky. His voice was quiet as he asked, "Do you need any help?"

"If it's something from my world, it'll probably be better for me to go alone. But thank you. I'll be back as soon as I see what this new fun is." She glanced at the murky opening, "Something exciting must be happening on the space station."

"Exciting good or exciting bad?"

"Not bad, but interesting, maybe." Her brother's emotions were a mix of excitement and curiosity.

He said, "Thank you again."

"You're welcome." He ducked through the door, disappearing on the other side. She took a moment to study the energy holding the exit open. She nudged her twin and shared the information she could gather from her side as he studied the other side.

"I'm going to go see what's happening at the exit back to our world, but maybe this will give us some insight into how these doors work on the space station."

"It can't hurt. Wes thinks the doors opened for him, Korbin, and the space pirates because of need. They were being chased by rampaging aliens on the loose, so that might have been the trigger."

"Strong emotional response to power it? I can see that."

"Yep, and now at least we can see how the exits are working."

She had shared the little bits of information with him the entire time she had explored. The idea that the space station might be the starting point was starting to sound more and more promising. Even though it didn't solve the whole problem with the ghosts and haunted houses, and who had opened those doors.

"This gives us a whole lot more questions than answers."

"Yeah, like who the hell put zombies in there with you?"

"Yep. But bonus, apparently using our powers is okay. At least so far." Her voice sounded more optimistic than she felt.

"Yeah, well be careful."

"Have Declan and Kya made it back yet?"

"Nope."

Skye reached out with her mind and laughed at Declan's grumpy reply. "They're fine. Just being chased by someone with a chainsaw."

"Seriously?"

"That's what he said. And Kya didn't contradict."

"I can't wait to hear about it. See you soon. Be careful."

"Yes, Mister bossy sir."

Sarah Eriksen

Chapter Twenty-Six

Skye felt a mental nudge followed by Eric roughly entering her mind. She had kept her light touch on his mind, so his clumsy contact was a little surprising.

"*I'm so sorry about that.*" He apologized.

"*It's okay. It wasn't as bad as Declan's attempt earlier.*" She laughed.

"*I could still feel your mind, so I figured I'd be able to talk. Then the door closed, and it wasn't as easy as I thought it would be. It's like stumbling in the dark and vaguely knowing where you are, then crashing into you.*"

"*That's a good description. I wonder why it's like that.*"

"*And why you have no trouble?*" He asked.

"*Pretty much. It's on the list of questions about this place I have no answer to.*"

"*Want my theory for the mind-to-mind talking?*"

She did want to know his opinion. He had a way of looking at things that made sense. "*I'd love to hear it.*" She pushed through the split in the hedge.

"*I don't think you see it as an obstacle, and your new powers give you a boost. I know Kya mentioned your strength with mind magic because of your twin connection. But that would imply that Trey would be able to communicate as easily.*"

"*Right, he wasn't able to reach Declan or Kya on his own.*" Her tone turned suspicious, and she asked, "*What are you implying with me not *seeing an obstacle?"* She could feel him shake his head and fight a laugh.

"In the time I've known you, any obstacles that come your way, you just push through them...past them...over them? Look at what you did with your ability to channel creation energy. We were in battles that were completely insane. The rest of us struggled, and you did what you had to do to fight." His voice held a note of apology but also a lot of admiration. *"I don't know if I explained that well, and I mean it as a compliment. You have the kind of strength that doesn't let things get in your way."*

"I understood what you meant. And thank you." She was surprised and flattered by his compliment. *"So, you think I have no issues communicating through the weird dimensional walls because I wanted to reach out and talk to you guys, and so I did it, blatantly ignoring whatever might have been in my way."*

"Basically, yes." His mental voice held a hint of a smile. If she was able to talk through a barrier across dimensions that was blocking everyone else, it was impressive. It meant she not only viewed it as something that wasn't an obstacle. It meant she could break down the barrier itself with her mind and make it so it wasn't an obstacle. She had always had a talent for adapting to things instantly. It was how her mind worked.

"Well, that makes more sense than most things this place has thrown at us. But please don't ever try and explain it to Declan because I'll never hear the end of it."

"Noted." He said with a laugh. *"I must admit I'm curious how Declan could still feel your mind while you were a few hours behind us in time. I couldn't sense anything until you caught back up to when we were."*

She hadn't even noticed that. It was surprising. *"Maybe he could find me since he's so used to the weird twin thing and time travel. He has been with us longer than you. But, curiosity aside, I'm sure you didn't pop in here to tell me all of that, so what's up?"*

"Right, sorry again. When we exited back to our world, it felt like something was trying to come in. The energy seemed kind of angry, and it sounded like something was attacking the other side. When I slid through, it was only a board banging against it with the current. I didn't

sense anything else once I was through. Something about it doesn't feel right to me."

"Don't apologize for things you don't need to apologize for. And, while it's a logical explanation for the sound at the door, your gut is telling you something was trying to come through that wasn't shipwreck flotsam?"

"Maybe I'm being paranoid." He sounded troubled.

"No. You're not prone to overreacting, so I bet there was something. We've now encountered a lich, a wraith, and a revenant at the doors we came through to enter this dimension. It makes sense that something could be at the exits."

"And something is messing with the exit where you are?"

"That's what it feels like."

"And you had zombies from our world inside." He was trying to wrap his mind around it.

"Yeah, try and figure that out. It feels the same right now, maybe more intense. Just like when the zombies popped out of the ground." She was walking through scrubby undergrowth and trees toward the door. It was like she had stepped into an unfinished garden that needed some serious weeding and maintenance.

"I don't know what difference it would make, but is the edge of the dimension under the ground? I tried to find the edge in the labyrinth, and it was kind of like an invisible wall. When I looked down, it didn't seem to go too far below the surface."

Skye hadn't thought about that. The zombies had been popping up from underneath, which was typical behavior. *"Hold on."* She searched with her mind back to where the zombies had been popping up, and sure enough, the dimension only stretched down a short distance, and there were some rough patches where they had ripped through.

"Well, look at that." She shared what she had found. "Whoever sent them here punched through the dimension."

"And other than the space itself being...annoyed by it, nothing else happened?"

"Yeah, nothing. And I used creation energy, at least enough to summon my swords and spells to kill the zombies and didn't draw any attention."

"I think the zombies alone would've been noticed."

Chaotic Haunts

Skye stopped mid-step, her foot dropping to the ground awkwardly, making her stumble and catch herself with a hand against a tree. *"This place is abandoned."*

"Abandoned?" Eric sounded incredulous.

"Think about it. Everything in here resets itself and starts over each night. It's connected to a space station with possible doors and maybe even a direct storyline from those doors. I'll have to do some digging there. But there hasn't been any signs of anyone here." Her mind dragged up the few moments when she thought she felt someone in the dimension. Each encounter had been too brief to be sure it was a person.

"I can feel you thinking harder than the words you're saying," Eric said, picking up her feelings.

"Yeah, I'm not sure...but there are some ideas churning in there. Let me wrap this up, and I'll see you back on the space station."

"Please be careful." Unlike Trey, he didn't sound overbearing, only concerned.

Instead of her usual flippant reply, she said, *"Always."*

Declan pushed his body back as far as he could in the tight space they had ducked into. Kya's dark violet eyes promised certain death if he said anything about the way their bodies were currently pressed together in the close quarters they were hiding in.

As much as he loved driving people crazy, he knew when not to push his luck. The massive man in overalls with a mask and chain saw who had leaped out at them and chased them into the town was enough to make him behave.

They had ducked into an alley that twisted and curved around the tall buildings in the town and found a small storage shed full of ale barrels. There was barely enough space for one person to hide comfortably. In their case, it was just enough space for them to squeeze together and close the door, with no room left. He was glad there was plenty of airflow above them.

They both tensed up as the sound of the chainsaw grew closer and the background music built up with disturbing intensity. He got ready to draw in creation energy to defend them, feeling Kya doing the same. The seconds seemed to drag out forever as a shadow paused outside the door, the chainsaw rumbling and sputtering.

Sarah Eriksen

The tension built up and then passed as the man finally moved away. Declan asked, *"Do we wait until the music tells us it's safe?"*

"That's probably the best idea. Correct me if I'm wrong, but the chances of another jump scare are pretty high?"

"You're not wrong. The music could be designed to fake us out." He considered how the dimension had played out so far with suspenseful tension. A jump scare would make them run again, which would seem to defeat the purpose. Everything had been linear so far. *"I don't know if chainsaw man would chase us again unless there's another clear path and hiding spot for us."*

"I guess it has been pretty obvious so far." The music shifted back to a calm and pretty background sound, with a hint of something upbeat. *"That's new."*

"Maybe there's a party in the town?"

Kya reached behind her to grab the handle, pushing the door open carefully. She turned her body slightly so she could peer out into the dark alleyway. *"I can't sense the chainsaw man anymore."*

"Me either. I guess we step out and be prepared to run again."

"I guess so." She pushed the door open the rest of the way and stepped outside.

Declan followed, allowing one wicked grin to cross his face without Kya seeing it. He did have good sense when it came to self-preservation, but it didn't mean he hadn't enjoyed the close quarters. He just knew better than to let her see it.

Kya said softly, "You can see his footprints in the dirt."

"Well, that's something, at least. Do we follow?"

"It's the right direction. Might as well."

"Maybe it'll give us a head's up if he's going to jump out at us." Declan followed Kya down the alley. The music kept shifting away from haunting to upbeat. He kept his eye out for the empty mind of the chainsaw man or any other scary construct character.

They were almost to the end of the alley when the footprints disappeared. They stopped dead in their tracks, exchanging a flicker of a worried glance and immediately shifting back to back, hands raised defensively.

"What are the odds he's going to do a last-ditch jump and *almost* get us as we leave the alley?" Declan asked sarcastically. This place was starting to push his limits on what he was able to find funny.

Kya felt the same as him. "I think the odds are high. Not that there's any place for him to hide, and he obviously disappeared into thin air."

"Might as well get it over with then." By unspoken agreement, they both bolted to the end of the alley and burst out into the open town square. The music spiked with violent intensity as the chainsaw man suddenly jumped out of the alley behind them, narrowly missing their backs with the blade.

Declan spun, ready to send a blast of energy out to knock back the man. He stared in shock as the figure was grabbed by tendrils of shadow from the alley and pulled back into darkness, struggling the entire time. The sound of the chainsaw abruptly cut off, and the music resumed its cheerful, upbeat tone.

"In what horror movie does the bad guy chasing you get eaten by shadows?" Kya asked.

"The one we're in, apparently," Declan replied with a laugh. "Awfully convenient that the scary bad things get eaten up by something else."

"Let's hope the monster-eating shadow doesn't decide to eat us too." She glanced around, taking in the new location.

It was a large town square lined with stalls and covered awnings. Brightly colored glass and paper lanterns hung from posts and wires that stretched overhead. The merchants and vendors hawked their wares and haggled with the villagers. Every one of them was a clear construct from inside the dimension.

"Declan, I've seen plenty of things in my travels that could positively blow your mind. But this *is* really strange, isn't it? It's not just me?" Kya was clearly at a loss on how to process the sight before them.

"It's not you. It's weird as hell." He answered. It was as if someone had taken every kind of nerdy collector item imaginable and stuck it in a middle age era village market. "I mean, this would be normal at a convention, but here—" He shook his head. It was one of the more peculiar things he had seen so far in this dimension.

"I'm not sure if that makes me feel better or not." Kya laughed as they walked through the market, carefully moving around villagers.

Sarah Eriksen

Declan said, "You've been a guardian in a very specific place for a long time now. I think you should give yourself more credit. Even with the size of the galaxy you work in, things would fit in ways you'd expect. A market on a world you've never been on probably has different kinds of merchandise that you haven't seen before, but it'd fit there."

He gestured around them. "Nothing about this place makes any sense. Being a guardian on Earth and dealing with the trouble that has come our way the last few months seems normal compared to this."

Kya's eyes were thoughtful as she studied his face. "It's always a surprise when you show this side of yourself instead of hiding it deep under all that charm and deliberately irritating attitude."

His smirk held a hint of self-mocking, and he deflected, "I don't know what you're talking about."

"You know exactly what I'm talking about."

Declan wasn't surprised Kya could see his outward behavior for what it really was. She was a lot like her cousin in that respect. Skye was the only person who had ever seen through the carefully constructed masks he had built over his entire life as a way to protect himself. She understood him better than anyone and accepted him for who he was in every way. It was why he considered her his best friend. And why he went out of his way to make sure he was there for her.

They left the market on the main road that headed toward the outer wall of the town. The music picked up a faintly ominous tone again. The wall was made of stone with a large gate for carts and a smaller door that could let a single person out. A guard post was built directly into the wall with a tower above. The rough wooden door into the guard post had a familiar feel.

"There's the exit to Earth." He pointed.

Kya studied it. "Same as the entrance door but opposite directional energies." She had an interesting perspective with her background in elven battle magic.

They exchanged surprised looks as Skye reached out to them to tell them she had something bad on the other side of her dimension trying to break in.

Declan grimaced. "Zombies from our world popping out of the ground and now bad things trying to come through the wrong door. The fun just keeps on going."

Chaotic Haunts

"I don't sense anything like what she is dealing with here."

"Me either, but it would make sense if the usual suspects that love hauntings were at the entrance points, they might show up at the exits too. At least now we know we can use our normal powers while we're inside. Which would have been nice to know earlier," he grumbled, knowing exactly why they had to be cautious the entire time. He was just done with the horror movie chase scene world they had spent far too long in.

"I never sensed any door back to the space station," Kya said as they walked to the exit.

"It's probably outside the town." Declan could feel the road going off into the distance a decent way before it got murky and hard to see. The ominous music picked up as they got closer to the gate.

"That would explain the music then."

"That or something is going to try and murder us as we leave," Declan said with a cheerful grin.

Kya sighed. His serious and thoughtful personality could only surface for so long before he reverted to his typical self. "If that's the case, I'm going through the door first."

"That's fine. We don't know what's going to be on the other side. It could be worse." He wasn't opposed to heading into danger first, but he was right. It was a toss-up as far as what was more dangerous…going first through the door or being the one who was still in this dimension.

"Either way, luck to both of us," Kya said as a faint purple glow formed over her body in a defensive shield. She stepped through the door.

The music spiked as soon as she moved, and Declan leaped back as a creepy clown jumped out of the shadows to the left of him. He had definitely had enough. He held out his hand, and a wood cutter's ax flew into it from across the clearing. He wasn't about to take a chance and kill a construct from this dimension with his powers. Skye had only used them to kill zombies from their world, after all.

He swung the ax with one powerful two-handed blow straight into the clown's head, splitting the comically small hat in half and lodging it firmly in its skull. He kicked his foot forward, knocking the now dead clown back and stepping through the door, muttering angry words under his breath. He hated clowns.

Sarah Eriksen

He stepped out of a small painted closet door and tripped over a haphazard pile of toys and stuffed animals, biting back a curse as he awkwardly regained his footing. He glared at Kya, who had navigated the clutter without stepping on anything. They were in a small room full of toys and cute frilly decorations.

"Are you a fairy princess?" A young girl asked Kya, excitement in her voice. Declan's less than graceful entrance had woken her up.

Declan fought back a laugh as he watched the surprise wash over Kya's face. She was tall, beautiful, and glowing with purple energy. Her clothing was more functional for combat and all black which didn't scream fairy princess, but the little girl, who was probably only five years old, didn't seem to mind.

The little girl's eyes lit up as she saw Declan. "He's your knight."

"This is suddenly not as humorous as it was a second ago." Declan's mental tone sounded irritated, but he gave the girl a charming smile and dashing bow, searching the house for creatures.

"I have some concerns over what she thinks fairies are like if she's mistaking us for them."

"Well, you are *an elf princess. It's close enough. I'm more concerned that she thinks I'm your knight in shining armor."* He was wearing jeans and a NIN t-shirt. *"But I think we should be more worried about the location of this door and the whole ghost thing."* He felt her wordless agreement.

Kya played along with the girl's story. "I am a princess. And I'm on a quest to save my realm. Have you seen anything scary come out of this door?" She wove a quick spell of silence over the room. The last thing they wanted was any more attention in the house they were in.

The little girl's eyes widened. "You're going to fight the monsters in my closet?"

Declan and Kya exchanged concerned looks, and Kya asked, "Do the monsters stay in your closet, or do they come out into your room like us?"

"They're just there." She shrugged, clearly uncomfortable. "Like the lady that walks in the hall. Mommy and daddy said they're not real." Her voice was sad, and her gaze dropped down to her blanket.

Declan reached out, *"Amonir, we have to do something immediately to protect this kid."* He relayed the information about the door. It was bad enough that real monsters were showing up in haunted houses that were full of adults. It was another thing for a door to a dangerous dimension to open up into a kid's room.

Kya knelt by the little girl's bed. "We believe you. And my knight protector here is going to make sure nothing bad comes out of this closet and gets you."

Declan felt Amonir's instructions and turned to face the closet, holding his hands out in front of him. His usual bright green energy took on a deeper hue as the god channeled his power through his guardian. Lines of verdant light spiraled out in a complicated knot that covered the door like vines. Small bursts of golden light like flowers blossomed where the lines crossed. The energy grew brighter and more intense and flashed once, fading back as the door was sealed with Amonir's powers.

"That will keep her safe. And you can reassure her that the lady that walks the halls doesn't want to hurt her. She's a faint residual memory. She was acting up because of the possible danger the door had presented. It should stop now, but I will personally look out for her."

"Thank you." Declan was relieved. No kids should have to deal with ghosts, monsters, and horrors, no matter their age.

He turned to the little girl, kneeling next to Kya. "No monsters will ever come through that door now. You have my word as a knight of this realm." He held up a hand, bright green light blossoming from his palm. *"Little help Kya."*

She saw the picture in his mind and held her hand over his, purple energy spiraling into the green, forming a stunning dark purple lily with a faint lavender glow inside. Declan's powers changed the energy into a perfect living flower. He handed it to the little girl. "This is for you. Any time you feel scared, hold onto it, and nothing will harm you. No monsters, and not the lady in the hall. And no one will be able to see what it is except you."

He had left a trace of creation energy that would react to her emotions. If she was scared, the energy would expand enough to make any ordinary ghosts go away. Anything else, a guardian would be called to take care of anyway. He trusted Amonir to keep her safe, but he didn't want her to be scared. At least he could help with that much.

Sarah Eriksen

The little girl's eyes grew wide as he handed her the flower, and she clenched it in her fists. Her mouth opened in wonder, and she stared at them.

Kya said, "Be brave little one. We have to go to finish our mission to protect the realms from monsters." She gracefully accepted Declan's outstretched hand to help her stand. She stood with her hand resting lightly atop his, and both of them glowed with radiant creation energy, faint hints of magic wings appearing behind them, and they disappeared.

"The wings were a nice touch." Declan laughed.

"She wanted us to be fairies. It seemed appropriate."

Trey stared at them as they reappeared on the space station and shook his head at their gracefully touching hands. "Do I want to know what the hell happened to you two in there?"

Declan raised an eloquent eyebrow and said, "When a little girl wants to believe you're a knight with a fairy princess, you give her what she wants."

"Knight and fairy princess?" Trey asked incredulously, taking in their appearance.

Kya was not above mischief and asked, "Is that so hard to believe?" She exchanged a look with Declan, and they both leveled challenging glares at Trey, daring him to say anything.

He opened his mouth and closed it a few times before surrendering to their united front. "Okay. You two win. But under no circumstances am I ever calling you your highness." He shook his head in disbelief.

Declan smirked. "Well, that's technically the correct way to address your cousin since she is, in fact, a princess. In case you forgot."

"Do you really want me to start calling you a fairy prince?" Trey asked acidly.

Declan burst out laughing.

Chapter Twenty-Seven

Skye hacked the grasping, rotting hand from its equally rotting arm with a slash of her sword. She held her left hand up, palm out, and a lance of bright energy shot into the zombie's head. The forest was filling with more and more undead clambering up through the mossy ground.

"This is getting ridiculous." She was never going to get to the door if she had to take out zombies every few steps. She slapped her sword to her back, magically sheathing it. She leaped upward with a spark-filled boost of energy, grabbing a branch and pulling herself higher into the tree. She straddled a large limb and leaned back against the trunk, ignoring the zombies gathering below her.

Ever since the attacks that had ultimately triggered her current new power levels, she hadn't had a lot of time by herself to process what everything meant. It was possible that sitting in a tree in a pocket dimension that made no sense, surrounded by hordes of zombies, was what she needed right now. Or maybe it was the fact that no one, other than Trey, could talk to her unless she wanted to talk to them while she was there.

It was time to analyze what she knew. Everything had started with sparks, and eventually, the dam burst open, and a massive amount of creation energy was available to her. She hadn't had any issues using it to foil the evil plot that was going to destroy the world.

Amonir had given her some tricks to mask the visual signs of channeling so much power. She could use more energy to make it invisible or control the amount she pulled, so it didn't have a visual manifestation. It seemed easy enough to manage, and it had worked.

But then, she had gone to Meriten and hadn't used her powers often. When she tried to use controlled amounts, the sparks had still been there, but they were faint. She had chalked it up to needing practice at pulling less energy. The times she let loose, she had been around people whom she didn't have to hide from. So, it hadn't mattered that she burst into flames and sparks.

She had struggled ever since she had returned home. It was hard to control the flow of energy. When she tried to do normal things, she sparked and flashed, and had very little finesse. It was like using a sledgehammer to stick a push pin into a corkboard.

The more she tried to control her powers, the harder it seemed to be. She knew she had kept her struggles to herself as she tried to figure it out. It was easier for her to work through things on her own most of the time.

It was also partly because she felt isolated and alone already and didn't want to burden her friends with things they couldn't fix. Whether she liked it or not, she was different now, and she had to deal with it. Her friends weren't treating her any differently. There was the teasing and banter about her powers, of course, but that helped maintain a sense of normalcy.

She could feel something big looming on the horizon. Things were changing. *She* was changing, and there wasn't much she could do about it. She had always struggled with loneliness, and she was holding tightly to how things were because it was comfortable. It was safe.

But she couldn't keep playing it safe. Not anymore. She had to get her shit together and get past all of this. She reached out to the one person she knew would understand.

"Hey, Declan."

"Yes, oh great and powerful, Skye?" He never could resist teasing her.

She wordlessly shared her feelings and struggles with him. His mental presence sobered as he took it in. He had seen and felt a lot of it, but she was showing him everything, and as usual, it scared her to open up that much.

He took a moment to process it along with what he had observed himself. *"Can I give you my honest and unvarnished opinion on all that?"*

"It's why I showed you." She blinked back tears of frustration.

"I think you're struggling because you're holding back. I think the tips Amonir gave you were to help you while you adjusted to things, not the permanent solution. You've been trying to force the sun to behave like a flashlight because you know how to work with a flashlight. You were trained to work with a flashlight. But it doesn't work for you anymore because you've outgrown it." He was blunt but also compassionate.

"So, since I'm trying to do things how I've always done them...forcing my powers into familiar levels, it's fluctuating and causing the sparks and flashy fire."

"Yes. I think you're always going to have the whole bursting into flames thing when you use your powers fully. But I also think if you stop holding back and stop trying to do everything the same, you'll have no issue doing things without the flashy fire show. You already do it sometimes. When you don't overthink it, you just use your powers, and it works without the internal struggle."

He could feel her processing his words and gave her a moment before he continued. *"I know that it seems backward to stop holding back. And I'm not saying to blow up stuff with no finesse and lots of energy. Although, that might be the solution sometimes. You know the 'whys' behind how we fight monsters. You just have to think outside the box. You did it with the revenant. Normal procedure is a long, drawn-out fight while you chip away at the defensive spells with your attacks until you can kill it. You can skip it and go right to the end."*

"But how do I stop holding back?" She wasn't asking about the process of using her powers. The real obstacle was herself.

Declan said compassionately, *"I think a part of you is afraid of acknowledging what you can do. Afraid of being different. Afraid of the loneliness that comes with it. Afraid of the changes it might lead to. I know you're smart enough to know that the people who truly care about you will accept you no matter what. Even if Trey has to be a bit of a drama queen about it at first."* He ended his observations with a light note to make her laugh.

Sarah Eriksen

She managed a smile at his attempt at humor but asked seriously, *"Do you think part of this is me reacting to how he reacted at first?"*

"I think you'd still have these struggles even if he had been accepting and supportive from the start. This is a big deal. Things are changing, and that can be terrifying. I've seen how hard it's been for you. The thing is change is a part of life for everyone. But at the end of the day, you're still you. And the people who matter will stick around and be there for you when you need them." He paused and said softly, *"At least, I promise I will."*

"Thanks, Declan." Her mind and emotions conveyed the depths of her gratitude for far more than the words alone could convey. She understood why he had been joining her on her investigations now.

"You're welcome. Besides, I might need an overpowered friend someday when I do something like piss off a super powerful entity."

"Well, that is inevitable."

He sent her an impression of his token smirk and wink and disappeared.

She considered his words. She had been holding back and trying to force herself to fit into what was familiar, comfortable, and safe. He was right. She had to accept it. All of it. She took a deep breath and opened her mind up to the flow of creation energy.

Coldfire blazed around her as energy filled her. There were no sparks, no dramatic explosion of unstable flame, only pure, limitless energy. She held her hands in front of her and watched the bright blue-white flames with small vortices of deep blue swirling around as the fire danced over her skin.

She could feel the difference. Before, it had been a slow build-up as she drew on more and more power until she couldn't contain it. But it wasn't about containment or drawing less to keep it hidden. It was just there, all around her. The flames disappeared with a thought, but the energy stayed.

Amonir spoke to her, pride in his mental voice. *"I knew you'd figure it out, guardian."*

"Even if Declan had to point out the obvious to me?"

"That's what friends are for. You had figured it out. You just needed him to tell you what you already knew." His mental voice faded away from her mind.

Chaotic Haunts

She swung her leg over the branch and dropped to the ground, coldfire blasting out around her in a wave, knocking the zombies back and disabling the reanimation spell at the same time. Flickering flames spread out around her far into the woods and into the ground below, taking out the horde of undead in seconds.

The flames faded back into her skin. She no longer felt off balance. She shook her head. All she had to do to learn control was to let go of control. "That's a little irritatingly deep, but I'll take it," she muttered to herself and leaped over the corpses at her feet, heading to the door back to her world.

She exited the woods into a large clearing with a lake off to one side and the crumbled remains of a stone tower. It had an oddly intact wooden door that was her exit. A rough wooden sign was stabbed into the ground on a small path leading to the shore.

The woods had felt like an unfinished part of a game, but the path and sign made her wonder. She couldn't help herself. She moved closer to the sign to see what it said. It was a warning.

She read it out loud, puzzled by the words. "Beware! Rodak Beavers?" She turned toward the lake, seeing the piled branches blocking the flow of water downstream. A small hint of a wake appeared in the water, and she shook her head, backing up. She didn't want to know what a Rodak Beaver was and why it required a warning sign.

She stepped out into an incredibly organized, dusty, old classroom. She was in an abandoned school building in Japan. With the dimension correcting her time jump, and the time she had spent inside it, it was early evening in Japan on the following day from where she had started. She stopped herself from overthinking the time jumps before a headache could set in.

The structure creaked softly, and wind whispered through hidden gaps. The entire place looked and sounded haunted. She had to make sure it was secure before she headed back to the space station.

She could sense three liches lurking below. She let out an exasperated puff of air and muttered, "Great." She wasn't surprised. If creatures were at entrances, it made sense for them to be at the exits. At least the building was otherwise abandoned, and she could test out her newfound inner mental peace of mind and blow some monsters up with magic.

Sarah Eriksen

The beautifully crafted door slid open easily despite its age. She stepped silently into the corridor, walking slowly to the end of the hall, and getting the layout of the entire building with her mind. It was easy to take things like that for granted. The strange dimension put things back into perspective.

She turned the corner and jumped back, a soft gasp of air escaping her mouth. The man standing in the hall jumped and ducked, turning at the same time. Skye stared at him, trying to process how she hadn't been able to sense him. She had looked for people, not just creatures. His presence was perfectly clear to her now, but something about it felt off. She didn't like it.

He whispered, "You almost gave me a heart attack."

Skye whispered back with a salty tone, "Probably not a smart idea to sneak around a haunted house if your heart isn't strong enough to handle scary things."

He fought back a smile and said, "I didn't know anyone else was here. Other than ghosts." He gave her a charming smile. "Are you a ghost?"

"Not that I'm aware of." She was normally one to joke and banter, but there was something about him that she didn't like. She couldn't quite put her finger on it, but she always trusted her gut instincts.

"Well, if you are, you're much more beautiful than the ghosts I saw downstairs." That charming and unsettling smile appeared on his face again.

Skye ignored the slimy compliment. "So, you saw scary ghosts downstairs, and you're hiding upstairs instead of getting out of the haunted house?"

He had to be referring to the liches. Skye moved past him to the balcony railing, her feet making no sound on the wooden floor. She peered over the edge. The landing was clear, and she could sense them further down the hallway toward the main doors.

"I didn't have much of a choice. They're blocking the front door." A wrinkle appeared between his brows. He didn't seem to know what to make of her. "How did you get in here? I didn't see any other cars outside, and there's only one road in."

"I walked." She wasn't lying. She had walked through the parallel dimension. He was lying, though. There were plenty of perfectly functioning doors downstairs he could have used to leave.

Chaotic Haunts

His charming smile appeared again. "Well, I'd be happy to help you get out of here and give you a lift back to town."

"That's a very kind offer, but no thanks." She turned to him. "Stay up here. I want to go see the scary ghosts for myself."

He reached out to grab her arm, his hand freezing in the air a few inches away from her as he caught the dangerous expression on her face. He pulled his hand back, smiling again and tilting his head in apology. "Sorry. I've been in a lot of haunted houses, and I've never seen anything like those ghosts. And while I don't like to admit it, I've never been scared in a haunted house until this one."

Skye's temper was short, and she was exhausted. This exchange was getting old fast, and she had places to be. "That's because they aren't ghosts. And you should be scared. They can actually kill you. You're lucky you got away without them noticing you."

To his credit, he appeared suitably worried, but something still felt off. Probably that he saw three liches who somehow had not seen him. And the fact that she hadn't sensed his presence at all, bothered her the most.

"Stay put. You're safe up here." She wasn't in the mood to try to explain things, but nothing told her she had to be completely sneaky. If he started to panic, she could always wipe his mind. It wasn't her first choice, but it was an option guardians could use in emergencies.

"What are you going to do? You said they could kill us." His concern seemed real enough.

"I said they could kill *you*." She corrected him with a point of her finger in his direction. "Look, just stay here. I'll go handle the not ghosts downstairs and tell you when it's safe."

"You're one of those people who fight monsters, aren't you?" He asked, his eyes wide.

That was surprising, but in the list of surprises from the last few hours, it was kind of underwhelming. "Yeah. I'm one of those people who fight monsters. Stay here." She felt certain he wasn't going to listen to her.

Surprisingly, he didn't protest again when she turned and walked away. Skye could feel his eyes following her in the dark hall, and she felt an inexplicable desire to hurry down the stairs.

"You made it out," Trey said.

Sarah Eriksen

"Yeah, and now there are three liches in an abandoned school in Japan and a weird random person."
"Weird random person?"
"I'll explain later."
"Good luck."
One of the liches was floating in the main entryway by the doors. Its shadowy tendrils drifted around it and reached into the darkness. The other two had moved into another room and further away. Normally she would put up a complicated shield and try to destroy its outer defenses first. And then kill its core with a spell. It could be time-consuming to get an opening while focusing on holding your shield up as it drained energy.

Skye tilted her head to the side in thought, then shrugged to herself. She held her hands together in front of her, and an incandescent ball of coldfire formed between her palms. It glowed blindingly bright as she poured energy into it and compacted together in seconds.

She turned her palms forward, her fingers spreading wide, and the spell blasted into the lich, ripping through its defenses and slamming into the bones at its core, exploding them outward. The tattered tendrils of dark energy ignited briefly with blue flames as it let out a shriek and died.

Skye's fingers curled toward her palms, and she lowered her hands. That had been much more efficient, and her body hadn't erupted with sparks or flames. She could control vast amounts of energy outside of her without the fanfare. At least when she was casting a direct spell.

"I'm not going to miss the sparks." She said to herself, turning to face the darkness to her left. The other two liches were hurrying toward her, invisible to normal eyes in the darkness but clear to her.

She lifted her hands out to her sides, and two bright balls of coldfire exploded into existence, lighting up the darkness and the shadowy nightmares lurking within. She sent both flying forward with a tiny flick of her fingers.

The spells performed with the same efficiency as her first one, killing both liches in a matter of seconds. Darkness fell as the faint hints of coldfire dissipated, and the last traces of the creatures faded away.

Skye let out a relieved sigh. Using creation energy like that had finally felt comfortable. She hadn't tried to fight them how she would have before. Instead, she had taken the general idea behind the familiar tactics and lumped it into one powerful spell that took care of it all at once. It had looked like a bright ball of coldfire but had been a complex and powerful spell.

She was sure it would still take her some time to get used to how to put everything together, depending on what she encountered. There would also be plenty of times where drawing on an insane amount of energy and blasting away with minimal strategy would be the right thing.

"That was really impressive." His voice was soft and full of admiration.

Skye bit back a curse and turned around. "Didn't I tell you to stay upstairs?" She almost wished he had stayed put so she could sneak away. Not that she would have left him in the haunted house, even with the liches gone.

The charming slimy smile appeared again. "When the light show died down, and nothing else happened, I figured it was safe enough."

Skye did her best to keep her irritation off her face. "You're lucky. They're gone now. But when dealing with monsters, don't make assumptions. It can quite literally lead to your death."

His face fell, and he apologized. "You're right. I'm sorry."

"No harm done."

"I'm Adrian." He smiled again.

"Skye." She replied politely, trying to ignore the unsettling feeling his presence gave her. She wished she could leave, but she had to do one more thing. "So, you've seen people like me before and monsters?"

He nodded an affirmative. "A couple of times, but only from a distance. There was some strange stuff a couple of months back with big scary monsters near where I lived. I was out for a hike and saw them, and a guy showed up and told me to hide, then went and fought off the ugly thing with a couple of others. He checked on me after the fact and kind of explained it."

It was a little unusual, but not impossible. Same as Ben with the monster he saw as a kid. With him, it hadn't been enough to even bother wiping his mind. With Adrian, there was probably some reason, but she didn't need to know it. If it was an issue, it would have been taken care of, or she'd have been given instructions already.

Sarah Eriksen

"Well, I would avoid haunted houses for a while if I were you. They seem to be attracting monsters lately, and they're more dangerous than they should be."

"That's a good idea. But if I did, maybe you'd come save me, and I'd get to see you again." He laid on the charm as he flirted with her.

Skye was sure her expression was less than flattering. "Well, there's no guarantee it would be me. It could be any number of people like me who would show up to save you." She was seconds away from looking for an escape route just to get away from him.

His smile radiated charm and slime, "I'm sure none of them will be as beautiful as you."

Skye didn't even bother trying to force a polite expression on her face this time. She knew he could tell she was not impressed as his smile faltered and faded away. "Stay away from haunted houses. If you'll excuse me," she managed to bite out politely, "I have someplace I need to be."

"Could I get...?" his voice faded away as she teleported back to the space station.

Chapter Twenty-Eight

Declan studied her face and then smirked. "You have your 'someone paid you a superficial comment on your looks, and you weren't having any of it' expression."

Skye was taken aback. "I have an expression for that?"

Trey answered without looking up from the door he was studying. "You do."

She shrugged and tilted her head to the side. "Huh. It seems awfully specific."

Declan said, "It's like a combination of super unimpressed, mildly disgusted, with just a dash of irritation thrown in along with a pinch of disbelief. It's a lot like your expression when Vincent screeches his undying love and affection in your general direction, only with less irritation and disgust."

"I can see that." She had been feeling a lot of those emotions.

"Who warranted this expression?" Declan asked with a laugh.

"There was some random guy in the haunted abandoned school house I exited to. Along with three liches lurking below."

"Lurking liches are so annoying," Declan said. "So, was he investigating or something?" He studied her face, his expression more serious as he picked up on her emotions.

Trey said distractedly, "You didn't like him whatever it was. I could feel it the whole time you were there." He was focused intently on the door.

"I didn't." She scowled. "I looked with my mind as soon as I got there and only felt the liches—no one else. Then I turn a corner and almost walk into him. And I could sense him clear as day."

Declan said, "That's really weird."

"Exactly. But then he was all charm and had a perfectly believable story about why he was there and hiding upstairs. Never mind all the other doors on the ground floor he could have used to leave. And he seemed to know about guardians and monsters, but again, believable story. Not plausible, but believable."

Declan said, "All good reasons to not like him, but then he started hitting on you."

"Yep. I told him to stay away from haunted houses because monsters. And he said if he went back, maybe I could rescue him again." Disgust dripped from her voice.

Declan's shoulders shook with laughter at her tone. It wasn't that she didn't like to be flirted with or even be complimented. But not when it was creepy and superficial.

Trey finally focused on her. "And that was it?" His voice held traces of laughter too.

She sighed. "I simply said anyone could rescue him, and then he decided to comment on my beauty." Her voice held a wealth of disgusted irritation. She'd accept a compliment on her looks if it came from someone who knew and appreciated who she was, not a total stranger.

Declan bent in half, laughter exploding out of him.

Skye rolled her eyes and said, "I'm pretty sure he was starting to ask me for my phone number when I teleported here."

Trey said, "That explains the expression then."

Skye glanced around the empty hallway. "Where's everyone else?"

Declan waved one hand vaguely as he caught his breath.

Trey answered, "Eric had to take a tech support call, and Kya and her crew went to secure one of the rampaging aliens that got out. Again."

Skye shook her head in disbelief. "How do they keep getting loose?" She felt her phone buzz in her pocket. She hadn't felt it while she was in the other world, so her usual connection must have been blocked. It only took the tiniest touch of energy to form the connection, so it would work no matter where, or when, she was.

She quickly scanned the messages. "Ian did some digging into the name Mary Ann Randall and found some stuff that's interesting and probably not helpful." It was morning back home, so he must have stayed up all night.

"Probably not helpful?" Declan laughed again.

"His words. But maybe we can figure out something useful."

Trey asked, "Should we bring him here?" They exchanged smiles. Ian would lose his mind with excitement at being on a derelict space station right out of a science fiction movie.

Declan said seriously, "We should, but if another alien breaks loose, you have to get him out of here immediately."

"No shit Declan." Trey scowled.

"So go get him, Trey." Declan mimicked his tone.

Skye intervened before the space station ended up with more human remains. "Trey, go get Ian, and get some food and coffee while you're at it. I'm starved, and I'm getting interdimensional travel lag, which is far worse than time travel lag. I need caffeine."

She could feel the irritation simmering in her twin's mind and gave him a glare that promised he would regret it if he continued bickering with Declan and didn't get her some coffee.

Trey disappeared with a grumble, and Declan managed to hold in his laugh until after he had disappeared.

Skye shifted her gaze to him and said, "You would think after all these years, he would know not to engage when you're being a pain in the ass."

"Now, where's the fun in that?" He smirked briefly, then gave her a searching look and asked, "You good?"

She knew he was referring to their conversation. "Much better. You were right."

It said a lot that he didn't make a big production out of her saying he was right. He just nodded and said, "I'm glad."

She changed the subject. "So, the doors?"

"Yeah, they have pictures on them that seem to give hints at where they go. They're kind of low and not detailed or bright, so it was pretty easy to miss. Wes and Rachel marked the doors they had an idea about and took some pictures of the rest to help us out."

Sarah Eriksen

Skye examined the depiction of a labyrinth. It wasn't fancy, but it looked like a simplified maze. "So, Wes was in the creepy pink ball of doom forest, Korbin was in the role-playing game place, and the pirates were in the tomb."

Eric spoke up from behind them, "We're guessing that's the labyrinth Trey and I were in."

"Alright, I can see that." She glanced at the two of them. "It's not that low, you guys. I mean, it is a little lower than my line of sight, but it's not impossible to see."

Declan snorted. "Try it from our height." He ignored her irritated scowl and said, "I'm serious. It's a very different picture from up here."

Eric said apologetically, "He's actually right. This time."

Skye sighed and lifted her body into the air a few inches, putting her head more level with the others, and looked down. The markings on the door did appear to be scuff marks from higher up. She dropped back down lightly. "So, the doors were marked for someone who's kind of short. And knowing that doesn't help much."

Declan shook his head. "It doesn't, but maybe it could if we learn anything else useful."

"Oh my god! This is a real space station!" Ian exclaimed.

Skye laughed, turning to watch Ian's reaction. "It's a space station." She took the travel pack of coffee from his hand and grabbed hers before handing it to Declan.

"That's seriously space out there." He pointed at the clear windows above them. "This is amazing."

Declan said, "It is. As long as the rampaging aliens don't break out. Again."

Kya spoke from behind them, "They are locked up. Again." She and her crew had returned from the latest round of handling the alien and pirate situation.

Ian's excitement faded, and his eyes shifted back and forth between them, pausing briefly on the mercenaries he hadn't met. "Rampaging aliens?"

Trey clapped a hand on Ian's shoulder. "Don't worry. If they break out again, I'll teleport you home right away."

Declan corrected him. "I think you mean 'when' they break out again."

Skye let out a long-suffering sigh. "Declan, knock it off. Yes, that is really space, and we're on a space station. And there are rampaging aliens that have a habit of breaking out. But we figured you'd still enjoy the experience as long as we keep you away from the aliens."

Tate said, "And disgruntled space pirates. They haven't been getting out as often, though."

Ian's expression was full of curiosity, and Skye could see the millions of questions piling up in his mind. She said, "Yes, there are also space pirates here. And doors to other dimensions." She gestured at the panel behind her.

He stepped back, shaking his head. "No thanks." The space station, pirates, and aliens were nowhere near as bad as the other dimension in his mind.

Skye gestured to Kya and her crew. "Introductions. You already know Kya. This is Wes, Korbin, Tate, and Rachel. This is our friend Ian, computer and tech genius extraordinaire on our world. And yes, our tech is significantly not as high-tech as yours, but don't hold it against him."

Declan said with a laugh, "Don't let him start asking you questions about your technology, or you'll never escape. His curiosity is an incredibly powerful force in the universe."

Ian did his best to copy one of Skye's irritated looks and mostly pulled it off. "I'm sure there's some rule against me learning new space tech from the other side of the galaxy? Universe?"

Skye answered, "Universe. This is not the Milky Way." She dropped to the floor, setting her coffee down and accepting a burrito from Trey.

He said, "I might have overbought burritos, but I wasn't sure who was hungry. So, I bought enough for everyone." He included Kya and her crew in his gesture.

Korbin looked at the foil-wrapped food. "I'm not sure what a burrito is, but they smell amazing."

Trey handed him one. "They *are* amazing."

Ian's face showed his sudden concern. "I wasn't sure how much coffee you guys needed, so I only made the usual."

Skye reassured him, "It's fine. I can always make some for these guys and teleport it here if they want."

Trey made a strangled noise of irritation. "Why did you tell me to get coffee if you can just make it and get it yourself?"

Declan burst out laughing. "She does it all the time. Her shop is this little magic place after hours, with coffee getting made when no one can see it. You didn't know?"

Skye's shoulder lifted in an indifferent shrug. "I have a whole system, so I don't overlap with myself if I have to time travel and need coffee."

Korbin whispered to Tate, "What's coffee?"

Tate shook their head. They were also mystified.

Everyone settled in with burritos and hastily made coffee or beverages of their choice.

Skye turned to Ian. "So, Mary Ann Randall, you said you found something?"

"Yeah, I did, but I don't know if it's going to help. A lot of my searches pulled up obituaries or old newspaper articles. The name itself isn't incredibly uncommon, so there were some hits on social media as well. Based on what you told me about the various movie references and memes, I fine-tuned my search. It made sense to assume that it would have to be someone who would be old enough to know and appreciate memes along with being alive when they could see those specific movies, which narrowed it down."

Skye held back a smile as she watched Kya's crew become more and more impressed. They had only had dealings with people like Kya and her family, or guardians, or the multitude of people in their galaxy. Ian was something very different, and they were surprised.

Ian looked at his tablet and froze in shock. "How is this even working if we are on the other side of the universe?"

Skye waved her fingers in the air and said dramatically, "Magic!"

He laughed. "Of course. Anyway, Declan had snuck out one of the newspaper clippings from the White Chapel place, and you provided me with a few descriptions of the statutes and things. So, I narrowed it down to possibly one person."

He turned the tablet toward them. There was a picture of a teenage girl, along with an obituary. "Mary Ann Randall. She's the only one I found who was the right age to fit the pop culture references *and* look like the missing person photo and other descriptions. She died over ten years ago from some kind of untreatable illness."

A somber silence filled the air, and Skye said softly, "Everything kind of looks like memorials in the dimensions. Other than the newspaper thing."

Eric said, "You told me you were starting to think it was abandoned. Maybe it was created for her and became a memorial after she died?"

Declan's usual snarky tones were missing as he said, "So a god built this place, on the other side of the universe, for a teenage girl from Earth who was terminally ill?"

Wes directed his question to Kya, "I don't know a lot about these things, but wouldn't a god be able to heal illness?" She had significantly more experience than the rest of them when it came to gods. Her world had the personal attention of a goddess, one they could call on and who gave them magic.

She answered, "Normally, yes. Gods can heal almost anything, including death, depending on the god. But there are some illnesses even they can't heal. Those usually only show up in their descendants, and it's incredibly uncommon. However, if the person in question didn't want to be healed, they are honor bound to respect their wishes if it's not from a race they created."

Skye said, "Whichever god created this place must have cared about her a lot, whatever happened." It was incredibly sad.

Trey interjected, "Not to sound too indelicate, but that doesn't explain the haunted house stuff. This place has been abandoned for over ten years, and the haunted houses and doors started showing up in the last couple of weeks?"

Skye said, "The place Korbin was in made more sense from a linear perspective to start where he was. It was a waiting room you had to escape from, with guards at the end of a hall who you couldn't get past without a key from a guard in the dungeon where I dropped in. Then you teleport to a maze, fight a boss, and come back here."

Eric ran his hand through his hair as he thought. "So, the doors to our world, are something else and something new. Who would have the power to open doors connecting our world to this place?"

Declan said, "I'm going to go out on a limb and guess probably another god."

Kya said, "Or a demi-god. In theory, at least. It would depend on what powers they got from their parent, and who their parent is."

"That's as bad as the idea of a god doing something like this," Declan said sarcastically.

Skye said, "We should figure out the doors and see if there are any others that go anywhere we haven't been before. And figure out how to make them open. Even with rampaging aliens breaking out, it would be nice to have a centralized location to fix things."

Ian asked, "Can I help with any of this?"

She said, "That was amazing research, Ian. And you probably could help us, but there's the whole rampaging alien and space pirates thing you don't want to get caught up in."

"How bad are the rampaging aliens? Like on a scale of Sci-Fi horror movies?"

Declan answered, "It makes anything you've ever seen look more like a rom-com for levels of terrifying."

"While I do find most rom coms painful and sometimes even scary, I would love it if one of you wants to take me home before I find out how bad that is. But let me know if I can help in any way that doesn't involve aliens or going into weird dimensions. And don't worry, Skye, Ryan is helping me with the shop, so we got you covered."

Skye felt a twinge of guilt. She hadn't missed too many days, but after her extended absence over the summer, she didn't like having to rely on everyone else to keep things running.

"Thanks, Ian. I owe you big time.

Chapter Twenty-Nine

Skye finished her coffee and sighed. She was feeling the lag from jumping between time zones, locations, and dimensions. Between that, the additional backward time jump, and the strange hours she had been keeping, she was exhausted.

"So, you found all the entrance doors to the places we know about and the corresponding exits for them." The doors to and from the dimension Korbin had been in gave them an idea of which ones were entrances and which were exits. They were scattered around the corridor in the ring, usually pretty close to the other door but not perfectly lined up.

Tate said, "That leaves two doors that go places you haven't been yet, and the matching exits. And, that covers all of the doors we couldn't open."

Declan said with fake excitement, "Progress! Now what?"

Skye frowned. "I guess we need to figure out how to open the doors?" She asked Wes and Rachel, "Did you have any luck?"

Rachel shook her head. "We don't know fancy magic stuff like you do, but they seemed to react to emotion. We decided it was better not to take a chance on opening things when none of you were here. In case something bad came through a door."

"That's fair. Guess we should see if you're right about the emotion thing."

"And then what?" Declan asked again.

Sarah Eriksen

"I need all of you to return to Earth at once. There are wraiths, revenants, and liches showing up at haunted locations connected to your mystery dimension." Amonir spoke to the guardians.

"Of course, there are," Skye said dryly, getting confused looks from Kya's crew.

"Thankfully, most of the locations do not have people in them, and I'm sending other guardians to help control the situations. I'm proud of all of you for piecing things together. Skye, go to Washington. That is the most critical location right now. Kya, stay with your crew and try to get your situation under control." The information on their destinations popped into their minds.

Declan smirked. "No rest for the wicked." He disappeared.

Trey shook his head. "Always with the parting line with him." He disappeared too.

Skye raised her eyebrows expectantly at Eric, who laughed and said, "See you later?" He shrugged and grinned at her laugh, and he teleported away.

A roar sounded from the lower ring, and Kya sighed. "And that's the situation he was talking about."

Tate pulled up their handheld computer and located the alien. "It's the one in the docking bay. How does it keep getting out?" Two more roars came from above them as the others got out. "And there go the other two. All three at once."

Rachel said with a sarcastic and somehow positive tone, "It's fine." She gestured for Korbin to follow her to the docking bay.

He asked, "What do you mean it's fine?"

"I mean, everything's *just* fine." The sarcasm remained.

Skye gave Kya an encouraging wave and teleported as close as she could to the haunted house in Washington. With all of the interdimensional jumping, it was only around four in the morning.

There were a handful of wraiths inside, and judging from the flashing lights of emergency vehicles, some damage had already been done.

She jogged up to the lawn, looking for one of the tour guides she had met previously and finding one sitting on a chair nearby, shivering from shock. "Hey, remember me?"

The man's expression was dazed, but recognition dawned. "You were here the other night with your friend. You went up to the attic, and then the ghosts and noises stopped."

She said, "Yeah, that was me. Can you tell me what's going on in there?" She scanned the location with her mind as she talked to him, feeling the presence of the wraiths along with a familiar mind that was full of fear. Ben had not listened to her warnings. The wraiths weren't close enough to him to be a concern yet, but she kept an eye on their locations to be safe.

"Same as it was when you were here. At least at the start of the night. The attic has been getting more and more intense, so we've stopped taking people upstairs, saying the structure wasn't safe anymore."

"I imagine the sounds alone were probably exciting enough along with the poltergeists and everything else." She spoke with an encouraging tone, drawing out some of his shock as he told her what had happened.

"Definitely enough to not lose any interest. But then, just a bit ago, a bunch of shadow figures appeared on the main floor and in the basement. Only, they weren't just shadows." His voice wobbled with fear.

"It's okay to be afraid. Those weren't ghosts. They were something much worse." It was true enough, and he would come up with his own idea of what they were. She could see two EMTs headed toward them. One of them was also a guardian.

The guide's voice was full of worry, and the words practically tripped over each other as he spoke in a rush. "I don't know if everyone got out. It was panic as people tried to get out. I don't know if anyone is still in there or not."

Skye patted his hand. "Don't worry. You didn't do anything wrong. If anyone's still in there, I'll make sure they're safe." She stood up and stepped out of the way of the non-guardian EMT.

He dropped down to a crouch in front of the guide and said, "Hey there, let's get you checked out."

The guardian met her eyes and spoke in her mind. *"I've contained what I can from out here, but the wraiths are still in there along with one person. I tried to drag out the confusion with the lists from the tour as long as I could. I'm about to volunteer to go in there since everyone else*

Sarah Eriksen

is occupied or taking statements. And I understand you'll be handling the wraiths?"

His words implied that the direction came from Amonir. It must have sounded more than a little odd. He gave her a puzzled frown as he noticed the strange echo in the back of her mind and blurted out in surprise, *"You're one of the twins, aren't you?"*

"Yes, I'm one of the twins." She managed not to sound irritated at the typical question. It was almost always the exact words every time. *"And as far as the wraiths, that's what I came here for. I'll meet you inside. I should probably fade out of sight a bit, so no one questions a random bystander suddenly running into a haunted house with an EMT."*

He bit back a smile. *"See you inside."*

Skye slipped away unnoticed and wrapped herself in invisibility before jogging to the entrance to the house. It was always nice how many guardians had jobs that allowed them to help in situations like this. Although, it had to be a lot harder to disappear as an EMT than it was for her with the shop.

She had another pang of remorse and guilt. She was lucky her friends always helped her out when she had to handle things, but it had been excessive lately. It had always managed to work out, but if her life kept on this path of bigger and more time-consuming jobs, she'd have to hire more employees.

She dropped her invisibility as soon as she was inside the door. She could feel a wraith in the basement and two more upstairs, along with the terrified presence of Ben. She checked. He wasn't in immediate danger, but the wraiths were close to him, and they needed to hurry.

The EMT was surprised. "Hey, you were fast."

She said, "I ran. We can probably leave the one in the basement for now and get rid of the ones upstairs." It was obvious that he could sense Ben's presence now as he agreed immediately.

She said, "I'm Skye, by the way."

"Brian. And I've never fought wraiths before." He managed an apologetic smile as they moved to the stairs.

"Well, I just blew up three liches a few hours ago without help. I should be able to handle some wraiths with no problem. Hang back and get to the guy up there if you can. His name is Ben, and he knows a little about us." She hoped she sounded confident but not ridiculous.

Chaotic Haunts

His confused expression told her she had missed the mark.

"I know. It sounded weird to me too. But trust me." She had to work on her approach as a highly overpowered guardian here to take care of shit. She could feel Ben hiding in the nursery. She could also hear crying, along with the faint thumping in the attic that let her know a mummy was up there.

Her eyes widened in surprise, and she turned to Brian. "You can hear the crying, right?"

He nodded, his expression shocked. "Is that a ghost?" He was as startled as her.

"I think so. My brother and a friend heard a ghost crying in a haunted house last night." She wasn't even going to try to give an accurate time stamp for when it had happened. "We think the doors to the other dimension have been ramping up the ghost activity and agitating them."

His eyes were wide, but with wonder, not fear. "That's kind of freaky sounding, but it's kind of neat too."

Skye knew how he felt. It was something guardians wouldn't normally experience, and it was awe-inspiring. "Of course, now we have to deal with ghosts on top of annoying poltergeists and wraiths. But it's fine."

She had gathered everything she knew about fighting wraiths and came up with something to try out. She stepped onto the landing, gesturing with both hands and directing creation energy to form rings of coldfire around the misty shape of the wraith by the nursery door.

The incandescent fire built in intensity, swirling violently around the wraith. It shrieked in agony as she flicked her hands together, and the spell constricted down, burning through its outer layers. She shoved her right hand forward, and a sharp lance of bright energy shot out of her palm and stabbed the wraith's revealed core of energy, killing it.

She could feel Brian's shock as he whispered, "I've never seen anyone use creation energy like that before."

"It's very new to me too. But it seems to work. Check on Ben, and I'll get the other one and be right there." She was relieved he didn't argue. She knew her skills were surprising, but it was promising if he could still ignore them to do his job.

She jogged to the end of the hall and the small room the other wraith was in. This one had had some warning and tried to blast her with debilitating icy energy as she opened the door. She waved her hand, and a wall of fire shimmered in the air in front of her, eating the spell. She redirected the fire toward the wraith, pushing its energy back at it and wrapping the flames around its wispy outer edges. She poured more energy into it and crushed it down, burning through its core and killing it.

"Guess I have more than one method that works now." Admittedly, her first attempt had been along the lines of how they were usually handled. She had just tried a few adjustments to make it more efficient.

Trey gave her a mental nudge and didn't wait before popping into her mind and dragging Eric along with him. Skye could feel Eric protesting Trey's rude mental interruption.

"It's okay, Eric. I'm used to it from him. What's up?"

"I keep forgetting to tell you about this strange thing that happened at the amusement park. I bumped into—"

A strangled scream came from the nursery. *"Shit, I have to go. Hold that thought."* She pulled away from them as Brian called her name with his voice and mind.

She turned abruptly, tripping over her feet on the edge of the carpet, stumbling into the hall as she tried to not fall on her face. She managed to regain her footing and saw the misty tendrils disappearing into the nursery.

The thing had moved fast to get up here from the basement. No time for finesse for this one. She bolted down the hall, sliding to a stop, swords appearing in her hands. Coldfire blazed around her body, protecting her from the wraith's cold, draining spell.

She poured energy into her swords, crossing them in front of her and slashing out and down at the same time, directly into its wispy body. Swords, or weapons in general, were not a suggested way of defeating a wraith, but standard tactics didn't seem to apply to her anymore.

The creature screamed as the glowing blades ripped through its misty body and destroyed its magical core. It disappeared in a flash of fire and misty motes of energy as its shriek faded into nothing. Apparently, swords worked fine if you could pour enough power into them.

She could tell the house was clear, of wraiths at least, and let her swords disappear and the coldfire fade from her body. Brian's fiery orange shield dropped as he realized the wraiths were gone too. He turned to Ben, who was pressed against the wall behind him, eyes wide.

"Hey, it's okay now." Brian placed a hand on Ben's shoulder, sending soothing healing energy into his body and calming down the panic and anxiety reeling in him.

Skye said gently, "Hey, Ben."

He blinked his eyes, fear still clear in his gaze. "Are they gone?"

Skye reassured him. "I took care of them. We should get you out of here."

Ben nodded shakily, and Brian helped him to his feet. Skye led the way out, and Brian stayed next to Ben, ready to catch him if he collapsed. They guided him to the ambulance and had him sit in the back. Brian did a more normal check-up while healing the shock in him with guardian powers.

"That's pretty nifty how you combine things like that. Looks like a normal process, and you'll magically find nothing wrong other than a little shock?" She always loved seeing how different guardians handled everything.

"Exactly." He smiled faintly, delighted by her compliment.

Skye turned to Ben. "Now I know you aren't going to want to hear this. But what did I tell you about not going to haunted houses?" She wasn't mad at him. She understood the curiosity.

He winced and said, "That I should probably not go back to them since they're dangerous, especially this one."

"Exactly. It's not just the ghost and the magic doors. They're attracting bad things. That's what you encountered tonight. Those were wraiths, and they are nasty creatures that happen to look very ghostlike."

She felt the strange sensation that someone was watching her, and she turned to scan the crowd, searching for the source. She was positive it was connected to everything else now. She turned to Ben, then snapped her head back as she caught a glimpse out of the corner of her eye of someone who couldn't possibly be there. A glimmer of an idea started to form in her mind.

"What are you looking at?" Ben sounded worried.

Skye shook her head. There was no one there now who wasn't supposed to be. "Nothing. I swear I saw someone who couldn't possibly be here through normal means of transportation. But it must have been my imagination." She knew it wasn't, but no need to make Ben worry more.

Brian told him, "You're fine. You have mild shock, and that's understandable. Sit here for a bit until you feel steady enough to get up by yourself. I'll leave you two to it." He smiled reassuringly at Ben and tilted his head respectfully at Skye before heading over to help his partner check on some of the other tour attendees.

Ben dropped his eyes in embarrassment. "I know you said not to go back. But I didn't think it would be anything other than what it has been."

"I know. And you couldn't have known. It's not like we can announce to the world that haunted houses are now attracting real monsters too." She got a smile from him. "I have to thank you. The locations you suggested were the real deal."

"Really?" He sounded happy and hopeful.

"Yep. Three new weird dimensions. And we were able to rescue a missing friend and figure out some significant things. Thank you. Truly."

"I'm glad I could help." He glanced hesitantly at her, pointing at the house. "Is that what it's normally like? The monsters and your magic?"

She did her best to answer truthfully. "Sometimes. It can be scary, or beautiful, or terrifying. But it's almost always dangerous."

"It was pretty amazing. I mean, your disappearing act was impressive, but this was unlike anything I could have imagined. And it was also frightening."

Skye felt the strange pressure inside the house. At the same time, Amonir said, *"Guardian, you need to—"*

"Go in there and stop whatever the hell is going on in the dimension?" She interrupted him. Whatever was happening, she could feel the angry energy of the dimension outside the house.

"And see if you can close down the door."

"On it."

Ben followed her gaze and asked worriedly, "What's going on now?"

"No clue, but it's not good." She pointed a stern finger at him. "No more haunted houses for a little bit. Hopefully, we'll have this situation locked down soon. I'll let you know once they're safe again." She patted his knee and ducked around the emergency vehicle, wrapping herself in invisibility again and running to the house.

"I swear I just saw the guy I bumped into in Queensland." Eric peered into the shadows around the grounds of the abandoned hospital.

"The one who snuck up on you?" Trey asked, following his gaze.

"I don't know that he snuck up on me exactly. I didn't sense him, walked into him, then suddenly I could feel his presence." Eric ran his hand through his hair in agitation. He was normally very calm, but the encounter had left him shaken, and that said a lot.

Trey's eyes widened as his mind pieced things together. "I completely forgot. Skye said she bumped into someone at the schoolhouse in Japan. She said she didn't notice his presence until after she saw him with her eyes."

Eric's brows furrowed in confusion. "I didn't hear about that."

"You were on a call when she got back, and then we had other things going on. It sounded weird, and she didn't like him at all. But I wasn't paying that much attention, and Declan was mostly teasing her. I didn't think too much about it at the time. Then we had the doors to work on and Ian helping, so I forgot."

Trey glanced at the hospital, searching for signs of life, human or otherworldly. There was another wraith, but no people this time. "The wraith is lurking in there, and there's no one living around. Let's bug her for a sec and see if it's the same guy."

Eric felt Trey pulling him into a mind connection with Skye without politely asking permission first and tried to protest.

He had barely started to explain the experience when something interrupted them. Eric gave Trey a troubled look and asked, "Is she okay?"

"I can't sense anything out of the ordinary. Probably whatever she was dealing with at her haunted house." He shrugged, his expression rueful. "With her new powers, she probably got the worst of it. So that makes us lucky."

Eric let out a humorless laugh. "Let's get rid of this wraith and wrap things up so we can figure out how the sketchy guy might relate to everything."

"Sounds like a good idea."

Chapter Thirty

Declan grumbled, *"Why do I have to fight a revenant by myself? You sent Trey and Eric together."* He wasn't annoyed at all, but he had to say something about it.

"Guardian, you are a truly powerful healer and more than a match for one revenant. I assume there was another reason you wanted to talk?"

"Two things." He could feel Amonir trying to hold in his amusement at Declan's typical outrageous behavior.

"By all means, proceed."

"First, I know that you know what Ian found out about Mary Ann Randall. Are you able to figure out who the god is who created this place?"

Amonir's sadness was contained but still present. *"I know who it is now."*

"I wouldn't ask this if I didn't feel it would be necessary. Would it be possible to arrange a meeting with them? I think there's something we should know about this place to figure out who has messed it up so much. But I'd understand if it would be too hard." He was the last person who would want to bring up bad memories of loss and grief for anyone, even a god.

"I can see if he is open to discussion. I can't make any promises, though."

"At the very least, please reassure him that we want to set things right, so it isn't being tampered with."

"Of course, guardian. Was there something else?"

"Yeah, are any of the rest of us going to get nifty powers in the future like Skye?" His smile was his most outrageous and charming rolled into one.

"Be careful what you wish for, guardian," Amonir replied blandly.

"So, is that a yes?" Declan laughed as Amonir disappeared without replying.

He walked up the stairs to the lighthouse. The haunted tours had been temporarily shut down after the panic from the night before when the lich had caused so much trouble. He stopped on the top step, feeling like he was being watched. He vaguely remembered Skye having fleeting hints of something in the haunted houses and inside the dimension.

He was going to find out who the hell it was.

He shifted, acting like he was taking a cautious look inside. He sent out his mind to feel for things that were much harder to hide magically, vital life signs. He caught a faint hint of a pulse that disappeared a few seconds later.

Whoever it was, they were a living being, and he had almost caught them. The smile that crossed his face could only be described as smug with a touch of wickedness. They had left in a hurry, but not because they noticed his mind had caught them. He knew he could find them now.

He strolled into the lighthouse, shaking his head at the snarling mindless revenant. Apparently, whoever had sent it, wasn't taking chances that it would reveal anything. As a rule, Guardians used the same tactics when they fought. Creativity was encouraged, of course, but there were basic foundations they stuck to.

Guardians who had significant healing skills had a bit of an edge every now and then. Their minds understood how bodies were supposed to function in order to put them back together. But they could reverse those same processes. It would be cruel to do things like that to a living creature. However, those same tricks, when used against an undead creature, could be devastating.

Bright green energy flowed from his hands and into the revenant while cords of power snared it into place. The revenant's protective spells had some serious flaws that let in his backward healing powers.

Sarah Eriksen

He sped up the decomposition process, making the bones brittle, the flesh and muscle sinking in as it rotted away. The revenant screamed, not in pain but in rage, as its body fell apart. Seconds later, it was gone.

He studied the remnants of the reanimation spell. It was the same as the one Skye had fought. It had been reanimated by something much more powerful than your run-of-the-mill necromancer. He was pretty certain it wasn't as powerful as a god of death. It would have been a lot harder for him to pull off that trick with something brought back by a god.

A cold sensation tickled the back of his neck, and he felt the air get heavy. He looked up, seeing a shadowy figure pacing on the metal grate of the landing above him. Eerie moaning sounds echoed faintly in the narrow lighthouse stairwell. A quick check confirmed what he suspected. It was a real ghost.

A sudden draft chilled him, and he glanced down, sighing at his bare legs. This was getting to be an expensive prank. He turned a suspicious gaze up at the shadowy figure on the balcony.

"Did *you* steal my pants?" he asked the ghost, knowing it was ridiculous. He couldn't say for certain, but he was sure the ghost was laughing.

Skye dashed into the house, feeling the angry energy of the dimension and a strange heavy feeling she had never felt before. She twisted her body, narrowly dodging a book that was thrown across the room at her.

"Would you *stop* throwing books at me?" She yelled in exasperation. "I'm trying to get rid of the other dimension that's pissing you off so much." The heavy feeling subsided slightly.

She bolted up the stairs, catching a glimpse of a strange misty figure in the nursery. The desire to look at the ghost was almost powerful enough to make her stop. But she had a job to do. She could hear the shuffling steps in the attic, along with mournful crying. The door to the other dimension was open and spilling angry energy out. But even worse, she could sense more than a handful of wraiths.

"Skye, what's going on?" Trey asked.

"Can't talk. Lots of bad things happening here." She tapped her finger on the lock on the door, and it clicked open. She felt his brief flicker of irritation and snapped, *"Seriously, there's like a few dozen*

wraiths in the damn tomb dimension. I can see and feel everything in this haunted house, including more than one ghost, and the dimension is extremely unhappy."

"Sorry. What can we do?"

"I wish I knew." She meant it. She could handle the wraiths. That wasn't an issue. It was getting everything resolved that was the problem.

"What did you do to annoy your ever so moody twin this time?" Declan asked her.

"Declan, I really don't have time—"

He interrupted, "I know you have a ton going on. Trey and Eric filled me in about a sketchy weird guy Eric bumped into at the amusement park, and he sounds exactly like the sketchy guy you bumped into. I just had one of your feelings like I was being watched at the lighthouse. I can't say the feeling is for sure the sketchy guy. But if it is, there's no way he could have been in all of those places that close together unless he isn't a normal human."

"That would track with the whole unsettling feeling of my encounter with him." She gestured and sent a mummy flying backward into the other, causing a collision that made them both crumble to dust.

"Eric's encounter sounded similar, minus the creepy flirting. Anyway, when I felt like I was being watched, I searched. For life signs, not a mind."

"You found him?" She was surprised.

"Well, I found someone, but they disappeared. I don't think it was because they felt me find them either. I think they just left."

Skye stopped in front of the door, staring blankly at the angry energy rippling in front of her. "Wait, what time did you sense him? Never mind, let me look?"

"Of course, oh great and powerful time traveler." Declan's smirk was clear in his mental tone.

Skye fought a grin at his attitude and searched his mind, following the flow of time backward until she pinpointed it. It wasn't quite the same as reading a memory so much as backtracking his steps in time.

"Got it. That was only maybe a minute before I saw the sketchy guy here."

"Eric thought he saw him at the hospital in Maine."

Sarah Eriksen

"That must have been when they reached out, which still puts it within minutes, if not seconds."

"I can feel the crazy thoughts bubbling in your mind. You go blow up some wraiths, and maybe look for mister sketchy guy's life signs. I'll get Trey to do the weird time thingie you just did and see if the other encounters we've had might match up. And see if we can open the door back to the space station from the dimension you're headed into."

"Thanks, Declan. You're the best." She meant it.

"I know but keep that shit secret. I have a reputation to uphold."

"Your secret's safe with me." She sent him a mental wink and leaped through the door.

She hit the sand in a somersault, pulling in creation energy at the same time and summoning her two swords. She came to her feet covered in vibrant coldfire, weapons blazing in her hands. She thrust her sword through the wraith directly in front of her before it even realized she was there. The blade ripped through its cold protective energy and destroyed its inner core.

Three more wraiths were floating further into the chamber, and she blazed brighter as energy poured into her. She crossed her blades and sent energy flying forward in a bright streak that ripped the three wraiths in half. She swung her right arm around and pointed her sword forward, using it to direct more energy into the remains. They ignited with more fire that obliterated them.

She turned to the door behind her. It hadn't closed as it had previously. She studied it, but the convoluted flows of unfamiliar energy would take her hours to figure out.

"Amonir, I'm not sure I'm going to be able to close this door any time soon."

"Don't worry about it. I have Declan working on something right now that might help. Just get rid of those wraiths."

She was feeling more and more comfortable using creation energy in vast amounts and new ways. Confidence in her abilities was returning, and it was wonderful.

She reached out her mind, finding the locations of the wraiths, and searching for vital signs. Declan was a lot better at this than she was, but all guardians knew how to look for a hint of a pulse pushing blood through veins.

Chaotic Haunts

There was a faint hint of life further in the tomb on the spiraling path with the traps. If it was Adrian, she wanted to get to him before he managed to get out. She was done playing around.

She ran through the room and into the hall, using a touch of energy to make her feet stable on the sloping corridors. She rounded a corner and swung her sword, sending another streak of energy flying off her blade into the wraith floating above the steep incline. It seemed to be a truly effective way of killing them. She didn't have to get close, and it cut through their defenses quickly.

The wispy remains ignited with fire as she ran past and slid down the steep stone floor. A touch of energy kept her from sinking into the piled sand at the bottom. She kicked off the wall to change directions and dashed down the hall.

The chamber with the quest sword was full of wraiths, and there was more than one mummy. And they were fighting. The dimension had woken up more of the constructs to fight the wraiths.

She threw her left-hand sword in a controlled spin into the room, grabbing the quest sword and magically sheathing it across her back. She wasn't sure if she'd need it or not for the boss fight, but better to carry the extra weapon just in case.

Her incandescent sword took out the mummies as easily as the two wraiths it ripped through as it curved through the room and landed back in her palm. She cut her way through the mummies swarming toward her. They didn't seem to be able to differentiate between her and the wraiths, and they were very much in her way.

She hacked the legs off of a mummy and jumped through the opening, turning her back to a large stone column. She found the wraiths with her mind, and columns of coldfire erupted around them, burning through their defenses. Within seconds they had all disintegrated.

She let out a deep breath. She didn't feel overextended at all. She had been pulling in a nearly constant amount of creation energy, and it was as easy as breathing. If anything, she felt more tired from all the running on minimal sleep and not from using her powers. She hadn't realized how hard she had been working to limit herself.

She finished off the mummies and hurried to the next part of the tomb. The two dead ends were still dead ends, with no wraiths at least.

Sarah Eriksen

She could see a handful of them drifting down the booby-trapped hall and sensed three along the corridor to the trap door.
The life sign was nearing the bottom. She had to head him off. She could kill the wraiths following him after. She bolted down the hall with the murals and memes, running as fast as she could through the narrow corridors.
A wraith was floating around the corner ahead of her. She twisted herself into a spin and swung her sword down, sending a streak of energy flying into it. She burst through the disintegrating cloud and kept going. Each attack and use of creation energy felt easier and more natural.
She slid to a stop as she reached the final narrow passage she couldn't run through. There was a single wraith on the other side, its cold energy drifting into the gap. She pointed her left-hand sword toward it, energy blazing bright as it turned into a lance that flew into the wraith before exploding outward and annihilating it.
The life sign was still below her. He hadn't made it out of the dimension yet, and she had the sword to kill the quest boss to open the door. She was starting to think the exit back to Earth was more of a coincidence and that the exit to the space station had to be in the same room.
She shoved the urn off the pedestal with more enthusiasm than seemed proper and fell down the shaft. She held her arms tight against her sides, slowing her momentum at the last second with a puff of creation energy and landing softly on her feet.
The anger of the dimension was more noticeable on the lower level. It had been calming down with each wraith she had killed. As odd as it was to have a dimension that seemed to have an awareness, at least it wasn't directing its anger at her.
Skye took a moment to reach out her senses to detect where the other person was, along with the wraiths. They were close by. She took a quick look with her mind, confirming the life signs belonged to Adrian. She kept her mental presence back from him to avoid detection.
It was strange, she could see him and could feel his life signs, but she could not sense him. All living things had a sense of presence and emotions. Even the calmest person had something you could feel with your mind. But there was nothing where he was.

Chaotic Haunts

He seemed unconcerned with the wraiths drifting around him, and his expression was mildly irritated as he gazed at the room full of mummies.

A person who stumbled into a strange dimension with wraiths everywhere and hadn't died in seconds should have been panicking. The fact that the wraiths didn't seem to register his presence was more than a little troubling.

Any question about his involvement was confirmed now. She just had to figure out who the hell he was and how he was connected to it. But first, she had to kill the rest of the wraiths and not give him a chance to escape.

Coldfire blazed around her body in a protective shield as she sauntered into the room. She lifted her hands slightly away from her body, bright energy flowing down to form her swords.

The wraiths turned toward the threat, cold energy billowing out of their tattered wispy forms. She felt the sudden presence of Adrian's mind as he realized he wasn't alone. It was almost comical how good he was at faking a terrified mind.

Skye knew he was something other than human, but she wasn't sure how much he knew about Chaos Guardians, and her specifically. The only way to make sure he didn't try to run was to kill the wraiths as fast as she could. She sensed him step back to a wall and glanced his way, seeing the perfect impression of a terrified person trying to hide from the big bad monsters.

She shook her head and raised her right-hand sword, crossing her arm in front of her chest and swinging across and away from her body. A broad streak of light ripped through three wraiths directly in front of her. She spun and repeated the same slashing movement with her right hand, aiming for two wraiths that were converging on her left side.

Skye sliced through a ball of icy, ethereal energy from a powerful wraith lurking in the back of the room. The spell fell apart, icy motes drifting down and fading before hitting the sand. She threw her sword in a powerful overhand movement, the incandescent blade swirling as it flew across the room and pierced the wraith lord's chest.

She saw Adrian inching closer to the room with the mummies and grabbed a spear from a statue, throwing it across the room with a boost of power. It flew a few inches in front of Adrian's chest, embedding itself deeply into the stone wall.

Sarah Eriksen

He flinched back and stared at the quivering wooden shaft. He turned a frightened gaze to her, and she shook her head, pointing a warning finger at him. He pressed his back against the wall, nodding his head shakily, a hint of real fear clear in his emotions.

Skye headed back to the curving trapped corridor, slashing her remaining sword and sending another powerful wave of energy into the three remaining wraiths. It was time to take care of the wraith lord.

It was clawing at her sword and screeching, its ghostly form phasing in and out around its dark core. Cold energy radiated off its body, trying to find emotions to consume for strength. It fed on fear and terror, and its spell would amplify the feelings giving it a bigger feast. The cold energy brushed against her, and the only emotion it met was irritation.

She snapped her fingers, and her sword exploded outward in a rush of fire full of shards of creation energy. They ripped through the wraith lord's body, shredding its protections and igniting the remains left in its wake.

She turned to Adrian and raised one eyebrow. "Care to explain what you're doing in a pocket dimension with not only a shit ton of wraiths but a wraith lord?"

He let out a relieved breath. "Thank god you're here. I thought I was going to die for sure. You saved me." He managed to sound grateful.

"Seriously?" Her tone conveyed her utter disbelief. "You're really going to go with 'oh, thank god you saved me'?"

Surprise flashed across his face, the first honest reaction she'd seen from him. "You did save me, though."

"No. I killed the wraiths that had no issue with you wandering around amongst them. You weren't in any danger. So, how about you tell me what the hell you're doing here with all these wraiths that seem to be your friends."

She felt the energy from the dimension calming slightly, but it was still agitated. It was clear it didn't like Adrian. She couldn't blame it. She didn't like him either. There was something about him that was just not right.

Adrian dropped his gaze like he was ashamed or embarrassed. "I'm sorry. I know how this must look. And, I didn't know that I wasn't in danger. These wraiths, as you call them, keep showing up and following me around. I can't seem to get away from them. I tried to lure them in here to get them away from me."

He met her gaze, his expression grateful and worried. "You did save me. Maybe they weren't trying to kill me, but I know they want something from me. I don't know what this place is, but it seemed better than having these things back out where there were other people."

Skye growled in irritation. He lied like a pro. The story was plausible, almost believable even, but nothing about it added up. She needed to get him to the space station so she could find out what other horrible things he had done.

She leveled a no-nonsense glare in his direction. "You're coming with me. Stay back, and do not even think about running."

He nodded and followed her to the room with the mummies.

"Can I ask you something?" His voice sounded contrite and hesitant.

"I suppose." She stopped at the entrance to the room.

"Why would you pick up a sword from here if you have those bright swords?"

"It's a quest item." She frowned. It was obvious he was familiar enough with these dimensions to drag wraiths into them, and she could almost guarantee he had pulled in the zombies. He should know there was a special weapon to kill the boss.

His face was comically confused as he tried to figure out why she needed a quest item.

She said, "Stay here while I take out the mummies." She almost admired his ability to stay in character. She just wished she knew who he was because every instinct she had was screaming that he was something bad.

Sarah Eriksen

Chapter Thirty-One

She walked past the coffins, knowing it was a little mean to leave him behind, but she didn't want him trying to run ahead of her, and he wasn't likely to make it back up the dangerous death ramp to escape. She wasn't sure if the collapsing ceiling would work differently if they went through it at different times. She had run through it with Declan at the same time. And she wasn't in the mood to get stuck in this place.

"Any progress on the door?" She asked Trey, swinging the quest sword at a mummy that staggered close to her.

"Possibly. I'm not going to lie, from what Korbin was saying about the one he came through, I kind of think it might open when you finish the level." Gaming references seemed to make the most sense to explain the weird place. *"How's the tomb?"*

"Same as usual, other than a shit ton of wraiths and a wraith lord, and one super sketchy dude."

"Super sketchy dude? The one you found in that schoolhouse and the one Eric bumped into?"

"The very same. I apparently saved him. From the wraiths that weren't remotely doing anything to try and kill him or hurt him."

"So even sketchier sketchy dude."

"Yep. I'm almost to the end boss part of the tomb, so we'll see if your theory about the doors is right. If not, I guess I'll drag this guy's ass into our world and teleport us there. I would rather not give him too many chances to escape, though."

She casually finished killing or disabling the mummies, enjoying being able to take it easy for a minute. She was running on fumes and a lot of coffee and could tell her body was about at its limit. She knew creation energy was flowing through her tired muscles, trying to bolster them, but it wasn't quite enough to compensate. Her mind was still holding up with no issues, though.

A mummified arm twitched and grasped at the sand near her foot. The dimension wasn't only increasing the number of mummies. It had also changed them in small ways. These were now moving around after she dismembered them. Not quite as active as the ones above, but it was different from before. It made sense that the dimension would protect itself, even if the methods were creative.

She decapitated the last mummy and beckoned to Adrian. He stepped cautiously into the room, his eyes wide. She knew he had watched the entire fight. His projected mind had seemed as impressed as it had when she was killing the wraiths. Still a plausible reaction, but she still didn't believe it.

"Watch out." She said as the dismembered hand grasped at his shoe. He let out a strangled yell and kicked his foot, sending the wriggling hand flying across the tomb. It crashed into the side of a sarcophagus and hit the ground, flailing around and crawling back toward them. He turned a horrified gaze in her direction.

She said blandly, "They don't stop moving, so we should get moving." She turned away, hiding her mischievous smile. That had been a genuine reaction. And she would never admit to purposely leaving a mummy's hand where it would grab him.

They entered the hall, and Skye paused by the two doors that headed into the treasure room. She turned to Adrian and said, "I would suggest not touching any of the treasure in there. I'm not sure if anything bad would happen, but this is my third time through, and I can say for sure nothing happens if you don't touch the treasure."

"I just want to get out of here in one piece. I won't touch anything."

"Good. I hope you can run too. The ceiling over there will try to crush us. We have to run through at the same time, and I'd recommend a solid slide at the end."

His dark eyes widened. "That sounds dangerous."

Sarah Eriksen

While it was possible that he had never been in this place before, it seemed unlikely he didn't have something to do with the doors. And that would mean he would have to know about the ceiling. She would love to keep him on his toes and acting like he was scared, but she wasn't that mean. "I'll make sure you get safely to the other side."

Adrian flashed his charming grin at her. "Thank you, beautiful lady."

Skye's eyebrow popped up, and she knew her face had shifted into the expression Declan had teased her about. "You can thank me when we get out of here." As soon as the words left her lips, she regretted it as his expression turned from charming into more of a smolder, and his grin widened.

She stalked into the treasure room, feeling him hurry to walk next to her. The temptation to leave him trapped in the tomb was high. Even Vincent, at his most obsessive, wasn't anywhere near as unsettling as this. But then, Vincent was genuinely harmless. Annoying as all hell, but not dangerous, at least not deliberately.

She felt a strange and sudden sadness wash over her. It felt silly, but just once, she'd like to have someone seriously flirt with her who wasn't an obsessive stalker or a sketchy liar who was up to some nefarious purpose. Lately, it seemed like the men who expressed interest in her were obviously bad news. Or, if they weren't bad, things were unlikely to work out for several reasons.

"Time to run." She nodded at Adrian, sprinting forward toward the exit as the ceiling started to drop. Adrian kept pace with her effortlessly. Not that it was saying much, his legs were quite a bit longer with his tall frame. If anything, he could have probably outpaced her without her ability to magically boost her speed.

She dropped into a slide as the ceiling lowered, Adrian gracefully following a split second later. She used a light touch of energy to ensure they both slid safely to the other side. Although, he had managed to drop into a competent and controlled slide that was at odds with his 'innocent bystander being picked on' persona. She wasn't sure he had needed her help to get through safely.

The ceiling thudded to the ground with a puff of sand and dirt. She was expecting it, and it still made her flinch. Adrian jumped and stared at it in shock.

She said dryly, "It does that. You could probably stroll through there, and it would adjust. Not that I would want to test that theory."

He shook his head. "I don't think it would be a good idea." He glanced around the room and asked dubiously, "More mummies?"

"Just one. Follow me." It was time to see if their theories were correct. If the story was linear from the space station, then there would be a door back to it somewhere nearby.

"Trey, I'm about to fight the boss. Let me know if the door opens on your end."

"Ready when you are."

She directed Adrian to stand off to the side, away from the door that would lead back to Earth. No point in giving him an opportunity to escape.

His gaze followed her as she walked to the door. "What are you doing?"

"Triggering the boss fight."

The sarcophagus cracked open on the other side of the room, and she threw the magic quest sword at it. It exploded as easily as it had the first time. She could sense the energy she now knew was the space station. She walked toward Adrian as the door opened, revealing the exit back to Earth.

"The door opened on our end," Trey confirmed.

"I can sense it, but I'm not seeing it yet."

She grabbed Adrian's arm in a crushing grip, shaking her head as he stepped toward the door to Earth.

"Well, you're in an ancient tomb. Maybe there's a secret door?"

"You're brilliant." She felt her twin's pleasure at her heartfelt compliment. She hadn't really thought about it. The door to Earth had opened, and there had been no reason not to leave. But this place was like a video game, so a hidden door would make sense.

She moved to the sarcophagus, keeping a firm grip on Adrian's arm and pulling him along. She glanced around and saw it. There was a small lever off to the side of the door back to Earth by a panel that appeared to be part of the wall.

Adrian tried to move toward the door again, grunting in surprise as he wasn't able to make her budge. She said, "That's not our way out."

His eyes moved to the door and then back to her. His confusion deepened as she pulled the lever and the stone panel slid back and off to the side, revealing another door full of energy.

Her grip tightened on his arm as she felt the tension and faint hint of him trying to pull away. His arm suddenly relaxed, and he nodded at her, a slight frown creasing his brow for a fraction of a second before the mask slid back in place.

He said, "I'm happy to be getting out of here." His charming grin was as fake as ever as Skye pulled him through the door to the space station.

Declan jumped to the location Amonir had given him. It was a small town on the east coast. He headed down the road toward the café he was supposed to meet the god. He knew Amonir wouldn't send him to a meeting if it was going to be a bad idea. But he still felt a slight hint of trepidation. He was going to be asking some difficult questions to a most likely grieving god.

He felt the powerful sense of presence, indicating the god was there, but it was muted to something more comfortable for the average human to handle. He found the source with no issue. A middle-aged man in an impeccable suit sat at a table. He was attractive with a well-trimmed beard liberally sprinkled with silver. He looked every inch the gentleman with a tragic history.

The god raised his hand in greeting, and Declan walked over to join him. He paused briefly, raising his hand to his chest and nodding his head. It was a modified version of the typical formal greeting, but one that wouldn't cause too much notice.

"You're very kind, guardian." The god sipped his tea. "Would you like some coffee or tea? This shop is quite respectable."

"Thank you. Tea would be great." Declan knew when to be polite.

"I'm Lucas." The god said and gestured to one of the servers to bring another tea.

"Declan. Thank you for agreeing to meet with me."

Lucas' dark eyes were sad, and he nodded. "Of course. Amonir had expressed your desire to talk, and it seems that it will be in the best interest for both of us if I am able to help."

Declan thanked the server for the tea she placed in front of him as a powerful weave of silence wrapped around them.

"It won't do for our conversation to be heard by regular ears. Now, how can I help you?"

Declan said, "I want to apologize first. I fear some of my questions may bring up unpleasant memories."

Lucas dipped his head in acknowledgment. "Your compassion is appreciated. Please continue."

"I'm not sure how much Amonir has told you about what's been going on. But the long and short of it is, someone has been opening doors to the dimensions you created."

"He had mentioned something about my dimension being involved. Please explain what you know." The sadness was there, but also a hint of anger simmering below the surface.

Declan said, "It started with doors opening in haunted houses on Earth. My friend Skye was directed to go and investigate. Throughout her investigation, she discovered doors from our world that led in and an exit door that went to another location on Earth. I joined her later, and we found a name that connected each unique location." He hesitated, "It's become apparent the name had been placed as something of a memorial."

Lucas' eyes closed in pain. "Mary Ann."

Declan's voice was compassionate, "I'm very sorry."

Lucas said, "Thank you." He blinked and took a sip of tea. "To save you the awkwardness of asking, she was human, like her mother. I had business here and found myself quite taken with both of them. Unfortunately, Mary Ann developed a serious illness when she was a teenager. She knew a little about who I was by then, and she asked me not to heal her."

"I'm so sorry, Lucas." Declan meant it. He was a healer who could heal almost any injury or illness that was possible for humans and many others to catch. But it was heartbreaking when he couldn't heal someone. He couldn't imagine being asked not to heal something he could.

"Thank you, guardian." He paused to take another sip of tea, visibly collecting himself. "I created the dimension for her. It was full of things she enjoyed, movies, books, and history. She came up with the ideas, and I brought them to life. It was our place to spend time together and go on adventures that she wanted to go on."

"That's beautiful. The detail you put into it is amazing." Declan was impressed. The weird dimension made a lot more sense now. One person's unique influence had combined the scenes with the strange pop culture references and random touches that made it so bizarre.

"She loved it so much. When she passed away, I turned it into a living memorial. It's a piece of her that will always exist."

Lucas looked at him, that same simmering rage in his eyes, "I built that station in a remote part of the universe and locked it down after...she was gone. No one should have been able to find it."

Declan said apologetically, "I don't know the entire story, but some space pirates found it and were using it as a base."

"Only a god would have been able to drop the cloaking spells I placed on it. I will look into who could be behind that. I would not put a Chaos Guardian at risk."

"Thank you." Declan took a sip of his tea and said, "So the station was designed with an entrance to each location, and then you follow the story and exit back to the station?"

"Yes, some had quests, some had stories, some were to explore and experience something different. But they were quite straightforward."

Skye had been right about that. Declan said, "The doors from our world seem to drop us into random places, and the exits made as much sense as the entrance. Who would have the power to open doors into your dimension from here?"

"We could assume it was the same god who took down the protections. But why bother with that if they were going to open doors to this world? Are they all in haunted houses?" Lucas asked curiously.

Declan corrected himself. "Well, haunted locations all over the world. The energy from the dimension spilling through the open doors seems to be riling up the ghosts at each location. Now wraiths, liches, and revenants are appearing too."

Lucas' face grew thoughtful. "The energy from the dimension itself shouldn't be enough to agitate spirits here. Not to any noticeable degree, at least. But if something is disturbing the energy of the dimension, that could explain it. And if creatures that are a product of necromantic energies are appearing, there would have to be a connection to a death god."

With the multitude of gods and goddesses in the universe, there wasn't a hierarchy of who ruled the souls of the dead. There wasn't a heaven or hell in a general sense. Gods had control over that for the souls in their keeping. It was a convoluted mess only the mind of a god could understand.

A death god was merely a term for a deity who preferred to have power over aspects of death. They favored necromancy and the continuation of life after death in a physical or spiritual sense. No god was truly like another, but some had similar interests depending on the worlds that were created.

Declan said, "We had no sense of any god around the locations, but there was someone who recently popped up at a few places with a clear ability to teleport. Two of my friends said they couldn't feel his presence until they physically saw him, and then he seemed normal. Well, more or less normal. They said he felt unsettling."

"Demi-gods can mask their presence much like a god. I would venture a guess that if this man is a demi-god, then his god-parent is probably a death god."

"He would have the power to open doors to your dimension?" Declan asked.

"I think that would be a safe assumption. Do you have this person in custody?"

Declan frowned, reaching out to Trey when Skye's mind felt murky and out of reach. "My friend Skye appears to have caught him and is going to bring him to the space station. If her assumption is right, he led a bunch of wraiths into the dimension. She is killing the wraiths as we speak."

"I had felt some disturbance in the energies. However, it is not an easy place for me to visit." Rage simmered to the surface, "But someone is defiling my daughter's world."

Amonir spoke from next to them, "Lucas. My guardians will handle the situation and close the doors to our world so that it is once again as you made it."

Declan raised an eyebrow at Amonir. "Eavesdropping boss?"

Amonir raised an eyebrow right back. "You should head back to the space station and help wrap this up for our friend here." He was dressed in an impeccable black suit, with a neatly trimmed goatee, his black hair styled tastefully. His clothing and appearance showed his respect for Lucas.

Declan felt the nudge from Amonir and said, "I promise Lucas, we'll do everything in our power to fix this. Thank you very much for meeting with me."

"Thank you, guardian. You do credit to your kind."

Declan stood up and touched his hand to his heart, bowing his head and leaving the two gods to discuss whatever it was gods discussed.

Chapter Thirty-Two

Sky tapped her foot on the floor in irritation, staring at Adrian, who was gazing up at the vast window with a lovely view of space above them.

A roar echoed through the ship, and he jumped, turning in the direction of the sound. One of the aliens had gotten loose again, and Kya was currently getting it contained. Again.

Trey was standing in a similar position to her, his foot tapping the same as hers. Eric was leaning against the wall nearby, staring impassively at Adrian.

"Are you sure it's safe?" Adrian asked, sounding truly worried. He had only freaked out a little about being on a space station nowhere near Earth for a few minutes when they had popped through the door. Eric stopped him from having to carry on for too much longer since they had recognized each other. The alien breaking loose had interrupted further conversation.

Skye shrugged and said blandly, "As long as the other two stay locked up, we should be fine." She wasn't lying. The other two were a bit closer.

Trey asked, "Can you explain your entire story? We're very curious." He didn't say exactly what they were curious about. They wanted to hear whatever story he was going to concoct for them.

Adrian cleared his throat. Skye believed his nervousness was real for once. He had been toying with them this entire time and knew or recognized each of them. Skye was convinced the strange feeling of

Sarah Eriksen

being watched had all been him. His story was going to have to be good to explain how he had pulled it off.

"Like I told Skye. My entire life, creatures like those wraiths seem to find me. They don't do much of anything, but they seem to be attracted to me. At first, it was only one here and there, and they didn't always follow me. In the last few weeks, it started to get worse. More and more of them were showing up. So, when I saw these doors appearing in haunted houses, I thought it would be a great place to get rid of them."

"It's just plausible enough that it's a great lie," Trey said.

"Yeah, other than guardians would know if there was a sudden influx of wraiths and liches harassing a single person." Skye pointed out.

"Pretty sure Amonir would have told us about that a long time ago, even if it was only one. He doesn't joke around with those creatures." Eric said.

Skye asked, "So how exactly do you travel around the world so fast?"

Declan popped onto the space station and answered with a smirk, "Because he's a demi-god."

All eyes went immediately to Adrian, who was suddenly uncomfortable under the intense scrutiny directed his way.

Eric said, "Well, that makes a hell of a lot more sense."

Adrian blurted out in surprise, "How could you know that?"

Declan smirked and winked. They could see Adrian's confidence take a hit as he realized he had confirmed his parentage.

Declan spoke to the guardians, *"He's the one who opened the doors. Good chance that mommy or daddy is a death god, which explains all the shit. There's a whole separate issue with how the space station cloaking was removed. But that is above our pay grade. Amonir and Lucas, the creator of this place, are looking into it."*

"Can I punch him?" Skye asked in irritation.

"We might have to draw straws," Eric said, his voice as irritated as hers. It had been a long handful of days, and while it seemed they were getting closer to resolving things, the one person who knew what was going on was a chronic liar.

Skye said, "You're a demi-god who seems to be friends with wraiths. I'm guessing probably liches and revenants too. So, who is your god-parent?" She was over it. She was tired, and this was getting ridiculous.

"I don't know." Adrian shrugged apologetically, "My mother told me my father was a god when I was a teenager, and I started noticing I wasn't like the other kids. She didn't tell me who it was."

Declan said, "Well, daddy dearest is clearly a death god. Otherwise, you wouldn't be able to control wraiths so easily." He nudged Skye to get her to go along with him in his line of questioning.

"What do you mean control? They show up and then follow me." He sounded aggrieved and annoyed at the accusation.

Skye asked, "Declan, are you accusing him of deliberately bringing wraiths to haunted houses and into the dimension?" She sounded incredulous. "You know those creatures are attracted to ghost activity. They could very well have followed him when he showed up." She sounded for all the world like she was defending Adrian's story.

Trey and Eric both gave her disbelieving looks. She deflected their mental inquiries, focusing on the ruse.

Declan scoffed, "And we have a rogue demi-god popping up in haunted houses that just happen to have doors to this dimension? Way too much coincidence."

Skye asked doubtfully, "Why were you going to those haunted houses?" She made it sound like she wanted him to convince her that he had a good reason.

"I'm not going to lie. I was going to those places on purpose. I've always liked haunted houses. I don't find them scary. Maybe you're right. If my father is a death god, maybe I feel an affinity for them. But, I noticed that wraiths, as you call them, were still showing up. They don't seem to want to hurt me, but there were people at some of the places. Since they're drawn to me, I figured I could get them away from people there and keep them safe." He kept his eyes on Skye as he spoke, watching to see her reaction as he pitched himself as a hero.

Skye smiled at him. "That's incredibly noble of you. I guess you used the doors to try to get them away from the others. Especially after the panic at the haunted house in Washington." She could feel Trey and Eric trying to get her attention. She was incredibly disappointed they believed her act as much as Adrian did. He was positively eating up her attention.

"It seemed like the safest bet. I didn't know exactly what it was, but it got them away from everyone else. I can't fight them like you can, but at least I could keep people safe."

Skye tried not to laugh as he latched onto the hero concept since he seemed to think it was what she wanted. She finally spoke to Eric and Trey, pulling Declan along, *"I'm seriously disappointed that both of you think I believe the bullshit this guy is spewing out."*

Eric's mind voice was apologetic. *"I'm sorry. What are you two doing?"*

"Good cop, bad cop." Declan's mind voice implied a shrug. *"He's obviously got a crush on Skye or a motive. Whatever. I push the logic, she defends him, and he slips up. He's already making a ton of mistakes. It's pretty pathetic."*

"I need popcorn," Trey said, relief that his twin wasn't completely losing her mind filling his voice. She had been consciously blocking him out, focusing to make sure Adrian believed her. Trey had gotten a confusing mess of emotions projected back at him because of it.

Declan said to Adrian, "You might as well drop the act. We know you opened the doors. Just like we know you've been watching us for the last few days."

Adrian's eyes flickered briefly to him, then returned to Skye, "You believe me, right? I'm trying to help people and get rid of these monsters that won't leave me alone."

Skye burst out laughing. "Your story is certainly…detailed. But the thing is, you have so many lies wrapped up that you can't even keep them straight. They followed you. You deliberately led them into the dimension to get rid of them. You were a ghost hunter hiding from wraiths."

The humor left her voice. "Enough with the bullshit. We know you deliberately opened the doors. We know you're responsible for pissing off the energy in the dimension, which has pissed off the ghosts. A single wraith or lich in a haunted house would make sense with the activity. But hordes of them? A wraith lord? Zombies bursting through the ground? And revenants? Sorry, but your story doesn't add up at all. None of them do."

A flicker of rage simmered behind his dark eyes, then his face fell. "You're right. I haven't been completely truthful. All my life, I've had a connection with death. I never thought about why. So, I go to haunted houses and explore. The ghosts always noticed me. It's kind of why I like haunted places. At least, at first. Sometimes a wraith or a lich would show up. I would always run away. But it's how I know about people like you who fight monsters."

His gaze dropped, but he kept peering at Skye. "Then, one day, I just wanted to get away from them. Away from everything. Next thing I know, there's a door to another world. So, I went in. It was strange and terrifying, but I was able to get out when I needed to. Then I went to another haunted house, and a wraith showed up, so I opened a door again. I knew how to do it that time, so it was easier." His story was still plausible enough, but not one of them believed him. It didn't help that these wraiths that had supposedly followed him as the doors opened were nowhere to be found until later.

He pleaded with Skye. "You have to believe me. I didn't know what I was doing was going to cause so many problems with the ghosts on Earth. I didn't know."

Declan said, "No one has to believe you. But we do have to fix what you've screwed up. To do that, we need to know how the hell you opened the doors in the first place."

Adrian's eyes widened, his mouth dropping open in amazement as Kya returned with her crew. Skye rolled her eyes at the expected and obvious reaction to her cousin. Not that she was jealous that his attention shifted. It was a relief.

"The alien is contained...again," Kya announced, leveling a frigid glare at Adrian. "Have you finished your interrogation?" Her lips twitched as she watched Adrian's expression change from raw admiration to discomfort.

Declan leaned against the wall, casually crossing his arms over his chest. "Almost. Our demi-god friend was about to tell us how he managed to crack into the dimension and create doors."

Adrian shifted as everyone's attention turned back to him. He might like trying to play the hero for Skye's benefit, but it was clear he didn't like his present situation.

He shrugged and said, "I've heard of things like doors opening to other worlds. Staircases appearing in the woods. Portals to other dimensions. I know there's not always an explanation for them, or not one I'm aware of. And doors in haunted houses are real things. I wanted to get away— from the wraiths and ghosts that wouldn't leave me alone.

Sarah Eriksen

I don't know exactly what I did, but I needed to get away. So, I reached out, and next thing I know, there was a door."

Eric said, "The doors open at specific times and are tied to the other dimension. How did you find so many locations without knowing about them?" His soft voice and pointed question made Adrian shift uncomfortably again.

"I didn't want to leave them open since anyone could stumble into them. I notice ghosts more often when it's late at night, so I put the two together. Once I was in the other dimension, I knew there was more to it. So, the next place I went to, I reached out again, and it connected to a new place. I know the exits were in other locations, but some of those dimensions were so bizarre and terrifying I didn't want to stay."

Declan asked, *"Skye, you're an expert with the whole spatial relation stuff. Do you buy any of this?"*

"Each part of the dimension is tied to a different set of doors here. And it occupies a space outside of our main dimension but overlaps with it. It's technically possible he could sense different parts of the dimension based on where he was in the world. I haven't mapped it out myself since I can only sense it when the doors open. But, like the other shit he's said, it's plausible enough to be true."

"But clearly not completely true. Even the timing of the doors isn't precise enough to make sense. Or the fact they stay open unless someone goes through." Trey finished her thought.

Skye said, *"They closed after we went through them. But the door going in didn't close after Ian went through the bed and breakfast. On the outside, that is."*

Declan glanced sharply at her, *"That would imply it was aimed at guardians."* An angry roar followed by pounding and scraping metal drew their attention back.

Eric said, *"We might have to look into that more, but we probably should wrap things up here first."* None of them could argue with that.

Skye said to Adrian, "I want you to picture, in your mind, exactly what you did to open the doors, both to the dimensions and out of them." She reached out to Amonir, *"I don't trust him enough to go into his mind. Can you help?"*

"I will protect you, guardian. He won't know the difference." Amonir agreed instantly.

Chaotic Haunts

Skye wasn't surprised he was willing to make sure her mind wasn't vulnerable to an attack while reading the demi-god's mind. But the fact he hadn't argued at all spoke volumes. She reached into Adrian's mind, seeing how he used his demi-god powers to open the doors. It hadn't been that complicated, but the power was pretty significant.

She drew her mind back and said out loud, "Well, I feel confident I can close them."

The ship groaned as the doors to the other dimension flickered, angry energy pulsing against them. Skye asked, "Did you guys figure out how *these* doors work for getting into the dimension?"

Declan said, "Oh yeah. Just put your hand on it and say open."

Wes covered his face with his hand, letting out a frustrated groan. "It's not emotions then?"

"The doors react to emotion, but they open with the word."

Korbin laughed. "I do believe I might have hit the door I went through and said, 'open gods dammit'."

Wes said, "I didn't say it out loud, but I do recall I was thinking it at the time."

"Kyadara, keep an eye on our new friend. Declan, stay and help her. Skye, the dimensions are full of creatures he lured in. Take care of them and seal off the doors from the inside. Trey, Eric, you can assist with the creatures that are getting drawn to the haunted locations on our side. Whatever Adrian has set into motion is increasing by the minute." He didn't have to explain.

They had already seen it all. The ghosts getting agitated enough to appear in front of guardians and at stranger times of day. The creatures being drawn to the energy from the ghosts.

The number of creatures Adrian had lured into the other dimension would only be a catalyst. One or two would be an inconvenience, but as many as he had drawn in were dangerous. The dimension was enraged, and that anger was bleeding out, aggravating the ghosts, which only attracted more creatures.

"Can't we help Skye close the doors?" Trey asked. It was a great question since it would be the fastest solution.

"She is the only one of you who can wield the amount of power required to close them." The guardians were all surprised, including

Skye. She knew her powers had increased, but he was implying they easily rivaled that of a demi-god.

Declan patted her on the shoulder and said with a smirk, "Glad it's you, not me."

Eric gave her an encouraging smile while Trey smacked the back of Declan's head. Skye held in a laugh. Declan had timed his comment perfectly to pull Trey back from the mental abyss he had almost fallen into. She couldn't ask for a better friend.

She had the information from the worlds she had been in and the ones her friends had been to. Now she just had to fight an outrageous number of creatures attracted to death and close off doors by wielding ridiculous amounts of power. At least she had gotten some practice in on the wraiths in the tomb. This should be a piece of cake.

"Good luck, cousin," Kya said to her.

Information flowed into her mind, and Declan winked at her. *"It's a gift from Lucas."* The maps of each part of the dimension were now complete in her mind.

Skye grinned and slapped her palm against the door to the tomb, saying dramatically, "Open!" The door shimmered, turning into a portal. She turned her head and gave her friends a grin and a wink before leaping through, feeling the door shut behind her.

Chapter Thirty-Three

The tomb was creature free since Adrian hadn't been able to lure anything else inside in the last few minutes. The entrance from the space station was one of the apparent dead ends. She let out an exhausted sigh and ran back to the door from the haunted house in Washington. She was looking forward to wrapping things up and sleeping for a few days, or at the very least not having to run anywhere for a while.

The tomb hadn't reset, and the emptiness felt oppressive. The energy in the dimension had calmed down considerably, but it still felt unsettled. It might not truly go back to normal until the connections to her world were severed.

She heard muffled conversation as she neared the door. Some avid ghost hunters had either picked the lock, or the people in charge wanted to see what was going on after the wraith attack. The blurry portal showed a handful of figures on the other side, one of them moving to the opening.

Skye bit off a curse and put on a burst of speed. She slammed her palm into the chest of the man who had started to step through the door, shoving him back into the attic. He tumbled into his friends with a strangled yelp, all of them staring in shock as her hand slipped back through the portal.

She yelled, "Sorry folks, this door is out of order." Creation energy blazed out of her hand, turning the portal back into the tomb wall. She severed the connection with a delicate slash of power, smoothing everything over. It had taken a lot of energy but was far easier than she would have guessed.

The booby-trapped hallway would be the faster route to get below. She made it across the first traps with a few well-placed jumps and bolted through the next section. She flipped over the last blade that popped up with no regard to the timing. She shook her head, another last-minute trap that would almost get you no matter what you did.

She slid down the ramp and launched herself over the pit. She ran through the halls to the treasure room, stopping and staring in irritation at the wall that was still firmly closed. Teleporting the short distance into the next room didn't seem like the best option. She accessed the mental map Declan had shared and found what she needed.

There was a narrow corridor behind a fake wall hidden behind a massive golden statue of a cat meme. She pulled a metal bracket holding a torch. A mechanism activated, and the stone wall shifted open into the boss fight room.

She muttered, "That would have been a lot nicer to navigate before this."

The two exit doors were still open in the final chamber. The energy in the dimension was settling down as it realized the outside forces were no longer a threat. She closed the exit back to Earth, cutting off all connections Adrian had created. The entire tomb fell into an eerie silence.

She hadn't realized how much background energy had been buzzing because of the doors. The dimension was intact and behaving as intended. The atmosphere was perfect for a creepy old tomb full of mummies. She exited back to the space station, feeling the door close behind her with a tranquil energy.

Loud thuds reverberated across the space station as a massive alien body slammed the door it was trapped behind. Skye was confident one, if not all of them, would get out again soon, but that wasn't her problem. She waved impudently at Kya and the others as she told the next door to open.

Wes asked Declan, "Does that mean she successfully closed off the doors back to your world?"

Chaotic Haunts

Declan said, "She came back fast enough and didn't look like she was going to murder everything in sight, so I'd say yes."

Korbin said, "I'm glad she's having a good time. Because things are about to get fun around here." He was watching a handheld computer that was connected to the security systems.

Kya sighed. "Who got out this time?"

"The pirates on the bottom ring."

Kya asked Declan, "Want to babysit the demi-god or capture some space pirates?"

Declan considered his options. "Well, they both sound super exciting, but there's only one obvious choice." Kya's crew looked at him expectantly. "Space pirates!"

Kya wasn't surprised at his answer. "Korbin, please go with him since you have eyes on all our other guests. We're about due for one of the aliens to break out again." A hint of mischief flickered across her face as she walked with them to the ramp.

Declan glanced sideways at her, hearing Adrian's panicked burst of questions fade behind them. "Are they breaking out of their holding cells with a time pattern? Or are you torturing the problematic demi-god?"

She smiled enigmatically and said, "Mostly the latter. I haven't figured out if there's a pattern of the aliens escaping yet. I sent Tate to the command center with Rachel. They should be safe in there, but Korbin, I need you to be a second set of eyes. Watch for anything out of the ordinary, along with the usual breakouts. I don't trust Adrian at all. I fully expect him to try to take advantage of any opportunity that might arise."

Korbin said, "Like aliens and pirates breaking loose, which keeps happening."

"I'm worried about the randomness of that, especially since the creator of this place didn't have an explanation. Something has to be letting them out."

Declan glanced over her shoulder at Adrian, who had finally stopped his panicked questions. "You think he might have something to do with it?"

She wasn't certain he was the culprit, but that didn't mean he wasn't involved somehow. Her instincts were telling her things were going to get worse. "Declan, can I count on you to protect my crew?" She knew she could, but she still wanted to hear it.

He studied her face, reading everything she wasn't saying, and nodded. "Of course."

Korbin glanced back and forth between them. "Should I be worried?"

Declan clapped his hand against Korbin's shoulder and said, "Nah, man. I got your back."

Skye stepped through the door into a narrow black and white street in White Chapel, taking a moment to get her bearings. She wasn't too far from the alley the door from Earth was in. The sooty sky had an angry red glow, giving a disturbing wash of color to the dreary place.

The dimension was full of zombies shambling around along with one nasty revenant. The placement of the NPC-style characters was strange and out of sync with their usual behavior. They were gathered on roads and filling alleys.

It dawned on her. They were keeping the zombies trapped in a small area encompassing the two doors to her world. She said out loud, "Thank you for the help." She wasn't entirely sure who or what she was thanking, but she felt a wordless acknowledgment.

She ran along the slippery cobblestones past dilapidated buildings that towered over the narrow alleys and roads, taking out zombies on her way to the door. She slid into the alley, plowing into a zombie and using it to stop her momentum. It dropped to the ground in a lifeless heap as she disabled it.

The hall on the other side of the door was dark and unnaturally quiet. She listened to make sure nothing dangerous was happening on the other side. Her job was to close the door, but something about the silence was disturbing. The darkness suddenly coalesced into a shadowy figure that screamed and moved down the hall on the other side.

Skye risked a quick peek with her mind. The ghostly figure had been lying in wait to surprise attack a wraith. She felt the presence of unfamiliar creation energy as the hallway lit up with a bright aqua light from a guardian she didn't know.

The bed and breakfast was handled, so she turned her attention to the door. It shimmered with coldfire, returning to a soot-smeared wooden door as she severed the connection.

Now all she had to do was get to the exit, past garden gnome Jack the Ripper, close it, and get to the door back to the space station. And kill the zombies and the revenant while she was at it. She mapped out a path through the streets that would let her accomplish everything with minimal backtracking.

She tore through White Chapel, leaving piles of dead again zombies in the filth-packed gutters. She sensed the revenant nearby, but she had to close the door first. She rounded the corner, interrupting the murder. The garden gnome brandished its bloody scalpel, screaming at her.

She twisted her wrist, and Jack the Ripper gnome flew into the air, ceramic limbs flailing as she held it in place with her mind. She could see a commotion through the blurry portal and felt a familiar presence.

"How's it going over there, Eric?"

"Oh, you know, just a couple of zombies and a wraith or five. And some super freaky ghosts. I'll never make fun of scary movies set in asylums again. I get it now."

"Need any help?" She glanced back, calculating how much time she might have.

"We got it covered. You can close the door."

An icy blue flash of light and a sense of another familiar presence appeared as she closed the portal.

Rhaeadr said, *"All this power and the ability to travel anywhere in the universe, and I'm still fighting zombies all the time."* He sent her a wordless greeting that felt like a hug.

Skye laughed at his dry humorous quip and closed the door, completely sealing this part of the dimension off from Earth. Now she just had to clean things up.

A terrifying, hollow screech accompanied by moans and shuffling footsteps sounded behind her. She turned to face the revenant, glancing at the angry floating garden gnome with its scalpel. She considered the situation for a moment, then shrugged, flicking her hand forward and launching the murderous gnome straight at the revenant.

Garden gnome Jack the Ripper wasn't too picky about killing anyone or anything in front of it. The small ceramic body was surprisingly fast as it hacked and slashed at the revenant, crawling up its towering form and screaming in a murderous rage.

Sarah Eriksen

Skye was impressed and more than a little disturbed at the sight, but it was effective. She threw her hand forward, and lances of energy blasted out, killing the zombies gathered in the street.

The revenant screamed one final time and collapsed to the ground. The ceramic gnome stood up, looking around for its next victim. Skye scooped it up with creation energy and ran down the alley, pulling it along with her. She rounded the last corner into an open square with more zombies milling about, along with a wraith lord.

She threw the gnome at a large cluster of undead to her left and ran toward the wraith, coldfire igniting around her. She held up her left hand, shielding herself from a blast of deadly power. Energy flowed down to her right hand, forming a sword. It glowed brighter and brighter as she channeled power into it.

She twisted her wrist and swung it in a powerful overhand blow that sent a crackling blast of bright light across the square. It ripped through the swirling mists and exploded through the wraith lord's body. The remaining energy flashed around the square, killing the zombies that Jack the Ripper hadn't gotten to yet.

A raging scream and clattering ceramic warned her she was next on his list. She snapped her fingers, and it exploded in a cloud of dust, the blood and gore-covered scalpel clattering to the cobblestones. The angry red tint faded away, leaving the eerie smoke-filled sky hovering over the black and white London.

She stepped through the door back to the space station and into absolute chaos.

Skye glanced to her right and saw Wes shielding Adrian from a barrage from the space pirates who were right in front of her. Korbin was on the other side of them, wielding a stun baton with impressive accuracy against a handful of pirates. He seemed to be holding his own, and no one had seen her yet.

She moved forward and slammed her foot into the back of a knee, pushing the pirate's shoulders forward so he fell face first to the floor. She twisted and slammed her fist into the face of the other one as he turned in surprise. She sent a touch of energy into both of them, making sure they would stay unconscious for a while.

Wes dropped his shield and turned to help Korbin, throwing his fist into a pirate's face to knock it out. Korbin got a few more hits in with his stun baton, taking out the last pirate.

Wes turned back to Skye, sparing a glance for Adrian to make sure he was still alive. "I'm sure glad to see you."

Korbin said, "I would love to say we had it handled, but I'm glad you showed up too."

"Where are Kya and Declan?" It wasn't like them to leave Adrian alone.

Declan said, "Oh, you know, shoving a very angry alien into a small room. And losing my pants in the process."

Skye had to ask. "Was the alien the cause of you losing your pants, or was this..." her voice trailed off, and she made a vague gesture.

"I would like to blame the alien, but no. They just disappeared. Again." He sighed, summoning a pair of shorts. "How's it going in there?"

"Oh, you know, zombies, revenants, wraiths, ceramic gnomes. I have to say, Jack the Ripper garden gnome sure did a number on that revenant." She could tell he could use a laugh.

"Are you saying you used the garden gnome as a weapon?"

She shrugged, her expression innocent. "Threw it right in the revenant's face. Then used it against some zombies while I killed a wraith lord."

Declan fell back against the wall laughing as she sent him the visual of the attack. He gasped and said, "That is the best thing I think I have ever seen." The others were staring at the two of them in confusion.

She winked, placing her hand against the next door and stepping through it.

The monster movie chase world Declan and Kya had explored was swarming with wraiths. The eerie background music had taken on a sinister tone. The entrance from Earth was a few feet ahead of her. The linear aspects of this dimension had forced Adrian's door to stay in line. She could hear a slight ruckus on the other side of the blurry portal as she closed it, but it wasn't anyone she knew.

Sarah Eriksen

She summoned both of her swords, stretching her body with a few twists and wiggles, then sprinted down the path. She blitzed through the woods, destroying wraiths with vibrant streaks of energy.

The music intensified as a covered bridge loomed ahead of her. The dimension was still operating within its set parameters. Her footsteps echoed in the closed space, and she heard the deep whinny of a horse behind her as she hit the halfway mark. Horseshoes clattered on the rough planks as she ran toward a group of wraiths clustered at the other end.

She crossed her arms in front of her and slashed out, sending a wave of fire that tore through the wraiths. Her feet pounded down the hard dirt road, the horseman still following. She bolted past the tree she was supposed to take cover in, wondering how the dimension was going to handle her not following the plan.

There was a sense of confusion behind her as the horseman slowed down. She glanced back and saw it shrug and turn its horse to head off into the woods. She couldn't resist a breathless chuckle at its reaction.

She slowed her mad dash to a jog and tried to catch her breath for a minute. She was used to running daily, but this was starting to wear on her.

The injured man who was going to turn into a werewolf was sitting on the side of the road ahead. It was time for another chase.

The man radiated confusion and surprise as she flew past. His mind caught up with the change in the storyline, and he shifted into the werewolf, pursuing her down the road. She sent a blast of coldfire into a wraith ahead of her and then flicked her wrist, lobbing the lantern backward. She heard a scream as it hit its target. Declan had been right. The lantern was designed to kill the wolf without needing an accurate throw.

She entered the town and thrust a powerful kick into the stomach of the chainsaw man as he started to leap out of the dark alley. She swatted the chainsaw with her sword and disintegrated it with a crackle of power.

The town square was a jumbled mess of people wielding all manner of objects as weapons against the wraiths that were attacking. The villagers were holding their own but hadn't managed to kill any of them.

She dove into the crowd, destroying wraiths and dancing around the villagers. She ducked under a well-aimed stuffed animal, flipping her sword around and stabbing backward into the wraith, igniting it with a burst of energy through her blade.

The villagers settled back into haggling and bartering in the market as the wraiths died. Skye was impressed with the details of this place. The creativity alone was astounding. She slowed to a stop at the guard shack, studying the door that glowed with a complicated energy shield created by Declan and Amonir.

"Want to drop your shield so I can close this one?" She asked him.

The shield shimmered and disappeared. She could feel Amonir's protective energy through the door. It was the one location that was completely safe from attack.

Her mind filled with simmering rage as she closed the portal. She already didn't like Adrian but opening a door into a kid's room and luring wraiths and things anywhere near it was messed up.

She turned to head to the gate out of the town when the clown jumped at her. She let out a shriek, and it exploded in a flash of coldfire, leaving nothing but a smoking spot of ash on the packed dirt ground. She lowered her hands, her body tense.

"Are you okay?" Trey asked in concern.

"A clown jumped at me."

"Oh." Understanding dawned.

"It's dead now. I blew it up."

"Okay good. Think you can hurry up with the doors? This shit is getting wild out here."

"Yeah. I can do that." She made a disgusted noise, wiggling her body to shake out the lingering tension from fear. She was ready to be done with this place.

She jogged out of the gate into the woods, the music changing again with a disturbing chiming tone, like an old music box. Something was sitting in the middle of the road ahead. She absently pointed her sword off to the side, killing the last wraith with a flash of energy.

She slowed down as she neared the object. It was an old porcelain doll sitting on the ground. Its head bent slightly to the side. The exit back to the space station was slightly past it in an old crumbling house.

Skye came to a dead stop and stared at the doll. It was going to move if she walked past it. There was no way it wouldn't. She steeled herself

Sarah Eriksen

and bolted forward. Its head turned to follow her as she moved past it. She dove for the door, not chancing a single look back.

Chapter Thirty-Four

Declan yelled, "Just die. God. Damned. Alien piece of shit!" He punctuated each word with a punch of his fist glowing with green fire. He dodged a glob of venomous spit and gestured at the alien's face, throwing a sticky blob of gooey green energy into its gaping maw as it prepared another venom attack. It fell back, clawing at its mouth, heaving and gagging, while letting out a stream of muffled shrieks and whimpers.

Skye somersaulted out of the door behind him, landing in a crouch. "Geez, Declan, what did you do to it?"

"I blocked its deadly spit channels with some goo. It's getting a literal taste of its own medicine." He was unsympathetic to its plight. There was a loud crash as another alien slammed into the wall above and charged down the ramp toward them.

Skye studied the outer wall of the space station and did a quick calculation while Declan let off a string of curses. She said, "I have an idea, be ready to push these bad boys outside."

His voice was confused. "Outside? What— "

Skye slammed her hand onto the floor of the space station, energy rising to form a seal around the area they were in. Bright coldfire surrounded her and Declan protectively as the metal wall of the space station disappeared. The aliens clawed at the ground, sharp claws sinking into the metal as they fought for purchase against the vacuum of space.

Declan used energy to pull their limbs away from the walls and floors, and they flew out of the space station. Skye reformed the matter, putting everything back the way it was, and dropping the protective energy around them.

She could feel Declan staring at her. She sighed tiredly and asked, "What?"

"I mean, I was sort of joking about blowing them out of an airlock when I suggested it. But I never imagined rearranging matter to make a hole in a space station." He was impressed.

"I didn't think we had time to drag them down to the cargo bay and try that. Hopefully, they can't survive out there, or at least drift clear of the space station." She felt confident they wouldn't be able to rip through the protective outer walls.

"Shit, Rachel is out there. With the space pirates getting loose, Kya wanted her to get their ship away from here." He tapped the communication device to open the channel. "Hey Rachel, we sort of sent two aliens out into space. You might want to watch out for them. They don't seem to be dead yet."

"Yeah, they don't die in vacuums, apparently. Who knew?"

Skye said, "Sorry about that."

"It's fine. I can take care of it. Probably better to get them out of the space station anyway, and it gives me something to do out here." Rachel laughed.

Declan placed his hand on Skye's shoulder, and she felt a soothing flow of healing energy rejuvenate her tired body. She gave him a half smile. "Thanks."

"Anytime. Better get back in there. I should probably go make sure Wes and Korbin haven't killed Adrian." He didn't sound thrilled at the prospect.

"So, you're going to take your time going back?" She placed her hand on the door to the labyrinth and gave him a questioning look.

He grinned wickedly and didn't answer as he strolled down the corridor.

Skye gazed at the miniature labyrinth from the slight rise she was on. It was only a few steps, at her current size, from the entrance. She could sense a lot of zombies, but she couldn't see any of them. A strange tug of a spell brushed against her, and she blocked it reflexively. The door back to the haunted hospital in Maine was in a stone arch higher up the hill.

Chaotic Haunts

The hospital was quiet on the other side of the portal. The boys must have cleared it out already. She sealed off the door, watching the opening in the arch clear to a view of dead grass and shrubs. She headed back down to the labyrinth entrance, feeling the same tug of a spell.

She paused long enough to analyze it. It was a spell to shrink anything that crossed it. The labyrinth was massive, if small in scale. The spell must have allowed you to experience a labyrinth at the right size. The creator of the dimension was just thrifty with space usage. She laughed as she realized what had happened to the zombies that had entered.

Sure enough, they had shrunk to a size much more appropriate to the scale of the labyrinth. A closer look showed her that most of them were not doing very well against the traps built into the twisting maze.

"Guardian, Eric could use your assistance in Queensland. The labyrinth can protect itself." Amonir sounded amused by the miniature death trap too.

"You got it, boss." She threw her leg over the first wall, hopping awkwardly to get her body up the extra inch needed to get over the top. She twisted, almost falling as she pulled her other leg over and glared at the walls with her hands on her hips. It would take her hours to navigate like this and running through the maze would be as bad.

She absently punted a calf-high zombie into a pit of spikes while she studied the stone wall, hoping it would hold her weight. She jumped to the top of the labyrinth and leaped across the walls, carefully landing between stone finials before finally jumping down into the open space by the exit. A rotting tentacle had pushed through from the other side and was feeling around.

"Of course. Giant zombie squid." She got a running head start, wrapping a bubble of air around her face and sliding feet first into the opening. She blasted through with a burst of energy preceding her feet and shoved the zombie squid away from the door. She splashed into the water, her momentum sending her to the sandy bottom of the wrecked ship.

Her eyes adjusted to the darkness of the cold ocean, and she saw a myriad of freaky deep sea fish scurry away. The giant squid pulled itself into view through a hole in the hull. She thrust her hand forward, and a massive ball of coldfire lit up the dark bottom of the ocean and destroyed

Sarah Eriksen

the zombie squid. She swam back to the portal and sealed it off, teleporting herself to the amusement park.

Eric was doing an impressive job holding his own against three berserk revenants. His hands crackled with silvery blue lightning as he threw spells at each one. He pulled his hands together, lightning concentrating into a tight spiral that he hurled into the ground at the feet of a revenant. It expanded outward with a crackle and tangled the creature's legs, slowing it down and giving him time to get out of range.

Skye gestured, and coldfire erupted around Eric's spell, burning away the protective layers wrapped around the revenant. Eric took advantage of the opening her attack had created, and a bolt of silvery blue light flew through the air and pierced its chest, followed by more and more bolts of energy hitting the same spot.

The other two revenants had moved in opposite directions to make them more challenging targets. Skye's lips twitched into a faint smirk, and she twisted both hands, flames dancing around her palms and fingers. Columns of fire erupted under the revenants' feet, burning with a cold intensity. Inhuman screams filled the air as the revenants died.

She turned to Eric, who had killed the last revenant. He looked at the smudge of remains from her attack and said, "You know, you're awfully handy to have around in a fight."

She burst out laughing. "Happy to help. Where's Rhaeadr?"

"He went to help with a zombie situation at another spot. How's it going in there?"

"Well, I have this dimension, and the RPG one, and the two I haven't been to. So, we're getting there. The dimensions seem to be helping out, so that's pretty neat."

She eyed the door with trepidation. She wasn't sure she was ready to see what was going on with the pink ball of doom. It was also a good excuse to let her breathe for a second. She blinked in surprise as she felt Eric's hand on her head.

"Sorry, you have some seaweed in your hair." He gently pulled the offending plant out of her hair and sent it back to the ocean where it belonged.

"Thanks." She felt oddly self-conscious all of a sudden.

Eric said, "It's weird seeing the door open in the daytime. Everything has been consistently late at night until now."

She appreciated the new topic. "I think Amonir or Lucas have something to do with that. The last thing we need is having to time travel on top of all the rest."

"Right. This is already complicated enough. Sounds like I need to go help on the space station now." He must have gotten instructions from the boss.

"Yeah, every time I've popped over there, it's been pretty...um...full of pirates and aliens running amok."

"Fun times. Good luck."

He hesitated, and she interrupted him, "No, *you* be careful." She stuck her tongue out and him and ran to the door, hearing his chuckle behind her.

The wind tore through the forest, bending the trees with ominous intensity. Leaves and twigs whipped through the air, and thunder rumbled overhead.

"For fuck's sake," she muttered, closing the portal behind her. She could feel the presence of multiple liches in this dimension. They were clustered around a powerful revenant in the small ruined town and cemetery.

She jogged down the path, watching out for falling tree limbs from the angry storm and cursing as debris collided with her. There was a sense of fear coming from the liches and a stronger one from the revenant. There was only one thing she could think of that would be able to scare creatures that were attracted to fear.

She gave herself a boost of unnatural speed on the familiar paths of the forest, reaching the ruined town in record time. The revenant was directing the remaining liches to attack the pink ball of doom, which had grown in brightness and size with each creature it killed. She tilted her head. Maybe it was absorbing them. It was fascinating and terrifying at the same time.

The portal to the space station was in the direction the ball had come from. There was no way she'd be able to get into the crypt, close the portal, and get out unnoticed. The pink ball of doom was destroying the liches with disturbing efficiency and speed.

Sarah Eriksen

Skye ran toward the crypt as the revenant screamed and charged at the glowing orb. She ducked through the door and crashed down the stairs in a cross between a fall and a controlled leap. She landed on her feet at the bottom as a final gurgled scream ripped from the revenant's throat.

She tore open the casket and shoved the remains out of the way, throwing herself through as a bright pink glow appeared behind her.

A young man clutching a handful of books let out an inelegant scream and jumped back against the wall as she burst into the library basement. She spun on her feet, throwing her hands up in front of the blurry portal that was glowing a terrifying pink as the ball of doom loomed nearer. Coldfire flashed across the opening, and the portal disappeared, leaving a simple wooden door.

She let out an explosive breath of relief and heard a clatter of books hitting the ground behind her. The emotions, namely fear and awe, rolling off the young man were intense. She sent out a soothing wave of energy and turned with a smile.

"What the fuck was that?" He blurted out.

She opened her mouth to answer and closed it. She had no clue what to use as a plausible explanation for what had happened. She shrugged and said, "That *was* an interdimensional door. And honestly, I haven't the foggiest fucking clue how to explain anything that was happening on the other side."

He blinked in surprise. "Is that why the ghosts down here have been so upset lately?"

It was her turn to be surprised. "Yeah. Yeah, it is. But I've closed it off now. So, things should go back to normal." An awkward silence descended between them.

She said, "Um...I've got to go. Probably don't mention this to anyone."

He nodded in agreement, his mouth falling open as she disappeared.

The space station was disturbingly quiet when she arrived. She reached out, finding Declan first. *"Why's it so quiet?"* Trey was still back on Earth, and Eric was with Kya in the cargo bay below them. Wes and Korbin were still with Declan. Tate was in the control center, and Rachel was outside the station in Kya's ship. She could feel pirates scattered in different locations and only one alien presence.

"Judicious use of duct tape." He replied.

"Did you—?"

"Tape Adrian to a wall and leave him to fend for himself? No, I didn't. But that doesn't mean I won't. We have things under control for the moment. I'm sure that'll change any second now."

"Fair. Off to the next dimension, then."

Tate spoke over the communication channel to Kya. "Something's been bugging me about this."

"I'm guessing it's something specific." She teased.

"Yeah, it is. When we first arrived, we had the three aliens, and Korbin was the living person left. No big deal. But then the pirates returned. There were twenty-two pirates in total and the three aliens, all locked up when Skye left. And then we had another dozen show up later."

"Okay." She was curious about where he was going with this now.

"So, we know we lost three of them through one of the doors, and they died, right?"

"Yes, Skye and Declan confirmed they were dead, and I verified it was the three who went missing."

"And I watched while Skye opened up the side of the station when she and Declan threw two aliens out into space." Their voice held a hint of terror. Anyone who worked in space as they did was not comfortable with holes in the walls of space stations. "Rachel killed both of those aliens. So, we should have one alien left and thirty-one space pirates, right?"

Kya said, "Yes. That's all I can sense on the space station."

"But I can see the one alien in the cargo bay by you, and there are two more in the hangar on the opposite side. And I'm counting thirty-four pirates."

Kya's eyes widened, and she spun in the direction Tate indicated, searching with her eyes and her mind. She only sensed one alien, but she could see the other two.

"Eric—" Words failed her, and she pulled him into a link with her, showing him what she was seeing.

He cursed. "How's that even possible? I haven't felt any energy or power that could have reanimated them."

Kya grimaced. *"Declan, has Adrian used any magic that you've been able to feel?"* The demi-god could mask his presence when he wanted to. But there wasn't a force in creation that could mask any kind of power being used. Not even a god.

"Not one spec. What's going on?"

"Someone reanimated the two aliens you blew out into space, and they're in the hangar."

"That's super neat. Let me guess, any pirates that may have died are back too?" His voice was positively acidic.

"Yes."

"Want me to knock him out?"

"I'm not sure it would work; it might not be him." Loud shrieks of anger and rage echoed across the station.

"Tate?"

They confirmed, "They're all loose, pirates and aliens."

Kya shook her head and spoke on an open channel. "It's about to get ugly, everyone. Do what you have to do. The only survivors I care about are you and the guardians." They understood what that meant.

Chaotic Haunts

Chapter Thirty-Five

Skye stared in speechless amazement at the sight before her. A revenant and a few zombies were holed up in a windmill, fully under siege by an angry mob. The trail of destruction in their wake was impressive, considering the mob was comprised of brightly colored stuffed animals wielding pitchforks, axes, and torches. The exit door was in the windmill. The entrance was a cellar door across the village square she was in.

She raised her hands defensively as an elegant deep voice filled the entire dimension. *"It was a typical autumn day in the village of Oak Spring. But something sinister was brewing in the castle."*

Skye's hands dropped, coldfire flickering in response to the confusion she felt.

"Our weary traveler stopped to rest in the empty town square, unaware of the coming danger."

The world had a narrator.

She turned back to the portal, staring in consternation as the blurry image of a handful of people moved toward it. Someone moved in front of the door, their arms spread wide. She heard an unfamiliar voice on the other side speaking.

"Sorry folks, we have to call an end to our haunted cemetery experience. We're getting reports of serious lightning in the area, and we can't stay here." A flash of lightning lit up the sky, caused by a powerful jolt of creation energy from the stranger.

Sarah Eriksen

He waved his hand, gesturing for the tour group to move along. He must have been sent to handle creatures at the location on the other side of the portal and was now doing crowd control.

The last of the people disappeared from her sight through the blurry opening, and he said, "You're clear to close the door now."

The narrator said, *"Our intrepid adventurer had rested and moved to head out of town."* The voice had a hint of impatience with the not-so-subtle direction to get things moving.

The stranger asked with a hint of a laugh, "What was that?"

"Oh, just a narrator in this alternate dimension trying to get me to leave the town so the story can progress. You know, business as usual."

He chuckled. "Well, better not keep it waiting. Good luck."

"You too." She raised her hand and closed the portal. She jogged to the outskirts of the town and the angry mob of stuffed animals. They were finishing off the revenant and—

"Our intrepid adventurer searched for a way into the windmill."

Skye tilted her face to the sky and said in exasperation, "Seriously?"

The stuffed animals turned toward her, and she raised her hands to try and show she meant no harm and was unarmed. Her hand shifted to point an angry finger at the sky as the narrator started to speak again. "Not a word."

She addressed the mob. "I have to get into the windmill to close the portal that let those things in. Your world should go back to normal once I do."

The cute furry faces turned to one another, no audible words exchanged. They must have come to some agreement because they stepped to the sides of the gravel path so she could go to the windmill. The interior was dark and dusty, but she could see the watery door easily enough.

Thin beams of sunlight shone down into a large old ballroom that appeared to be abandoned. It was silent. Whatever might have been there had been handled.

She closed the door and got an urgent update from Declan about the pirate situation. They were going to need her help, and she still had two more locations to take care of. It was time for a reckless gamble. She strode out of the windmill and considered the waist-high plush mob.

"Our adventurer had come up with a clever plan to save the day."

Chaotic Haunts

"I'll take that as a sign it might work." She addressed them. "There are more creatures like that in other places in your world. I could use the help if you want to follow me. But I can't promise your safety."

"The villagers considered what she was asking. It would be dangerous, but they would all safely return to their homes to sleep tonight, as though it was a dream."

"Okay, shall we?" The mob of stuffed animals brandished their weapons in a silent roar. She booked it toward the castle, her new allies following behind her.

The evil scientist's castle and lab were empty, giving her a clear shot through cobweb-filled corridors to the exit. The dimension was cooperating with her to take care of the problems. She ran into the space station, followed by her angry mob of stuffed animals.

Pirates were scattered along the curved corridor of the space station between her and the next door. They were trading shots with Korbin while Declan held up a bright green shield of energy to protect them.

Skye charged down the hall, kicking, punching, and knocking over the space pirates so her short allies could finish them off.

Declan dropped his shield with a laugh of disbelief. "What the actual fuck, Skye?"

"No time to explain." She ran past him, a horde of stuffed animals on her heels, and dashed through the door to the RPG world.

Korbin looked at Declan with a comically confused expression. Declan patted his shoulder sympathetically. "Don't worry. I have no clue what the fuck is going on either."

They piled into the small waiting room, and Skye grabbed the useless sword, slapping it into a magical sheath on her back. She waded through the mob and pulled the candlestick down, opening the door into a hall full of zombies with a wraith at the end. A handful of guards were pinned down by another wraith near the stairs to the dungeon.

The stuffed animals roared silently and charged into the fray. Skye fought her way through the crowded hall, using her fists to slam spells into the zombies to kill them. She burst into flames and threw her hands forward, sending a ball of coldfire into the wraith.

Sarah Eriksen

She slid to a stop in front of the guards, who held their swords up in case she was a threat. A tense handful of seconds passed, and they lowered their blades. One guard handed her his key ring with a respectful nod.

"Thanks." She said and dashed to close the portal in the dungeon. She ran back up the stairs, stopping to catch her breath. She never wanted to run again after this insanity.

"Are you doing okay?" She pulled her friends into a mind link, taking a moment to breathe and catch up on everything.

"Just peachy," Declan replied flippantly.

Trey sent a mental impression of a slap to Declan and said, *"I'm helping calm down some panicked ghost hunters and thrill seekers in an old factory. This place is a total safety hazard as it is."*

Eric said, *"I'm keeping space pirates, living and dead, out of the command center on the space station. Are you okay?"*

"Oh yeah, just really, really, really...sick of running." Her mental voice sounded as tired as she felt.

"How's your mob of stuffed animals doing?" Declan asked.

"They're very effective against zombies and revenants."

Eric said, *"Space pirates too clearly."*

"What are you guys even talking about?" Trey asked with a laugh.

"Fill him in, you two. I need to round up my angry mob and finish clearing this place now that I've caught my breath."

The upper hall was littered with dead zombies and only a couple of brightly colored plush bodies. The rest were waiting near the teleportation wand. She moved through them and grabbed the wand, all of them appearing on the grass-covered hedge path, which was packed full of wraiths.

She narrowed her eyes and said, "Stand back." The stuffed animals shifted to either side. Coldfire blazed around her, growing incandescent as she drew in a ridiculous amount. She thrust her hands forward, and a massive ball of blindingly bright fire barreled down the path, disintegrating every single wraith. She lowered her hands as the light and coldfire faded away.

"Let's go." They rushed to the courtyard, and Skye unsheathed the useless sword, repeating the light show and killing the end boss. Her angry mob barreled through the gap in the bushes, and she followed, laughing at the site of the brightly colored stuffed animals scattered around the woods fighting zombies.

She left them to it and ran to the crumbling tower, closing off the door. A strangled shriek made her turn toward the lake with its warning sign about the Rodak Beavers. A revenant flailed and screamed as it was pulled under the murky waters of the lake.

She nodded to herself and shook a finger at the lake as she walked back down the hill to go back to the space station. There was only one part left to clear out.

"Rachel, think you could do me a favor?" Declan asked, his voice strained as he dragged the massive struggling undead alien behind him in a powerful web of creation energy. The weight wasn't the issue. The flailing limbs with sharp claws and the power from the reanimation spell were making it difficult.

"Sure. What did you have in mind?"

"Do you have like a tractor beam on your fancy little ship out there?"

"Yes." She said cautiously.

"Okay good. Do you think you could grab onto this giant fucking alien, drag it far enough away from the space station, and hold it safely away from you so I can incinerate it?"

There was a pause, and then she said, "Okay, if I disregard the fact that fire normally requires oxygen to burn, because I'm guessing you're just going to ignore that, the answer is yes. But can I ask why?"

He grunted and dragged the alien onto the hangar floor. "Because some asshole reanimated this thing once already. It can't reanimate a pile of ash, especially ash that will be scattered across space when I'm done."

He wasn't taking any chances. He also didn't want to ignite a giant alien inside a space station. He was confident he could contain the fire and not ignite the air and blow them all up, but better safe than dead.

"I like how you think." The ship flew into the hangar, a beam of pale light latched onto the alien, and he let go of his web as soon as Rachel got it outside the station.

He walked to the energy shield at the edge of the hangar watching as she flew away. This was going to push him to his limits, but it would be worth it.

"I'm good to go when you are. I've got heat shields up, so I should be fine as long as you don't send any unnatural fire my way."

He closed his eyes and raised his hands, drawing in as much energy as he could. A bright green ball of liquid fire formed between his outstretched hands, growing brighter and brighter and then disappearing with a snap of power. It reappeared in space and exploded into the side of the alien that was away from the ship. The liquid fire was like napalm and splattered across the alien's body.

His jaw clenched as he used more power to force the energy to spread and eat through the armor-like skin. His hands started to glow with a dark emerald light, and the fire deepened to the same color before the alien's body exploded into tiny particles that spread out in a verdant wave of light.

"That was amazing, Declan." Rachel's voice was quiet.

He dropped to his knees with a groan, watching the emerald glow fade from his hands with a perplexed frown. He said with a hint of his usual irritating smugness, "I'm not going to argue with you. That was pretty amazing."

Skye tripped over the body of a space pirate as she ran through the door, tumbling into Korbin. His reflexes prevented them both from falling to the ground as he caught her. The stuffed animals piled into the corridor in a much more graceful heap.

"We really need to stop meeting like this." She said, getting her balance again. "Thanks."

"You're welcome." He said with a flirtatious grin that wavered as he looked askance at the stuffed animals.

"I know, it's weird. But they're incredibly helpful." A roar heralded the entrance of a massive alien.

Korbin aimed his energy rifle at it. "That's one of the dead but not dead ones. Kya is fighting the living one with your brother, and Declan dragged the other one down to the hangar. He was...um—"

"Less than thrilled and using a lot of colorful language?" She lifted her hand, coldfire swirling into a ball above her palm.

"Exactly." His eyes widened as he watched the coldfire grow brighter.

She raised her arm further and twisted her wrist, sending the bright, compact orb at the undead alien's face. It slammed into it, spreading out and burning through its eyes to reach its brain. The coldfire latched onto the reanimation spell and ate at it, speeding up as Skye channeled more energy into it.

The alien dropped to the ground with a gurgle, dead again. Skye twisted her hands, and it disappeared in a flash of light along with the pirate corpses.

"What did you do?" He was awestruck.

"I teleported them into the heart of a nearby star. No one's reanimating any of them anytime soon." She smiled at him. "You good? I have to go…do the door thing."

"Yeah. I'm good. I should go and help Wes with the last of those pirates." He watched in bemusement as the brightly colored stuffed animals followed her down the corridor.

Dry heat blasted her face as she stepped through the door. She immediately adjusted her body to feel more comfortable in the unbearable temperature of the desert. The stuffed animals crowded in behind her. She put her hands on her hips, watching the scene unfold in the valley below.

Wraiths, liches, and a couple of revenants were fighting every monster, alien, and creature from every movie she could think of from the 1950s and on. A revenant ran screaming out into the desert, chased by a flying saucer. She glanced at the stuffed animals that were watching the carnage unfold and gestured. "Go for it. I'll get the doors."

They ran past her, plump, plush legs moving with disturbing speed as they entered the fray. She jogged along the edge of the ravine, avoiding the majority of the battle that was well in hand. A revenant screamed and flailed past her, its hand covered in gelatinous goo that was creeping up its arm.

She slid down a sandy hill through various desert plants and watched a pair of dapperly dressed vampires stalk past, capes billowing in the hot wind. A flicker of mist caught her eye, and she turned, seeing a handful of wraiths hiding in a pile of tumbleweeds.

She called out, "Hey, Draculas. They're over there." She pointed at the wraiths. The two vampires grinned seductively and ran past her into the tangled weeds to attack the wraiths. She could have helped out and killed them, of course, but she was in a hurry.

Sarah Eriksen

The screams of the wraiths faded behind her as she jumped into an old shipping container and closed the portal inside it. The last door was in a nearby cave.

She moved through the battlefield, past werewolves, bizarre aliens, giant bugs, stuffed animals, and a lot of dead creatures that didn't belong there.

The cave mouth loomed in front of her, and she ducked inside. She closed the final door to Earth with a sigh of relief and headed back out to help wrap up the battle.

She surveyed the carnage spread out across the desert. The creatures were all dead or dying. A final blast of a laser from a flying saucer killed the last one.

The various monsters turned toward her, and she said, "Thanks for the help. Everything should be able to go back to normal now."

The stuffed animals disappeared as the aliens and monsters slinked, crawled, and floated away back to their respective haunts scattered about the desert. She trudged to the exit, which was in a crashed spaceship in the center of the desert and returned to the space station.

Chapter Thirty-Six

The station was quiet. The pirates and aliens were dead, or dead again, and her friends were gathered by the command center in the middle ring. Skye trudged up to them and dropped to the ground between Trey and Declan, leaning back against the wall and pulling her knees up to her chest.

Eric was leaning against the wall nearby but still miraculously on his feet. Tate was perched on top of a crate, looking at their handheld computer intently, with Wes leaning over their shoulder. Rachel sauntered in with an impudent wave. Kya's hand glowed a gentle purple as she healed a nasty wound on Korbin's temple.

Skye's eyes narrowed, and she looked around for the conspicuously missing demi-god. "Where's Adrian?"

Korbin answered in a pained voice. "He took advantage of the pirates to get away. I did try to stop him, but—" he gestured toward his head which was now healed. His remorse and guilt were intense enough that they could all feel it. "I'm sorry, it's my fault he got away."

All of the guardians responded with some form of protest, surprising him. Kya said, "You can't blame yourself. He was a demi-god. He could have gotten the slip on any of us. I'm just glad you're alive."

Declan turned his head toward Skye and asked, "Are all the doors closed?"

"No. I'm taking a break while all hell breaks loose," she said sarcastically. "Of course, they're closed. Everything has returned to normal in the other dimension."

Sarah Eriksen

The sense of two powerful presences filled the space station. Kya's crew had varying degrees of shock on their faces. It was the first time most of them had encountered a god.

Lucas raised a hand as the guardians tried to get up to show their respect. "Please. There is no need. I am the one who owes you." His voice and face were sad as he looked around the space station. "You have done me a great service, and I won't forget it."

Amonir said, "You have done exceedingly well. And I do mean all of you." He nodded respectfully at Kya's crew.

Skye said to Lucas. "Thank you for the help I got inside your amazing world." She meant it. It had been crazy at times, terrifying, or downright weird. But the care and detail were astounding.

He smiled gently. "It was the least I could do. Although, I don't think you needed much help. Your skills and power are impressive." He glanced around at all of them. "As soon as you are safely away, I will take this place somewhere more secure, so this will never happen again."

Kya asked, "Would you like us to help with anything before we leave?" The space station was covered with a lot of dead bodies, after all.

He shook his head. "I will take care of everything." He turned to Amonir and said, "We need to talk." Amonir gave him a searching look, then dipped his chin down in a brief nod. They walked away together, wrapped in silence.

Tate blurted out first, "Those are gods."

Kya replied, "Yes. They are."

Declan pushed himself to his feet with a tired groan. "You get used to it after a while."

Korbin said in a strangled voice, "You get used to gods thanking you for things?"

Trey pulled Skye to her feet, and she said, "Well, Amonir is our boss, and he's pretty polite." She walked over to her cousin and hugged her. "This has certainly been weird, cousin."

"Isn't it always?" Kya said with a laugh. She glanced at her crew, feeling their melancholy emotions at everyone returning to their respective parts of the universe. No one liked a goodbye, especially after surviving something like this.

She gave Trey and Skye a stern look. "Don't forget that mother is expecting both of you to come to the lunar solstice celebration next month."

Identical expressions of dismay flashed across nearly identical faces. Declan burst out with an evil laugh that died down as Kya leveled her gaze at him. "You're invited to." She smiled politely at Eric, "And of course, you're welcome to come."

"Thank you." He fought back a grin at the others' discomfort.

Kya looked at her crew. "I might even bring all of you along." Korbin looked confused, but the rest smiled in understanding at what she was offering. It was a way for them to see their new friends again.

Declan whispered to Trey, "How do we get out of this?"

Trey shook his head, defeated. "This is not a battle we can win."

He grumbled, "How did I get roped into this?"

They made the rest of their goodbyes and Kya's crew headed to their ship, ready to leave and return to their normal space mercenary jobs. The guardians returned to their respective homes. Skye was dead on her feet, but after all the running and fighting, there was one far more important thing that she needed. A shower.

She finally crawled into her bed, pulling the covers over her head, not even noticing what time it was. She felt a warm furry body curl up against her back with a rumbling purr and fell asleep.

Skye walked into the shop early, feeling awkward after missing out on so much work. The entire haunted houses and other dimension excitement and recovering from it all had only taken about two weeks, and she still felt guilty.

She held in a laugh as Gwen did a double take. She hardly ever came in early as it was, but she knew it was more than that.

"Hey, stranger! I hope your time off was nice."

"Busy, but it was fun." Her cover story had only been that she wanted some downtime after spending the entire summer helping an unspecified relative with things.

"I'm glad you took some time for yourself. You've always worked so hard here after your dad died. I worry about you." She gave Skye a conspiratorial wink. "Since we both know you have to keep an eye on your wayward brother."

Sarah Eriksen

Skye laughed. "Oh, come on Gwen. He's grown up a bit in the last few years. Not a lot, but a little."

She laughed too. "You're right. He's been great helping out around here while you were off." Her eyes were full of compassion. "But I'm glad you took some time. You've always put others before yourself. Always looking out for your brother, that holy terror Declan, now Ian, and even me. You need to make sure you take care of yourself too. Or find someone nice, like that friend of yours, Eric. He's got his head on right."

Skye smiled to cover the emotions Gwen's comments had stirred up. She knew her friend meant well, but she didn't want to encourage her. Especially where Eric was concerned. It always seemed like everyone wanted the two of them to hook up, but it wasn't something that ever seemed to come up between them. They were close friends, which meant a lot.

Gwen noticed her silence and said, "Sorry, hun. I don't mean to try to play matchmaker. I just want you to be happy."

"Thanks, Gwen. I appreciate it. How are your grandkids doing?" Gwen let her change the subject without question, and Skye managed to pay enough attention to respond while her mind spiraled around the things Gwen had said.

Relationships were complex as a guardian. There was so much secrecy needed with what they did. It was dangerous, and for her now, even more dangerous. It was hard to find people who could accept who and what she was. And all too often, they ended up backing away. Not to say guardians didn't form lasting relationships, they just had more complicated things to navigate than most.

Her phone buzzed, and she pulled it out of her hoodie pocket. It was a text from Ben. He wanted to know if everything had gone okay. Stories were popping up about haunted houses not being as haunted.

Rumors of money-making schemes discouraged the thrill seekers and avid hunters. Plausible reasons and theories spread and took the focus off the real ghosts and dangers, making it out to be something boring. All in all, it was a fairly typical conclusion after a big guardian-involved situation like that.

She texted back that everything was taken care of, so haunted houses were as safe as they ever were. She watched as he started and stopped typing a few times. Then he finally sent his message. He thanked her for saving his life and wished her luck with her monster-fighting job. She knew a goodbye when she saw one.

She wasn't surprised or even hurt, honestly. She had enjoyed his company in the haunted house, and he was a genuinely nice person. But a goodbye, on top of the emotions Gwen had stirred up and her recent struggles, set off a strong wave of loneliness. She immediately squashed it down before Trey noticed how powerful of an emotion it was.

She had her friends, and she had the shop. Well-intended matchmaking friends aside, she wasn't desperate for a man to make her life complete. She was complete. But that didn't mean she didn't want someone who cared about her. Someone she didn't always have to be strong around. Someone who wasn't bothered by her powers.

She pulled out her headphones and turned on one of her favorite songs from her favorite band. Their music always helped when she was in a mood like this. Temporal resonance rippled around her as the music played, making her wonder, for the first time in a long time, what it could mean.

Her musings were interrupted by the only thing she would bother acknowledging when she was in a mood like this.

Amonir asked, *"Do you have a moment, guardian?"*

That was odd. He was always polite and understood his guardians' needs and moods. But he usually just got right to the point. *"It's quiet right now, but I can't leave the shop."*

"Not a problem."

The door chimed, and a tall, dark-haired man with bright green eyes wearing dark jeans and a bright blue hoodie walked in, his presence muted so he would go unnoticed.

Skye winced and blinked her eyes. "I don't think that color blue exists in nature, boss man."

He smiled. "Funny." He gave her a searching look. "How are you?"

"Better than I have been." It was true. Her confidence in her powers was back, even if she felt like a bit of an emotional train wreck at the moment. She knew he could read her emotions, so she wasn't going to lie. "Want a coffee?"

"I'm glad." He let her change the subject and asked her to make him one of the most sugary concoctions she could feasibly create that still had coffee in it.

He sipped his drink and said, "I'm going to require your help with something. After your time on Meriten, it's come to the attention of several gods that Nekros has broken some significant promises and possibly several cosmic laws. I won't bore you with the details, but it was enough to cause concern. Chaos is also concerned, although I have yet to get a straight answer as to why." He was irritated. "But that being said, I need help looking into what Nekros has been up to."

"You want me to spy on a death god?" Skye asked blandly.

"Not directly, of course. I need you to investigate some things that have happened and see if there is any connection to him."

Skye glanced sharply at him and said, "Adrian is Nekros' son, isn't he?"

A genuine smile flashed across Amonir's face at her accurate assumption. "You are correct. I did a little digging into his involvement with the haunted houses. We know he opened the doors, but I studied the spell after you got the information from his mind. The doors were designed to close after a guardian went inside."

"Any guardian? Or us specifically?" She shook her head, "It'd be hard to make it that specific to us with all those locations. But regardless, it was directed at guardians."

"Yes. It wasn't likely that he could have trapped a guardian in there for any specific amount of time, but it still is cause for concern."

"Did you have a chance to find out how a ghost hunting group online would have known about the door inside a heavy marble coffin?" Her gut was telling her that Adrian had to be behind that too.

"I asked for your friend Ian's help. He did whatever magic he does with computers and tracked down the user who posted the helpful information. It was Adrian." It was almost funny that an all-powerful elder god with a direct connection to Chaos was impressed with a nerdy computer genius.

Skye's eyes narrowed. Adrian had not only opened the doors, made them specific to sort of trap guardians, but had also gotten into online ghost hunting groups and dropped hints to lure people in.

Amonir continued, "It seems too coincidental that he managed to get much-needed information onto sites that Ben would be able to access and get to you. But he was watching all the haunted locations, so he might have taken a gamble that you would remain in touch with Ben."

"That makes sense, even if he didn't think that plan through very well. Of course, he seemed fairly incompetent at even coming up with plausible stories, so that's not that surprising, actually."

Amonir chuckled. "His ineptitude is mind-boggling." His face turned serious again. "This is not going to be an easy job. It ventures into dangerous territory dealing with gods and demi-gods, even inept ones, and their schemes. You can say no, and I will not think less of you for it."

Skye thought about it and asked, "I'm the only guardian you have who could potentially protect myself from a demi-god, aren't I?"

"I believe it's possible you have the power to protect yourself from a god. At least briefly. However, I'd prefer not to test that theory."

"Okay. I'll do it. But you know my friends are going to want to be involved."

"I already planned on it. Because if I didn't, we both know Declan would somehow insert himself into it anyway." They shared a fond smile.

"Thank you, guardian." He glanced around the shop and said, "Have you ever thought about letting someone else take over the day-to-day of this place? Or even giving it up?"

His questions surprised her. She had never thought seriously about giving up the shop for many reasons. The least of which was that it was her source of income. The rest was the emotional attachments to it. There were days she dreamed of moving away, taking her life in a different direction, dreams that anyone would have.

That being said, she answered, "Ever since the whole power thing, I've felt that it's a little difficult juggling both jobs. I feel guilty when I'm not around a lot. And that seems to be happening a lot more now." She knew there was a reason he had asked.

"If it ever gets to be too much to juggle both jobs, as you say, you know you could become a guardian full time and not need a normal source of income." He smiled at her shocked expression. "Think about it, at least. I'll be in touch."

Sarah Eriksen

Made in United States
Orlando, FL
31 May 2024